PENGUIN BOOKS

THE KILLER NEXT DOOR

Alex Marwood is the pseudonym of a journalist who has worked extensively across the British press. Marwood lives in South London.

Praise for *The Killer Next Door*

"If you read Alex Marwood's *The Wicked Girls*, her new one—*The Killer Next Door*—is even better. Scary as hell. Great characters."　　　—Stephen King

"Chilling, suspenseful, and darkly comic, *The Killer Next Door* is not only a terrific crime novel, but also a fascinating exploration of memorable characters, each individually lonely and secretive, and yet inextricably tied to one another by circumstance."　　　—Alafair Burke, author of *All Day and a Night*

"This tightly plotted story that grabs you from the opening paragraphs and will keep you up far too late at night is highly recommended for fans of Laura Lippman, Tana French, and Gillian Flynn."　　　—*Library Journal* (starred review)

"Taut, assured, and reminiscent of Ruth Rendell's psychological novels, Marwood's second book more than lives up to the promise shown in her splendid debut, *The Wicked Girls*."　　　—*The Guardian* (London)

"Even better than her debut *The Wicked Girls*. It's a compulsive, unsettling read that will leave you wondering how well you really know your neighbours."
—*Bella Magazine*

"Nasty, compelling, and original, the author has done it again."
—*The Sun* (London)

Praise for *The Wicked Girls*

"The suspense keeps the pages flying, but what sets this one apart is the palpable sense of onrushing doom."
—Stephen King, "The Best Books I Read This Year,"
Entertainment Weekly

"Harrowing . . . While the received wisdom on violence committed by children seems to be that 'some people just are born evil,' Marwood makes a strong case that these crimes are more likely rooted in poverty, abuse, and parental abandonment."　　　—Marilyn Stasio, *The New York Times Book Review*

"In addition to being an excellent intelligent dark thriller in the vein of Gillian Flynn, *The Wicked Girls* presents an intriguing insider's account of salacious British tabloid journalism."　　　—*BoingBoing*

"The swirling mass of perceptions and happenings behind the main drama of Kirsty and Amber's past crime is what makes *The Wicked Girls* more than a plot-driven mystery novel. (Not that it isn't also that; Marwood sacrifices no speed, no engaging details, or cliffhangers for the sake of the book's spiky undercurrent)." —*The Rumpus*

"[Alex] Marwood is equally at home with terrifying, potentially violent scenes and quieter ones revealing the tensions of work and family life. She is also adept at depicting the subtle and not so subtle ways differences in class shape the lives of the girls and the women they've become." —*The Columbus Dispatch*

"A dark and beautifully executed first novel."
—TheMillions.com, 2013 "Most Anticipated" books preview

"Riveting from first page to last . . . A suspenseful, buzz-worthy novel."
—*Kirkus Reviews* (starred review)

"*The Wicked Girls* is ingenious and original—a novel that surprises and rewards its readers, delivering a twist of an ending that I never saw coming, then realized it was the only ending that could truly satisfy. Real, chilling, true to its world and its characters. In short, a knock-out."
—Laura Lippman, *New York Times* bestselling author of
And When She Was Good and *What the Dead Know*

"Genuinely disturbing and emotionally unsettling. *The Wicked Girls* is irresistible."
—Val McDermid, author of *A Place of Execution*
and *The Vanishing Point*

"*The Wicked Girls* is utterly compelling. It's psychologically rich, complex, and masterfully plotted. I couldn't put it down, even when I sensed it was taking me somewhere very dark indeed. I can't wait to see what Alex Marwood comes up with next."
—Jojo Moyes, *New York Times* bestselling author of *Me Before You*

"I loved it. I thought it was a brilliant exploration of the sins of the past colliding with the mistakes of the present; really well-written, multifaceted characters, who behave in ways you wouldn't expect them to: in other words, like real people. It was cleverly plotted and pacy, with all the storylines thundering towards a final, gripping conclusion."
—Elizabeth Haynes, *New York Times* bestselling author of
Into the Darkest Corner

"I devoured *The Wicked Girls* over one weekend and loved it. I held my breath during the last few chapters."
—Erin Kelly, author of *The Dark Rose* and *The Poison Tree*

"The most gripping novel I've read in years. Dark, haunting, thought-provoking, brilliant—I couldn't recommend it more."
—India Knight, author of *Comfort and Joy*

"You're never quite sure which side you're on in this brilliantly taught psychological thriller. One of the best debut novels of 2012."
—*Bella Magazine* (Books of the Week)

THE
KILLER
NEXT DOOR

ALEX MARWOOD

PENGUIN BOOKS

PENGUIN BOOKS
Published by the Penguin Group
Penguin Group (USA) LLC
375 Hudson Street
New York, New York 10014

USA I Canada I UK I Ireland I Australia I New Zealand I India I South Africa I China
penguin.com
A Penguin Random House Company

First published in Great Britain by Sphere, an imprint of Little, Brown Book Group 2013
Published in Penguin Books 2014

ISBN 978-0-14-312669-0

Printed in the United States of America
1   3   5   7   9   10   8   6   4   2

Set in Sabon LT Std

For Cathy Fleming
A wonderful sister and a brilliant friend

Acknowledgements

All writers have many, many people to thank by the time a book finally reaches the world. I'm always terrified that, in the rush to thank, I will forget someone crucial. If this is so, please forgive me.

Laetitia Rutherford and her colleagues at Mulcahy Associates for their inspiring, supportive and generally above-and-beyond agenting. I feel immensely lucky to have stumbled into their offices.

The hugely talented team at Sphere: particularly Catherine Burke, my editor, Thalia Proctor, Kirsteen Astor and Emma Williams. It's such a pleasure to work with such professional, imaginative and thorough people.

Hannah Wood, whose cover designs make me almost dizzy with joy.

Dad and Patricia, Mum and Bunny, Will, Cathy, Ali and David. And Elinor and Tora and Archie and Geordie, who make me very happy about the future of the world.

The Board, for over a decade of support, friendship and back-room cackling.

ACKNOWLEDGEMENTS

Those enabling bitches, the FLs, who not only make me laugh daily but are usually awake when the Brits are asleep, which is damn useful for an insomniac. Prostitution whores, the lot of you.

Off the top of my head: John Lyttle, Chris Manby, Charlie Standing, Brian Donaghey, Helen Smith, Lauren Henderson, Jane Meakin, Angela Collings, Dawn Hamblett, Claire Gervat, Bottomley, Paul Burston, Antonia Willis, India Knight, James O'Brien, Lucy McDonald, Diana Pepper, Merri Cheyne, Stella Duffy, Shelley Silas, Jenny Colgan, Lisa Jewell, Jojo Moyes ... oh, Lord, if I haven't mentioned you here it doesn't mean I don't love and value you.

All the brilliant people who lurk on Facebook and Twitter, who make every day a party. Without your help I'd have written at least one more book by now.

And finally, my Sweet Felice, who protected me for many years and whose last book this was, and Bad Baloo, whose first book it is. If it's good enough for Sam Johnson, it's good enough for me.

As is your mind
So is your sort of search; you'll find
What you desire

ROBERT BROWNING

Prologue

He checks his watch and downs the last of his coffee. 'Okay. Miss Cheryl should be done with her fag break. Let's take you down to her.'

She follows him down to the interview rooms and he surreptitiously checks his reflection in the wired glass of a door as he passes it. DI Cheyne's a bit older than he usually goes for, but she's a good-looking woman. Slightly hard-faced, but a life in the Met doesn't make for a lot of childlike innocence. Doesn't hurt to keep your options open, anyway. Women who understand your unorthodox working hours are few and far between; attractive ones even fewer.

'You should probably know,' he tells her, 'she's pretty tired and upset, and we've still got a lot to get through, so if you could keep it shortish, that would be good.'

'Sure,' she says. 'I don't suppose it'll take that long, anyway. How is she? Cooperative?'

'Pissed off,' he says. 'In the custody of social services, so you can't blame her. She's a bit sulky. And she's not the sharpest tool in the shop. No point asking her to read anything, for a start.'

'That's okay. Think she can look at a photo?'

'Oh. I should think so. We'll give it a go, anyway.'

Cheryl Farrell is back in the interview room after her cigarette break, right elbow on the table and tear-streaked face resting wearily on her bandaged hand. She's pale and, DI Cheyne guesses from the dampness of her forehead, still in some degree of pain. The orthopaedic pink of the shoulder brace that holds her collarbone in place does nothing for her complexion. Could be pretty, thinks DI Cheyne, if it wasn't for the generally sulky demeanour. Golden-brown skin, curly African hair that she's bleached until it's a coppery shade of bronze, over-plucked eyebrows, almond-shaped brown eyes that she rolls at the newcomer.

The lawyer looks as if he hasn't shifted from his seat in a decade. He's scribbling furiously. The social worker sits, sensible hair and sensible shoes and an air of New Labour sanctimony pouring off her, in the chair next to the girl. 'All done!' she says brightly. 'She's had her cancer stick.'

'Oh, fuck off, you.' The girl gives her a look that would melt ice.

Merri Cheyne is longing for a smoke herself. Those nicotine tabs give her terrible indigestion. She ignores the social worker – best thing to do in most circumstances if you can manage it, she's found – and takes a seat on the other side of the table, next to Chris Burke. Cheryl turns back to DC Barnard and looks at him sullenly.

'So what were you on about?' Her strong Scouse accent is surprising in one who's been in the south so long.

'The television,' says DC Barnard.

'Oh, yeah.'

There's a silence. The girl looks like she would be slumping, if the brace would let her. Truly, thinks DI Cheyne, not the sharpest tool in the shop. He did warn me.

DC Barnard clears his throat. 'So tell us about the television, Cheryl? How did it come to be in your possession?'

'You what?'

'How did you get it, Cheryl? Where did it come from?'

'Oh.' The girl sniffs heavily and wipes her nose with the back of her hand. 'He said it was spare,' she says. 'Said he'd bought a new one and did I want it?'

'And you didn't wonder why he was offering you televisions?'

'I knew exactly why he was offering it,' she says, with a glare of defiance.

'And you accepted it?'

'If you're asking if I shagged him to get a second-hand telly, no I didn't. But there's no law against letting a fella give you a present because he thinks it might get you to, is there?'

'Fair point.'

'Anyway, I needed a telly. D'you know how bloody boring it is if you've got no money and no telly? I wasn't going to give him a ...' she sneaks a look at the social worker to see if she's going to get a rise, '... blow job, but I wasn't going to tell him to fuck off either, was I?'

'Well, I can see that there might have been some chance that things could get a bit unpleasant when he realised—'

'Whatever,' Cheryl interrupts. Most of *your* lot –' she narrows her eyes at her minder again '– think they can get a feel for a bag of crisps and a Fanta. At least I *wanted* a telly.'

The social worker stiffens beside her, offended. Amazing, thinks DI Cheyne. Even after a deluge of scandals, they're still blanking suggestions that their own might not be perfect.

'And when was this ...?'

'Don't know. Two, three weeks? Ages before the weather broke. It was still boiling bloody hot and he kept looking at my tits cause I was wearing a vest. I just thought he was another dirty old bloke. C'mon. Nobody else thought he was up to anything, either. D'you think I'd've stayed in that house, if I did?'

'So you don't think any of your neighbours had any suspicions, either?'

'No! I've told you! Place smelled like shit, but it's not exactly the first time I've been somewhere that smelled like shit. Anyway, they all had their own stuff to worry about, I should think. We hardly talked to each other, until it happened. It wasn't a flatshare or anything. We weren't *friends*.'

DI Burke opens the cardboard folder that DI Cheyne gave him earlier. On the top, an A4 photo of a woman: short, caramel-streaked blonde hair, low-cut white minidress, white slingbacks, white handbag, Versace jacket, oversized sunglasses perched on the top of her head. As unmistakeably Essex as Stansted crotch crystals. She's looking away from the camera, holding a half-drunk glass of champagne. It looks like a picture taken at a public event of some sort, the races, perhaps. He studies it for a few seconds. Wonders if this will be the picture the papers go with. Clears his throat pointedly, and DC Barnard stops and turns.

'Sorry, Bob,' he says. 'Cheryl, this is DI Cheyne. She's from Scotland Yard.'

The same bovine unresponsiveness. Cheryl pouts and rolls her eyes again.

'The Metropolitan Police Headquarters?'

'Organised Crime Squad,' interjects DI Cheyne. 'You can call me Merri, if you like.'

4

Usually, announcing this will produce some signs of interest, but the girl just gives a don't-care shrug of her good shoulder.

'DI Cheyne's not working on this case,' he says, 'but we think there might be a connection with something else she's working on.'

'Right,' says Cheryl, suspiciously.

DI Cheyne smiles at him and takes the folder. Lays it on the table in front of the girl. 'Cheryl,' she asks, 'does the name Lisa Dunne mean anything to you?'

Cheryl shakes her head, her face a mask. Cheyne opens the folder and slides the picture across the table so she can see it. 'Well, can I ask you, Cheryl? Do you recognise this woman?'

The girl slides the photo towards her, mouth turned down. Looks up, her spidery eyebrows arched. 'That's Collette!' she says. 'I thought you said Lisa something.'

DI Cheyne and DI Burke exchange a look. Damn, it says. It really was her, then. 'Collette?'

'She lived in number two. Didn't look like this when she was there, but it's her. Where did you get this?'

'Collette?'

'Collette. She moved in in, ooh, early June. After Nikki went ...' she suddenly looks sick again, and her eyes fill with tears, '... went missing.'

'And have you seen her lately?'

'No.'

'What sort of no? Can you be a bit more specific?'

The girl looks blank. DI Cheyne simplifies. 'Can you remember when you last saw her?'

'Not for a few days,' says Cheryl. 'But I didn't really think about it. She was never going to be here long, though. I think she only took the flat for a bit, while she did some ... business or something. Something to do with her mum. I don't know, really. She wasn't friendly, exactly. Sort of person who wouldn't recognise you if you passed her in the street, if you see what I mean. We said hello on the stairs a few times, that sort of thing. Why?'

Chris Burke puts his prepare-yourself face on. 'Cheryl, I'm afraid that there were some body parts in the flat that didn't match up with the known victims. The ones in the flat, I mean. There was more in the surrounding area. Down on the railway embankment. In the old bonfire at the end of the garden.'

Cheryl looks as if she's been socked in the face. Grips the table as though she's about to faint.

'Are you okay, Cheryl?' asks the social worker. 'We can take another break, if you need.'

'Are you saying there were *more*?'

'Um ... We've not established it as fact. But yes. Things are pointing that way, I'm afraid.'

'Oh, God,' she says.

'And there were ... among the remains ... you know he was keeping stuff in the freezer compartment of his fridge, right? Well, there were a couple of fingers in there. So we took prints, and ran them, and, well, they matched up with this woman. Lisa Dunne. She's been missing for a while. Three years, as a matter of fact. We've been looking for her.'

'Why? What's she done?'

'Doesn't matter, now. She was a witness to something – you don't need to know the details. But ... well, we just need to confirm if this is her.'

'Oh, God,' she says again. She's visibly shaken, her brown skin gone grey and her eyes as big as soup plates. 'Oh, no. He can't have. She was in Nikki's room. It's like he was ...'

The police wait while the news sinks in. Well, thinks DI Cheyne. That's one avenue shut off, and we were days off tracking her down. All that work, and Tony Stott's still scot-free.

'I'm sorry,' she says. 'I know it's a shock. But we need you to tell us what you remember about her.'

'What do you want to know? Oh, God. I can't take this in.'

'I'm sure,' says DI Cheyne gently. 'It must be a terrible shock. But we need you to concentrate, Cheryl. For Lisa's sake.'

Cher Farrell swipes an arm across her eyes and clears her nose. Glares at the police, the lawyer, the social worker. 'Collette,' she insists. 'Her name was Collette.'

Chapter One

Three Years Ago

She wakes up with a stiff neck, slumped across her desk. The heating's gone off and her circulation has slowed, and the cold has woken her. If it hadn't, she'd probably have slept through until lunchtime. Wouldn't be the first time ...

She sits up, her head fogged and her mouth dry. Checks her watch and sees that it's very nearly six. She's tired. She's always tired, these days. Night work really only suits the very young, and Lisa's thirty-four – no spring chicken, in clubland. As of her last birthday, some of the girls who work here are literally young enough to be her daughter, and she's feeling it. She used to get through the cashing-up by four-thirty on a Saturday morning, but tonight even the quadruple espresso she took up to the office hasn't kept her awake.

She pushes herself up from the chair and stretches. At least she's finished. She remembers, now, deciding that maybe she'd take ten minutes just to close her eyes before she took the cash to the safe, to try and ensure she wouldn't crash the car on the way home. I've got to leave this job, she thinks. I don't want to spend my nights seeing men at their worst, all slavering with lust and googly-eyed from whatever they've been at in the toilets, and I'm too old for these hours. These hours and the stress and the worrying I might end up in jail.

None of it adds up. It never does. She knows how many bottles of champagne are left in the cellar, and how many there would be if they'd sold them in the numbers the bar tabs add up to. It's the same every week. Two hundred people in the club on a good night, and though sometimes they're footballers or the modern robber barons of the City, slumming it among the tarts and the yobs, or silly young actors who think their stint in the soap they're in will last for ever, £998 for a bottle of champagne is still steep enough to make them think about the choice between drink and dance; and most of them opt for a bottle of Absolut at four hundred and fifty pounds and a bunch of private dances at fifty pounds (plus tip) a pop. But every Saturday, according to the bar tabs, they sell a hundred, hundred and fifty bottles of fizz. And all of it paid for in cash.

She slaps herself about the face a couple of times to try to wake herself up. Come on, Lisa. Sooner you get this finished, the sooner your day off begins. You can think about this when you've slept. Think about handing in your notice before there's police swarming all over this place. The Adidas bag is back by the desk, where Malik always drops it after he's been to the bank in the morning. She picks it up and starts counting the bundles of notes into it, one by one. For God's sake, she thinks – some of them are still in their wrappers. He's not even trying to make the notes look used any more.

Of course she knows what Tony's up to. Basildon lads with no obvious source of capital don't end up owning nightclubs by twenty-six, with no investors. But a place like Nefertiti's – yeah, get the pun; great name for a lap-dancing establishment, all flash and splash and paps on the door – is a licence to print money. Or if not print it, at least wash it greyish clean. That's why he makes sure they're always in the papers, why he bribes the grabby whoremongers of sport and pop and TV to come here with free drinks and girls all night in the VIP lounge. Get a reputation for being where the high rollers go, and nobody will question what you claim they spend, because everyone reads about such crazy profligacy every day in *The Sun* and everybody knows that footballers are stupid. Those clubs in town, the big ones, can take half a million easy on a Saturday night, on maybe twenty grand's worth of booze, though they probably actually hand over some goods in exchange for the money, of course.

And here it is: she finishes counting and confirms what she already knows. The bag contains a hundred and eighty-five thousand pounds, give or take a few hundred, in fifties and twenties. And on Monday morning it will go into the bank, and from the bank it will go into the white economy.

She does a last check round the office. Now all she has to do is take the cash down to the safe that's sunk in concrete in the basement store cupboard, do a last visual round the bar, and then she can lock up and leave it to the cleaners. She quite likes this time of night, despite the smell of spilled drink and sweat and poppers, the lonely smell of spooge from the back rooms. She likes it when the lights are fully up and she can see how this place the punters think is fairyland is made of smoke and mirrors. Velvet benches in pure, liquid-shrugging nylon; the light-up dance floor that's black with sticky muck, the ornate Louis XV-style mirrors whose frames are made from purest polystyrene. Even Nefertiti herself, presiding over the entrance lobby with her black bangs and her golden crook, titties out for the lads, was cast in stone-effect resin in a factory in Guiyang. She turns out the office lights, turns the key in the door and walks down the stairs.

The bars are based along a white-painted brick corridor lined with curtains in more velvet, royal blue trimmed with gold fringes this time, all hanging from long poles that allow the staff to pull them across and cut off rooms for privacy or move the VIP area around to suit the crowd that's in, and even close off sections altogether. The reputation of all nightclubs rests on the punters having felt that they were in a crowd, and in Nefertiti's they can make a crowd of a couple of dozen people if they have to. She walks along the corridor, checking each room as she passes it, making sure no strays have stayed, or passed out unnoticed behind a couch, turning off the lights as she goes. It's only when she's halfway to the end that she realises that she's not alone.

Something's going on in the Luxor Lounge. Something physical, repetitive and energetic. Sex? Is someone shagging in there? Who is it? Someone left behind? Her own staff, doing the worker's fuck-you to the bosses?

She slows her pace, quietens the sound of her steps. The corridor is thickly carpeted in black with a gold border and little gold stars. Just a small amount of pattern will hide a multitude of sins. As she approaches, she becomes less sure that it's sex she's hearing. There are grunts, and sighs, but also, she's sure, the sound of groans; and, behind it all, low laughs and chat, as though whoever's making the sounds is providing the entertainment for a corporate shindig. As she nears the curtain that's pulled across the entrance, she slows her walk down to a creep, positions herself against the wall and peeps in through a crack in the cloth.

The Luxor Lounge is black and red, dark colours that don't show the dirt. A good thing, because what's coming out of the mouth of the man on the floor will never scrub away.

There are six people in the Luxor Lounge. There's the man who lies still on the floor, as though he has long since given up protecting his vulnerable parts, whose face is so swollen his mother wouldn't recognise him; Tony Stott, her boss, the big man, the wunderkind, four years younger than she is and millions of pounds richer, all designer suit and gold cufflinks, clean-shaven even at this time of night, his tight curls cut close to his head; a woman she's not seen before, low-key in a grey suit that, from its cut, she knows didn't come from Debenhams; a much older man, late fifties, maybe, who wears a dark wool overcoat as though he's at a funeral. The three of them stand by the bar with an open bottle of Remy, drinking from snifters, watching Malik Otaran and Burim Sadiraj kick and kick and kick. As she watches, she sees the man's head snap back on his neck. A spurt of blood arches from his crumpled nose, beautiful in its elegance. Malik stands on one foot, lifts up the other to knee height, and stamps down.

She gasps.

The Luxor Lounge falls quiet. Five heads, smiles freezing on faces, pupils still distended with arousal, turn and look in her direction.

Lisa runs for the exit. Knows that she's running for her life.

Chapter Two

He's a magnificent cat. Rangy and black and swaggering, with great vampire incisors that extend most of the way to his jawline. Green eyes and a kinked tail that speak of oriental blood, and a scarred left ear that shows that he's not afraid to fight.

Today he is asserting his mastery of his territory by visiting. He's been attached to the house for so long that no one remembers who originally brought him here, or if, indeed, anybody did. Some tenants shoo him away with angry hisses, afraid of his panther grace and unblinking stare, some sweep him into their arms with coos and growls of admiration, give him a warm place to sleep, and weep when they, as they all do, have to leave him behind. Twenty-six tenants have passed through the house on Beulah Grove since he took up residence, and he has never gone hungry enough to move on himself. He has had many names and for now it's Psycho.

He stands in the window – The Lover has thrown it open because the heat inside is so stifling he's afraid he'll make the air damp with his sweat – and surveys the space, then leaps on to the back of the chair where the girl sits. He leans forward and sniffs her ginger hair, touches an ear with his fine damp nose. Affronted by her failure to respond he raises his face and looks up at the man. Blinks.

The Lover is weeping. He sits in a folding chair against the far wall, his face buried in his hands, and rocks. The tears come more quickly every time. He used to have a few hours – even a day or two – in which to savour the company, enjoy the romance, before the despair overtook him; to hold the hand and stroke the cheek and take pleasure in togetherness. But each event seems less delightful than the last, seems to pass so quickly that, almost as soon as it's done, the yearning begins again, the loneliness breaking over his head like a wave.

He's apologising, as he always does. 'I'm sorry,' he says, and the words catch, salty, in his throat. 'Oh, Nikki, I'm sorry. I'm so sorry. I didn't mean it.'

She doesn't reply. Stares, vacant, past his shoulder, her mouth half open, surprised.

'You just . . .' he says. 'I was afraid you were going to go away again. I can't bear it, you see. Can't bear it. I'm so alone.'

He continues to weep. He's consumed with self-pity, eaten up with the emptiness of his existence. My life is full of busy-work, he thinks. I do and I act and I help and I organise, and at the end of the day it's always the same. Just me. Me, alone, and the world going on as though I had never existed. They wouldn't notice – none of them – for months, if I disappeared. Families like mine, no money, fractured marriages, siblings only half-related and homes already full to bursting, we drift apart when someone goes away. I don't speak to my half-brother or sisters from one year's end to the next, just bump into them sometimes when I make the trip back at Christmas. Worst of all, my mother always sounds surprised to hear my voice on the phone, though she hears it, regular as clockwork, first Sunday of every month, while *Songs of Praise* is on. They wouldn't notice. *Nobody* would notice. I would vanish in a puff of smoke and make a nasty clearing-up job for someone further down the line.

He raises his eyes and looks at Nikki, the source of his suffering. A pretty girl. Not spectacular, not anything that anyone would say was out of his league, though he supposes that eyebrows might be raised at the difference in their ages. It was all I ever wanted, he thinks. A nice girl. No great ambition, no overwhelming passion like they play out in the movies, no champagne and roses. Just someone to stay with me, someone who wouldn't go away.

The cat is standing by the wardrobe now, sniffing at the crack between the doors. The Lover leaps to his feet and shoos it off, claps his hands and hisses so that it tenses; then, with a baleful yowl, it jumps on to the bed and out of the window. He considers closing it to keep the cat out, but in this heat his dwelling space has become stifling, overwhelming, and he's afraid that the smells it draws out will spread through the house. He wipes his salty face on his sleeve and tries to pull himself together. We can have a nice evening, at least, he thinks, as he looks back at his silent companion. I'll have a glass of wine, hold her hand. Maybe she'd like to watch a film with me, before we begin.

Her right hand, knocked by the cat's passing, slips suddenly from the arm of the chair and hangs in mid-air, still and soft. Such a pretty hand, he thinks, the nails always clean and scrupulously shaped. I noticed that about her the first time I saw her; always wanted to take that hand in my own, to press its smooth skin between my palms.

No time like the present. He fetches the fold-up chair and plants it beside the armchair. Funny, he thinks. She looks smaller than she used to. More fragile, more frail. More like someone who needs my protection. He puts the forearm back, along the chair's arm, and goes to the kitchen drawer to fetch the scissors. Cuts, very slowly, very carefully, through the duck tape around her neck, then lifts the plastic bag it holds there – thick, heavy, transparent from her head, carefully, so as not to mess up her lovely hair. He'll give her a bath, later. Strip off her stained clothing and run it through the washing machine, shampoo her sweaty locks and comb them down, dust her with baby powder. In heat like this, it'll all be dry in no time.

'There,' he says kindly and plants a loving kiss on her temple, where no pulse beats any more. He takes his seat and lifts the hand, just briefly, to his lips. 'There,' he says again, and enfolds it between his own, larger, rougher palms, as he has always imagined.

'This is nice, isn't it?' he asks, rhetorically.

Chapter Three

Despite the cloying heat he wears a cardigan that smells of tobacco, frying, and those dark creases on the body that the air never reaches. His male-pattern baldness is accentuated by a scurfy comb-over, and a pair of smeary spectacles hide his eyes. And he's fat, front-buttock fat, bulge-over-your-waistband fat. He wheezes as he leads the way slowly up the front steps, his bulk making a flight that was designed as a graceful decoration for a house of substance look narrow and mean as he climbs.

The wheezing, she thinks. It's not just the weight. There's something more to it. He's excited. Feeling pleased with himself. There's ... lust in those laboured breaths. I can feel it. The way he looked me up and down on the steps; he wasn't just deciding if I seemed respectable; he was checking out my tits.

She dismisses the thought, impatiently. Get over yourself, Collette. And so what, anyway? A dirty old man getting a thrill: it's not like you're not used to *that*, is it?

The Landlord stops for a rest on the small landing outside the front door, one hand leaning on the wall, and stares down at her. She shifts the Adidas bag further up her shoulder, giving herself a chance to surreptitiously pull her scarf over the open neck of her shirt. She's as modestly dressed as the heat of the day will allow, but she's suddenly uncomfortably aware that her clothes are clinging damply to her skin.

He takes a couple of breaths before he speaks. 'I wasn't expecting anyone yet, you see,' he says, clearly believing that he is offering an explanation for something.

She stands and waits, unsure how to respond. The bag is heavy and she wishes he would just move on to their destination, so she can drop it on the floor and shake out her arm.

'They usually start coming round the next day,' he says. 'Or in the evening, anyway. After the advert goes in. Not, like, an hour after. You caught me on the hop.'

'Sorry,' she says, not sure why she's apologising.

He takes a key from his cardigan pocket, whirls it by the tag around his index finger. 'Luckily I was here anyway,' he says. 'Had a bit of admin to deal with downstairs. Thing is, it's not ready. I was going to get a cleaner in to deal with it, but I thought we had all day.'

'Oh, that's okay,' says Collette. 'I'm good with a bottle of Flash. There's a hoover, right? In the house?'

He has wet lips. They smack together, a nasty shade of blueish pink. 'Sure,' he says. 'We've got one of those. But it's not that.'

He turns to fit the key into the front door. It's a heavy door, two panels of glass patterned with etched ivy leaves allowing light into the hallway beyond. A graceful door, made to match the aspirations of a Victorian on the way up, not the security needs of a run-down rooming house. 'It's the last tenant, you see. She skipped out on her rent and left her stuff behind.'

'Oh,' says Collette.

'Must've wanted gone in a hurry, is all I'm saying,' he says. 'Because she's left pretty much everything. I kept it all for as long as I could ... but I'm not a charity.'

'No,' says Collette. 'Of course not.'

'So it'll need clearing out. Just so you know.'

'Mmm,' she says, uncertainly. 'I was hoping to move in today.'

'Well, that doesn't give me much time to check out your references,' he says, smugly. '*Does* it?'

'No,' she says. She wishes he hadn't followed him into the hall. It's airless in here, even with the door open. The smell from his clothes bursts over her in gusts as he reaches round and pushes it to. She peers into the gloom and sees a stained grey carpet, a Utility table piled with post and a payphone attached to the wall. Haven't seen one of those in years, she thinks. Wonder how much he gets out of it each month?

A drop of sweat works its way loose from beneath the bag strap over her shoulder and trickles down into her cleavage. From behind the door to her left, to her surprise, she hears the strains of a violin playing some classical air. Not what she'd expected to hear in a place like this. If she'd thought about music at all, she'd have put her money on hip hop. 'But I really don't want to have to spend money on a hotel, if I can manage it,' she says.

'Haven't you got anyone you can go and stay with? In the meantime?'

She's got her story all lined up and ready to go. 'No,' she says. 'I've been living in Spain for the last few years. I've sort of lost touch with a lot of people. But my mum's in the hospital and I want to be near her. And, you know, you come back and you realise you don't really know anybody, any more. You know how people move around, in London. I lost touch with my school friends, and we never had any other family. It was just Mum and me ...'

She stops, and, just as she's practised in countless mirrors over the last few years, turns big, hurt eyes up to look at him. This look has helped her though more awkward situations than anything else. 'Sorry,' she concludes. 'You don't want to hear about my problems.'

Lying is easy. It's so, so easy once you've got into the swing of it. Just say what you've got to say confidently, keep it as close to the truth as you can get away with, then look vulnerable and find an excuse to duck out of the conversation as quickly as you can. Ninety-nine per cent of the time, people will just go along with whatever you tell them.

The Landlord looks faintly pleased. He thinks he's got me, she thinks. Thinks he's sussed me out. He'd be twirling his moustaches, right now, if he had them. 'Well,' he says, his voice full of speculation, 'I'm sorry to hear that.'

'It's not your problem,' she tells him, humbly. 'I understand that. But it means that I ... you know ... I don't really have anything by way of references, because I always lived at home, before I went away.'

'What were you doing in Spain?' he asks.

She tells the prepared story, the one that nobody ever wants to hear. 'I got married. He owned a bar on the Costa del Sol. More fool me ... Anyway, here I am now, no husband. Life, isn't it?'

He eyes her, speculatively. The pound signs are lighting up behind his spectacles. 'I daresay we can come to an arrangement,' he says.

Who are you kidding? You're a cash-in-hand landlord who rents his rooms out through cards in newsagents' windows. I don't suppose you've checked a reference in your life, as long as the money comes on time. Of *course* we can come to an arrangement.

'Maybe if I gave you an extra month's deposit?' she offers, as though the idea has only just come to her. 'I think I could probably manage that. I've got a bit put by. At least I managed to salvage *that* much, even if my dignity's still in Torremolinos.'

He looks pleased, then wolfish. 'You know it's already first, last and damage, don't you?'

'I thought it would be,' she says evenly, and looks at a greasy stain on the wall, at a level with her face. Someone – people – obviously feel their way up here in the dark, the flats of their hands against the wall to steady themselves. I bet none of those light bulbs works.

'Well, maybe you'd like to see the studio,' he says.

'Studio' is an exaggeration, but she had expected that from the fact that she'd found it advertised on a slightly grubby file card in a newsagent's window rather than on a glossy photo stand in an estate agent's. Northbourne is gentrifying fast, but City money has yet to drift this far south, and these Victorian streets still play host to a dwindling number of plasterboard walls and two-burner stoves and halls full of bicycles.

It's a decent-sized room, at least. At the front of the house, it must have been the drawing room once. But it smells. It's stale from sitting through a heatwave with the large sash window that overlooks the street firmly closed and her predecessor's discarded clothes in a heap in the corner. But also, she notices, because there is a small pile of food on the countertop to her left. A bag of potatoes, blackened and liquefying, half an onion, a block of cheese, an open jar of blueish pickle and the stump end of a sliced loaf, barely recognisable beneath blankets of hairy mould. In the sink, a bowl and a mug have been left to soak in water that has taken on the scent of a sewer. There's the drip, drip, drip of a tap.

The Landlord has the grace to look slightly abashed. 'Like I say,' he says, 'I haven't had the chance to get it cleaned up.'

Collette puts the Adidas bag down on the floor, relieved to be rid of it after another journey during which she kept hold of it constantly, fearfully, terrified to let it out of her sight. Without it, she'd be sunk, but she's heartily sick of the sight of it.

'Where's the bathroom?' she asks.

She'd known it was too much to hope that a 'studio' in this neck of the woods would have the luxury of an en-suite and she's glad that she's always had a strong stomach with a relatively insensitive gag reflex, because she's tired of running. She tries to persuade herself that it's not so bad. Once the window's been open a while and all that stuff's safely out for the bin man, and I've burned a couple of scented candles – it's not for ever, after all. Just until you've done the right thing. God knows what's in that fridge, though.

'So the other people ...' she says. 'Who else lives here at the moment?'

He gives her one of those goggling looks that suggests that the question is somehow impertinent. 'If I'm going to be sharing a bathroom,' she adds, 'I wouldn't mind knowing who I'll be sharing it with?'

'Oh, don't worry about that,' he says. 'Nice quiet man, Gerard Bright. Recently divorced, I think. Music teacher. The others are harmless enough. No junkies or anything, if you're worried about that. And it's only Mr Bright you'll be sharing with. The two upstairs have a bathroom between them, too.'

He shuffles over to the window, pushes back the half-closed polyester curtains and throws up the lower sash. She's pleased to see that it moves easily, as though the groove in which it runs has received a recent application of lubricant. The increased light does little to improve the prospect before her, though. Every surface is covered with dust, and the unchanged bed-clothes look grubby and worn.

'I'll get someone in to bag it all up,' he says, and jangles his keys. 'It shouldn't take too long.'

Collette perches on the edge of the armchair – she doesn't want to sit in it fully until she's given it a proper inspection – and tucks the bag behind her feet. 'It's okay. I'll take it and I'll sort it out. It's nothing a few bin liners and a vacuum cleaner won't fix.'

The Landlord raises his eyebrows.

'Oh, sorry,' says Collette. 'I didn't think. Unless you ... you know ...' she waves a hand over the abandoned junk, the tiny TV, the pile of George at Asda dresses, '... yourself ...'

He looks so offended that she knows immediately that this was exactly what he had been planning, and that, now the option has been cut off, offence is his only option. She gazes at him innocently. 'I mean, I ... I guess some of it could go to a charity shop or something.'

The Landlord huffs and turns away. 'I doubt it,' he says.

'So.' The bag is burning a hole in her ankle. She wants some quiet, some space to get her head together, and get it hidden away. 'How about it, then?'

She sees him startle. Fuck's sake, he thinks I'm proposition-ing him! Just look at you, man. It's astonishing how some men can believe they're gods among men even when they're standing next to a mirror. 'The room?' she adds, hastily. 'Can I have it?'

He knows he's got the upper hand. No one who had any options would be offering to move in on some stranger's discarded knickers, their unwashed crockery. 'Depends,' he says.

No way, she thinks.

'What with the no references, I'll need a bigger deposit. You know. For security. I'm not a charity. I'm already out a month on this little ...' He gestures round the room, at the evidence of the hasty departure.

Collette blinks: once, twice. Waits.

'And no cheques,' he says. 'I'll need it in cash. Like the rent. I've done enough bouncing cheques to last me a lifetime.'

'That's okay,' she says. 'I guessed that would be the case. Is the extra month not enough, then?'

He stands there, pretends to consider the question. She should have held back, earlier. He's got the measure of how few choices she has available. 'Six weeks,' he says, 'on top of the normal deposit. And the rent's in advance.'

'So that's ...' she says, thinking. She's got two grand in her bra, counted out from the bag in her hotel room this morning. She didn't think she could possibly need more, even in this market.

'Twenty-one hundred,' he says. 'And you don't move in until I've got it.'

She takes a deep breath. It's okay, Collette, she tells herself. He's not going to mug you. Not in his own house. But, Jesus, he's making Paris look like a holiday camp.

'I can give you two grand now. I'll have to go to the cashpoint for the rest tomorrow.'

His tongue runs across his lips and he shifts on the spot. Cash clearly has a near-erotic effect on him. He narrows his eyes at her, and licks his lips again.

She stands up and turns her back. She has no wish to put her hand near her breasts in view of this grubby old lecher. But it's perfect, the room. It's off the radar in every way. No one from her old life would look for her here and she needs this place, needs the time to regroup, see to Janine and work out what she's going to do next.

The cash is warm, slightly damp from contact with her heat-soaked skin. She turns back and holds the money out. The Landlord pinches it between thumb and forefinger, and stares her in the face. I must hold his gaze. I mustn't be the one to look down first. If I do, he'll know he's the boss and I'll never see the back of him.

'I'll need a receipt for that,' she says.

Collette closes the door, tries to put the snib down on the flimsy Yalelock. It slides, but doesn't engage. She waits, her ear pressed against a wooden panel, and listens for the sound of his leaving. Hears him hover in the hall outside, feels the weight of his labouring breath. After a minute or so his shuffling tread moves away, starts slowly up the stairs. He lets out a small grunt as he takes each step.

She looks round her new home. Yellowing magnolia walls, thin polyester curtains in a pattern of geometric colour blocks on a field of blue that she recognises from several one-star hotels she's stayed in over the years, the unmade bed, the armchair, the small Formica table below the window. The previous tenant's hairbrush lying on the windowsill, a few red hairs caught in the bristles. What sort of person moves on without even taking their hairbrush? she wonders.

Someone like you, she replies. She remembers her last room, in Barcelona: the clothes she will never see again, her make-up scattered across the top of the chest of drawers, her books, the necklaces hanging from panel-pins knocked into the back of the bedroom door, the sounds of café life in the street below. At least, thank God, she'd put the bag in a locker at the station, because once she'd seen Malik in the street outside she could never risk going in there again. She feels tears prick the back of her eyes. Someone will come along, eventually, when the rent runs out, and throw it all away. No one will wonder where she's gone, why she left in such careless haste. She feels a certain fellow feeling with the vanished tenant. She's part of the easy-come, easy-go world now and only Tony Stott wants to know where she is.

Collette goes over to the bed and pulls back the bedclothes. They smell of someone else. She saw a big Asda nearby from the window of the train. She'll head there and buy a couple of sets when she's had a rest; maybe even treat herself to a new duvet and pillows, too.

You mustn't spend it all, she thinks, automatically, the way she has each time she's started again. Don't go blowing it. It's all you have, Collette.

She fetches the bag from under the chair. Sits on the bed and checks, as she's checked every hour since she fled for the station, that the contents are still there, pulls out the small stash of emergency belongings she stored in there and lays them out to mark her territory. A couple of summer dresses, a cardigan, flip-flops, a couple of pairs of knickers, a sponge bag with a toothbrush, a tube of face cream and a small collection of eyeliners from her handbag. All she's salvaged, this time. Not much to show for nearly forty years, but it's better than no life at all.

She sits, then lies, on this stranger's bottom sheet. It's mercifully free of stains, at least. She can't face the thin, sad-looking pillows, though. Uses the bag and what remains inside as a rest for her head instead. It's firm, unyielding. Who'd've thought? she wonders, that you could be this uncomfortable lying on a hundred thousand pounds?

Chapter Four

The signs are everywhere that Northbourne is coming up in the world, though it still has a way to go. There are new businesses springing up: a deli that sells sun-dried tomatoes and the sort of cheese that smells of armpit, an estate agent with a one-syllable name that hands out free cappuccino if you look smart and old enough, a dedicated greengrocer and a café with pavement tables and extra-wide aisles to accommodate the buggies. But most of all, Cher has noticed that there are new signs. One has appeared on the lamp-post on the corner of Station Road and the High Street since she passed by this morning. She stops to read her way slowly through it, her lips moving as she does so.

THIEVES OPERATE IN THIS AREA.
TAKE CARE OF YOUR BELONGINGS.

She raises her eyebrows. A sure sign, if ever there was one, that there are people living here now who have something worth stealing. Cher instinctively checks the breast pocket of her denim jacket, where her money is stored. Feels the slight bulge and smiles. It's been a good week. She's got the rent, and cash left over, and three days until it's due. She might even take a couple of days off, do her roots, give herself a manicure. There's a new range of glitter varnishes in the chemist on the High Street. She might pop in, buy some emery boards and treat herself to one of those while she's there.

She hoists her floral backpack to her shoulder and turns on to the High Street. It's the tail end of lunchtime, and the street is relatively busy, filled with savoury scents from the food outlets scattered among the charity shops: curry, fried chicken, Greggs' sausage rolls, the smell of chips from the greasy spoon.

Cher dawdles along the pavement: no rush to be anywhere; no rush, ever. But her eyes, behind her Primark sunglasses, are watchful, take in everything around her in the search for opportunities. Life can't be just about making the rent. There needs to be more. It's hard to remember on a day like today, but winter will be coming – the long dark nights, the days spent mostly sleeping because it's too cold to get out of bed. She needs to start saving to top up her meter card – there are some things you just can't get for free.

She scans the road. Wherever there's a crowd, there's an opportunity. Today she's done a circuit of the redemption stores of Tooting, Streatham and Norbury – no need for any great stealth, just confidence and an air of shame, a talent for playing the embarrassed, cash-strapped student who's spent their loan on tech and run out of food. She rarely works her home patch, though, apart from the occasional foray into the Co-op when she's forgotten to get cat food for Psycho. The West End, where people are distracted and careless with their tech, and she's just one of thousands of girls in short skirts, is a richer and safer place in which to work. Only junkies and other people too wasted or desperate or tired to get themselves further afield work their own home patch. But her eye roams, automatically, and logs the chances available.

In front of the Brasserie Julien – one of the new arrivals, all brass and wood and marble table tops – a group of Yummy Mummies has gathered. The new breed of Northbourneite, driven further out by the rising prices of Clapham and Wandsworth and Balham in search of period fixer-uppers with room for a conservatory kitchen extension in the side-return. They're drinking cappuccinos in the shade of the canopy, designer sunglasses perched on heads like hairbands, a couple of toddlers strapped into jogging buggies beside them, talking loudly about what a joy it is to live in such a multicultural area. Their handbags sit carefully between their feet, but a bag from the White Company hangs from the back of a buggy and all three have lined their iPhones up on the table like badges of identity. That's £200, right there, she thinks. Just trip over one of their kids, and I'd have all their Apple products before they'd retrieved the organic low-fat apple snacks. Though their prices are going down as they get commoner and commoner, Apple products still have a greater resale value than any other tech because people still think they make them look rich. That's why she specialises in scrumping.

She walks on, past the dusty display of dead pensioners' unwanted knick-knacks in the window of the Help the Aged shop, the shuttered Citizens' Advice, the Asian grocer that only seems to sell cumin and evaporated milk. She pauses at the window of Funky Uncles and sees that the eternity ring she sold there six weeks ago has gone on sale for three times what they gave her for it. It's a mug's game, this, she thinks. When I'm older I'll have a pawnshop of my own. It's a licence to print money.

Outside the new deli, a woman her mum's age – well, the age her mum would have been – pauses and delves in her shoulder bag at the sound of a ringtone. Snatches the phone out, turns away from the street and starts to talk, the flap left hanging, unsecured. It's like they're tempting me, thinks Cher, as if they've heard my thoughts.

An old lady, auburn wig faded to rusty lilac, drags a wheelie bag past her, a leather wallet bulging from the pocket of the tweed overcoat she wears despite the heat. A sitting duck, thinks Cher; thinks of her nanna, tumbling to the floor in Toxteth, the hip that never really healed, and reaches out to touch her sleeve.

''Scuse me, love,' she says.

The old woman regards her with half-vacant, faded blue eyes. Hairs like fuse wire sprout from her upper lip and chin. Cher smiles, encouragingly. 'You don't want to be leaving that sticking out like that,' she says. 'Someone'll have it off you.'

She sees the woman struggle to interpret her accent. Fuck's sake, she thinks, I'm only a Scouser. It's not like I'm from Newcastle or something.

She points towards the purse, waits as the woman looks down, sees understanding dawn as she fumbles with knotted old knuckles to ram it deeper into the pocket. I don't want to get old, thinks Cher. There's nothing in the world will make me live like that, smelling of piss and my tits round my knees and not even able to keep warm on a day like this.

The woman looks up at her and bestows her with a snaggled smile. 'Thanks, darling,' she says, the tones of London almost as impenetrable and jarring to Cher's ear as those of the Mersey were to her. 'That was nice of you.'

'That's all right,' says Cher.

'Not many young people bother, these days,' she says, and Cher realises, too late, that she's befriended a talker. 'You're all in such a rush. I'm surprised you bothered to stop – young people are so selfish.'

Her tone has changed from the brief flash of gratitude to one of reproach. Oh, God, thinks Cher, never a good deed goes unpunished.

'In my day, we respected old people,' the old lady says, 'and we got a clip round the ear if we didn't.'

The urge to roll her eyes is almost overwhelming. 'You're not allowed to do that any more. It's against the law.'

The old woman purses her lips like a cat's arse. Not a sweet little old lady at all. Not her nanna. She's always wondered how people manage to believe that old age automatically bestows some sort of saintliness when they are so convinced – if the platitudes she's heard mouthed at funerals are anything to go by – that only the good die young. 'And more's the pity,' she says.

Cher considers tipping her wheelie bag over, but settles for saying. 'Never mind, you're *welcome*,' pointedly, and walks on shaking her head. You can't win if you're young these days. You're damned if you do and damned if you don't. She helps herself to an apple from the display outside the Knossos mini-mart, turns the corner on to Beechcroft Road and takes off her jacket. It really is hot today. Too hot. She'd like to ditch the wig as well, but she's too careful for that. Nowhere in England is built for this sort of heat. It's stupid, having to walk all this way to get back to pretty much where she started. If she could get over that chain link at the station, she'd be home in less than a minute. There's even a gap in the garden fence that leads straight on to the embankment.

Beechcroft Road is full of skips. There are four along its hundred-yard length, their bricks and laminate-kitchen-cabinet contents bearing witness to the arrival of the home improvers. Cher scans them as she passes for usable gear, but it's all builders' rubble and some hideous patterned carpet. She once saw a beautiful Persian rug in a skip off Kensington High Street, but she had no way of getting it home.

A telly, she thinks. That's what I could really do with. If I had a telly, I wouldn't need to go out so much. It's going out that costs the most. You can't do anything for free in this town, unless you're ready to pay in other ways.

She crosses over on to the opposite pavement to turn into Beulah Grove. This side of the street basks in full sun, and it's like stepping into an oven. She hurries round the corner, crosses over into the shade, suddenly aware that her mouth is parched. One of the Poshes' kids – Celia, Delia, Amelia, whatever – has dumped a pink bicycle at the foot of the steps up to number twenty-one. I could have that, thinks Cher. Probably get twenty quid for it in the Royal Oak. Some people don't know they're born. Some people deserve to get ripped off.

She passes by, pauses at the bottom of her steps to find her keys, and glances down to see if the net curtains covering the basement window move. If Vesta is back from her holidays, she'll be looking out: she's always looking out, constantly on the watch for life passing by her window. But nothing moves. Cher shrugs. She'll be back soon, she's sure. She runs up the steps to the front door.

She smells the Landlord before she hears him. Knows for a fact that he's been in today, from the aroma he's left behind: Old Spice and Febreze and, below all that, something cheesy, old and rotten. It's got worse, lately. The smell of him seems to hang around in the communal parts of the house even when she's seen no sign of him all day. Bugger, she thinks, and closes the door as quietly as she can. Her rent's not due till the end of the week, but that's never stopped him from popping in to 'check up' on her, breathing and snuffling and trying to see her nipples.

She hears his voice, and the boards on the upstairs landing creak beneath his weight. He's talking to Hossein, walking towards the stairs. He'll corner her by the front door, subject her to his leery flirting, his innuendo, his knowing smirk. Cher looks back towards the front door. She's almost at the bottom of the stairs, and it'll take too long to get there and get it open from here. She can see the toes of his trainers on the top step. He'll see her from halfway down and she won't be able to get away.

She glances down at her hand and sees that Nikki's key is still on her keyring. The door to her bedsit is three steps away. Cher tiptoes to it, scrabbles the key into the lock and slips inside the room.

Chapter Five

Collette snaps from her sleep at the sound of a key turning in the door lock. She had only meant to lie down for a few minutes, but those minutes plunged her into the deep, black unconsciousness of exhaustion. And now she's awake again, head fogged and nerves jangling, kicking her way up this strange bed, coming to rest against the headboard with the bag clutched to her chest as though it will shield her against a bullet. Oh God, oh God, oh God, she thinks, as she's thought every time she has been surprised in the past three years, they've found me! They've found me and I'm dead.

A slight figure enters the room. A girl: brassy blonde hair, floral backpack with leather-look straps hanging from one shoulder, skin dyed Egyptian mummy brown, closes the door, turns and gawps as she catches sight of her.

'Oh,' she says in a Mersey accent and the high tones of someone who's barely got used to her hormones. 'What the fuck are *you* doing here?'

Collette can't find her voice. Her heart is fluttering in her chest and she's still waiting to breathe.

'This is Nikki's room,' says the girl. 'Don't tell me he's gone and let it already.'

Collette's heart slows.

'She's only been gone two weeks,' says the girl. 'Less than that. You'd think he'd have left it a *month*, anyway.'

She starts forwards, and Collette stiffens, tightens her grip on her bag. The girl stops, widens her eyes and holds her hands up in the air, palms toward her.

'All right, all right,' she says, 'keep your hair on.'

Then suddenly, as if she's reminded herself by saying it, she reaches up and pulls her own hair off. Stands, blonde mop in hand, and releases a mass of loose curls, bleached so the hair has gone an interesting metallic shade, from the confines of a stocking cap. She runs the fingers of her free hand through it, ruffles up the sweaty roots. Not fake tan at all, thinks Collette. She's mixed race. Amazing how a change of hair can completely change the way you interpret someone. Don't I just know that?

'Phwoar,' she says, 'that's better. I thought my head was going to come off, it's that hot under there.'

Collette finds her voice at last.

'What are you doing in my room?'

The girl looks surprised, as though this is an odd question. Then she smiles, and shrugs. 'Oh, yeah, sorry about that. But to be fair, I didn't know it was your room, did I? Nikki gave me a copy of her key. So I could come in and watch telly when she was out. I really love *Real Housewives*. D'you like that? And *Judge Judy*. Anyway, I heard the Landlord coming down the stairs, and I popped in to get away from him.'

Collette doesn't say anything, just stares, and waits.

A little frown crosses the girl's face; the look of someone struggling to make herself understood by a foreigner.

'You've met the Landlord, right?' She pantomimes waving a hand in front of her face, holding her nose. 'Yeah, course you have. You're gorra've done, if you rented a room off him. Unless you're a burglar. Are you a burglar? There's not much to nick in here, you know. Even the telly's from a car boot.'

'No,' says Collette, 'I'm not a burglar. Are you?'

The girl bursts out laughing. 'Only on weekends. You're all right.'

'I moved in this morning,' says Collette.

The girl looks around her, disbelieving. 'So you've just ... taken over someone else's life?'

'I ...'

'Cause you've not exactly put your stamp on the place, have you?'

'My ... my stuff's coming after ... I ...' she stammers, then stops. Hang on, she thinks, what are you doing? It's not like I've done anything wrong, is it? 'Anyway,' she says, 'I don't see how it's any business of yours.'

'Nikki's my friend,' says the girl, 'I'm looking out for her.'

'Well, if she comes back, she can have anything she wants,' says Collette. 'It's not like I'm putting it on eBay.'

A silence. They stare each other down. Then the girl drops her bag from her shoulder and says, 'I'm Cher, anyway. I live upstairs.'

'Collette,' says Collette.

Cher puts a finger to her lips and presses her ear against the door. Outside, heavy footfalls plod up the passage and keys jangle in a hand. While the girl's face is turned away, Collette takes the opportunity to tuck the bag down the side of the bed, get it out of Cher's sightline. The last thing she wants is for anyone to see its contents.

Chapter Six

It's a long journey from Ilfracombe to Northbourne by public transport. Vesta's been on the road for eight hours, hobbling from bus to train to bus again, and is feeling her back and the arthritis in her knee. The walk from the High Street, dragging her suitcase behind her on its wonky wheel, seems to take as long as the trip from Victoria. I'm not sure how many more times I can do this, she thinks mournfully. I feel my age more each year. But, oh – if I didn't have my two weeks by the sea, what would be the point of any of it? Just Northbourne day after day, the hoodies in the bus shelter and the litter on the common, the rattle of the suburban trains passing by at the end of the garden. Damn you for a coward, Vesta Collins, she chides herself. You always wanted to live by the sea. You should have gone when Mum died, not taken the easy route and tied yourself to a sitting tenancy.

On the corner of Bracken Gardens, she sees Hossein sauntering up the road towards her, dapper in a shirt of cotton brocade, his beard neatly trimmed. She waves, and his face is suddenly wreathed in smiles. He hurries up to her and stretches out a hand to take hold of the handle of her case.

'You're home!' he says. 'I've missed you.'

Vesta laughs, and pushes at his upper arm. 'Oh, go on, you. You're all charm.'

He takes the bag and starts pulling it towards the house. 'What are you doing?' she protests. 'You're on your way out!'

'Don't be ridiculous, woman. I can go later.'

'But you—'

'Enough,' he barks. 'Do as you're told.'

She subsides, content. The magazines she read when she was young, when feminism was a mere glint in Germaine's eye, were full of warnings about Middle Eastern men and how controlling they were. Never said anything about the gentlemanliness, though, she thinks. Catch an Englishman dropping his trip to the bookies to drag an old lady's suitcase home.

'Did you have a good holiday?' he asks.

'Oh, lovely, thank you. It's so beautiful down there. Even with that silly statue they've stuck in the middle of it.'

'So I heard,' he says.

'Yes. You should go and see it,' she says. 'Silly, being here and not seeing anything of the country.'

'As soon as I can, I will,' says Hossein. 'There are a lot of places I want to see.'

Vesta remembers. 'Sorry, poppet,' she says. 'Mind like a sieve, me.'

Hossein gives her his lovely smile again. 'It's okay. I take it as a compliment.'

'Where were you off to, anyway?'

'To sign my little book,' he says, 'so they know I haven't run away. Then I'm going to Kensington.'

'Kensington!' says Vesta. 'Posh!'

He laughs. 'Iranian shops. I'm going to see my cousin. He lives in Ealing.'

'That's nice,' says Vesta. 'It's nice to have family. Even if they *are* in Ealing.'

'Yes,' says Hossein. 'It is. Do you have any family of your own?'

She pauses, sighs. 'Not any more. I had an auntie in Ilfracombe, but she passed away a few years ago, now.'

'No brothers or sisters?'

'No, nothing like that.'

She sees him glance at her from the side of his eye. Don't look at me like that, she thinks. It's a fine old day when *you* feel sorry for *me*.

'You don't miss what you never had, dear,' she says. 'It's not like I don't have friends, is it?'

'No,' he says. 'You're good at that.'

Vesta smiles. Such a charmer. But still, she feels warmed by the compliment. 'So how's life at the old homestead?' she asks. 'Any gossip? How's that little girl? Not got into any trouble, has she?'

Hossein shrugs. 'No. She's okay, I think. No trouble. There's a new woman, moved into Nikki's room.'

'Oh! Nikki didn't come back, then?'

'No. Not a sign of her. And her rent's run out, so boom, she's history.'

'That's weird,' says Vesta. 'She was a nice girl. I didn't think she would be the type.'

Hossein shrugs expansively, as is his habit. 'I know. But there you go. And you know what he's like. Not going to leave it a day longer than he needs without getting some money.'

'Well,' says Vesta. Then: 'She just went? I can't believe it. She didn't say goodbye? Not even to Cher?'

'Not as far as I know.'

'Well,' says Vesta, again. The itinerant movements of the young never cease to amaze her. 'Maybe she went back to Glasgow. Did she make up with her folks, did you hear?'

'Vesta,' says Hossein, 'nobody tells me anything. I sometimes think you're the only one who realises I speak English.'

'Well,' says Vesta again. 'So what's she like?'

'Don't know,' says Hossein. 'She only got here today. I heard the Landlord letting her in, so I ... '

'Oh, you big scaredy-cat.'

He shrugs again. She's right, of course. A man his age shouldn't be hiding from strangers, even if they do have Roy Preece attached. They reach the steps and he bends to slide the handle back into the case. Picks it up and starts towards the door. 'Good God, woman. What have you got in here?'

'Oh, sorry,' she says. 'I didn't have anywhere to dispose of the bodies. It was only a bed and breakfast.'

'How many people you killed? Have you no self-control? You've only been gone two weeks.'

She starts up the steps behind him, winces as she bends her knee. She can't wait to have a sit-down and put her feet up, have a cuppa. There's not much in the flat, but she at least had the foresight to lay in a pint of UHT before she left. Not as good as fresh, but better than nothing, and there's no way she's leaving the house again today. There's a packet of digestives in the tin, she's pretty sure, and a block of cheddar in the fridge. There are times when the reduced appetite of age is a great convenience.

Hossein opens the front door, and stands by to wait for her

to pass. From behind Gerard Bright's door a piece of music, all piano and sobbing cello, plays on and on as it had done the day she left for Ilfracombe; it's as though she'd just popped out to the corner shop. She steps in to the hall and notices that the familiar smells of her childhood – dust and impermanence, and a slight whiff of damp – have had another layer added to them. Something ... meaty, she thinks; like something's died under the floorboards and has yet to desiccate. We need to get this place aired out, she thinks. There's no ventilation on this stairwell, with all the doors shut most of the time.

She stretches, her journey finally over, and leafs through the mail on the hall table. A couple of circulars – the usual stuff, animal charities thinking she's a sucker, old-people insurers reminding her she's going to die. 'Oh, but it's good to be home,' she says, and isn't sure she means it.

'No place like it,' says Hossein, but she misses the faint irony in his voice.

She puffs out her cheeks and drops the letters into her bag, ready for the recycling bin. 'Can I tempt you to a cuppa?' she asks Hossein. 'Before you go out?'

He checks his watch. 'Sure. I don't have to hurry.'

She fetches her key from her handbag. 'I'll put the kettle on, then.'

She knows the moment she ducks in through her narrow door under the hall stairs that something isn't right. The air in the flat is too fresh. For a moment, she wonders if she forgot to close a window before she left for Devon, but then she switches on the light at the top of the stairs and sees that her umbrella stand – her mother's umbrella stand – is lying on its side.

For a moment, her brain freezes. The sight of the unexpected where all is so familiar leaves her grasping for thought. 'Oh,' she says. Then, catching sight of *The Crying Boy*, his frame askew on the wall, she suddenly knows what has happened and her guts lurch. 'Oh,' she says again.

She hears Hossein drag the bag in through the door as she feels her way wordlessly down the stairs, clutching on to the banister as soon as it starts, like a proper old person. Her legs are weak, her breath watery. Sixty-nine years she has lived here, the world changing around her and neighbours coming and going, but this has always been her place of safety. No one has ever come in here without invitation. No one has ever invaded.

She reaches the bottom of the steps with a flood of relief and dread as she feels the solid ground beneath her feet. The hall is scattered with umbrellas and walking sticks, her father's precious books tossed out from their shelf on to the faded Axminster, her coats, her mother's hats – globes of fake fur and fabric roses she could never bear to give to the charity shop – ripped from the hooks above and trodden into the ground. 'Oh,' she says again. Hossein, concentrating on balancing his burden down the steep staircase, has yet to see the chaos, is yet to remark upon it.

She doesn't want to go any further. Wants to turn tail and run, go back to Ilfracombe, not have to face it. Glancing up the corridor towards her tiny kitchen, she can see light where the outside door should be. It's hanging open, on its hinges, kicked or jemmied during one of the nights she slept unknowing in her bed and breakfast, lulled by the sounds of gulls and water.

Vesta puts a hand on to her breastbone, feels her heart thud in her chest. It's too much. This is too much. She steps over the fallen umbrella stand and peers into the living room. The curtains are open, the nets still drawn, but the light that penetrates here, even on a blazing summer day like today, is thin and pale. She switches on the light, looks around her, feels tears spring into her throat.

'Oh, Hossein,' she says. 'Oh, my Lord.'

Chapter Seven

She lies on the bed, listens to the sound of voices in the corridor outside. There's something going on beyond her door; something's happened. She hears a man's voice, foreign; the guttural aitch of the East raised over the classical music that started up an hour after she arrived and continues to pierce her party wall. From somewhere in the distance, floating through the window over the sticky air, the sound of sobbing, a woman's voice saying, periodically: 'No! Oh, no! Oh, no!'

Collette rolls on to her side, picks up the pillow and presses it to her ear. She's exhausted, wrung out after her journey, after three years spent looking over her shoulder, dreading the weeks or months to come. She's desperate to sleep, desperate to feel that, even for a few days, a few weeks, she can let her guard down and rest while she finds out what's going to happen with Janine. It's okay, she tells herself. You don't have to get involved. Just keep yourself to yourself and—

A series of loud bangs on her door wrenches her upright. Someone's thumping on it as though they plan to break through.

Collette sits on a stranger's musky sheets and stares as the wood judders beneath a fist. A man's voice, the foreign accent that she heard passing out in the hall earlier, an edge of intemperate urgency. 'Hello? Hello?'

Angry men. The world is full of angry men. She can't face an angry man today. She feels like she's been running from them all her life.

He thumps again, rattles at her door handle. 'Hello? Are you in there? I need to talk to you.'

Maybe if I just keep quiet ... at least this one doesn't seem to have a key ...

Another burst of hammering. 'HELLO?'

She pushes herself off the bed and crosses the room. No spyhole, no chain, no bolts: it's as secure as a sauna, this room. She steels herself, throws the door open, ready to fight.

The most beautiful man she has ever seen stands in the corridor, clenched fist raised at her face. Golden skin and sad, almond eyes, glossy black hair and a beard trimmed close to sharp, angular cheeks. A generous mouth that, even in what is clearly a state of some disturbance, is dimpled at the sides by good humour. Collette gasps, and blushes.

He misinterprets the sound. Looks at his upraised hand and drops it to his side. 'Oh,' he says. 'I'm sorry. I didn't know you were going to open it.'

It's a precise diction, its foreign edge poetical, educated, the consonants carefully separated. He's learned his English from the BBC, not CNN.

Collette feels her blush begin to subside, says: 'That's okay. Just lucky I didn't open it a second later or you would've broken my nose.'

He laughs. 'I was just ... ' She sees him look her up and down, take in her crumpled face, her crumpled clothes. 'I'm sorry, you were sleeping.'

Up the corridor, by the front door, the door to Flat One opens and a man – washed-out sandy hair and skin with the strange plasticky quality that always makes you think that the top few layers have somehow been burnt off – steps out and stares. Collette leans out of her own door and gives him what she hopes is a friendly smile. No point in being stand-offish with her neighbours. It's not like they can't all hear each other. The man blushes and looks down, then retreats into his domain. The sound of his music dies back as he closes his door again.

'It's okay,' she says, hurriedly, not wanting to admit that this is how she's been dressed all day. 'Stupid thing to do, in the middle of the afternoon. I'll be up all night, now.'

He offers a hand. 'Hossein Zanjani,' he says. 'I live upstairs. Above you.'

'Hello, Hossein.' She shakes the hand, leaves it a beat. 'I'm Collette.'

'Collette,' he says. 'That's a pretty name. French?'

Collette shakes her head. 'Irish mother who spent too much time reading romance novels.'

And a useful name, as it turns out, given that she shed it in primary school after two terms of playground banter and used her second name. It was the work of a moment to swap it back to the front when she applied for her Irish passport.

She deliberately steps out through the door, into his territory. She already feels that the room behind her is her safety zone, but she learned a lot from watching Tony and Malik and Burim, in the time when they weren't her enemies: watching them assert their authority with a single forward footstep, a cold smile, a refusal to allow their arms to cross their bodies. She pulls the door to behind her, leaving it slightly ajar but blocking off his view of her space.

'What can I do for you?' she asks.

He takes a step back, cedes the status.

'I – so, you moved in this morning?' he asks.

'This morning,' says Collette. 'That's right.'

'The Landlord didn't scare you away?'

'Beggars can't be choosers,' she says, and sees him blink with incomprehension. Okay. His English is good, but not *that* good. He's not been here all that long. Either that, or he doesn't get out, much.

'I just,' he says again, then takes a moment to formulate his next words. 'I wanted to ask you. Vesta ...' He gestures towards a doorway under the stairs that she hadn't noticed when she arrived. 'The old lady downstairs. She's been burgled.'

'Oh, no,' Collette makes the appropriate sounds of sympathy, though her thoughts stray immediately to the bagful of cash lying by the side of her bed. 'How awful.'

'Yes. It is. Poor lady. She came back from holiday, and ... anyway, I was wondering if you'd ... noticed anything. You know. Anything unusual.'

'Oh,' she says. 'I'm so sorry. Poor lady.' She wants to ask more, like: is this something that happens a lot? Should I be worrying? But contents herself with saying, 'No. No, I haven't. Though I suppose I've only been here a few hours, so I wouldn't know unusual from not.'

He looks impatient, as though she's not being helpful. Well, what do you expect me to say? she thinks. And by the way, you turning straight up here at my door the second there's been a burglary doesn't exactly make me feel welcome.

'No ... you know. Someone moving around downstairs? You didn't see anybody?'

Collette shakes her head. 'I'm sorry. Mind you, it's hard to hear anything over the free entertainment.' She jerks her head towards the flat next door. Hossein rolls his eyes and grins.

'Poor lady. Is she okay? She wasn't hurt, was she?'

He's backing away already. 'No. No, she's okay. She was away. She's just ... upset.'

'Yes,' says Collette, and puts a hand on her door handle. It's clear the conversation is coming to an end. This beautiful man hasn't come to welcome her to the house, but to interrogate her about her movements; to check her out. She's not going to get involved. She's only here for as long as it takes to see Janine through to the end. 'I should think she would be. Has she lost anything valuable?'

Hossein shakes his head. 'I don't know. It's a mess. And, you know, she doesn't have much. Family things ...'

A fleeting look of inexpressible sadness crosses his face. For a moment, he's a thousand miles away. He snaps back into the room, gives her a sorrowful smile. 'She's still, you know ...'

'Oh, dear,' says Collette. She knows she should offer condolences, offer to help, because that's what civilised people do. But *I'm not civilised*, she thinks. *Not any more. You fall asleep at the job, and before you know it ...*

Their attention is diverted by the sound of someone jogging up the outside steps, whistling tunelessly. It's a semi-familiar tune, more from its rhythm than from any actual musicality. A key slips into the street door and turns. A man comes in: an unremarkable forty-something, a courier bag in one hand and a supermarket carrier in the other, looking at his keys as he wiggles them from the lock, as yet unaware of them, still whistling. Thinning hair, slightly tinted spectacles and Hush Puppies. A brushed-cotton shirt with a tiny, faded check let into the weave, like a farmer in a documentary. I know what that song is, she thinks. 'I'm Leaning on a Lamp-post at the Corner of the Street'. Now I know I'm really back in England if the neighbours are whistling George Formby.

The man looks up, jumps and claps a hand over his heart. 'Jesus!'

He's instinctively raised his courier bag in front of his chest like a shield, lowers it as his eyes focus on Hossein. He glances from him to Collette and back again. 'My God,' he says, 'you nearly gave me a heart attack.'

'Sorry,' says Hossein. He doesn't sound particularly sorry.

'Hot, isn't it?' The man's eyes run up and down her, like Hossein's before them. Differently, though. His spectacles glint with a gleeful sort of curiosity. 'Visitor, Hossein?'

'No,' says Hossein. 'This is Collette.'

She looks over at him. That's not madly helpful, is it? 'I – I live here, actually,' she adds.

The eyes glint behind the specs. A likely story, they say.

'Nikki's room. I've taken over Nikki's room, I just moved in today.'

The man's face clouds with doubt. 'Nobody said anything to *me*,' he says.

Were they meant to? She tries again. 'The Landlord let it to me. Roy Preece? This morning?'

This seems to be the password, the Open Sesame. 'Oh,' he says. 'Well, sorry about that. You can't be too careful.'

He gives her one of those toothy smiles that looks like he's practised it a lot, but doesn't get too many opportunities to use it in real life. They're not great teeth. Small and pointy and yellowed from lack of cosmetic care. 'Thomas,' he says.

She realises the word is an introduction, shakes the hand he offers. 'Hi, Thomas.'

'Welcome to Beulah Grove. I live upstairs.' He points upwards, in case she is in any doubt as to where it might be.

'In the attic,' says Hossein.

'Oh, right,' she says. 'I didn't know there was an attic flat.'

'It's a Tardis,' says Thomas. 'I keep thinking I'm going to stumble across a secret portal to another dimension. How are you?' he asks Hossein.

'I'm okay,' says Hossein. 'But I'm afraid poor Vesta's been burgled.'

Thomas drops his courier bag on to the carpet. 'No!'

Hossein nods solemnly.

'Christ! I knew it. I knew it would happen. It's that girl. I swear she doesn't understand how a door works. I can't tell you how many times I've just found it hanging open. Oh, poor Vesta.'

'It wasn't the front door,' says Hossein. 'Whoever it was came in through the garden.'

Thomas seems to simply tune this out. He turns to Collette and puts a hand on her upper arm. Instinctively, she goes to pull back. It's overfamiliar, this touch. Grabby. 'You need to make sure you keep your door locked, even when you just go to the loo, young lady. Especially living in *that* room. Easy access from the street, you see. Opportunists. They can be in and out in a minute. Poor Vesta.'

'I don't think it was opportunists,' says Hossein. 'It looks as if …'

'You can't be too careful,' Thomas continues, as if Hossein

hadn't spoken. Hossein looks irritable, then forces a look of patience on to his face. He's clearly used to this man talking without listening. 'I don't even like leaving my windows open, when I go out. Even on the top floor.'

She slides her arm out from his clutch, steps back towards the sanctuary of her door. 'Thanks,' she says. 'I'll bear it in mind.'

'Seriously,' says Thomas. 'I wouldn't even go to sleep with your window open, if it was me. Someone could easily ...'

'Yes, thanks,' she snaps. 'I feel *much* safer now.'

'Well, I'm just *saying*. I mean, I don't suppose Vesta ...'

She's got the door open. 'Yes, thank you.'

He starts walking towards her, as though he's assumed that the open door is some sort of invitation. 'Why don't I ...'

'Yes, maybe some other time,' she says. Hossein meets her eyes behind her back, and winks. He's biting his lower lip, and his eyes shine with merriment. Ah, the house bore, she thinks.

'It's no problem,' continues Thomas. 'It won't take a—'

'Thanks,' she says. 'Ooh! There's my phone! Got to go!'

She skips inside and closes the door.

Chapter Eight

There's a new tenant in Nikki's room. Barely time for her sheets to get cold. Thin and nervous-looking, creamy skin – Scottish blood, perhaps? Or Irish? – thick fair curls pulled to the back of her head with a rubber band and a smattering of freckles across the bridge of her nose. She doesn't look as if she belongs here. But then, he wonders, which one of us *does* look like we belong here? Maybe that's what all the people who live in houses like this have in common: that we all look like we're just passing through. And, of course, most of us are.

I'll have to get to know her, he thinks. Find out her story. She looks … interesting. Like she might have a tale or two to tell. Like she might be one of those strangers who could one day become a friend.

He thinks about her as he makes his preparations. Marianne, with her long dark hair and her scarlet manicure, watches him silently from the armchair. Today, she is dressed in an olive-green silk shift dress, size ten from the Monsoon sale. It hangs off her in folds, far too large, but it's a good colour and an elegant cut, and he can always take it in; he's become handy at many skills, over the years. He picked it based on the labels in the clothes she was wearing when they met, but of course she has lost weight since then, gone down to the level of emaciation you generally only see in famine zones, or Hollywood. He needs to remember this, for the future. His lovely friends are thin. Fashionably thin, and then some.

He has bought a new set of plastic sheeting from the builder's merchant off the Balham High Road. The Lover doesn't like to attract attention to himself by buying his supplies too close to home, or too many from the same source. It's time-consuming, but he knows it's worth it. He could, for instance, have bought the bicarb at £29.99 for twenty-five kilos on eBay, the washing soda at the cash and carry, but he doesn't want to do anything that will cause remark. So every day, he goes into each super-market he passes and drops a single pack into his Bag For Life, carries it home bit by bit to store in his cupboards. The bicarb he buys from the craft shop, two, three, kilos at a time, along with bottles of essential oils, which work wonders for smells. The nice, home-knit ladies behind the counter believe he has a hobby business making bath bombs which he sells on Etsy. It's an unorthodox pastime for a man, but in this increasingly met-rosexual age, not odd enough to attract attention.

He rolls out his plastic sheet. It is heavy – the heaviest gauge he could buy – and transparent, so the faded flower pat-tern on the carpet shows eerily through from beneath. As he crawls across the floor, he brushes Marianne's shin with his elbow.

'Oh, I'm sorry, my darling,' he says. 'Excuse me.'

The skin on her legs looks dry, today, her hair low in lustre, her make-up faded.

'I've been neglecting you,' he apologises. 'I'm sorry. I've been busy ... you know how it is. I hope you won't hold it against me.' He needs to pay her a bit of attention once he's finished his ministrations for Nikki. It's not fair to give someone else all the love, when Marianne has been with him so long, been so pleasing. Tonight, when Nikki is safely stowed, they can watch *Big Brother* together. He'll maybe paint her nails and brush her hair through. He bought a bottle of spray-in shiner at Sally Hair and Beauty when he was up in Soho the other day. Hopefully it will make all the difference.

He's judged the size of the sheeting wrong, and has to fold it under itself when he reaches the bed. No matter, really, and definitely preferable to leaving a gap. This part of the process is always messy. There are always spillages, however careful one is. He smooths the plastic out, tucks it in, and goes to get the rest of his tools from the kitchenette. There's a bucket under the sink, and a trowel inside it: he's learned through trial and error that, for this particular job, a trowel is the best possible equipment, and a wire brush for the fine work. It will be hot work, but the air-conditioner is turned up full and the flat is blissfully cool and dry, despite the heat. The heat has been a problem for him. He had only a few lovely hours with Nikki in her soft, pliable state before he was forced to go to work.

The Lover pulls on his pink Marigolds and returns to the bed. He's proud of the bed, of his ingenuity in spotting its potential and buying it. To the casual observer, it's a dull old divan in muddy brown, the faded duvet cover and sagging pillows giving no indication that it is, in fact, the seat of his heart.

The Lover bends down, takes hold of the two woven tabs that protrude from the side of the bed, and lifts. With a hiss, the top of the bed, mattress and all, rises into the air, propelled by a gas hinge within. Inside, two compartments, each the width of the bed and half its length. In one, half a dozen humidifiers, each in need of emptying. The other is filled with white crystals. No, crystals that were once white, but have become tinged, over the past two weeks, with brown.

'Right, my darling,' says the Lover, 'let's get started.'

Chapter Nine

Out on the landing there's a cupboard set into the wall, by the stairs up to Thomas Dunbar's flat. It's where the Landlord keeps his tools, whatever tools those are, and he keeps it locked. But today she finds the door hanging open, and can't resist the urge to have a look. And in the back of the cupboard, barely visible in the gloom, she finds the door.

This isn't right, thinks Cher. That's an outside wall, I'm sure it is. If I open it, I'll just step through to three storeys of thin air.

But she steps inside anyway, and closes the door behind her so no one can see what she's doing. Aside from the door, the cupboard contains nothing much beyond a broken vacuum cleaner and a collection of rags, which hang from nails hammered into the risers of the stairs above her head. There's no one out on the landing, and the house sounds quiet, but she feels uncomfortable, as though the silence is a sign that someone is hiding nearby, listening. In the stifling darkness, she feels her way over the back wall with her fingers until she finds the latch, lifts and pushes. The door resists for a moment, as though it's not been opened in many years, then it scrapes back over dusty floorboards and her world is once again filled with light.

It's a grey light, a dead sort of light. A light that bleaches the colour from the world, makes everything dusty. Cher steps over the threshold and finds herself in an attic room, all sloping rafters and thick cross-beams, the light seeping in through a single skylight ten feet from where she stands. This is not right, she thinks, even as she steps in. It shouldn't be here. But here it is: a jumble of beds and bassinets, all scratched and broken and covered in dust.

She jumps as she sees a figure move into view from behind a curtain; breathes again when she sees that it is just herself, blurred by a haze of crackled silvering in a console mirror half-covered by an old sheet. A miniature rocking horse, skewbald, its mane missing in hanks, sways back and forth on its rockers, as though its infant rider had leapt from its back and fled at the sound of her arrival.

It's not right, she thinks again, and walks out to where thin air should be. But, oh, look, it's three times the size of my room. Four times. It just goes on and on. Look at that big pile of velvet curtains. I could have those for my window, not be woken up at dawn every day, and that tapestry cover would look great on my bed. I could come back tonight, when nobody's looking. Imagine: all this space, and nobody knows it's here.

Except *him*, says a small voice by her shoulder. *He* knows it's here. And he knows *you're* here, too.

She starts awake, paralysed for a few seconds beneath the sheet by the force of her dream. Her limbs are pinned to the mattress, her muscles prickling as though pierced by a thousand red-hot needles. Her eyelids open before she is able to move, and she is briefly confused to see the same old dingy bedsit, the scuffed flat-pack wardrobe with the peeling laminate, the brave little splashes of colour she has tried to add by Blu-tacking photos of models and pretty rooms, carefully cut from the pages of glossy magazines, to the faded flowered wallpaper. Psycho the cat sits near her on the bed, and purrs with pleasure to see that she's awake. He's not been as cuddly, lately. Until the heatwave hit he would have inserted himself into her arms as she dozed, and slept along with her, but he prefers just to be nearby at the moment, to submit to the briefest of hugs and extend his chin for rubbing.

She pulls him into her arms and feels him settle against her chest. Kisses his satin forehead, speaks low, soft words of love into his twitching ear. My first love, she thinks, and it's a cat. How sad is that? Then: where is it? Where did it go? The dream-room behind the stairs was so real – its smell, its dry air still somewhere inside her so that she can barely comprehend that she isn't there. It was a dream, Cher, she scolds herself, but a bit of her wants to go right out on to the landing and jemmy that cupboard door open, just to check.

She stretches out and checks the time on her phone. Gone half past six. She's slept the afternoon away again. She sits up in her frowsty bed. She's fallen asleep with the window closed, and the room is like an oven. She is sticky with sweat, her hair glued to her scalp. No wonder I'm having mad dreams, she thinks. My brain's boiling.

She slides out of bed and pulls her dressing-gown – satin, kimono-style, £16.99 in TK Maxx, or it would have been if she'd bought it – over her pyjamas, goes over to the window and throws it wide. Psycho drops down from the bed and pads across the floor, jumps up on the windowsill in search of coolness. The heat hasn't even started to leave the day and, though the shadows are changing in the garden below her, there's no sign of an evening breeze. A fan, she thinks. I'll probably have to buy one of those: too damn bulky to slip under my coat. But it would be so good, being able to just lie in bed with the air running over me like water.

Her thirst is pressing. She wanders over to the sink and fills a pint glass – all her crockery and cutlery comes from the outside tables of pubs and cafés, slipped into her bag, ketchup remains, beer froth and all, as she passed. The water's lukewarm from the pipes, but, this far up the house, the wait for it to run cold is worse than drinking it that way. She drains it in a single breath, refills it and takes it back to bed. Gets out her hand mirror and starts to repair her face, licking a finger and wiping her eyeliner back into place.

Now she's awake she can't stop thinking about the new woman downstairs. That wasn't a good start. She looked as if she thought she was going to be stabbed in her bed when Cher came in through the door. It doesn't do to be in bad odour with your neighbours. But aside from that, Cher is a kindly girl. The woman looked like she had lived through a train crash and it's her first night in a new house. She deserves cheering up – even if she has taken over Nikki's room.

I should tell her, she thinks. Let her know, before that lady throws all her stuff away. She might want it.

She grabs her phone – a Samsung because she doesn't believe in iPhones herself – and scrolls through the contacts. It doesn't take long. Nikki is the third of six numbers the phone contains. She hits the button to send and listens as the phone rings out. No voicemail. Nikki doesn't do voicemail. Says if anyone really wants to get hold of her they'll keep trying.

Okay, thinks Cher. Whatevvs. Sod her if that's her attitude. She tucks the phone into her bra, in case, and jumps from the bed, finds her flip-flops and ties her hair up off her face with a scrunchie. She can't shake off a feeling of melancholy about Nikki, though. I thought she was my friend, she thinks. I'd've at least thought she'd have said goodbye. Then she shrugs the sadness to the back of her mind and starts to clean her face. In Cher's life, no one lasts for long. If you let it get to you, she tells herself, you're done for, so let her go. If she doesn't want to talk to you, then fuck her.

She wonders about putting on more make-up and dismisses the thought. 'We're all girls together,' she tells the cat, who blinks his jade eyes to show that he's listening. 'We don't need slap.'

She heads for the fridge. The supermarkets have become a lot more canny about tagging their branded goods, but the own-brand equivalents don't seem to matter to them in the same way. Apart from sherry. Sherry, the old tramp's standby, often has a big black bold alarm strip round its neck. But Cher has yet to develop a taste for the grown-up things: olives and sherry and vermouth and red wine. Her favourite drinks of all are neon blue, but they're surprisingly hard to nick.

In the fridge, along with the cheese slices and the ketchup, she has a bottle of Sainsbury's own-brand Irish Cream, just a couple of inches taken off the top. She snatches it up, along with a bar of chocolate and a multi-pack of meat-flavoured Golden Wonder crisps, and heads down the stairs where her knock is greeted by silence. But she feels, as much as hears, that movement has stopped behind the door. She knocks again and listens. Gerard has turned his music off, which must mean that he's gone out. He never stops with it, from when he gets up in the morning until eleven on the dot each night. The only times there is silence is when he goes out. Weird bugger, thinks Cher. Far too much time locked up in there, if you ask me.

She hears Collette call out to ask who it is. She doesn't sound friendly. She sounds like she might have had one visitor too many already today.

'Only me,' she says. Then, when the announcement is met by silence, adds: 'Cher. From upstairs.'

'Oh.'

She hears the sound of the snib being slid off the Yale lock before the knob turns. Not taking any chances, then. I did that to her, thinks Cher, ruefully.

The door cracks open, and Collette peers at her. Cher brandishes her gifts and flashes her a wide smile. 'Peace offering.'

'Oh,' says Collette. 'Thank you. But really, there's no need. I'm not offended. Don't worry.'

'All right, then,' says Cher. 'Housewarming present.'

'I – no, really, I'm okay. I don't need anything. You don't have to …'

'Oh, come on,' says Cher, 'I'm doing my best, here.'

'I'm really tired,' says Collette, and her face looks for a moment as though it might crumple into tears. 'Really. I should just go to bed.'

Cher's not taking no for an answer. She stopped taking no for an answer when she left the Wirral. 'It won't even start to get dark for a couple of hours. Call it a nightcap.'

Collette sees that she's not going to get away with rejecting her and reluctantly lets the door swing open. Walks ahead of Cher into the room and stands in the middle of the carpet, looking around as if she doesn't know what to do next. 'Sorry. It's a mess.'

She's clearly been sleeping again – or lying in bed, at least. The duvet is thrown to one side, and there's a deep indentation in the thin pillows she's piled on top of each other. On the floor, there's a small pile of clothes.

'That's okay.' Cher reassures her, 'you should see mine. And I've been here months.'

'It's not – it doesn't help that the place is full of Nikki's stuff,' says Collette. 'I don't really know where to put anything. I can't help feeling she might want it all back, some day.'

Cher looks around at her former friend's familiar belongings. Waste not, want not, she thinks. If Nikki doesn't want it ... 'Well, anything you want to send my way ...'

Collette whirls round, looks shocked. 'I can't do that! It's someone else's stuff!'

Cher shrugs. 'It's not like I'm going anywhere, is it? If she comes back, I'll give it her.' She waves a hand at the sweatpants, the emerald green vest top Collette is wearing. 'And anyway, it's not like *you* mind helping yourself, is it?'

Collette blushes, looks at the floor. 'I'll get them laundered,' she says. 'It's just till – you know. All my clothes are dirty. I've been travelling. It's just till I ...'

Cher dismisses the protestations with a cackle. 'Don't worry. I won't tell if you don't. So ... We having a drink, or what?'

Collette springs into life like a clockwork doll, starts bustling about, pantomiming busyness. 'Of course. Yes. Let me just ...' She picks the pile of Nikki's clothes off the single armchair, drops it against the wall behind. 'I don't know where the glasses live, I'm afraid.'

'That's okay.' Cher goes straight to the left-hand wall cupboard of the kitchenette, gets down two tumblers. 'I know my way around. Plates and stuff are down here,' she pulls open the door by the sink, 'with the saucepan, and there's this drawer here, for knives and forks and stuff. Have you got any ice?'

'Ice?'

'Nikki always had ice.' She crouches down in front of the little fridge and opens the freezer compartment. A half bag of frozen peas, and an ice tray. 'Thought so. You might want to throw that milk away without opening it. It's probably been here since before she went away.'

She gets out the ice tray and runs it under the tap. Bangs a couple of cubes into each glass and fills them up with Irish cream. Takes a big gulp from one, sighs and tops it up again. 'There. That hits the spot.'

Collette sits down on the bed. She looks hopeless, tentative. 'I got crisps as well,' Cher says, handing her a glass. 'D'you want me to put them in a bowl?'

Collette takes the glass and looks at it as though she's never seen the stuff before. 'Nah,' Cher answers herself, 'what's the point in making washing-up?' and flings herself into the arm-chair, hooks a leg over an arm and takes another swig. 'Trouble with this stuff,' she says, 'is it doesn't really feel like booze at all, does it? And once you start drinking it, it slides down your throat like it's coming out of a spittoon.'

Collette takes a sip, raises her eyebrows. 'I've never drunk this stuff before. I though you just put it in cocktails, like curaçao.' She takes another sip. 'It's delicious.'

'Never drunk it? Girl, where've you *been*?'

The look Collette gives her is startled, suspicious. It's like we speak a different language, thinks Cher. 'Oh, you know, here and there,' Collette replies, eventually. Then adds: 'It's been Cristal champagne for me, 24/7.'

They fall awkwardly silent and sip their drinks, eying each other. She looks like my friend Bonny, thinks Cher, only older. I wonder what happened to Bonny? She was meant to be going back to her dad, but I know she didn't want to go. Not like *that* matters to social services.

'So how are you settling in, then?' she asks, to fill the silence.

Collette shrugs. 'Oh, you know. Okay. It's all a bit strange.'

'Better once you've got your stuff.'

'Yeah,' says Collette, and looks away again. That can't be it, wonders Cher. That tiny bag I saw her with earlier? No one moves in somewhere with that little stuff, do they? And then she remembers the duffel bag she'd arrived with herself, seven months ago, and does an internal shrug. Hossein had a suitcase, but from the way he hefted it one-handed up the stairs, she doesn't think it was full.

'It feels a bit like moving into someone else's grave, though,' says Collette, suddenly. 'What happened to this Nikki? Where did she go?'

'I wish I knew.' This much is true. Cher's had few friends in her brief life, and has felt the loss of Nikki surprisingly strongly. Nikki was kind to her, let her watch the telly, used to make her fry-ups on Saturday mornings, the two of them nursing their come-downs in companionable silence. 'She just – I mean, I know she was bothered about making the rent, but it's not like he could just have thrown her out on the street or anything.'

'What was she like?'

Cher remembers. What do you say? Bright orange hair and a ginger complexion; a tendency to eczema on her ankles, and an embarrassing passion for Johnny Depp ... 'Scottish,' she says, eventually. 'She came from Glasgow. I guess maybe she went back there.'

'Mmm,' says Collette.

'She didn't even say goodbye,' says Cher, mournfully.

Chapter Ten

The Landlord doesn't suit the heat. Or the heat doesn't suit him. Either way, on a day like this, he would usually spend most of it in his flat, the curtains drawn. On a day like today, he likes to lie beached on his leather sofa, naked, watching his DVDs with a fan playing over his flesh, drinking Diet Coke from the bottle and occasionally lifting up his belly to let the air get to the crevices beneath.

But today is rent day, and rent day gives him purpose. He is out on the street by eleven o' clock, shuffling up Beulah Grove in his Birkenstocks, sticking to the shade to keep the sun off his pate. Behind him, he drags a shopping trolley in Cameron tartan. He likes to take this with him when he goes to Beulah Grove, not just because of the convenience, but because no one would ever assume that someone pulling a shopping trolley might also be carrying large amounts of cash. The Landlord is a lot wealthier than most of his neighbours, but they'll never spot it from the way he looks.

He pauses at the foot of the steps to take a breather, and surveys his domain. Though he doesn't have a lot of time for beauty, Roy Preece can see that number twenty-three is a handsome house, in a road of handsome houses. If it were in one of the gentrified boroughs – City-money Wandsworth, perhaps, or Media Putney – it would be worth two, three million, even in its current state, even with the railway running past the bottom of the garden and the old bat in the basement. As it is, with the Farrow & Ball front-door paint going up all over and the front pull-ins full of SUVs, he'll have enough to live like a king for the rest of his life when he gets shot of the place. Go somewhere where life is cheap, and buy as much of it as he can.

The Landlord reaches into his back pocket and pulls out a handkerchief, mops his glistening face and the top of his head, and tucks it back in. The exertion of walking up from the station in the heat has left deep, damp stripes down his shirt. But it's *clean* sweat, he thinks, and sets off up the steps.

Thomas Dunbar has left an envelope on the hall table, neatly separated from the piles of junk mail, most of it addressed to long-gone residents. He's the only one of his tenants, as far as he can work out, who is actually gainfully employed. Punctilious, quiet, respectable. He works at the Citizens' Advice and, since the hours there were cut back, has involved himself in some organisational role with a furniture recycling charity. He has paid his rent on time in every month of the thirty-six he's been here. Never any trouble, with Thomas. Or, it seems, with Gerard Bright. His envelope's there next to Dunbar's, the Landlord's name in neat block capitals on the front. The Landlord tucks them in his pocket, doesn't bother to check their contents. He knows that Dunbar's will contain a cheque for the precise amount of his debt, made out in careful, neat script, the gaps scored through with a ruled line and a capitalised ONLY, and that Bright's will – God help him for leaving it out for anyone to nick – contain cash. Of course, he's probably in there anyway, he thinks, listening, although there's no music playing. Watching through the keyhole, for all I know. Anyone tried to nick it, he could be out there before they got to the front door.

He knocks on the door of flat two. Hears the sound of a bolt being pulled back and a chain being slipped on, raises an eyebrow. Collette opens the door in a knee-length cotton dress, her hair pulled back from her face with a rubber band. She looks better than she did when he first met her. I bet she'd brush up nicely, he thinks. Quite a looker, our Collette, if she'd wipe that don't-touch-me look off her face. 'All right?' he says.

'All right, thanks.'

'I see you've added some extra security,' he says.

She shrugs. 'Yale lock's not a huge amount of protection, is it? Specially given what happened to the old lady downstairs.'

'I hope you've not damaged my door,' he says.

'You can take it off my deposit if I have.'

She looks him straight in the eye. The look of someone who's used to handling stroppy clients. Managing that bar in Spain, he wonders. But he's never believed any of her story, never will. Policewoman? Could be. A no-questions-asked rooming house like this attracts all sorts, and where all sorts are, the plod are rarely far behind. Teacher? He considers for a moment. Yes, that's it. She's another teacher. Split with her husband and on the downward slide, but she'll never shed that air of judgement.

'Settling in?'

'Yes, thanks,' she says. 'I've got the rest of that money for you inside. Hang on a sec.'

She turns away and closes the door. He's used to that. His

tenants rarely seem to want to let him look inside their quarters. Ironic, really, considering that he has keys to every room in the house. He presses an ear against the door, hears the sound of things being moved around, and a zip being drawn. He is back in the middle of the corridor by the time she returns. She extends an arm from behind her chain, a sheaf of notes in her hand. 'There you go,' she says. 'I think that's the lot.'

The Landlord counts. Three hundred and twenty pounds, all present and correct. 'Yup,' he says. 'That's you done till next month.'

'You'll be giving me that receipt I asked for, of course?' She gives him The Look again. No one's asked him for a receipt since he made a brief, unsatisfactory foray into student accommodation back in the noughties, though Vesta Collins is a stickler for her rent book. He has a receipt book somewhere in his desk, he's sure of it. It might be a bit yellow by now, but he doesn't suppose that matters. 'Sure,' he says. 'I'll drop it in next time I'm passing.'

'Thanks,' she says, and closes the door, firmly.

Rent day's not a lengthy procedure at the moment. The Government pays the rent for Hossein Zanjani directly into his bank account. It's swings and roundabouts with these asylum-seeker/single-parent DSS accounts. The tax is a nuisance, but at least the pay is regular. No feckless bimbos skipping out on their bills, no I-swear-I'll-have-it-next-week types. A bit of a wait for payment to start, sometimes, but it always come through in the end.

He tucks Collette's money into the pocket alongside the envelope, takes his Filofax from the shopping trolley and leaves it parked in the hall. Hauls himself slowly, step-by-laboured step,

70

up the staircase, gripping the banister like a mobility aid. Good God, this heat is heavy. It's been threatening to thunder for weeks, but nothing ever happens. He wishes it would. It's like wading through treacle. If the fun bit weren't on the first floor, he would leave it until later.

He stops on the landing to mop his brow again and takes the bunch of keys from his pocket. The padlock key stands out, polished by the rubbing of his fingers. He likes to feel it sometimes, when he's sitting on his sofa; touching it somehow makes him feel closer to the contents of his cupboard. He leafs past it, finds the key marked Three. He always likes to have the key to the room in his hand when he comes knocking, in case the tenant doesn't answer. Sometimes they try hiding until they think he's gone, to wriggle out of paying up. It gives them the shock of their lives, when he comes in anyway.

He stops outside Cher Farrell's door and has a little listen. Faint sounds of movement, then the hiss of the tap being turned on and off. She's in there. He'll be interested to see how she responds. He knocks.

To his surprise, her footsteps cross the room immediately, and she throws the door open as though she'd been expecting him – something of a contrast with last month. He had to make three trips back before he caught her in then, and in the end he only managed it by waiting in his cupboard until he heard her thunder her way up the stairs. 'Hiya!' she cries, and beams at him. It's a false, over-bright greeting, too friendly.

'Hello,' he says, suspiciously.

She's stunning, today. Her hair's pinned loosely to the back of her head with a chopstick, brassy tendrils falling loose against a neck so smooth it could be made of alabaster. Skin that's like that all over her skinny body, he knows. He's thought about

touching it many, many times. Her make-up is relatively light –
in smoky browns and taupes – her eyelashes not coated into
tarantula legs like she so often wears them. She has on a pair of
pedal-pushers, like the ones the young girls used to wear when
he was a child, and a crop top, which they certainly never did,
and a pair of platform shoes so high you could use them as a
step-stool. Her legs go on and on, colt-like, and her belly is flat
and brown and muscular. He knows she's been sunbathing in
the garden and she looks young and fresh, and fragrant and,
standing before her, he feels squat and sticky and ungainly. He'd
thought he'd got over his resentment of all the young girls, their
careless beauty, the eyes that turn away as he shambles down the
street as though he's something they don't want to exist, but
Cher is something else.

'I suppose you'll be wanting the rent,' she says.

'That's right,' he replies.

'Hang on a tick. I've got it right here.' She turns back into the
room, striding across the threadbare carpet to her knock-off
Chloe handbag, which lies beside the bed.

The Landlord follows her in, and closes the door.

She whirls round at the sound of the latch clicking to, crosses
her arms over her small breasts and backs against the sink. All
legs and wide, wide eyes, she looks like a fawn overtaken in the
forest. She's taller than me, he thinks, but I'm so much bigger
than her. I could do anything I liked, really.

The vulnerability doesn't last for long, a couple of seconds at
most. Then she masters her fear and the street-smart Scouser is
back. 'I thought I said to hold on,' she says, and digs in the bag
for her wallet.

He can see her surreptitiously glance through her lowered
eyelashes in case of sudden movement, enjoys knowing that,

however insouciant her demeanour, she is still ill at ease. A lot less friendly than last month, he thinks. But then she came up short and had to suck up, last month. 'I thought you might want to give me a cup of tea,' he says.

'No milk,' says Cher. Finds the wallet and starts pulling notes from it, fanning them out of the top of the slot like playing cards. Fifties, twenties ... she's had a good month, he can see that. 'And no tea either. I don't do tea. It's the devil's drink.'

'Never mind,' says the Landlord. 'I'll have a glass of water instead.'

He goes to the sink. She totters backwards on her stupid shoes, not fast enough to avoid a brush from his arm as he approaches. For a brief moment he feels the softness of that little breast against his forearm, through her flimsy top. Feels goose bumps raise themselves where they've touched. Then she's away, striding purposefully over to the bedside table and picking up her cigarettes as though this was always her intention. She turns back round, lights one and blows smoke towards the ceiling, amateurishly, without inhaling.

The Landlord slows his movements down as he selects a glass from the choice of two, mismatched, on the drainer. An Arcoroc tumbler, like they had at school, and which the bistro on the High Street affects for wine, to stimulate the nostalgia of the local self-improvers, and a pint glass, complete with Weights and Measures markings. She's got a few more bits and bobs than she had last month: nothing matching, all cheap; stuff that pubs and cafés use on street tables. A couple of side plates, a soup bowl, a chunky glass latte mug in a metal cage. Teaspoons, a knife, a fork. Building herself a home, bit by bit, with pickings from the edges of other people's lives. There's a saucer on the floor, encrusted with the remains of something brownish. She's feeding that bloody cat, he thinks. Oh, well. If I ever need to get rid of her, I can add it to the list of Whys.

He chooses the pint glass – the heat and the climbing have made him thirsty – and runs the cold tap for a half minute to pass off the warm. Fills the glass and turns back to face her, drinking. Looks her up and down over the top of his hand.

'Aaaaah,' he says, 'that's better. So how are you, then, love? All cosy? I see you've got yourself some new bedclothes.'

She looks affronted that he would mention the place where she sleeps, though they are both standing in full view of it. There are etiquettes to bedsits, and one of them is that you treat the bed, in company, like a sofa. The duvet is pushed over to one side, a polycotton sheet rucked up where she's clearly been sleeping. Too hot for proper bedclothes. He wonders if she wears anything under that sheet, hopes that she doesn't.

'Fine,' she says. 'Ta.'

She finishes counting out her money, steps forward and places it, at arm's length, on the drainer. Steps back, refolds her arms, tries to stare him down.

The Landlord gets out his handkerchief, takes off his specs, polishes them, then mops his face again and picks up the notes. Starts to count them, relishing her mounting tension as he does so. 'You'll find it's all there,' she tells him. Sucks another drag off her cigarette and flicks the ash into a grimy saucer on the nightstand.

'You're not smoking in bed, are you?' he asks, once again violating the unspoken rule. 'Only that's a fire risk, you know.'

Cher shrugs. She's not going to rise to the bait. The Landlord finishes counting, starts to count again, for the pure pleasure of it. 'All right?' asks Cher.

He reaches the end, rolls the notes up and snaps them in alongside Collette's in his rubber band. Slips the money back into his trouser pocket. 'Yup,' he says. 'That's fine.'

'Good,' says Cher.

He picks up his water glass and takes another drink, studies her again as she taps her foot on the carpet. He wonders if he might extend things by sitting down for a minute, but the chair is piled with clothes. Her clean laundry, he assumes, as there's a small heap of underwear and a couple of skirts kicked into a corner beyond the bed.

'Well,' she says, uncomfortably, 'I must be getting on. People to do, things to see.'

The Landlord finishes his drink and puts his glass back on the draining board for her to wash up later. 'Thing is, I wanted a little word.'

A little frown plays across her face. Suspicion, mixed with boredom.

'Thing is,' he continues, 'I've been charging you well below market rent for this place. I felt sorry for you. Wanted to help you get on your feet. But I'm afraid the rent's got to go up next month,' he tells her.

Cher's chin jerks up. 'What?'

'Yes,' he says, and gives her his oiliest smile. 'I'm afraid so.'

She doesn't look so bored now. 'But ...' she says, 'hang on a minute!'

'Yes?' he says.

'I've only been here four months.'

He spreads his hands in the air before him. 'Sorry. Prices are rising all over the shop.'

'How much are you talking?'

'I was thinking three hundred.'

Cher's face colours. 'I ... are you *serious?*'

If there's one thing the Landlord likes more than a young girl, it's a young girl over a barrel. 'You can always go somewhere else,' he says. 'No skin off my nose. There's people queuing up for a room like this.'

'But you can't just ... it's not legal.'

The Landlord raises his eyebrows and smirks. 'I think you need a contract for something to be legal, Cher, dear. And I'm sure you've got your pick of places that take tenants without a reference or a direct debit. It's all the rage, in this day and age. Still, if you want to report me ...'

He lets the sentence hang in the air as her blush spreads. She knows she's stuck. Doesn't stand a chance.

'The council, perhaps?'

She looks away, covers her stomach with her arm and takes another puff of her cigarette.

'Social services?'

She glares at him, defiant in defeat.

'We could call them now, if you like,' he offers, to ram his advantage home. 'Give them your details?'

'No, that's okay.' Her voice is dull, stripped of the lilt he found so irritating.

'Good,' he says. 'That's settled, then. Don't worry. It's only starting next month. Plenty of time. How is everything? You comfortable?'

Cher shrugs. 'Whatever,' she says.

He's not going to get any more from her today. Launches himself off the kitchen counter and lumbers to the door. 'Well, I'm always at the end of the phone, if you, you know, need anything.'

He turns in the doorway, and smiles at her. 'Oh, and you

really shouldn't be smoking at your age,' he says. 'It's not good for you.'

She doesn't answer.

Out on the landing, he gets out his keys again and checks the house for noises. There's music from the downstairs front, but otherwise the place is quiet. There's not a sound from behind Cher's door. He imagines her standing where he left her with her face in her hands, and smiles.

He goes over to his cupboard door. Undoes the padlock and lays it on the carpet, pulls the door wide to allow himself to pass through. It's a tiny space – a triangle beneath the stairs, four feet deep, the street window, whitewashed, saving him from having to pay to light it – and there's barely room for him, but the Landlord is skilled at manoeuvring his bulk through a thin man's world. He squeezes in, plops himself into the old office chair – no arms, because there's too much Landlord to fit between them – that sits inside, and pulls the door to behind him.

On shelves built neatly into the underside of the staircase treads, red lights blink at him. One disc has filled itself and popped out of its slot. The Landlord unzips the leather case that holds the rent book, and swaps the disc for a blank one in a slot in the side of the case. Entertainment for later. It's going to be a good night.

Chapter Eleven

'*Hola, chica.*'

Oh, Christ, he thinks he's so witty. When she had a French SIM, it was '*bonjour, chérie*', in Italy '*ciao, bella*', Switzerland '*grüss Gott*'. Everywhere she hides, they find her, and every time he does, he announces himself in the local language.

But at least he doesn't know where I've gone to, yet, she thinks, not if he's still saying hello in Spanish, reminding herself to buy a British SIM.

'*Carrer de la Ciutat,*' he says. 'Nice. Classy. Glad to know you're still in the money, anyway. Shame it's *my* money.'

Collette doesn't speak. She always hopes, somehow, that if he doesn't hear her voice he'll think he's mistaken. She's cleared out just in time. That clearly *was* Burim she saw in the street, not a figment of her imagination. Six whole months she managed in Barcelona. One of her better runs. She wonders if she's brushed up against whoever it was who tracked her down as she walked down the street, as she locked and unlocked the flats' front door, sat at a table in Catedral. It's the worst thing about her situation:

that every stranger on every corner could be the man who's watching out for her.

Tony waits for her to speak. Cat and mouse: a game that's been going on for three years. Collette hiding away, scrabbling herself into dark corners, and Tony toying, pretending to have turned his back and lost interest, letting her think she might, this time, have escaped, and all the time ready to pounce the moment she allows herself to breathe.

How is he getting my numbers? How? They're pay as you go, for God's sake. I buy them in station booths.

'Nice flat, too,' he says. 'Shady. I like that. It can get hot, at this time of year. Burim says he liked your décor, by the way. Very Mediterranean, he said. All that turquoise.'

There's sweat trickling between her breasts. She's had the window shut all night, after that doomsayer Thomas cursed her sleep with it open, and the room is like a sauna. In Barcelona, even away from the front where she lived, there was always a movement of air off the sea, and shutters that kept the light and burglars out but let through the sea breeze. This room is close and smelly. Sometimes she thinks that the smell is coming in through the air-brick where the fireplace used to be, but it's just as likely that her predecessor's hygiene skills were not of the best, and she's not got round to buying new bedclothes, despite her resolve on the day she arrived.

Ah, Tony, if you could see me now, she thinks. You'd proba-bly walk straight past me in the street without blinking.

'So isn't it about time you gave it up?' he asks. 'Haven't you had enough, yet? We only want to talk to you, you know.'

Chapter Twelve

Did I forget? Did I? Am I losing my mind? It's too early for dementia, isn't it? That door has been open all summer. Maybe I was just too excited about my holiday to remember to lock it ...

She goes again to look at the back door, as though the mystery of how it came to be hanging open, unbroken, will somehow reveal itself if she stares for long enough. All my life, she thinks, I've made the safe choices. I've never taken a risk, always stuck to the featureless lowlands. It seemed like such a good thing, a secure lease at twenty-seven, but now ... now it feels like I was putting myself in prison. I should have got up and gone, when Mum and Dad died, not stayed on here because it was all I'd ever known. What sort of life is this?

Each time Vesta sits down to rest, she starts to shake, so she carries on cleaning, powered by ibuprofen and PG Tips, trying to wipe away the traces of whoever it is who's been here. Her home, barely changed since her parents' passing, genteelly threadbare with decades of respectable dusting, feels suddenly changed, now some stranger has torn through it like a tornado.

The day-after-day, the making do, the blind eyes turned to wear and tear because it was easier than confronting the Landlord, or his grabby old aunt before him, and stirring up their resentment of the sitting tenant. When did my expectations get so small? she wonders. While everybody else got caught up in the self-improvement race, while they found themselves and stretched their worlds and travelled, I stayed in the 1930s, in the decade before I was even born, living by my parents' values, knowing my place.

She stretches her aching back and catches sight of her expression – the face she used to pull when dosed with cod liver oil from a teaspoon as a child – in the mirror above the mantelpiece. She's been seeing her face in this carved wood frame for the whole of her life. Still feels a sense of profound shock every time she glances into it and sees an almost-seventy-year-old woman staring back. Where did it all go? Did I really do so little, that I'm still living here, surrounded by reminders of my parents' tenancy before me – the Waterford vase, Mum's collection of ceramic cottages, the framed photos of long-dead ancestors on the tallboy, *The Crying Boy* in his frame on the wall, Nan's good teaset behind the glass of the display cabinet – with hardly a mark of my own life added on top?

Her own death looms large in her mind these days. She looks around her living room, and suddenly sees it through the contemptuous eyes of the outsider who has treated it with such gleeful disrespect. She's made the occasional attempt to stamp her own personality on the place, with the frugal resources of a spinster dinner lady. The upright suite with its lace-edged antimacassars has been replaced by a flower-pattern settee and a tub armchair, her mother's fussy wallpaper painted over in neutral colours, but most of the things this stranger has destroyed come from a time before she was even thought of – the plates, glasses, books, pictures, the occasional table, the Coronation plate that used to hang on the wall and the Murano bird brought back by her dad after the war ended. Even my bits of jewellery that came from Mum, she thinks. And when I go, what will I leave behind? And who, anyway, is there to leave it to?

Vesta has lived her whole life in this cave beneath Beulah Grove, in the basement half-light, never knowing what the weather was like without opening the back door. She has seen the neighbourhood go from genteel lower-middle to Irish-rough to Caribbean poor and, over recent years, swing gradually into the hands of people who sound like they should be running a village fete. She was born here, in what is now her bedroom, and is beginning to suspect that she might die here, too. Grew up in her own little nook, walled off by her father in plyboard and woodchip, in a corner of the lounge, has eaten nearly every meal of her life at the little gateleg table by the back wall, nursed her elderly parents as, one by one, time took them, and took over the tenancy when her mother died, in 1971, back in the days when tenants still had rights. She's seen off three landlords and, from the look of this one lately, might well see off a fourth. But Londoners are meant to be adventurers, she thinks. You're not meant to come *from* here. You're meant to come *to* here.

I'm luckier than some people, she thinks. A secure tenancy is a secure tenancy. At least I won't end my life out on the street. But oh, what happened to my life?

She doesn't know what, if anything, her invader was looking for. The tea caddy where she keeps the scratched savings of a life lived frugally on the old-age pension hasn't been raided, and her mother's engagement and wedding rings, the eternity ring with which her father marked her own belated birth, still nestle in their felt-lined boxes on the bedroom mantelpiece. Her electrical equipment is outdated and chunky, but a junkie would probably have got a tenner for the telly. It's spite, she thinks. Pure spite. He just broke in to spoil my home. Why else would you upturn a funeral urn and tread the ashes into the carpet?

Holding on to the table, Vesta lowers herself to the ground and starts to sweep together the contents of her memory box, tipped out randomly among her parents' cremains. She hates herself for having fallen prey to such indecisiveness about what to do with them. They only hold a space for so long at the crematorium and after that, you're on your own. For forty years, she's meant to take them to some beauty spot, some place with a view, and scatter them there, but every time she's tried to remember a place they might have loved, her mind has gone blank. They didn't *do* much. Her mother's whole world encompassed errands on the High Street and the occasional walk on the common, a trip to the shops in Kingston a major undertaking. They never even went into town, as far as she remembers. For all the use they made of London – big, scary, exciting London – they might as well have lived in Cardiff. No wonder I've never done anything myself, she thinks. It's over a decade since I last went in to Oxford Street, even.

Such a paltry little box of keepsakes; nothing of value, nothing that will mean anything to anyone else. When I die all alone in a hospice, she thinks, they'll send in the house clearers, and the whole lot will go in a skip. Oh, stop it, Vesta, she scolds herself. Pull yourself together. The world is full of nice people. You can't let one spite-filled random act of vandalism ruin it for you. Such kindness I've seen over the past couple of days. I have to remember that, hold on to that. There's more kindness than nastiness in the world.

From above, she can hear Gerard Bright's music thunder through the floorboards. Normally she tunes it out, adopts a live-and-let-live approach, but he seems to have been playing *The Ride of the Valkyries* since breakfast time, and the sound of the new girl in the back room, walking up and down, up and down, has driven her out of the bedroom. She goes over to the window, where there is light, and leafs through her handful of photos – relatives long since dead, friends and neighbours moved on, moved up, returned to their countries of origin – and feels a surge of loneliness. I was always good at making friends, she thinks. But I haven't the first idea where they all are, now. That's London, for you. There's more of a sense of community than outsiders give us credit for, but the communities don't last.

She hears footsteps rattle up the pavement, and glances up at the window. The little girl from the first floor, Cher, walks past, all legs and backpack from this angle. She's wearing that wig again, hiding her lovely hair as if she's ashamed of it, and is dressed as if she doesn't want anyone to notice her. She goes out a couple of times a week like that, and the sight makes Vesta melancholy. Enjoy it, my love, she wills the girl. You have no idea how much you'll miss those looks when they're gone.

Cher peers down and sees her, and waves airily down from on high. Such a pretty face. Vesta feels herself touched by sunshine, smiles broadly, and waves back. Lovely girl. A bit lost, she senses, a bit aimless, as if she's waiting for someone to point her where to go. And so young. She barely looks old enough to have left school. Mind you, I long since lost my knack for telling how old people are, she thinks. Policemen have been looking young to me for decades. Maybe it's just one of those things about being nearly seventy that everyone under thirty looks as if they're barely out of nappies.

She slides the window open. 'Hello, love.'

'Hiya,' says Cher. 'How's the clearing up going?'

'Oh, you know,' says Vesta. 'Where are you coming back from?'

'College,' says Cher. They both know it isn't true, but it's their unspoken agreement that Vesta won't say anything if Cher at least looks as if she's trying to improve herself.

'You're back early,' says Vesta. From the state of her reading Vesta guesses that Cher's still not enrolled anywhere as she'd suggested. I must do something about that, she thinks. Maybe I could teach her myself? Because it's not stupidity that's stopping her.

'Short day,' says Cher. 'It's so bloody hot it's hard to concentrate.'

'I bet. You got time for a cuppa?'

Cher mimes checking the watch she doesn't wear. 'Sure.'

'Back door's open. Come on down.'

She potters through to the kitchen to put the kettle on. Pulls a face at the smell coming in through the open door. She's got to catch the Landlord about those drains, again. Her kitchen sink is taking the best part of an hour to empty, cooling greasily an inch below the overflow. Five pounds a week she's been spending on chemicals to keep the outlet moving, but the drains barely seem to work at all, now. That bottle of something he poured down the outside drain before she left has done no good at all. Probably just a gallon of bleach from Poundstretcher, anyway. He'll never spend money if he has a choice about it.

The gate in the side-return creaks, and Cher appears at the top of the steps, picking her way delicately between the plant pots. Psycho the cat trots complaisantly in her wake. He must have been waiting somewhere in the shade for her to come home. He's really attached himself to her, thinks Vesta. That's nice. It's nice to think he's found himself a good friend. She would love to have him herself, but the Landlord would use it as an excuse to break her lease before he'd got through his first tin of Whiskas. Cher has shed her wig, and dangles it from one hand like a Regency lady holding a fan. Her hair is tied up on the back of her head, her neck exposed to let out the sweat.

'It's a stinker out there,' she says, and starts down the chipped brick steps. Catches the whiff of the drains and pulls a face. 'Feee-you,' she says, and waves the wig in front of her face as though that will make the smell go away. She's such a kid, thinks Vesta, again. It's so bizarre, the way teenagers are: twenty-five one second and seven the next. 'That's a bit rank, isn't it?'

'It's the drains,' says Vesta. 'They're blocked again.'

'He needs to call Dyno-Rod, that mean old bastard.'

'I keep telling him. It's all those kitchenettes. Emptying their bacon fat down their plugholes.'

Cher shakes her head. 'Not me.'

'Yes, well, that's because you live on pizza and chocolate. These drains were built for a family house, not a block of flats, and he needs to deal with it. Someone's going to go down with food poisoning, and it'll probably be me. Milk and two, is it, love?'

Cher bounces down the last two steps, tittups over to her door. 'Ta.'

'Let's have it in the garden,' says Vesta. 'Get away from the smell.'

She hands Cher her cup and follows her up into the sunshine, passing through her potted herb garden. Sweet aromas of sage and rosemary, basil and mint rise off the heated bushes as they brush past. Now, this is what a garden *should* smell like, she thinks. Feels a little swell of pleasure at the patch of civilisation she's carved out of the dilapidation beyond.

It's a big garden, bigger than normal for London, the railway tracks at its end having saved it from being carved up for development. Vesta has kept the front third tidied and cultivated all her life. It was her contribution to the family when she was a child, bringing flavour and colour to her mother's sepia household, and the green-finger bug has stayed with her ever since. Narrow beds of bright annuals, fetched back, one by one, from the greengrocer's discount shelf, surround a tablecloth of manicured lawn on which two old-fashioned deckchairs recline in the dazzle. Beyond the beds, a tangle of foot-long grass, run to seed so often it's almost a hayfield, a blind rhododendron that contrives to look dank even in this weather, a couple of aged plum trees, stunted by some bug that's way beyond Vesta's knowledge, a mess of rubble and bonfire ash and goosegrass surrounding a tumbledown shed.

'Looks lovely out here,' says Cher.

'Thanks,' says Vesta, and they sit in the deckchairs with their back to the chaos. Each takes their first sip of tea and lets out the great British 'ahhhh' as they settle back. The generations may look completely different, thinks Vesta, but some things never change. The cat finds a patch of sun and rolls on to his back to show the handkerchief of white on his belly. She smiles.

'You look more cheerful,' says Cher. 'You almost done in there?'

'Not completely. But at least I can sit down, now.'

'Christ. They really made a mess, didn't they?'

'Yes.'

'Ooh, that reminds me.' Cher leans over her backpack and rummages inside. 'I got you a present.' She finds what she's looking for, and holds it out, a small hard object wrapped in a T-shirt. She looks pleased with herself. 'I hope you like it.'

'Oh, Cher, you shouldn't waste your money on buying me ...' begins Vesta, then stops dead when she sees what's inside the bundle. It's a dancing lady, bone china, imperial purple ball dress swirling around impossibly thin ankles, a blaze of carmine hair improbably stiff on a single shoulder. Round azure eyes and a snub nose, tiny mouth hand-painted in shiny crimson. It's the spit of one of her mother's that lies in pieces with the rest of the collection, wrapped in newspaper in her kitchen bin. 'Oh, Cher,' she says. 'You shouldn't have. What on earth did you think you were doing? You can't afford this.'

Cher shrugs. 'Didn't cost much. Hardly anything.'

'No, but ...' Vesta knows exactly how much they cost. She and Cher looked at them together only a few weeks ago, in the window of Bentalls in Kingston, and she was shocked to see that they cost very nearly a week's old-age pension. All these years, she had had no idea. Her burglar has taken out very nearly a thousand pounds she never knew she had with a single swing of the poker from the fireplace. '... I can't believe you've done this.'

Cher's face clouds over. 'Don't you like it?'

'It's not that. It's ... Cher, you shouldn't have done this. You should save your money. You shouldn't be spending it on things like this. What about your rent?'

She looks up and sees that Cher has visibly shrunk. She swings her legs from the knees like a little kid, wide-eyed with disappointment. 'I thought you'd like it,' she says. 'I can get you something else, if you want.'

'No, love,' says Vesta. 'I love it. I love, love, love it. C'm'ere.'

She holds her arms out and enfolds Cher in a hug. They're both so thin it's not a very comfortable hug; more a clashing of bones. Cher smells of salt and hair conditioner, and some floral chemical they all spray over themselves these days. She hugs like someone who's not used to hugging: comes into it gingerly, as though she's nervous that something will break, and then clings on far too long, as though she's afraid to let go. They stay there, awkwardly, in the sunshine, for longer than either of them is easy with. Poor little love, thinks Vesta. Whoever dragged her up, they didn't make her expect people to like her.

Slowly, slowly, she disentangles herself, and lays the figurine gently down on the grass. 'It'll look lovely on the mantelpiece,' she assures her. 'I shall treasure it for ever.'

But where the hell is Cher affording this sort of thing? she wonders. It's not off the dole, that's for sure. And how do you ask someone if they've stolen your present, without offending them? Cher is always popping in with stuff: usually biscuits, or a cake or something. But always premium quality, branded stuff. No Every Little Helps about young Cheryl's presents. But oh, I would feel terrible if she got caught nicking nonsense to lay at my feet the way that cat brings her mice.

'What's the new tenant like?' she asks, changing the subject because she knows that if she stays on it she'll have to ask. 'Have you met her yet?'

Cher plops back down into her deckchair. 'Ooh, yeah,' she says. 'I dropped in, the other night.'

'Oh, you,' says Vesta. 'You've got no shame, have you?'

Cher shrugs. 'It's not Buckingham Palace. You don't need a tiara and a fanfare. Anyway, I took a bottle of Baileys.'

There she goes again, thinks Vesta. She's partial to a drop of the creamy stuff herself, but she doesn't even buy Baileys at Christmas.

'She's all right,' says Cher. 'Posh. Talks like someone off *Made in Chelsea*. God knows what she's doing here.'

'Divorce?'

Cher shakes her head. 'She's been travelling, that's what she said. Lucky for some. I haven't even got a passport.'

Vesta laughs. 'I have. Every ten years, I renew it. Always think I might, you know, *go somewhere* some day.'

'Anyway, her mum's in a maximum security Twilight Home. I think she's on her way out and she said something about wanting to be near her, in case.'

'In case. I've always liked that phrase. You can cover a lot of ground with an "in case". Shall I ask her down, you think? Would that be nice?'

Cher shrugs. 'Could do.'

Vesta closes her eyes and listens for a moment to the neighbourhood noise: the laughter of the kids from what they call the Posh Family on the other side of the fence playing in their paddling pool, the tannoy playing a recorded announcement on the unmanned station platform, a jet changing speed as it cruises in towards Heathrow. You would only have heard one of those sounds when I was Cher's age, she thinks. 'I wonder,' she says. 'Maybe I ought to throw a party?'

'A party?'

'Not a huge party. Just us. Well, it's silly, isn't it? All of us living on top of each other, and we've never all been in the same place at the same time. And it would be nice. A thank you because you've all been so nice, about the burglary. You and Hossein. Even Thomas. And it would be a good way to kill two birds with one stone. Welcome her to the house; thank everyone.

And get him in Flat One to leave his lair. He's been here ages and we've barely said a word. And besides. It's been ages since I had a party.'

'How long?'

'God, it must be ...' Her mind flashes back to Erroll Grey and the Khans, sitting on her mother's old settee. Really? She's not had a party since that went on a skip? 'Good Lord. Seven years, at least. I can't believe it. I used to have people down all the time. And I've still got Mum's old teaset. I spend my life washing the damn thing up, and it never gets used. Might as well celebrate the fact that at least he didn't smash that, eh?'

'Tea,' says Cher.

Vesta laughs. 'Oh, sorry. Were you expecting cocktails?'

Cher pouts, just a little bit. Of course she was. She's a teenager. She wants to be out carousing, not eating finger sandwiches with a crew of middle-aged strangers. We must all seem ancient to her, Vesta thinks. Practically mummified. Same way she looks like a baby to me.

'We could have some cider, at least,' says Cher.

'No,' says Vesta, firmly.

Chapter Thirteen

The Lover is a great reader. He loves to read. He lives in a world where not many people do, where his learning is an anomaly and treated, often, with suspicion, but without reading he wouldn't be the man he is. He wouldn't know about the forty days, or about ritual and how its basis often lies in accidental coincidence and pragmatic use of the surroundings in which it developed. And besides: reading helps stave off the loneliness, in more ways than one.

The things he has read about Ancient Egypt, for instance, and its burial traditions. While venerating the corpses of the great is common all over the world, the means of disposing of them often reflects the circumstances of their lives. Thus the Vikings, facing solid, deep-frozen soil for much of the year, would, unsurprisingly, dispose of their heroes in fire and water. And a country in which the combination of climate and shallow topsoil would frequently turn up desiccated corpses from shallow burials might well eventually ritualise the natural order. Egypt's arid plains, dotted with salty lakes that threw up great heaps of sodium, was ideal for experimentation. With skilled evisceration, and the right combinations of salts and herbs, forty days would be the perfect time to turn wet and putrefying dead bodies into leathery facsimiles that, at least passingly, resembled the original owner as they were in life.

But in a south London suburb – even a suburb that is going through the longest heatwave in living memory – the process needs a little help.

He's learned as he's gone along. Practice, after all, makes perfect, and besides, he's had to learn two sets of skills where his teachers only had to master one. In Egypt, two sets of priests were responsible for rendering their royalty fit for the afterlife: the *parichistes* and the *taricheutes*, the cutters and the salters. Necessity has forced the Lover to master both roles, and there were bound to be errors along the way.

He doesn't like to think about his first two attempts at making himself a girlfriend; is just grateful that he didn't live in this crowded house when the first experiment failed, at least. A body is easier to move before the rot has set in. Jecca left the house in a series of carrier bags, flesh falling from bone like a five-hour pot roast; but at least, coming from a garden flat, she didn't have to go through any communal areas. Katrina, her body cavities cleared more studiously, was a steep learning curve. His incision, down the front of the abdomen the way a pathologist would do it, left the trunk loose and floppy, and her nose was ruined by his clumsy attempts to remove the brain with the crochet hook. The parichistic entry, via a slit in the left-hand side, though it means having to plunge himself arm-deep in viscera, produces a neater, more human-shaped final product. He discovered the barrel drill in Homebase soon after that. He figures that the Egyptians would have used one too, had they had access to electricity and geared motors. He thinks of them sometimes, his two lost loves: Katrina sacrificed to fire and Jecca to water. He wonders if they are lonely, now, as he no longer is.

But he's not happy with Alice. She's an improvement on the two who came before, but it was only once her forty days were up and he had to break her from her crust like a salt-baked chicken that he understood that he needed to change the desiccation salts as the process progressed. The Egyptians had the help of the blazing sun to preserve their kings. For his princesses, he has dehumidifiers, and the close quarters of their confinement means that the juices have nowhere to go.

He moves Alice and Marianne to the sofa to watch the TV while he attends to Nikki. Some tender part of him wants to spare her the indignity of exposing her half-cooked nakedness to the gaze of his more finished beauties. As he carries Alice, he sees that her smile has spread again, as her skin is contracting back towards her hairline. He can almost see her wisdom teeth and is painfully aware of the bones beneath the surface. I haven't done you justice, my dear, he thinks. I should have read more. If only I'd known before it was too late that a girl like you deserves her share of moisture once the natural wet is gone. He puts her gently down in the armchair, unwinds her arm from round his neck. She settles with a rustling whisper. Her hair is thin and brittle, her eyes sunken and hollow beneath their drooping lids. I wonder, he thinks. Soon you'll be nothing but skin and bone, flaking and shedding over my carpet. Perhaps it's time that we started to think about parting company.

He goes back to the bed, to his Princess Nikki.

The base of the bed is covered with a thick plastic sheet, liberated from a building site. Sleeping above his girls has never been a problem for him – indeed, it gives him a feeling of warm companionship – but the process of transformation, even with the alkaline, deadening effect of his home-made natron, tends to produce sudden bursts of smell that wake him, gagging, in the night. He props the mattress – lovely soft, lightweight memory-foam mattress – against the wall and peels the plastic off. Waits, breathing through his mouth, until his stomach settles, then tugs on the cloth ties and allows the lids to lift on the two compartments below. He spent a long time making his choice on the internet once he'd seen the possibility of such a bed, clicking through faux leather after faux leather, until he finally settled on this workmanlike black hessian covering. Cloth tends to soak up smells, but it's breathable; and when the bed is empty and the plastic cover off, the memory of its former contents dissipates over time. He has drilled air holes where the walls meet, to allow the bank of dehumidifiers in the head section to do their work. The collection tank of each one – and there are six altogether – is nearing full. This was where he went wrong with Jecca and Katrina. You can never believe, until you experience it first-hand, how much moisture there is in a human body. It comes and comes, for the first few weeks. In week two, once the natron really starts to work its magic, he has to empty the chambers on a daily basis.

Two by two, he unclips the chambers and carries them to the kitchenette sink. The water is strangely greasy, as though it has been used to wash up with after a full Sunday roast. He doesn't bother to flush around the sink. He'll be chasing it down soon enough, after all. He grabs the bucket and the trowel from the cupboard under the sink, and returns to his darling.

The natron has settled, as it often does, and one shoulder peeks out from above the surface. This is one of the reasons that he's opted for the weekly fuel change. He left Alice alone for the full forty days, and chipping and scraping her out from her hard-set casing was the full work of an afternoon, a chore that made him admire the stoical patience of archaeologists in a way he never had before. And he has been forced to dress her in sleeves since he got her out, to hide the deterioration of her exposed left arm. No little sundresses for Alice; no pretty evening gowns. Every time he looks at her, he feels sour and sad. So close, and yet so far.

'Never mind,' he says to Nikki. 'I've got *you*, now.'

He digs from the walls inwards. The powder is still dryish in the corners away from the flesh. It pours like sand into the bucket, almost good enough to use again. But the Lover no longer believes in shortcuts. Precision, he knows, means the difference between failure and something to treasure for ever. He fills the bucket and takes it to the sink. His natron, made by mixing simple washing soda with equal parts of bicarb, has the added advantage of acting like a drain cleaner. Everything that goes down his sink – tea leaves, bacon fat, scraps of visceral matter scrubbed from his parichistic hands – is periodically dissolved and flushed away from the pipes as he changes his preservatives. He upends the bucket, turns on the cold tap and watches, pleased, as the natron fizzes, smokes and vanishes down the plughole.

He works with the windows thrown wide, but the heat is heavy on his shoulders and, as the digging becomes harder, his breath is damp and stuffy behind the surgical mask he wears to protect his lungs. Three weeks in, and Nikki has given up the greater part of her moisture, but still the natron has solidified around her and needs prising out in lumps. He sweats as he works, sees drops of it run over his goggles, feels it drip from the end of his nose to mingle with Nikki's body fluids. It takes a full half hour of digging and flushing before he has her uncovered, and can brush the final sticky coating off with the help of a stiff paintbrush in preparation for the final cleaning.

He never likes this part. She is lying on her left side, so he has to roll her over to access the entrance to her abdomen, to get at the packing that both dehydrates her torso and prevents it from losing shape as it does so. Then he goes in with a serving spoon, scooping out the natron like stuffing from a Christmas-day turkey.

This packing is more solid than that on the outside; interiors are more permeable than skin designed to keep out the rain. And it's dark brown in colour, where that which surrounds the body is a blend of khaki and yellow. And it stinks. The stench that rises from the depths of Nikki makes him gag repeatedly as he buries his arm to the shoulder and scrapes out its filling. This won't wash down the sink so easily, either. It's one for the toilet. Once again, he makes a mental note to keep a bucket of clean powder back to chase it down the drains.

It's worth the effort, though, he tells himself. Two more weeks of this, and she'll be perfect.

Chapter Fourteen

He thinks you're still in Spain. Don't sweat it. He's not looking for you here; he still thinks you're in Spain.

It's only two or three miles to Collier's Wood, but the trip involves two trains and a tube. Five stops to Clapham Junction, two stops to Balham, then three on the Northern Line. London's transport system almost invariably involves going round an unnecessary corner, the neighbouring boroughs often the most laborious to get to; she'd forgotten that factor, when she picked Northbourne on the map. It will be almost two hours to get there and back each time, and because of the change of transport and the enforced trip into Zone 2, would cost the best part of a tenner without an Oyster card. Suddenly, the thought of taking one of those minicabs from the kiosk at Northbourne Junction seems less of an extravagance.

She makes sure to travel well out of rush hour, but still, by the time the tube doors open, she is bathed in sweat and nursing a dry, crackly throat. The air as she comes up the escalator, usually a moment's pleasure, provides little relief. The day is still, hanging over the streets like punishment.

She buys a bottle of water at the little shop by the station, and searches the phone menu for the satnav. She's not bothered to buy a new handset this time, just replaced the SIM. She's getting better with each move at slowing down her spending, finding new ways to move to a new city on the cheap. If she wants to keep ahead of Tony Stott, she needs to string the cash out for as long as she can.

The thought of Tony makes her check, instinctively, over her shoulder. Fuck's sake, Collette. He doesn't know where you are. He doesn't know where your mother is. It's not like we've shared a surname since I was eight. And it's not like anyone at Nefertiti's spent their nights having cosy chats about their families. He thinks you're still in Spain. But still, the years in hiding have taken their toll on her, made her fear each passing shadow.

Sunnyvale is a ten-minute walk away, in a cul-de-sac off Christchurch Close. They're always a way away from public transport, these places, though there's a bus stop at the end of the road for the people who've really mastered this city's labyrinthine routes. It makes sense, really: it's not as though the residents are going to be going anywhere, and a lot of them don't get a visitor from one month's end to the next. God preserve me from dementia, she shudders. She sets off up the main road past the bookies and the Royal Mail sorting office, weaves her way between midmorning knots of uniformed smokers. The bottle of water vanishes down her throat as though it were just a thimbleful. It's the sort of weather that makes you wonder if you're diabetic, she thinks. Christ, I'm getting middle-aged.

All these suburbs, blending into one. Collier's Wood is slightly newer than Northbourne and lacks, from what she can see, the networks of Victorian artisan terraces and solicitors' villas that have made Tooting, and now her own area, so appealing to the fixer-uppers with an eye on the Cotswolds thirty years down the line. She passes a sad little arcade, a pretty church marooned in a field of 1930s semis. Edwardiana is right back in with Londoners, now, so how long until these stuccoed porches and low-silled windows begin to look attractive to generations who no longer remember them as nasty-modern? It's the way of the British, she muses. We like old things. And when we can't afford the old things, we start seeing newer things as old, stake a claim of our own, and drive the renters and the drifters and the immigrants on to somewhere newer.

She turns off the main road into Christchurch Close, and the tarmac gives way to cement block paving; a high, wire-topped wall along one side and blocky 1950s brick housing on the other. When her mother was young, she thinks, these were the sorts of places people dreamed of being located to: the bomb-sites filled in with affordable housing. There's a symmetry to Janine coming to somewhere like this on her downward slide.

Collette turns up the Sunnyvale cul-de-sac, skirts the metal bollard that blocks off its maw, there to stop stray cars from seeking out a parking space but allow the ambulances in when the need comes. The home straddles the end of the road, forty feet up past the garden fences, its concrete turning circle jollied up by resin pots of dying geraniums. A line of hanging baskets – busy Lizzies, salmon-coloured, jarring with dark purple petunias – droops in the sun trap of the yellow brick frontage. It's clear that someone's tried their best to cheer the place up, alleviate its functional air, but no amount of watering can combat this heat. The little border of grass on the far side of the pavement is dusty and frizzy, like neglected old-lady hair.

Collette stands for a moment and looks up at the white

plastic lettering that runs along the parapet of the lean-to porch. SUNNYVALE, it reads. She's found her mother's final home.

Inside, it smells as she had expected: floral disinfectant, floor polish, the graveyard scent of chrysanthemums in a vase on the reception desk, food cooked till it no longer needs chewing and the faint, unmistakeable odour of unchanged nappies. A woman sits behind the desk, in polyester scrubs. She's turned a fan straight on to her face and leans back, eyes closed, cooling herself in its blast, until she hears the door open. She looks up and assumes the robotic smile that seems to have become part of the healthcare canon. 'Can I help you?'

'Yes.' Collette advances across the small lobby, glimpses a huddled figure, dressing-gown tied tightly round a shapeless torso, making its way slowly up the corridor to her right with the help of a walking frame. 'I'm Elizabeth Dunne. I called this morning.'

The woman shifts through a list on a clipboard, importantly. 'And you've come to see . . . ?'

'Janine Baker.'

She runs her pen down a list, ticks something off. 'Ah, yes, Janine. I saw she was due a visitor.'

Since when did they stop giving old people the dignity of a surname? 'That's right,' says Collette.

The woman presses a bell on the desk beside her. It sounds out, Big Ben chimes with a shrill electronic top note, somewhere not far away within the building. 'Someone'll be along in a minute,' she says.

'Thanks,' says Collette. Looks about her for somewhere to sit and, not finding anything in the Spartan lobby, stands awkwardly before the desk like a supplicant.

'We've not seen you before, I think,' says the woman, and

there's an edge of judgement to her voice. Your mother's been here for three months, now, says the tone. Where have you been?

'No,' says Collette, and feels the blush creep further up her cheeks. Cheeky mare. You don't know anything about it. 'I've been away.'

'Away?' Lucky for some, says the single word. Wouldn't it be nice for all of us, if we could be *away* when responsibility called?

'Abroad,' she says. Adds, defensively: 'Working. I couldn't get away before.'

'No, dear,' says the woman. 'Well, it can be a terrible inconvenience.'

Oh, fuck you, thinks Collette. Who do you think you are? Do you really think that the ones who end up here, the ones with no one to take them in, are totally innocent of their situation? Don't you think we'd have at least tried to have them with us, if they'd been nicer when we were young? And it's not like I haven't been drip-drip-dripping my cash into her bank account, to pay for your services and keep her out of council care.

She doesn't voice it. It can't be a greatly rewarding job, this. Making the families feel guilty must be one of the few pleasures she gets.

'Well, I'm back now,' she says. 'For as long as it takes.'

'Good for you,' says the woman, patronisingly.

I just hope it's not too long, thinks Collette. God help me, I shouldn't be wishing her life away, but it's only a matter of time before they find out I'm in London, even if they don't know why. They seem to have contacts *everywhere*.

'Actually,' says the receptionist, 'while I've got you, we probably need to update your contact details, if you're not in Spain any more. Have you got a phone number? In case of – you know – emergencies?'

She's not memorised it yet; has to look on the menu to reel it off. The woman types, hits the tab key. Looks up. 'And where are you living?'

She's about to say the address when her natural suspicions stop her. There's no need for them to know. It's not like she'll be switching the phone off. She tells the woman the address of her mother's flat, because it's the first thing that springs to her mind.

Footsteps soft-shuffle down the corridor and a man appears, wearing what look like chef's whites. He wields a bunch of keys, like a jailor, and peers enquiringly past the flowers at the receptionist.

'Visitor for Janine Baker.'

He raises his eyebrows. 'Oh, *riiiight.*'

'Her daughter,' says the woman, significantly.

He turns to Collette and gives her an up-and-down look. 'I was beginning to think she was all alone in the world.'

'Yes,' says Collette. 'I couldn't get here sooner, I'm afraid. I've been abroad. I had to make arrangements.'

'Fair enough.' He turns and starts walking back up the corridor. She hesitates for a moment, unsure as to whether she's supposed to follow or not, then, when he turns and looks over his shoulder, hurries to catch up.

Deeper into the building, the smell of nappies is stronger and the smell of polish weaker. They pause at a double fire door as he unlocks it. 'It's a toss-up,' he explains. 'I know you're meant to keep them unlocked, but whoever made that rule clearly wasn't trying to herd cats like we are. I'm Michael, by the way.'

Collette nods and mutters a second greeting. On the far side, the atmosphere is slightly damp, slightly feral, like the air in the underground she's just come off, the walls a soothing mint green. She walks beside him, glimpses an empty dining hall,

Formica tables and a wall-length window overlooking a garden full of privet and the corrugated iron wall of a warehouse. I must start stockpiling opiates, she thinks. I don't want my last view to be of this. A seascape, a bottle of gin and a bottle of Oromorph: that'll do me if I make it that far. In a lounge, shrivelled forms sit on non-absorbent surfaces and stare silently at Jeremy Kyle on the television. Each chair has a built-in tray sticking out from its right arm, each bearing a medical-pink earthenware teacup. There are no visitors, no people standing up by themselves who aren't in uniform. Wrong time of day, thinks Collette. At least, I hope so.

'Your mum's in her room,' says Michael. 'She likes to stay there most of the time. Till lunchtime, at least.'

'Fair enough,' says Collette. Janine was never a very sociable sort, in between boyfriends. God knows how she managed to replace them, sitting in her chair smoking and gazing at the telly while her peers went out arm in arm to the bingo, but she did. Even got three of them to marry her, for a bit. 'How's she doing?'

They reach a junction and the wall colours change abruptly. To her right, sky blue, to her left, where he leads her, candy pink. Even in second childhood, the genders are distinguished by decor. 'She's fine,' he says soothingly.

Always good to get a medical opinion. 'Sometimes she's a bit confused, but mostly she's quite content,' he adds.

So why did they decide she needed taking away? wonders Collette. This is how I remember her all my life, though I suppose the Temazepam and gin might have had a bit to do with that. Cardiac-related dementia, they called it when they informed her. Her heart's failing and the oxygen's just not getting through to her brain.

They reach a door, which sits ajar like all the others she's passed, so the staff can see the inhabitants without going inside. No real privacy in a twilight home. Collette wonders if they even close the doors at night and suspects that they don't. From behind the door they have just passed, a reedy voice rises in a wail. 'They won't let me they won't let me they won't *let* me! Bugger them. Why can't I? All I want is ...'

'Here we are,' says Michael, drowning the voice out. 'Now, don't be surprised if she's gone downhill a bit since you last visited. It can come as a shock, I know, but Mum's still inside.'

Last time she saw her was in the garden of Collette's flat in Stoke Newington: her hard-won respectability, her move into home-ownership. Three-odd years ago, looking unimpressed as she smoked her Bensons under a monstrous parasol, gin and tonic rattling ice in her hand. I loved that flat, thinks Collette. I was so proud of it. It was my proof that all the work I'd done was paying off. I wonder what's happened to it? Taken back by the bank, I suppose. Someone else is living there now, enjoying my kitchen, probably using my parasol and congratulating themselves on their auction bargain. And Lisa's probably credit-blacklisted until the end of time.

'Thanks,' she says. 'I'll remember.'

He calls in through the gap in the doorway. 'Janine, love? Are you decent?'

He mother's voice, but not. It's gone reedy, like that of the weeper next door, and breathless. 'Yes, thank you, dear.'

'I've got a visitor for you,' he calls, and pushes the door full-open.

Janine sits in a high-backed faux-leather fauteuil in front of a window that looks out on to a blank wall, two plastic tubes hooked into her nostrils. She looks up with childlike curiosity and a big smile, then her face falls, fills with confusion.

'Are you sure you've got the right room?' she asks, between breaths. 'Who are *you*?'

Collette feels a lurch. She was never much of a mother, but she can't have forgotten me, surely? 'It's me, Mum,' she says, and walks further into the room. Crouches down beside her mother's chair and looks up. 'Lisa.'

Janine's shrunk. She looks like a facsimile of herself, like someone's run her through a photocopier that's running low on toner. Last time Collette saw her, her hair had been loose-permed and lowlights ran through a base of yellow blonde. Now, she's grey: grey skin, grey eyes, grey greasy hair that looks like it's been cut with the kitchen scissors, charcoal lines running up from her lips and into her nostrils. She stares at Collette for a long time, then shakes her head. 'No,' she says, decisively. 'Don't be ridiculous. Lisa's only seventeen. You're bloody ancient.'

'She comes in and out,' says Michael. 'Don't let it worry you. Next time you come, she'll remember everything, most likely.'

Collette puts a hand on her mother's. Wrinkled, spotted, big blue veins standing out on the back. When did she get like this? She's only sixty-seven, for God's sake. It can't have all happened since I went away, surely? Was she getting like this and I just didn't notice?

'And Lisa's pretty,' says Janine, snatching the hand away.

Collette finds that she is trembling. She busies herself by looking down at her bag and searching out her packages. 'I brought you some stuff, look. I thought you'd like them. See?'

She holds up her gifts, like prizes. 'Those chocolates you like. And some nice smelly stuff. Chanel, look. You always liked Chanel.'

'Ooh,' says Janine, all sunny smiles again. She snatches the box of Ferrero Rocher from Collette's hand, delves within with the fervour of someone who's eaten nothing but mash and pudding cups for months. 'Mmmmm-mmmmm,' she says, mumbling them between blue gums and gasping for breath between smacks. She's grown a moustache. Thick hairs like wires, blacker by far than the hairs on her head. She holds up the bottle of Chanel N°5, always her aspiration scent, the one she longed for, the one Collette would save and save for from her Saturday jobs, to buy her for Christmas. Wrinkles her nose and drops it on the patterned carpet as though it were an empty box.

'So what was it you wanted?' she asks. 'I haven't got any money, if that's what you're after.'

Collette perches gingerly on the pink candlewick bedspread on Janine's bed. 'No,' she says, gently. 'I just wanted to know how you are.'

'It's my daughter who's got the money,' says Janine. 'Not that she can be bothered to come and see me. D'you want a chocolate? They're nice, these.'

'Yes,' says Collette, 'that would be nice. Thank you.'

Chapter Fifteen

'These are lovely,' says Vesta, and helps herself to another. 'What did you say they were called again?'

'Shirini Khoshk.' Hossein hovers a finger over the white card presentation box, selects a heart-shaped sandwich covered with shreds of something green and pops it whole into his mouth.

'I'm never going to remember that,' says Vesta. 'You know what they remind me of? Biscuits.'

'Yes,' says Hossein, solemnly. 'That's right. They are like biscuits.'

'Well, I never knew Persians ate biscuits.'

Hossein smiles. 'What did you think we eat?'

Vesta sits back in her lawn chair, dunks a pastry in her PG Tips. 'Oh, I dunno. Babies and that, I suppose.'

'Only on Eid,' he says. 'They are very expensive.'

They lapse into contented silence and gaze up at the azure sky. The garden is prepared for Vesta's party: blankets from her airing cupboard and her mother's full tea service laid out on a side-table Hossein has carried out, and water bubbling on a primus stove left over from the Three-Day Week. The others are due any minute, but she doesn't really mind too much if they don't show up.

This is nice just as it is, she thinks. To be honest, I could do without having to make polite conversation with people I hardly know, though of course that's the way they become people you *do* know. I bet him from Flat One doesn't bother to show. Didn't answer his invite. Not that I'm bothered if he doesn't. All sandy hair and pale lips and not meeting your eye in the hall. Not a party animal, Gerard Bright. No great loss to one, either.

Who would have thought, thinks Vesta, glancing across at Hossein, that at nearly seventy my best friend would be an Iranian asylum seeker half my age? Not Mum and Dad, that's for sure. They thought the Pelcsinskis at number seventeen were suspiciously foreign, with their weird cabbage-based food. What on earth would they make of the world now? We hadn't even heard of Iranians before the 1980s, and now they're all over the place. Like Somalis. Haven't had many of them down here, though. They seem to be more of a north London thing.

'Ooh, I saw your article in the *Guardian*, by the way,' she says. 'Very interesting.'

He raises his eyebrows. 'Thanks, Vesta. I didn't think anyone I knew would see it.'

'Oh, you know. I like to go through the papers in the library. If there's one thing you have a lot of when you're retired, it's time. So tell me something.'

'Yes?'

'I thought you weren't allowed to work?'

'I'm not. They don't pay me. They make a donation to the Medical Council for the Victims of Torture.'

'Oh. I see. That makes sense, I suppose.'

'It does. They were good to me. They deserve something back.'

'Still. Seems like a pretty pointless rule. All these people moaning about scroungers and they won't let you work.'

Hossein shrugs. 'It keeps my hand in.'

'True.'

'And it'll make it easier to get a job when I get my papers.'

'That's true too.'

She starts to reach down to take the cling film off the food, but Hossein puts out a hand, pushes her back by the arm. 'I'll do it.'

'I'm not ninety, Hossein.'

He tuts and gets down on his knees. Looks up as Cher comes round from the side-return, with a tall, fair-haired woman in tow. Vesta gets to her feet to greet them, like an old-fashioned hostess at a cocktail party. 'You must be Collette,' she says. 'I'm Vesta.'

Collette blushes slightly, and shakes her hand. 'This is very nice of you.'

'Oh,' Vesta waves a breezy hand over her bounty, 'it's nothing. A pleasure. Always a pleasure to get to know your neighbours.'

'Hello, again,' says Hossein, and she stutters a greeting, the colour on her pale cheeks deepening, but only meets his eye for a split second. My my, thinks Vesta, our new lady's got a thing for the handsome lodger, and it's only been a split second since she moved in. How cute. He could do with a nice lady friend. I've not seen him with a woman since he got here. 'How are you settling in?' he asks.

Her eyes are tinged slightly pink. Crying, or hay fever? 'Okay,' she says, and looks up at the sky.

'Here,' says Vesta, 'sit down, do. Have the chair.'

'Oh, no, I couldn't. Someone else must …'

'You're the guest of honour,' says Cher. 'Just take it.'

Collette lowers herself self-consciously into the spare deck-chair. The beautiful man has his back turned to her now, uncovering a collection of old-fashioned teatime foods laid out on elegant antique plates. The old lady has a stack of matching cups and saucers and one of those big brown earthenware teapots at her side, on a spindly table. She studies her as she pours: she's the only neighbour she's not seen in the flesh before. She's a surprising-looking woman. Tall and dignified, with nut-brown skin and steel grey hair, and the sort of profile that wouldn't go amiss on a Cherokee brave. Not what you think of when someone says 'the old lady downstairs'. Somehow that always conjures up pictures of walking sticks and buns full of Kirby grips. This woman looks like she'd be running an intensive care ward, if you let her.

Cher has sprawled herself on the edge of a blanket, platform soles like orange boxes on the ends of her skinny legs. The man keeps his eyes studiously away from the bare flesh, concentrates on the task at hand. What am I doing here? Collette wonders. I don't want to make friends. All I want to do is go and lie down and think about Janine.

As soon as the wrapping is off, Cher's hand darts on to the sandwiches. 'I'm starving,' she says.

'Have a sandwich,' says Hossein, and she laughs and flicks his upper arm with one fuchsia fingernail.

'Did you make that cake, Vesta? Ooh, Vesta-cake. I knew you'd make a cake.'

She's so kiddish, thinks Collette. And these people: they're enablers. They treat her like some cheeky niece, indulge her.

'We're not cutting it till we're all here,' says Vesta. 'Offer those sarnies around, Cher. Don't just hog them. Would you like a cup of tea, Collette?'

'Um,' she says, 'yes, that would be nice, thank you.'

'Got better manners than you have, anyway,' says Vesta to Cher.

'Probably wasn't drug up in care,' says Cher, and stuffs a sausage roll whole into her mouth. She's as skinny as a string bean, though she has a pair of surprisingly large breasts for such a small frame. Probably doesn't eat much when it's not given to her. Those kids never do. Cheese doodles and diet Coke, most likely, and the lack of calories made up with Baileys.

'Milk and . . . ?' asks Vesta, and picks up a teacup.

'Just milk, thanks. That's a pretty service.'

'It was my mother's. Booth's silicon china. It was a wedding present to my gran, before the Great War.'

'Oh, how lovely,' says Collette. She has nothing of family, now. Not that there ever was much. The one thing her mother achieved with her own life, as far as she knows, was to get out of Limerick and cut off her ties. After that, once she got to London, once she was pregnant and alone and the council gave her a flat, it was as if all the fight went out of her. She just sat there waiting for a man to save her and weeping as, one by one, they never did. There will be nothing but pound-shop china and second-hand pans for the council to clear out of her flat when they get round to it. She didn't even have many friends to swap Christmas presents with. That's how a lot of people amass decorative stuff: gifts and inheriting.

'I would have died if the burglar had broken these,' says Vesta. 'I wouldn't have been able to stop seeing my mother's face.'

'I'm sorry about your break-in. That must've been horrible. Did they get much?'

'Scary, more than anything,' says Vesta. 'I've lived here all my life, and nothing like this has ever happened before. I just hope ... you know. Now they've been in, they could come back. They do say they do that.'

'It's okay,' says Hossein. 'I'll fix a chain lock on that door. They won't get in again. Bastards.'

Vesta laughs. 'My knight in shining armour. He's an absolute godsend, this one,' she says pointedly to Collette; lets her know she hasn't missed her attempts not to look at him. 'He'll do anything for you, if you ask him.'

'Well, not *anything*,' says Hossein. He turns his golden smile on Collette, and Vesta sees her glow in the reflected light. 'So, how are you settling in, Collette? Are you enjoying your luxury accommodation?'

'All mod cons,' says Collette, and waves away a sandwich from the plate Cher holds out. She remembers her gift, blushes and digs in her bag. Finds her pack of chocolate HobNobs and offers them to Vesta. 'I brought these. A ... a contribution. I'm sorry. They look really poor, against all this ...'

'Nonsense,' says Hossein, as Vesta takes the biscuits and hands them on to him. 'HobNobs are one of your country's finest foodstuffs.'

'Thanks, love,' says Vesta. 'What a treat.'

'Don't let him get started on food,' says Cher. 'He'll go on for hours about his mum's lamb with rhubarb if you let him.'

'Lamb with rhubarb?' says Vesta, 'I don't like the sound of that.'

'Oh, God, it's beautiful,' says Hossein, and his eyes glow with liquid nostalgia. 'The lamb is cooked for hours, so it falls off the bone, and she used to throw in fried mint and parsley at the last minute, so it's still crunchy when you eat it ...'

'Told you,' says Cher. 'What are these? Arab cakes?'

'Iranian,' says Hossein, and pronounces the 'a' long, like an aaah. 'Not Arab. Iranian.'

'Whatever,' says Cher, and pops a little baklava in to chase down her sausage roll. 'Nnnnfff,' she says, and sprays pastry flakes over the blanket, 'that's sooo good.'

'I know,' says Hossein. 'Really, it's hard to believe that such beauty could come from an evil empire, isn't it?'

'Can we start the cake?' interrupts Cher.

'Not till Thomas gets here.' Vesta waves a finger in the air. 'It's easy to make young people happy with food, isn't it?' she says to Collette, confidingly. Oh, Lord, thinks Collette. Does she see me as closer to her generation than to theirs? She must be the same age as my mum.

Cher's face drops. 'Oh, Christ on a bike, is *he* coming?' she asks.

'I told you I was asking everybody. I asked him up there, too,' she gestures towards the upper ground floor. 'Although I somehow doubt we're going to be graced with his presence. I saw him go off with his overnight bag this morning. I think he's gone off to see his kids again.'

'Thank God for that. He's not exactly Mr Party, is he? Between him sitting there staring at the air like he's trying to catch flies and Mr Chatty going on about the Second World War or something, we might as well pack up and go to sleep now. We'll never get a word in once he turns up.'

Vesta raises an eyebrow. 'Said the pot to the kettle.'

'No, but I'm *funny*,' says Cher, with the petulant assurance of the young. 'He's just such a ... a fuckweasel.'

The side-return gate scrapes open, bangs to. They fall quiet and crane round, none of them sure, really, what a fuckweasel is, but fairly sure that Thomas won't have liked being called one if he has heard. He can't not have. Cher's voice could warn ships on the Mersey.

'Hello, hello!' he calls, and his voice is unnaturally jolly. Yes, he's heard, thinks Collette, but he's going to pretend he hasn't. 'A beautiful afternoon for it!'

He comes round the corner. He's wearing a polo shirt today – the minor bureaucrat's smart-casual. It has obviously been maroon at some point in its existence, but has faded to a dark pink. He wears clip-on sun lenses over his spectacles; they're smudged, and a small chip has come off one corner of the left lens so he has the look of someone who's fallen on hard times, whose self-maintenance has slid downhill. The scuffed shoes and the slightly dandyish shirt suggest someone who clearly once cared about his appearance. Collette sighs inwardly – he looks like someone who's lost hope.

'Well!' he says, marching across the lawn with a box of Milk Tray held out before him. 'What a treat! So good to see the garden being used, as well. I love looking down on your little patch of green, Vesta. What a treat to come and be in it for a change. Hello, Hossein, hello, Collette. I've brought you some chocolates, Vesta. Maybe not the best present in this heat. I'm sorry. I didn't think. About the melting issue.'

He doesn't look at Cher, doesn't include her in the greetings. Yes, he heard, thinks Collette again. And he's not happy.

'They'll be lovely,' says Vesta, taking the chocolates. 'You *are* kind. Milk Tray! You shouldn't have!'

'Not at all, not at all, it's nothing.' He rubs his hands together like Uriah Heep and beams around him – at Collette, at

Hossein, at Vesta's begonias, at anywhere other than Cher. 'Well, it's another beautiful day, isn't it?' he says. 'Though I suppose some people might find it too hot. Nothing's ever perfect for everybody, is it?'

He stands awkwardly above them all, looking about for somewhere to sit and radiating an aroma of suppressed astonishment that the chairs have run out. I bet he's one of those people, thinks Collette, who always gives off a faint air of reproach, one of those people who's never truly happy unless he's hard done by.

Collette gives it a go, anyway. 'Here,' she hauls herself to her feet. 'Have a seat.'

'Oh, no, no,' says Thomas, 'I couldn't possibly. *You're* sitting there.'

'No, you're all right,' says Collette. 'I'm more of a floor sitter anyway. And I've been in chairs non-stop today. It'll be nice to get on to a rug.'

'No, no,' he begins again, but Collette practically dives on to the blanket next to Cher. 'Look, I'm here now,' she says, and he tuts sheepishly and sits himself down, takes the cup of tea Vesta holds out across the gap. 'Isn't this nice?' he says, again, and this time no one bothers to respond.

'So can we have some cake, now?' asks Cher.

'Yes. Collette, do you want to play mother?'

'Sure.'

'There's a knife in the basket.'

'Okay.' She reaches in and closes her hand around a handle that sticks out from under a chequered teacloth. Feels a tiny jolt of surprise as it brings the whole cloth with it. It's a chef's knife, best part of a foot long: a pointed end and an edge that looks like it would cut silk in mid-air like a Samurai sword. 'I thought

I was just meant to cut the cake,' she says, holding it up, 'not stab it to death.'

'Sorry,' says Vesta. 'My old man was a butcher. I've got all sorts. Knives, sinew scissors, cleavers ...'

Hossein bursts out laughing. 'It suits you,' he says, looking at Collette. 'It's like it was made for you.'

Collette wrinkles her nose and makes a stabbing gesture through the air. They grin at each other and Vesta sees a small, indefinable moment pass between them. Then Collette bends to cut the cake.

'So tell me, Collette,' asks Thomas, 'what brings you to our fine neck of London?'

This is why I didn't want to come. Questions. They're going to ask me questions. And I don't know what to tell them. She lets her hair drop forward and cover her face, pretends to be concentrating on making the slice just so. 'Oh, you know,' she replies. 'This and that. I've been abroad for a while. Just getting myself back together and working out what to do next.'

'Do you come from here originally, then?'

No harm in telling them that, surely? Millions of people come from here. 'Further over,' she says. 'Peckham, really. Over towards the Elephant.'

She sees the shutters of lost interest clamp down. No one cares about Peckham. London has invisible borders way beyond the north–south divide. To someone from the south-west, any-thing east of Brixton might as well be Berlin. It's one of the reasons she had Janine sent to the home she did, one of the rea-sons she hopes she may get away with staying here: that in London terms, Leyton is as far from Ealing as Mars.

'So what brings you to Northbourne?' asks Vesta. 'That's a bit of a way from home, isn't it?' She can count the number of times she's been to the West End herself on her fingers and toes. Even now she's got a pensioner's Freedom Pass, she can't think of any reason to go.

'I – my mum's in a home. In Collier's Wood. This seemed like, you know, near enough, but far enough away at the same time, if you get my drift.'

Hossein grins. 'Oh, yes,' he says. 'I know what you mean.'

'In a home?' asks Vesta. 'Oh, I'm sorry to hear that, love. That must be hard.'

Collette shrugs. 'It is what it is. But I didn't want her to … you know. Alone. Not that she knows who I am, really, any more.'

'Dementia? How old is she?'

'Sixty-seven.'

'My God!' Vesta looks stricken. 'But that's younger than me!'

Collette doesn't know what to say to that. It's never really occurred to her that someone of Vesta's age would think themselves still outside the zone when it came to the diseases of old age. 'It's her heart,' she says. 'It's because of her heart. She's got heart failure, and it's affected her brain.'

What do you say? That she lived her life on a cocktail of prescription drugs and high-tar cigarettes and London Gin, and now she's paying the price? A memory of Janine's slack face swims up before her, and she wants to cry again. It's not been much of a life, has it, Mum? I wonder if you ever wanted anything different for yourself?

'My granddad had that,' says Cher. 'It sucks.'

'How much longer do they think she's got?' asks Thomas, and the party freezes. Even Cher looks a bit shocked. You don't encompass impending death with strangers. Not unless you're in a hospital. He doesn't seem to notice the change in atmosphere: just sits forward with his elbows hooked round his knees, curious. 'Only, I work for the Citizen's Advice,' he says, 'two days a week. It's not something we handle, but if you need, you know, to know what to do, I'm sure I can find out.'

What a funny man, thinks Collette. I honestly think he actually means well. 'I – thanks,' she says. 'Not much longer, I don't think. It's hard to tell.'

She glances up and is surprised to see an expression that looks like deep sorrow in Hossein's eyes. Gosh, she thinks. You've seen some stuff, haven't you? There's someone you really, really miss. Then he looks away, awkwardly, and starts arranging the remaining patisseries on to the empty sandwich plate.

'Who's for cake?' she asks, brightly.

'Me,' says everyone.

Chapter Sixteen

The Landlord's settee is made of leather. Black leather, bought at the height of the 1980s black-leather boom and still going strong with its wipe-clean ways and smudged chrome frame. He bought it on the Tottenham Court Road when he still thought of himself as up-and-coming, soon after his aunt died and he became a man of property. Now, he just likes the feel of it beneath his naked buttocks.

He still has the smoked glass coffee table that came as part of the set. It sits in front of the settee, within easy arm's reach of a supine arm-stretch; the whole area within reach of his free left hand is set up perfectly for his solitary pleasures. The tablet computer lives beside the telephone, on the armrest behind his head, and lined up on the table top are an icy tin of beer whose temperature is kept down with the help of a neoprene stubby holder emblazoned with a picture of a windsurfer in front of an improbable sunset and the word AUSTRALIA (he's not been to Australia, but clearly someone who donates to the MIND shop on Northbourne High Street has), an ashtray, which contains two cigarillo butts and a pile of Werther's Original wrappers, the remote controls for the TV and the DVD player and a box of tissues. Man-size.

The Landlord loves to come home and shed his clothes. He likes the freedom. He likes the draught from the fan playing over his skin, to be able to lift up the apron of fat that hangs down over his thighs and let his privates breathe. He likes the feel of sweat – and goddamn, this heat makes him sweat – turning to vapour, without the close confines of cloth soaking it up. And he likes to touch himself.

The Landlord strokes himself from shoulder to nipple and marvels at the efficacy of the Internet if you're curious. It's not just the things that turn up online that help you learn about people – and he loves to know more about his lodgers than they think he knows – it's the things that don't. The fact that Thomas Dunbar's name no longer appears on the trustee list of the Northbourne Furniture Exchange, and the announcement that the Citizen's Advice has cut down its opening hours to go with the prevailing Austerity. He's noticed him about the place more, lately, fussing and gabbling and sticking his nose in. These bits of information look like an explanation. An underemployed nosy-parker is no one's idea of fun.

On the TV, the Landlord's camera footage plays out images from the motion-operated cameras he's set up in two bathrooms. The casual eye would interpret them as smoke alarms, and so far no one has questioned the need for such a thing in a bathroom. Currently, Gerard Bright is lathered up in the tub, shaving his buttocks. The Landlord glances, then glances away. Bright shaves and exfoliates and soaks himself in oils each day of the week. Nothing to see here: just a middle-aged narcissist in a prison made of glass. Besides, Collette Dunne is more interesting in every way. He Googles her as he waits for her to follow her neighbour in.

He can't find a thing about her. Hossein Zanjani gets thousands of hits, hundreds of photos. The Home Office wouldn't need to string out 'investigating' his asylum claim, if they were just to use Google, though they might be interested to see that he's writing for every left-wing media outlet that will have him. Even old Vesta has a dozen entries – marketing lists, surveys, the flower rota at the Anglican church. But Collette Dunne? Dozens in the world, millions of hits on Google, but none of them are her. They're dentists and dancers and strategic consultants. They're fifty and seventeen and dead, and black and blonde and redheaded, and not one looks like the one in Beulah Grove.

There are only two reasons why someone wouldn't show up on Google. No one cares a damn about them, or it's not their real name.

Bright leaves the bathroom, and the TV screen, after a couple of seconds of empty room, goes blank. He fixed motion sensors on to his camera in when he realised that 98 per cent of his DVDs were blank. Then the door opens and the subject of his web-search comes in. She wears pyjamas and a satin dressing gown, her hair tied up into a curly knot at the top of her head. The Landlord pulls up his knees and props the tablet against his thighs. His freed-up hand begins to stray downwards, fingers running over belly, back up again to the cleavage between his breasts, as he clicks through to Cher Farrell's Facebook page. He likes to use his fingertips; they make him feel like a cat.

Cher Farrell. Now here's a story. Collette may be pretending to be someone else, but this one, it seems, nobody cares about. Since he discovered this one desultory trace of the girl, the Landlord has developed a taste for Facebook. The place is riddled with pages for missing teens, and no one ever remembers to take them down once the drama is done. They sit there for ever, long after the subject has come home, been found, been buried; pottages of condolence and trolling and digital love-hearts. 'Come home, Keely, Granny loves you'; 'OMG XOXOEMMA-BABE LUV YA 4 EVR DRLIN <3 XOXO'; 'Deepest condolences from Lesley, Keith and all at WonderPackaging'; 'I'd give her one if she wasn't dead LOL'; 'Come back, Tyra. Nobody's angry'.

Cher Farrell's page hasn't changed since the last time he looked. It's not changed, in fact, since it was posted eighteen months ago. It has no likes, no comments, no shares, no nothing; just a photo, barely recognisable with the passage of time, and a barebones appeal from social services. Have you seen this girl? We've lost her. We've done our bit. Our budgets don't stretch to more than this, not for someone no one cares about. Even the page admin hasn't been back for a while, to clear off the spam advertising for sex toys and free iPads. It's the loneliest Facebook page he's ever seen.

He looks up to watch his newbie. Collette crosses the room, puts a toilet roll on to the cistern, hoicks up her dressing gown and drops the pyjama bottoms. Sits on the toilet and lets out a visible sigh of pleasure. The time-stamp says it's 10.17 and her last visit to this room was some time around midnight. Her bladder must be full to bursting. The Landlord caresses the thin line of damp hair that links his belly button and his *mons pubis*, twiddles it round his index finger and lets it slide out. The image is a long way from HD, too grainy to afford him much view of the dark place between her legs, but he thinks he sees a wisp of hair as she reaches back to the toilet paper. An unusual sight, these days, if it's so. Young Cher, like Gerard, has skin as naked as the day she was born; scrapes it clean each week with a tube of Nair and a plastic spatula. All the young girls, signalling their adulthood by making themselves look like five-year-olds. He's often wondered how this fits with society's obsession with paedophilia.

He slows down the action as she wipes herself and stands up, pulling her trousers up as she goes, but the movement is so fluid, the dressing gown falling across her body beneath her arm, that he fails to see more. Nonetheless, just the thought is enough to make him feel a tiny stirring in his groin. One of the advantages of his peripatetic clientele is the constant chance of change. He'd been beginning to tire of Nikki, her red hair and her heavy breasts; she had heavy thighs to match, and they got in the way of his fantasies.

The Landlord's fingers stray down, start to tickle at the hood of his penis; to tease his foreskin gently back from the tender glans beneath. Collette crosses to the bath, puts the plug in and turns the taps. The Landlord feels his breath begin to falter in his nose, to speed up. He licks a finger and brings it, spittle-lubed, down to rub in tiny circles around the outlet of his urethra. As she walks over and looks at herself in the mirror over the basin, takes her hair bobbles out and allows that mass of curls to tumble down about her shoulders, he feels another twitch as his cock begins to harden. He may not have seen it for a decade, but, with a little help, it all still works fine. The Landlord sinks down further into his sofa, and lets his knees fall open, the soles of his feet pressed together, as he takes the whole member in his hand and starts working it to full erection. To someone watching him he would look like nothing other than a frog pinned out on a sixth-form dissection table, but in his mind he is a king.

Collette lets the dressing gown slip from her shoulders, and comes over to the door, below his camera and hangs it on the hook on its back. She looks up for a moment and seems to be staring straight into his eyes. Creamy Celtic skin, dark eyebrows, lips clearly defined, full and strong; the sort of mouth that . . .

By his head, the phone rings.

'Fuck!' He considers ignoring it, but the mood is broken. As Collette Dunne turns back to the mirror and begins to wash her face with some product from a tube, he presses the answer button and holds the phone to his ear. 'Hello?'

A pause at the other end and then a single beep. A female voice, old-fashioned London accent, the semi-refined cup-of-tea-luv sort of accent you only hear on old Ealing comedies these days, shouts down the line as though trying to be heard without electronic aids. 'Hello?'

'Hello?'

'Mr Preece?'

'Yuh,' he says, though he still thinks of Mr Preece as his father.

'Oh, good. Hello, Mr Preece. It's Miss Collins, from number twenty-three. Vesta? Vesta Collins?'

The Landlord sighs and shifts and the sofa cushions fart in protest. He really must get that phone taken out of the hall. She's the only one who ever uses it, and she only uses it for nagging. 'Oh, right?'

Collette Dunne is testing the water in the bath with her hand and tugging at the back of her top. Trust that whiny old bag to spoil the mood. 'I haven't got long, Mr Preece,' says Vesta. 'Forty pee, you have to put in to these things before you call, these days, and I've no idea how long it lasts.'

Well, get on with it, then, you old bat, he thinks. If you weren't so mean, you'd have a phone like every twelve-year-old in the country. 'Fire ahead,' he says.

'I waited in when you came on rent day. You usually come down.'

'And you usually complain when I do,' he says.

'No,' says Vesta, 'I complain because nothing ever seems to get done, no matter how often I ask. I'd be perfectly happy for you to come down if I thought for a minute you were going to mend something.'

Moan, moan, moan. 'You can't expect a new Schreiber kitchen every couple of years on the rent *you* pay,' he says, resentfully. Vesta's sitting tenancy has been a thorn in his side since they put paid to any new ones in the 1980s. Squatting there in the bowels of the house, rendering it unsaleable while paying less than he gets for a single room upstairs. If it weren't for Vesta he would have sold up years ago. If it weren't for Vesta he'd be sitting pretty, running a complex of maid-service holiday lets somewhere warm instead of trudging back and forth up Northbourne High Street. Letting her drain him dry.

'You know perfectly well I'm not asking for that sort of thing. When have I ever? It's those drains. You've got to do something about those drains. Every time someone flushes the loo upstairs, stuff comes up out of the area grating. It's disgusting. I'm going to get ill soon.'

'Didn't that drain cleaner I put down work?'

Collette pulls her top off and he freezes the image while her back is still turned; a muscular back with a well-defined waist that suggests that she has, at some point in her life, at least, taken care of her figure. He wants to get back into the mood before she turns to face the camera. His genitals are still sensitive with interrupted excitement, and if he can get the old bag off the phone, stop listening to her ladylike vowels and her I-know-my-rights complaints, he might still be able to get there.

'Do you think I'd be calling if it had? I've been spending the best part of five pounds a week on bleach, and heaven knows how much it's costing on the immersion, pouring gallon after gallon of hot water down there. Not to mention the environment. All that bleach going into the water system . . . '

Everyone's an environmentalist, these days. Especially when they want something. He toys with a nipple and eases himself upright on the couch. Picks up his tinnie and takes a gulp.

'You need to call the drain people,' she says. 'I'm going to get ill.'

Good, he thinks. Hope you bloody die. That would sort a lot of things out. He takes another gulp of beer and raises an arm to let the fan play into the matted hair in the pit. 'I'll come and have a look,' he says.

'When?'

'When I get a minute.'

'Well, it needs to be soon, Mr Preece. I'll have to call the Health and Safety, otherwise. And another thing. That lock.'

'Lock?'

'On my back door.'

'What about it?'

'It needs replacing.'

The beer repeats on him, and he makes little effort to disguise the sound. Unwraps a sucky sweet and pops it in his mouth. 'Be my guest.'

'It didn't stop that vandal getting in at all. Just popped straight out of the latch.'

'Well, help yourself.'

There's a silence. Then she tries again. 'I think that's up to you.'

The Landlord screws up the sweet wrapper and adds it to the pile in the ashtray. 'No, I don't think so. If you want to beef up your security, that's up to you, but as far as I'm concerned there's a door and a lock. Maybe,' he says spitefully, 'you should ask your insurers. They might upgrade it for you.'

He hears her suck in her breath. 'You know perfectly well I'm on a state pension. You know I can't afford insur—'

He hears beeps on the line. The forty pee has run out. 'When are you—' she begins, and her voice is cut off.

His mood is almost lost, Collette frozen with her arms above her head. Irritably, he polishes off his beer in a single chug and throws himself back against the cushions. Every time he talks to that stubborn old cow, it puts a frown on his face, reminds him of the money she's depriving him of. That flat alone, even in its current state, with the kitchen that time forgot and the drains of doom, must be worth a hundred and fifty thousand. A big house like that, with a big garden, on a road the estate agents are calling 'popular', is worth half a million, easy, even without modernisation. Vesta Collins is cheating him out of his dreams.

He levers the remote out from under his left buttock, and presses play. Collette turns round, and shows him her breasts.

Chapter Seventeen

As in life, so in death: a woman needs a good moisture routine to maintain her beauty, both inside and out. Even after desiccation, the process of putrefaction continues, albeit more slowly, and a woman exposed to the open air – and the bacteria and fungus spores that float in it – deserves protection.

Once the forty days was done, the *taricheutes* would take the sacred corpse, now a hardened shell, and wash it in palm wine. The Lover has made do with Asda budget vodka. Even at eight quid a bottle, the alcoholic proof must be higher than anything they produced on the banks of the Nile, he guesses. The body was then massaged back to suppleness with scented oils, and the empty torso packed with resin and herbs and sewn up, for scent and verisimilitude. It was then wrapped in resin-soaked bandages before being placed in its ornately painted coffin, en route to the hereafter.

But an Egyptian mummy was only destined for the afterlife. Keeping his ladies user-friendly requires, as he has discovered, more regular attention. Once a week, the Lover gives Marianne her ritual ablutions. He only wishes he'd worked out the need before it was too late for Alice. She's almost beyond salvage, now. The last time he oiled her, he rubbed a little too hard with his home-made strigil and took a strip almost a foot long from her thigh, so that the bone showed through. And he has to admit that, with her abdomen unsealed, the smell coming from her is hard to ignore. Now he leaves her well alone, feels the reproach beaming from her shrivelled breasts as she sits in her chair and watches Marianne receive the attention that should have been her own. The rictus on her face has turned cynical over the past few weeks, as her nose has dried out and turned up. So much for loving me for ever, it says. You've barely given me a year. She's like one of those suburban wives who lets herself go, then sits about in a onesie, complaining about men.

Ah, but Marianne. Not a first wife, but certainly a trophy wife. Renewer of love, restorer of faith; the basis of his new family, harbinger of happiness to come. If anything, Marianne has improved with age. The slightly lumpy chin, the faint pot belly, the chunky thighs that used to irritate him when they were courting, have vanished in the preservation process, and she is as slim as a supermodel, her cheekbones like Audrey Hepburn's, her nose snipped like Paris Hilton's, the three-point jawline of Alicia Silverstone. Dressed in hipster jeans and a little broderie anglaise top, she reminds him vaguely of Kate Moss.

He lays her gently out on the plastic sheeting, lights his neroli candles and starts the ritual. He tests the temperature of the oil, warmed gently on the stove, on the tender skin of his inner elbow and, judging it right, pours a drizzle on to her beautiful shoulder. Watches it spread. Inhales the aroma and smiles: sweet almond, white soft paraffin, and essential oils – neroli, sandal-wood and vanilla – from the hippy shop in Balham. It's a ladylike scent, spicy yet clean, and it hides the smell of decay.

Palms flat, he reaches out and helps the oil on it way. Strokes his way over the shoulders, down the arms. Takes each hand and massages it all the way up to the fingertips, one by one. He is proud of his skill, of the fact that he has given her eternal life. Her fingernails, buffed and filed back to evenness, though a little short after her struggle to break free, are still perfect, still flexible and roundly pointed, painted once a month to match her toes. He talks to her as he rubs; makes circles with his fingertips and works the magic potion in. There, my darling. We'll keep you beautiful. Her skin so cold in the muggy air, so soft, almost papery, beneath his hands. You like that, don't you, my love? he asks. You know it's all for you.

He works slowly, methodically. Is determined that no breath of outside will taint his darling, damage her purity. It takes nearly an hour to oil her head-to-toe, then he dresses her, gently, gently: pink silk French knickers and a white lace bra (padded, but only slightly, just to replace what has been lost), and then a chic little black dress from the Trinity Hospice shop: a cast-off, he knows, but as good as new with its short pleated skirt and light crêpe bodice. Two silver bangles on the delicate wrists, a single stone of amber on a pendant between the jutting collarbones, matching droplets in the holes in her ears.

When he's done, he sits her in a chair and slowly, delicately, cleans her face with Clarin's cream cleanser, massages it with oil, pressing in above the jaw to encourage the plumpness back upwards, and replaces her make-up. Marianne needs little work. Black liquid eyeliner and a set of eyelashes, a couple of coats of mascara to bind them to the fading originals. Some blush to emphasise her spectacular angles and a touch of burgundy to thicken her slightly thinning lips.

He steps back to admire his handiwork, Alice glaring balefully, neglected, from the corner. I really must get rid of you, he thinks, spitefully. I hate the way you make me feel so bad. It's not her fault she came out better than you did. It's not her fault she's beautiful. He snatches up a tea towel from the draining board and throws it over her face. If she can't be good, she must live with the consequences.

Marianne sits, poised and graceful, in her chair, her green glass eyes gazing in rapture at the light fitting. Just one more duty, one more gesture of care, and they're done. He opens one of his fold-up chairs and puts it behind her, fetches the bowl of almond oil and dips into it the soft bristles of a Mason Pearson hairbrush. One hundred strokes for beauty; it's in every manual from the Romans to the Victorians. One hundred strokes for beauty.

He counts out loud as he brushes, enjoys the feeling of her hair running through his fingers. You like that, don't you, my darling? You like it that I make you lovely. Her hair is long and dark, and lustrous because of the oil, though every week a few more strands come away on the bristles of the brush.

Chapter Eighteen

The trick is to know the territory better than the punter does, and to look so out of it that he's off his guard. And not to let him see your face, much. Not that most of them are looking. They don't look at your face much, when they're thinking with their dicks.

She may have the reading age of an eleven-year-old, but Cher knows what makes the blood rush away from the brain. There are things you learn in school, and things you learn in Britain's better care homes. You need to look young, you need to look dirty and you need to look desperate. She's good at that. She's had a lot of practice.

On Brad Street, there's a house with a broken side gate where no lights have shown for months. She rings on the doorbell, waits for a response and, when none comes, slips into the dark little cave of the side-return and organises herself.

She is already wearing her wig, with the fringe brushed forward over her face so that her brows and eyes are partly covered. Squatting over her bag, she pulls off her fake Uggs and pulls on a pair of peep-toe mules – easy to kick off when the need arises. She sheds her denim jacket and pulls her knee-length dress over her head. Tucks it all away into the bag, but leaves it open, ready for action.

I hate him, she thinks, but I have no choice. I can't go back to sleeping rough again. It nearly killed me, last winter, before I found him. I need this room. He knows I need it. And shoplifting's all very well for your daily essentials, but you never get more than a tenner for anything. What am I meant to do?

She stands up in hot pants and tube top, and steps back out into the street. It's all quiet, down here. You'd never know you were two hundred yards from streets of bars and restaurants, the Old Vic theatre and a busy tube station tipping tipsy office workers who've stayed too long at Happy Hour on to their suburban trains. London is such a city of contrasts: one of those places where you can turn a corner and drop off the edge of the world. Where the IMAX cinema now stands used to be a subway full of the homeless known as Cardboard City. Back then the South Bank trendies would take mile-long detours to stay above ground.

These Dickensian mazes are perfect for her purpose. Rows of heavily restored black-brick cottages that sell for close on a million pounds, whose inhabitants come in and out by cab after dark, to avoid the dripping shadows under the railway arch. It's dinky in the day, all potters and delicatessens and artisan bread, but once the wooden shutters close, it echoes. A significant advantage for her, for someone giving chase in shoes will drown out the sound of someone fleeing barefoot.

Two corners away from her bag, someone from some council past has planted a bench by a stunted tree: a sad little gesture towards recreational facilities for the echoing maze of the Peabody Estate behind. Cher once tried sleeping there for a few nights, which is how she knows that these roads are a shortcut for drunken men staggering through to the Embankment from the bars of Waterloo. She sits down, arranges her long legs, lights a cigarette and waits.

It doesn't take long. He's old – must be nearly thirty – and sweating slightly in his unbuttoned pinstripe suit. The tail end of a tie sticks out from a pocket, and he walks as though he's trying to avoid the cracks in the pavement. Cher shifts around so he catches a good look at the lean length of her thigh, then looks up at the streetlight as he stops and looks again.

He crosses the road and sits himself down at the other end of the bench. It's not a very long bench. She can smell the beer on him from where she sits. It's a smell she remembers well.

He stretches one arm along the seat back in a parody of the casual, like a sixth-former in the cinema, and digs the other fist into his trouser pocket. She hears him breathe through blocked-up nostrils and feels him looking clumsily from the side of his eye.

He takes in a big whoosh of air and turns jerkily towards her as though he has only just spotted her. 'Nice night,' he says.

Cher shrugs, sucks on her fag and turns to look at him. She tends to keep the talking to a minimum during these transactions. He looks straight at her tits, then down at the imagined treasure between her thighs. 'You all alone, then?'

It's the sort of voice that puts her teeth on edge. A fat voice, full of plums and promising that its owner will soon be having to trade his suit up for a larger size. A voice that's never had to struggle, that's only slept outdoors on Officer Training Corps weekends. Cher pouts her frosted pink lips and shrugs again.

'Are you, er ... looking for company?'

Would it make any difference if I wasn't? she wonders. And replies: 'Sure.'

He almost starts dribbling. Christ, men. Are there any out

there that don't drool at the prospect of a feel? That don't want to be at you with their poky fingers, to hump at you like a bull terrier? None that Cher's met, anyway. The ones that are meant to take care of you are the worst, though. At least there's an honesty to a transaction of this sort. At least he's not telling her he loves her and talking about Little Secrets.

'Have you got a place?'

What do you think this is, Shepherd Market? 'No,' she says. Nods over at the path that runs up the side of a language school. 'That over there turns a corner round the back. Into a yard. We can be private there.'

She sees him look at the signage, conclude that a private education establishment can't possibly be a trap. He turns back, blearily.

'How much?'

'What for?' she asks. He doesn't look like he'll be up to anything much, but Cher is counting on that.

He runs through the vocabulary he's heard in films. He's not a habitual buyer of pussy. He's practically congratulating himself on his audaciousness. 'How much for French?'

'French?' She can't resist taunting him, taking the piss out of his attempts at sounding like he knows what he's doing. 'What's that?'

'I, er . . .' His sweaty fatboy face falls as he realises he's going to have to be more graphic; grapple with vocabulary he usually only uses with other men. 'You know. Blowjob.'

'Oh, riiiiight. Why didn't you say so?'

'I . . .'

'Never mind. That'll be sixty.'

'Sixty?'

'Oh, Christ. You're not going to start haggling, are you?'

Cher shifts, deliberately; flashes a bit more cleavage, slightly, ever so slightly, parts her thighs.

His eyes glaze. 'No. No, all right.'

She sits and looks at him; starts to slip off her shoes. It takes him a moment to work out why she's gone quiet, then he reaches into his jacket pocket and brings out a fat, card-filled leather wallet. She waits silently as he counts out three twenties: one, two, three. Even in this light she can see there are quite a few more in there. He hands them over, fanned out like they're a prize. Fat drunk rich boy wants me to suck his cock. Just like the fat old Landlord thinks he can get me to do, when I can't come up with the rent. Fuck them. Fuck them all.

His phone rings and she takes her chance while he's distracted. Waits until he's got it out of his pocket and is looking at the screen – it's an iPhone, of course it is, but it's probably not worth her while to try to get that too – then bats it lightly out of his hand, so quickly he barely registers the blow. It skitters away across the pavement, lands up in the gutter. Fatboy looks up at her, lower lip quivering, cross and confused. She smiles. 'Oops. Sorry.'

'Ssss,' he says. Wobbles to his feet, wallet carelessly in his hand, and walks over to the kerb. Silently, on bare feet, shoes in hand, she creeps up behind. As he bends and stretches, Cher snatches her moment. Runs forward and, with all her might, shoves at the unstable backside.

Fatboy goes 'oof', and goes down flat on his face. Change and keys and fountain pens jingle out of his pockets and the wallet flies from his fingers, lands on the tarmac four feet away.

She's leapt over the top of him and snatched it up before he's even drawn a breath. She is fifteen feet away before she hears his bellow of rage. Cher runs for her life.

No lights show in windows as she flies down Roupell Street,

hammers her bare feet along the flagstones and hopes to God she will encounter no broken glass. Thudding footsteps, thumping heart; the wig is starting to slip on her head and she clamps a hand to hold it on. Lets go again, for running one-armed slows her up. If it comes off, it comes off, as long as she's out of sight before it does. Cher has always been fast on her feet. If she'd been given the chance, she would have run for the county. She's almost reached the alley that opens to her right before she hears the scrape of his pursuing footsteps, the howling voice. 'You ... fucking ... *bitch*!'

She reaches the mouth of the alleyway, skids into it without looking. Hits the dumpster belonging to the Thai restaurant and recovers herself before she can feel the pain. Slaps her way round it and barrels forwards into the dark. Steps in something that squelches, collects something sticky on the sole of her foot. No time to shed it; she can hear him coming towards the mouth of the alley. He's seen her go up here. She must get out the other end before he sees her go.

The path narrows towards its top end; she has to pull her arms and shoulders in to navigate it, loses the skin on her elbow anyway.

He cannons into the dumpster, as she did. Another 'oof', a swear word. He's puffing like a walrus already. He'll run out of breath altogether long before she does.

Then she's out, at the four-way junction on Whittesley Street. Cher turns right again. It's less than a hundred yards to Theed Street, and if she makes it there, gets round the corner and out of sight, he will have no idea which direction she has taken. He is still sliding about at the foot of the alley. She takes the opportunity to snatch the wig from her head and runs on, dangling it like a designer handbag.

A diet of Chipsticks and Haribo, and still she makes the corner in under fifteen seconds. Rounds it to her right and lets her pace drop slightly. She can hear the train announcer in Waterloo East station as her pulse begins to slow. She turns right again and trots back to Roupell Street, retraces her steps to the foot of the alley. There's no sign of him now, though she can hear him, cursing and casting about under the Dickensian street-lights, peering through the gloom and realising he's lost. She hangs a left and returns to Brad Street.

The house is as she left it, the gate still on the latch. Cher glances up and down the road and steps inside. Bends double and lets herself breathe. Drops to her knees, then collapses back against the wall, chest heaving, and holds her hurty elbow. She is dizzy from adrenalin, her night vision impaired by lack of oxygen. She drops the wig on to the top of her bag and closes her eyes, holds the wallet against her stomach like a talisman.

This is shit, she thinks. It's crazy. I can't keep on like this. One day someone'll catch me. I'll get beaten up for the sake of an iPod. Chucked in YOI because I needed the price of a tin of beans and a pot noodle. Or I'll start thinking it's easier just to give them the blowies, and then I'll want crack or something to block it out, and before I know it I'll be my mum. Maybe I'm stupid. Maybe I should just give up and hand myself back.

For a moment she stops breathing altogether. Remembers why she can't. Remembers Kyra, two years out of care, on a street corner for real, her eyes as dead as dolls' and track marks on her ankles. Damned if you do and damned if you don't, really, she thinks. But if I'm going to end up a red-veined junkie whore, at least I'm going to do it on my own terms.

She opens her eyes and opens the wallet. Counts the notes: another fifty quid. He's got six cards. Six. Cher can't even get a bank account. She leafs through them. They're not top of the range. There's no blacks or platinums among them. But they're cash, they're credit, they're all the things she's not allowed. And tucked into the stamp pocket, a folded piece of paper, a four-figure number scrawled on it. A PIN. Just the one, but it's a PIN. If she makes it back to Waterloo before midnight and uses the cards one by one she can straddle the witching hour and get herself a few hundred before they get cancelled.

She gets back to her feet. Unpacks the bag, pulls on the dress and a pair of leggings, replaces the Uggs. Unties her hair and frizzes it back into its messy Afro, ties a scarf round the roots. Adds thick-framed specs – one pound fifty from Primark, if she'd paid for them – and a chunky metal cross on a leather thong. Shrugs the jacket back on over the top. By the time she steps back on to Roupell Street, she's just another office cleaner, coming off her shift.

Chapter Nineteen

Alice lies on the floor, face-up and grinning. The Lover kneels beside her and surveys his tool collection. Lidl and its special offers are a godsend. Disposing of Jecca and Katrina was a long, sweaty business, filled with noise and the fear of discovery, but thanks to Polish tradesmen and the European retailers who supply them, he feels, for the first time, fully equipped. Lined up in a row on the groundsheet he has a circular saw (£29.99), an electric carving knife (£8.99), a mini-tool kit for hobbyists (good for getting into inconvenient corners) (£19.99) amd a set of hacksaws (£6.99) – and a sledgehammer (£13.99) tucked in behind the shed in the garden, for later. God bless the Common Market, and God bless China, he thinks. All your DIY needs catered for, on the cheap.

Sic transit gloria mundi: nothing lasts for ever. The Lover knows that now. He'd hoped his ladies would carry him through to his life's end, but it seems that, in the British climate, even the best of preservation is not foolproof. That's why they keep the mummies in airtight boxes in the British Museum, of course. It wasn't only the skill of the embalmers that ensured the longevity of the ancient world's kings and queens, but the aridity of the desert winds.

Alice has become unbearable to be around. She splits and flakes, and her teeth drop from her mouth when he moves her, and he can't ignore the fact that she smells any more. Her nails are coming away from their beds and slide about beneath the brush when he paints them. Superglue seemed to do the trick for a while, but with each passing week the dry flesh beneath deteriorates at a faster pace and they loosen again. He finds himself resenting her slightly more each day when he wakes and sees the wisps of faded hair that cling to the leathery scalp, the shrunken ears whose lobes seem to have slipped downwards until they are nearly touching her jawline, the razor-edged scapulae poking through her once-smooth shoulders. He knows that the state of her is mostly his fault, that he should have done his research more thoroughly, but still he resents her.

It's the disappointment, he thinks. You go to all that trouble, you lavish such love and attention on someone, and they leave you anyway. No wonder I've started to resent her. It's always best to end it first. But I'm tired of it, so tired of it: of picking up the pieces and carrying on, of getting fond and getting hopeful and still ending up alone.

Her eyes are closed. They have been since he held her in his arms and felt her heart stop beating. It's another thing he holds against her: that she cannot gaze at him the way Marianne does. Discovering that you really can buy anything you like on eBay has been a huge boon, too. Marianne has beautiful green eyes; Jenaer glass dating back to the Spanish Civil war. They cost nearly fifty pounds each, but they were worth every penny. When Nikki comes out from her hiding place, blue eyes just like the ones that made him want her in the first place will be waiting to grace her face.

But, meantime, he must make space for her. There's no room for freeloaders in his life, or in this room. And yet, he's not without nostalgia. She had soft, soft skin. He remembers noticing it first of all about her. Lovely English skin, touched with roses, flawless. He loved to touch it, to stroke it, to feel it smooth beneath his fingertips. Hard to believe that this saddle leather is the same substance.

She grins at him, toothlessly, appealing for mercy. But he's over her now. It's strange, he thinks, how quickly love can be replaced by indifference. I adored her, once, but now she's an inconvenience, a chore that must be done to make room for better times.

'I'm sorry, Alice,' he says. 'It was never going to be for ever. You knew that, surely?'

He picks up the circular saw.

Chapter Twenty

And here he is, as she knew he would be. Standing at the foot of her bed, come in, no doubt, through the open window, toying with his BlackBerry and smiling at her in the half-light. His thinning hair is swept back with gel and he wears a slick Armani suit, like the last time she saw him. His eyes catch the shaft of light that comes in through the crack in the curtains, and gleam. His smile widens, and she sees that his teeth are sharpened into daggers.

Collette is instantly awake, but is slowing herself down by the time her feet hit the floor. Tony, or Malik or Burim, turns up almost every night, at some point; always the same, always smiling. Some nights he holds a knife, or a length of electric flex. Some nights he just stands over the bed and grins. She hasn't slept straight through since the night she ran. Sleep is a luxury whose price is security. Those who can shut the world out and leave it at will are usually blessed by a world that doesn't want to shut them up.

She collapses back beneath her sheet, the pillow hard and lumpy beneath her head despite its newness, and stares round the room in the light that filters through the curtains, checks the corners as though he might just have stepped back into the shadows, to toy with her. He was always the sort of man who loved to toy. The sort of man who would tell a joke so his business rival would throw his head back in hearty laughter and expose his throat.

There are noises, despite the hour. The tinkle of a piano sonata, turned down but still audible through the wall. From the basement window with its safe, strong bars, American voices arguing on the TV. Cher, talking to her cat in a baby voice, and the drone of Thomas's voice, intermittently, seemingly unanswered, the way it sounds when someone's on the phone. In the street, quiet footsteps pass the house, surprisingly many for a road that leads nowhere. A couple walk past, laughing. In the distance, the shrieks of a fox and a tomcat disputing territory.

He will find me, she thinks. It's only a matter of time. For all I know, he's found me already. For all I know, he's right outside the window.

The thought makes her cold, despite the clammy night. She throws herself from the bed and slams the window down. Slips a hand between the curtains to secure the catch, afraid, suddenly, to show herself to the world outside.

The sounds are cut off and the night goes still. I should have bought a fan. I know I can't sleep with the window open. I'll buy a fan tomorrow. Oh, God, I mustn't keep spending money. I know it seems like a lot, but it's not, when it's all you have left, when you've nursing home fees to pay, when you never know when you're going to have to run again. This air's so still. It's like it's pressing down on my head. Can I live like this? Can I live like this for ever?

She sits back down on the bed, her foot brushing against the bag as she does so. I need to find a place to hide that lot, she thinks. Can't just have it lying about. I don't really know anything about these people, and *someone* has to have burgled that old lady downstairs. You're nuts, Collette. You need to get it out of sight. Split it up and get it out of sight.

She checks the street through the chink in the curtains before she turns on the light. The pavements are empty and, apart from a pool of light falling against the street wall from Vesta's basement window, show no signs of life. Closing the window hasn't made her feel safer. If anything, with his presence still permeating her subconscious, it's made her feel hemmed in. The clock on her phone tells her it's nearly two. She won't sleep again until dawn, at least.

She upends the bag across the bed. So little, for so much: nineteen bundles, less than a couple of centimetres thick, and one broken one, doubled over in a rubber band. Twice as much, three years ago, but even then it was little enough that it fitted into a sports bag. She takes one bundle in each hand and starts to work her way round the room, searching for hiding places.

Three years ago: red blood on white skin, and stupid Lisa frozen to the spot. Tony laughing by the bar with his whisky glass, the man on the floor coughing up a tooth, a middle molar. It bounces on the carpet, tittups up against his shoe.

Their heads, turning ...

All rooms are full of hiding places, if you're looking. She's become a past master at finding them. She kept half her money taped in plastic bags to the back of a heavy old commode, in Paris; five thousand pounds in a Tampax box in Berlin. The trick is to remember where you've put it, not to lose ten grand when you move on, as she did in Naples. The armchair has a loose cover, to hide the holes and stains beneath. She tucks half a dozen bundles round the edge of the cushion, tweaks the cover to hide the bulge. Goes back to the bed, picks up two more, moves on, thoughts churning.

Should I have run?

She asks herself that every day. Maybe I could have brazened it out, stepped round the curtain and played the hard-face, one of them.

You saw what they were doing to that man. That wasn't execution. No clean dispatch, no merciful bullet to the head, like a dog. That was torture. That was getting their kicks from watching a man choke to death on his own blood. You saw how they were enjoying it. You think they would have hesitated to use you up for afters?

And what if they didn't? What if they took you in and made you one of their own? You know you would never have got away, right? No four weeks' notice and bringing in doughnuts for your colleagues on your last day. Just: life as a possession, always thinking of the consequences for not doing as you're told. You put yourself in this position the day you accepted that job, she tells herself, even if you did lie to yourself about it. No bar manager gets paid that sort of money. Not unless someone's buying their silence.

Maybe I should have taken that policewoman up on her offer. Gone in and handed myself over. Surely a life in witness protection would be better, more stable, than this?

The man next door turns off his music and the silence is so sudden that she finds herself checking once again to ensure that she is alone. Upstairs, Cher paces, paces, paces. Collette looks in the cupboard under the sink, finds a butter dish, of all things, covered in greasy dust, and stuffs it full with money. I should get some tape tomorrow. I can stick a bundle to the back of both those drawers; that'll take care of two of them.

And she knows the answer about the police. Has known it since she started noticing the cash pass through. He *owns* the police. No one operates that casually, throws his presence about, keeps his profile above the parapet, unless he feels safe. And no one who basically runs a knocking-shop feels safe from raids unless the raiders have been paid off. Someone's in his pocket, at least one someone. And she doesn't know who. Never will, even when the knock in the night lets her know she's been found.

Scarlet blood on white skin, fingers crushed and bent like Twiglets. That won't be me. I won't let it be me.

She's sweating like a mule in the airless room. Stops to run a glass of water, leans against the sink to drink it, runs her eye over her hiding place, looking, looking, for more.

Chapter Twenty-One

Vesta rifles through the post on the hall table, divides it into neat piles for its recipients – whole armfuls each week – gathers the junk for departed tenants into a bundle to put in the bin. It's not a task that takes long. Half a dozen windowed envelopes for Thomas, a couple – brown paper, official stamps – for Hossein. Something from the council for her – her tax rebate, she hopes. Old ladies, she's noticed, get less and less mail as pensionable age recedes behind them. Even the *Reader's Digest* doesn't want to give her fifty thousand pounds tax free any more.

Gerard Bright has a postcard, addressed in a childish hand. She mostly notices it because it's the first piece of handwritten mail to come through the door in a month. She has a cousin in Melbourne who sends cards with clockwork reliability on birthdays and Christmas, though it's over twenty years since they last saw each other at her auntie's funeral in Ilfracombe. She sends them back with the same dedication: the last of her family, a single precious jewel among the seven billion. He includes a Xeroxed round robin yarn of children and grandchildren, a second wife and a land cruiser. Vesta just sends good wishes. She has little to boast of. No one wants news of friends they have never met. It's one of the reasons people have children, that blood relations lend legitimacy to boasting to strangers.

She puts the card on top of his bank statement. Something to brighten his face up, she thinks. He always looks so grey and mournful when she sees him, the only person in London not to sport a suntan this summer, as though he spends his life in a cave, like a fungus.

There's nothing, as usual, for Cher – she's not had a single letter since she came here – and nothing, she notices, for the new girl, either. If you pay your power on a meter key, it's still possible not to exist at all in the modern world, whatever the government says.

Seeing Gerard Bright's card reminds her that she's not had a single card herself this summer. She used to get them from time to time, from former neighbours, old colleagues from the primary school kitchen in their static caravans down on the coast, even the odd friend from school. She would prop them in pride of place on the mantelpiece, to look at and make her feel remembered, to give her dreams of a seaside escape of her own. One day, she thinks. If he ups his offer to twenty grand – God knows, that would still only be ten per cent of what the flat is worth – I could just about do it. A little static near a pebble beach, just a patch of patio to see out my days ... but eight? Once I'd paid the movers, I'd barely have enough for a deposit.

She hears a key in the door and slips the junk mail into her Budgens bag, along with the potatoes and the eggs and the bit of bacon she's bought as a treat. Smiles as Cher lets herself in, pretty and normal today, no wigs, no fake glasses, just an orange cotton dress above the knee and a pair of gold plastic flip-flops, white earphones in her ears, a Pucci-patterned headscarf tied round the base of her Afro making her look older, more sophisticated, like a model on the front of an album from the 1970s. 'Hello, love!'

'Hiya.' Cher pulls out a single earphone and she hears a tinny scritch of music. She looks down at the little gadget in her hand – all smooth and shiny with a circular thing at the top – frowning as though she's unsure how it works, then presses and holds a button on the side. Takes out the other 'phone and wraps the wire round the machine. 'You been out?'

'Just for a bit. Went up the High Street for a few bits and bobs. What've you been doing with yourself?'

'Went and had a sit on the Common,' says Cher. 'Did a bit of scrumping. Loads of people up there.'

'Scrumping? I never noticed any apple trees on the common.'

'They don't always grow on trees,' says Cher, mysteriously, and tucks the iPod into her pocket. 'How've you been? How're your drains? He been and done anything about them yet?'

'Good grief,' she says. 'Don't remind me. I was in a good mood a minute ago. If he has, he hasn't told me. You in the mood for a cuppa?'

'I'd kill for something cold. You seen my cat anywhere?'

'I'm sure he's about. He'll be asleep on your bed at this time of day, I should think. I've got bitter lemon in the fridge. I made it yesterday.'

Cher looks incredulous. 'You *made* bitter lemon? I thought it was one of those things they made in factories. Like Pepsi.'

'Oh, good grief, you young people! You don't know *anything*, do you?'

'No,' says Cher, complacently. 'We're young, innit?'

She strides past Vesta, all legs and ankle bracelets. 'D'you want a hand with that?'

'No, love, I'm fine, it's not heavy. You go ahead and put the kettle on.'

''kay,' says Cher, and pulls the door open. Puts her foot on the top step, shouts in surprise and falls forwards into the dark. Vesta hears an 'oof' and the sound of tumbling. She runs to the doorway, grabs the frame and peers into the gloom. 'Cher? Cher! Are you all right? What happened? Cher?'

She feels above the door for the light switch, clicks it on and puts her head into the stairwell. Cher is halfway down the stairs, hanging on to the banister at the point where it begins, one leg buckled beneath her, the other straight out down the steps, her flip-flop dangling from her big toe. 'Fuck,' she says. 'That was close.'

'Are you okay?' Vesta suddenly feels nervous and tottery and old. She puts her bag down and works her way towards her with a hand on each wall.

Cher sits up, unfurls her leg and rubs her upper arm. 'Ow.'

'What happened?'

'I don't know. I – there was something on the top step. I trod on it and it went right out from under me.'

Vesta reaches her and sits down beside her. 'What on earth ...? I didn't leave anything on the stairs.'

Cher groans and gingerly tries her legs. Emits an inward hiss of breath as her right foot hits the carpet. I don't want to wish anyone ill, thinks Vesta, but thank God it was her, not me. That would have been a broken hip and an ambulance, if it were me.

'Are you okay? Anything broken?'

'No,' she says. 'I've fucked my ankle, but I don't think it's anything worse than that.'

'Language, Cher,' Vesta corrects automatically. She pulls

herself up by the banister and follows the girl as she hops down to the hall.

Cher leans against the wall and switches on the light with her shoulder blade. Rubs at the carpet burn on her thigh. 'So what the hell was it?'

Vesta looks up the oatmeal stair carpet. On the top step, there's a nasty, wet-looking stain; black and brackish. 'I don't ...' Her eyes trace back down the stairs, look down at the floor beneath their feet. 'Oh, God!'

There's a rat resting up against her shoe. A rat the size of a Pomeranian, yellow incisors hanging from its open mouth, dark fur matted and oily, bald pink tail winding round and knotting itself in the pink viscera that hang from a bulging, flattened torso.

Cher follows her gaze, stiffens against the wall, pushing back against it as though she hopes it will open up and let her through. 'Oh. Oh, God, oh no, oh ...'

'Well, I'll be blowed. Where on earth did that come from?' Vesta is simultaneously fascinated and repelled. The rat smells like her drains; old and foetid and long, long dead. Its eyes are milky-white. As she watches, a bluebottle crawls from the half-open mouth and bumbles away up the corridor towards the kitchen. 'It looks like it's been dead a while. It can't have been lying there all this time. I would have noticed.'

'I don't care,' moans Cher. 'It stinks. It's that bloody cat. He's fetched it in. I *knew* I shouldn't have adopted him.'

'Psycho? No, it can't be Psycho. That's carrion, that is. He's not a hyena. I don't understand. How did it come to be here?'

Absently, Cher lifts up her sprained foot and looks at its underside. Claps a hand over her mouth and stares at Vesta, wide-eyed. Her sole is coated with blood and slime. The contents of the creature's guts have smeared themselves up her leg as she fell, green and black and ...

When she moves her hand, her words come out in a rush, strangled and small. 'Oh, God, I'm gonna be sick.'

Vesta feels the skin on her neck crawl. 'No! Don't you dare! Don't you *dare*! Come on. Let's get you to the bathroom.'

She grabs the girl by the arm and manhandles her up the passageway. Cher is gagging as she hops and her cheeks are filling. 'Don't you *dare*, Cher. Don't you *dare*! If you throw up on my carpet, so help me, I'll ... I'll ...'

As they pass through the kitchen, she notices, to her surprise, that the outside door is open. She's sure she remembers putting the bolt on before she went to the shops, but right now all she can think of is the hurricane that's about to hit. She drags Cher into the bathroom, her own hand clamped over the one the girl has over her mouth, throws her down like a sack of potatoes over the toilet and feels a cold sweat of nausea break out on her own forehead as Cher's lunch – a hamburger and fries by the look and smell – explodes into the pan. Oh, God, she thinks, there's a rotten sewer rat squashed flat into my carpet. It looked like it had been run over by a truck and it's in my carpet. I'm going to have to scrape it up.

Cher makes a noise like a wildebeest trapped in a crocodile swamp as Vesta rushes to the sink and adds the fug of cheesy croissant and milky coffee to the odours in the air. Heaves again at the sight of the solids caught in the drain cover. Runs the taps and splashes her face, then collapses on the floor, leaning against the bath.

'Oh, God,' Cher mutters. She wipes her face with a forearm, flushes the chain and crawls back to join Vesta. 'Fuck,' she says.

'Yes,' says her friend, and lets the word that would have had her beaten within an inch of her life when she was Cher's age slide pleasurably from her tongue. 'Fuck.'

'It's all over my leg,' says Cher.

'I know. We'll wash it off with the shower hose.'

'That rat was *rank*.'

'That's what I love about you,' says Vesta, 'you're so obser-vant.' And they begin to laugh.

Chapter Twenty-Two

'Carry your bag, miss?'

She swims out of her fugue and sees Hossein standing in front of her. She's not seen him coming, not noticed anything, really, about the street around her. For all she knows, she's passed Tony, pulling faces, and is none the wiser. Visiting Janine wears her out. When she comes home after her daily hour, she's so drained that even the walk home from the station is enough to make her long for a nap.

She blinks and forces a smile on to her face. 'No, don't worry, it's not heavy. I'm fine, thanks.'

Hossein tuts. 'You Englishwomen are so independent it hurts. Come on. Letting me carry a bag for you doesn't mean I'll take away your right to vote.'

He holds out a hand and smiles, and suddenly she's relieved to hand the weight over. She finally stopped into Asda on the way to Sunnyvale and bought some bedclothes, and she's surprised how heavy they seem. The bag is a big woman's shopper in pink leatherette, but he swings it unselfconsciously over his shoulder and grins as he sets off towards Beulah Grove. She falls into step beside him.

'So how are you getting along?' he asks. 'You've been to visit your mother?'

She nods.

'And how is she?'

Collette sighs. 'Fairly much the same.'

'Does she remember you yet?'

'No. Most of the time, she doesn't even remember I came yesterday. She doesn't mind the chocolates, though. She eats a box a day, but she never seems to put on any weight.'

'It's hard,' he says.

'Yes,' she says, and they carry on in silence to the High Street. I need to find a change of subject, she thinks. We can't just walk all the way home without saying anything. It's embarrassing.

As they turn the corner, she says: 'So you're Iranian, then?'

'Yep,' says Hossein.

'That's Persia, right?'

'Sort of.'

'What's it like?'

'Lovely,' he says. 'It's a lovely country. It's not Syria, you know.'

'So why did you leave?'

'Because it's ruled by arseholes,' he says, 'and I kept saying it out loud.'

'You're a politician?' She's surprised by the distaste she hears in her own voice. She's never met a politician before. Hadn't ever thought she would want to.

'I taught economics. And I did some journalism, wrote a blog. These things don't go so well with the powers that be when your students start joining in.'

'Oh,' she says. 'I'm sorry. Did you … were you …?'

'It's what happens,' says Hossein. 'I wasn't exactly the only one. Anyway, I'm here now. And soon –' he hams up his accent and curls his spare arm so that a lean, hard muscle pops '– I weel be beeg, beeg Englishman, *inshallah*. So it's a beautiful day, isn't it?'

Collette looks around her as if she's seeing it for the first time. The heat has been heavy for the past few days, but a breeze, she notices, has got up and the air is surprisingly pleasant. 'Yeah, it is, isn't it?'

They reach the corner of Bracken Gardens and turn down it. 'It's swimming pool weather,' says Hossein. 'Have you ever been to the Serpentine?'

'What? The river?'

'The Lido.' He pronounces it Lee-do, like an Italian, not Lie-doh, the way she's used to, and it takes her a moment. 'I was thinking maybe I'd go tomorrow. In the afternoon.'

'Oh, God,' she says. 'I can't think of anything worse. Right in the middle of the city. All that duck shit.'

'I bet you swim in the sea.'

'Well, yeah.'

'You know they have fish and seagulls in the sea, don't you?'

'Yeah, that's … oh, whatever.'

'So I'm going to go,' he says. 'It's fun; old ladies with no tops on on one side of the river and old ladies in burqas on the other. An ice cream and some clear water to swim in. What could be nicer?'

'Not dying of salmonella poisoning?'

'You just don't want to get your hair wet,' he teases.

'Well, fair enough, Hossein. I look like a dandelion without the proper product.'

'Dandelion?'

'Never mind. It's a sort of flower.'

'I'm sure.'

'No, it – oh, never mind.'

'So are you going to come? We could take Cher, maybe.'

'Do you think Cher can swim?'

'She can swim like a porpoise, as long as she takes her shoes off.'

She's embarrassed, faintly uneasy. Is he asking her on a date or just being friendly? 'I'll have to see,' she hedges. 'Depends when I get back tomorrow.'

Hossein sighs and gives her the big brown eyes. 'Okay,' he says. 'I know what that means.'

'Oh, no, I—'

He laughs. 'You're very easy to embarrass,' he says.

'Piss off,' she replies.

'Ah, now I *know* you like me,' says Hossein. 'English people only tell their friends to piss off. It's a cultural rule.'

He stops on the corner of Beulah Grove and takes the bag off his shoulder. Holds it out to her. 'Okay,' he says, and there's a sweet twinkle in his eyes. 'Have a nice day.'

'Aren't you coming home?'

'Oh, no. I was going to the station.'

She gawps. 'You ...?'

'Oh, hush,' says Hossein, and lopes off up Bracken Gardens.

She stands on the corner and watches him go, feels odd emotions course through her. Confusion, pleasure. And then fear. She's had three years of avoiding involvements. I mustn't, she thinks. He turns on the far corner and gives her a wave, and she's waved back before she's thought about it. He's lovely, she thinks as she crosses the road and climbs the steps of number twenty-three, but I mustn't. I can't afford friends, and I can't afford lovers. Not when I might have to go at a minute's notice. It's bad enough when you're alone, but if there are people to leave ...

Her phone rings in her bag. She gets it out and looks at it, surprised. She's only given the new number to the care home. No one else knows it. No one. It's a withheld number. It must be Sunnyvale. She picks up as she comes in to the hall.

It's a woman. 'Lisa?'

She almost says yes, but something stops her. The fact that she's called her by her first name – and not just her first name, but her nickname. She's always been an Elizabeth in all her dealings with Sunnyvale, and they're quite scrupulous about calling her Ms Dunne; some gesture of respect to the bill-payer. 'Sorry,' she says, 'you've got the wrong number.'

She's about to hang up when the woman says: 'Lisa, it's Merri here. Merri Cheyne. Please don't hang up.'

Collette's heart jolts. She thinks about doing it anyway, for a second. Then thinks: she'll just call again. She's found me already and she knows it's me. I'm not going to put her off by not talking to her. 'Detective Inspector Cheyne,' she says. 'How did you get this number?'

She uses the rank with a faint note of insult attached, to emphasise the distance, walks up the corridor, clutching the phone so hard that the tips of her fingers go white.

She hears that her tone has hit home, for the voice that replies is changed, more formal, less pally. 'We're better at this stuff than you seem to think, Lisa. We've known you were back in the country since you caught the Santander ferry. Computers don't just go to plugs in the wall, these days.'

She unlocks the mortise on the door to her room, turns the

Yale, throws the door wide and checks the interior before she enters, as she always does. It's stuffy and hot and smells of the washing-up she didn't bother to do last night, but it's empty. She steps inside, closes and locks the door, shoots the bolt and throws open the window.

'So what do you want?'

She doesn't really know why she's bothered to ask, because she already knows the answer. The calls from DI Cheyne began just weeks after she ran from the club.

'Same as I ever wanted, Lisa. You know that. I just wanted to reiterate our offer.'

'No, thanks,' she says.

'Think about it, Lisa,' says Merri. 'It's really your best choice.'

'It really isn't,' she says bitterly. 'Thanks all the same.'

'Well, you may think that ...'

'I *know* that,' she snaps.

A sigh. 'Okay. Well, look, just so you know, the offer's still open. We still want you as a witness. We'll still protect you and you can sort this whole thing out, now. Tell us where you are, and I can come and pick you up and put you somewhere safe in the time it takes you to pack. Get Tony Stott behind bars and your problems are over.'

They don't know where she is. That's one hit in her favour. 'You know that's not true,' she says. 'They'll never be over. Tony doesn't exist in a vacuum. They'll always be after me.'

Merri laughs, and the laugh has a nasty edge. 'I don't know if you've noticed, Lisa, but they're after you now.'

Collette gasps.

The policewoman carries on, presses her point home, 'And Lisa? Remember. We have plenty enough evidence to prosecute you too, you know. It doesn't look good, from where I'm standing; we know Stott's using that place to launder money, and when we bring him down, every single person who handled money in that place will be going down with him. So then it won't just be Tony Stott who's looking for you. It'll be Interpol, too. Your shout, Lisa.'

You bitch. You *bitch*.

'And Lisa?'

'What?'

'One other thing you need to think about, Lisa. If *we* know you're back, how long do you think it'll be before other people do, too?'

Collette hits the off button, hurls the phone at the bed. Lets her tension out in a single roar, stifles it by biting the back of her arm. Leaves a ring of teeth marks in the flesh. Shouts once more and throws herself on to the chair to punch, punch, punch weakly at its padded back. Fuck! I need some exercise. I'm shut up in this damn room all day, or staring at Janine, and – how did she find me? How the hell did she find me? I've been so careful. I didn't even give a name when I bought the SIM. How did she find me?

Well, she found you before. Just like she always has. Her and Tony. All of them, on your arse, catching up every time you run; you're a sitting duck.

Her head throbs. Outside in the corridor, she hears Gerard Bright's door open up, hears him pad down the corridor and stand outside her door. He stands there for thirty seconds. He must have heard her shout. She's starting to hate this house. Hate the way everyone knows everything about each other here.

She gets up and runs a glass of water, pops four ibuprofen from their foil and swallows them down. The room feels like a prison, the walls closing in, the ceiling pressing down on her shoulders. She massages her temples, tries to think. She doesn't know where I am. She's just got the phone number. And even if she finds me, she can't make me *do* anything unless she arrests me. Oh, God, why did I take that job? Why? I could have worked anywhere. I should have *known* that nothing that paid that well was on the up and up. I *did* know. Who am I kidding? I knew, and I stayed there anyway.

A blast of music through the wall makes her jump. Christ. The bloody *Ride of the Valkyries*. He must have the amplifier up to ten. How does someone living in a place like this have speakers that size? It's crazy. It's impossible. What sort of person thinks it's okay to do that to everyone living around him? He's not bloody fifteen. He's a full-blown adult. He probably thinks that because it's classical that everyone's admiring him for being an intellectual, the bloody arsehole. No problem letting other people know they're bothering *him*.

She tries hammering on the wall. Thumps until her fist hurts, but the music carries on. Her blood pressure has soared since the music started, she can feel it. Her pulse is hammering in her ears and her face is burning. 'Shut up!' she shouts. You're going to bloody kill me, she rages to herself, never mind Tony Stott. 'Shut up, shut *up*!'

She throws herself down on the bed, grabs the pillow and crams it over her head. Hot and dark and unbearably stuffy, but still she can hear it: trumpets, trumpets, trumpets and squealing violins and the thump, thump, thump of her angry heart.

Collette swings out of bed and grabs her keys. It's too much. It's just too bloody much. She unlocks the door and throws it back, and storms up the corridor. Hammers on the door, her heart ready to burst out of her chest. You will not. You *will not* do this to me today.

The music turns down, but no one responds. She guesses he's listening, not even sure, the noise has been so loud, that he's really heard her knock. She raises her fist and thumps again. 'THANK YOU!' she shouts. 'And bloody *keep it down*!' Finds that she's panting, hear heart still racing.

He cracks the door open and stands in the gap, blocking her view into the room, and she's shouting before she notices that he's half-naked. 'What the FUCK!' she shouts.

It's the first time she has heard his voice. It comes out weak and prissy, self-consciously posh like a man who's spent too much time explaining grammar to schoolchildren. 'Can I help you?' he asks.

'Seriously? What? Can't you hear your own fucking music?'

He recoils at the swearword. 'Excuse me—'

'Jesus! Have you gone deaf or something? Is that it? Turn it down! Turn it the fuck down! How can you be so fucking selfish?'

He blinks at her.

'Have you any idea how thin these walls are?' she demands. 'Just because you think it's some kind of *classy* music I have to share every bloody note. Just turn it the fuck *down*!'

He blinks again. Upstairs, she hears the creak of a door, the sound of quiet footsteps creeping along the landing. Someone come to listen, but she knows they won't join in. Her rage builds. DI Cheyne and Tony Stott and her daft, mad, drunken mother, and that dirty old sod leering at her as he takes her rent and thinking he's entitled to the deposit because she's improved his property with a door lock, and everyone wanting, wanting, wanting the money she soon won't have.

'I'm sorry,' he says. He is sweaty, as though he's been

exercising in this heat, and his throat and chest are flushed, and his eyes are puffy and red.

She's too inflamed to stop, now. 'Sorry? Sorry's if it's just once. This is all the time. *All. The. Bloody. Time.*'

She stabs a finger through the air to emphasise each word. She had no idea she had this aggression in her. Maybe if she had, she wouldn't have decided running was her best way out of her situation. 'Do you get it? Turn it down. Turn it the *fuck down*, or I'll come in and smash your fucking stereo!'

Gerard Bright just stands there and lets her stab uselessly at the air. There's a big bruise on his upper arm; fingermarks, as though someone's gripped him there with a vice. 'I already have,' he points out.

'Oh, don't give me that. You'll just turn it straight back up again when I'm gone.'

Her voice rises to a shriek. My God. Where's all this anger coming from? I'm going to hit him in a minute and I won't be able to stop myself. 'Do you hear me? You can hear me now, can you, now that you've turned that fucking noise off?'

'We can all hear you, dear,' says a voice behind her. 'I should think they can hear you in Brentford.'

Collette whirls round in the narrow corridor. Vesta stands in the door under the stairs that leads to her flat, wiping her hands on a tea towel.

'What on earth is going on?' she asks.

Collette's rage collapses. Suddenly she feels weak and powerless and foolish, yelling out her frustration at this man who doesn't care. She opens her mouth to speak, and bursts into tears.

Chapter Twenty-Three

If I had a quid for every girl I've had in tears on this settee, thinks Vesta, I could probably have bought that caravan. It's very strange. They've all got mums somewhere. I've heard enough about them. But it's always me, in the end, that they come and cry to – and not just the girls, either. It breaks your heart, how sad so many people's lives are. How many people they miss, how far they feel from home. You'd have thought we'd have organised it all better, somehow.

Collette is crying her eyes out. Upstairs, she hears Gerard Bright's door go and his footsteps walk along the hall to the front door. She glances up through the window when it closes and sees his legs come down the steps. Such a strange man. In and out with that briefcase every afternoon and every other weekend going off to sit in McDonald's with his kids, or wherever it is they go these days, and the rest of the time he's locked up in that room like a hermit. Barely meets your eye if you meet him in the hall, and I could swear that half the time he looks like he's been crying, though maybe that's just his colouring. It's pitiful, really. So much loneliness in the world, and it's not like most of them started off meaning it to be that way. A few small slips, a moment of forgetfulness, and before they know it they're all on their own.

She sits quietly on the sofa and waits for Collette to compose herself. Doesn't know her well enough to give her a hug, feels awkward doing the Dot Cotton arm pat you see on the telly. So she sits, and waits, and hands her a new tissue from time to time. I'll give her a cup of tea in a bit. Tea always helps, though from the look of her she might prefer a large brandy.

Crying fits never last for long if you let them play out and don't add fuel to the flames. It's an unnatural way to be; too much strain to sustain. Collette sobs for three minutes after Vesta's helped her down the stairs and got her settled, then her breathing slows and she starts to make those tired little 'oh' sounds that precede the onset of calm. She sniffs through her blocked nose, blows it on a crumpled Kleenex and dabs at her crimson eyes. 'Thank God I wasn't wearing make-up,' she says. Then: 'Sorry. Sorry about that. I don't know where that came from.'

Of course you do, thinks Vesta. What you mean is you want me to *think* you don't know. 'I should think you're worn out,' she says soothingly. 'It's a strain, with your mum and that.'

'It's this house. I think it's this house. Don't you feel it? It's – oppressive. Like someone's listening to you, like they're watching all the time. Don't you feel it?'

'Can't say I do, but I've lived here all my life,' lies Vesta. 'If it is, I've got so used to it I don't notice.'

But there is, she thinks. There *is* someone watching me, I'm sure of it. That door didn't get open by itself. Not twice. I don't feel safe here any more. But I can't talk about it. I can't. I can't even *think* about it too closely. Because I don't have choices. There's nowhere else I can go.

'He just – I've been having trouble sleeping at night, and then, you know, I think maybe I can get a nap, and he starts up again and it's …'

'I know,' says Vesta. 'But at least it's not that boom-bada-boom-bada stuff the young boys are into these days, eh?'

'What's his deal, anyway? What's he doing, locked up in there all day?'

'I have no idea,' says Vesta.

'You don't wonder?'

'One of the tricks to living in a place like this is not wondering too much, unless someone wants to tell you.'

'Really?'

'Come on, love,' she says. 'We all deserve a bit of privacy. You wouldn't want everyone asking where you've come from, would you?'

Collette looks startled. He eyes widen and she almost jumps off the sofa. Hah, thinks Vesta. Thought so. There's more to your story than just an ailing mum, isn't there? Honestly: it's the House of Secrets, this.

Collette blushes, flusters her way through an apology. 'No, no, I didn't mean …'

'It's all right,' Vesta smiles, and finally lays her hand on her arm. 'I was just joking.'

Suddenly, Collette's words come out in a rush, as though she's been storing them up for a very long time. 'It's just – I … stress. Yes, that's what it is. Stress. I just can't … people just won't leave you alone, will they? I thought if I left, if I just made myself scarce, they'd all forget about me and I could just get some peace, but it's like … I don't know. I feel like I'm under siege. All the time. It's like the walls are pressing in on me. And this house, where I don't know anyone, I feel like everyone's looking at me … like they're … you know …'

'I wouldn't worry about them,' says Vesta. 'They're far too caught up in their own troubles. What was it? You don't have to tell me, but frankly you look like you want to tell someone. Debt?'

Another laugh, hard, sardonic, and another nose-blow. 'No. Not debt.'

'It's all right, you know, Collette. You're hardly the first person who's used this place as a refuge. Probably won't be the last, either.'

Collette plucks at her tissue, stares round the room. Takes in the old-lady décor, the framed photos faded to sepia, the china dogs Vesta managed to glue back together, the whatnot with the spider plant, the net curtains that block out the light. She's trying to make a judgement. Decide whether Vesta is trustworthy. Then she sighs and clears her throat.

'I'm in trouble,' she says, 'and I don't know what to do.'

It's never occurred to her that she could actually just tell someone. So many things stop you. The fear of shame, the fear that they'll be a spy, simple force of habit. Right from when she was a kid. Janine drummed it into her. Don't tell people. Don't talk to those nosy teachers. Too many do-gooders wanting to take you away. They'll take you away. You want to get me into trouble, is that it? Janine trained her, and life since then has sunk the training in. But she's tired. Exhausted by living her life in secret and bearing her burdens alone.

She's surprised by how easily it comes out. She has no idea why she trusts this woman. She's not really that different from all the other people she doesn't trust. Steel grey, sensible, hair and elasticated trousers and wrinkles round the mouth, like she's been pursing her lips all her life. Like someone's granny. Though grannies, in Collette's book, are women who throw their pregnant daughters on to the street.

Vesta's eyes widen a few times as she talks, but she doesn't panic, doesn't throw her out and, most of all, doesn't disbelieve her.

'Crikey,' she says, when her story is finished. 'I should think you could do with a drink. I know I could!'

She gets up and opens the little cupboard under the television. Brings out a bottle of brandy – the sort Collette used to use for cooking back when she was Lisa on the way up – and two old cut-class snifters. Pours two generous measures and brings them back to the sofa.

Collette waits for her to say something. She's all talked out. Too tired to try to argue her case, if there's an argument to be had.

'And it's three years?'

She nods.

'And how do you know they're still looking for you?'

'Because people like that don't ever stop,' she says, simply, and knows it's true. 'And the phone calls. He's toying with me. Enjoying it. If I'd put my hands up and taken what was coming to me there and then, there might have been a chance, maybe ...'

'I doubt it,' says Vesta. 'When people get caught up in these sorts of things, it doesn't usually end well for them. I lived through the sixties, love. I know. They're not cheeky-chappie loves-his-old-mum types, these people, whatever they like to say.'

'I thought if I ... you know, disappeared ... you know, when I saw Malik outside my flat ... He actually got there before I did. Christ knows how. And it's not just the witness thing, is it? It's the money. I can't believe I took it. I sort of forgot I had it till I suddenly noticed it on the passenger seat of the car. And then it was too late. I wasn't going to go back, was I?'

'No, no, I can see that. But yes. And really, the police ...?'

Collette shakes her head, vehemently. 'There were police in that club all the time. Getting free drinks. Backslapping. I know, because I was the one who had to make sure the drinks kept coming. I don't think I'd last a week, if I handed myself in. I might as well just turn up at Tony's house direct. That DI Cheyne – she's no bloody idea.' Collette drinks a large gulp of brandy. It burns, but it's good. 'What I don't get is how they've been getting the numbers. It must be the home. It has to be. I've only given it to them. I mean, I always gave it to Janine, in case, you know ... but she wouldn't. She wouldn't have.'

'Well,' says Vesta, 'the police have been getting hold of it, and frankly, if the police know something then everyone in the country can find it out for a couple of bob. But that man Stott clearly doesn't know where you are and nor do the police.'

'So do you think I should ...?'

'No. Oh, no, no, no!'

She's surprised. Vesta has struck her as a backbone-of-society type until today. The sort of person who thinks it's her duty to vote, who always trusts the authorities, no matter how many times they let her down. 'I've seen far too many of my neighbours' kids get sent down on stop-and-searches to think that,' she says. 'The police are just as dodgy as anybody else. Just as many prejudices, same proportion of people only out for themselves, probably more, maybe. It takes a certain type of person to want to be a copper in the first place. You don't want to be a copper if you don't want to tell other people what to do, do you? Only they've got power. Actual power, not made-up power, and everybody wants to think they're on the side of the angels, so it's really hard to persuade them that they're not. I'd be very careful of the police. The law's not set up for people like us.'

People like us? Funny how all those years I thought I was working my way up the ladder to be People Like Them. 'So what should I do?'

Vesta bites the inside of her lip. 'Search me,' she says. 'I could ask Hossein, if you like. He knows everything.'

'No! God, no! Are you kidding?'

Vesta pats her arm. 'Okay. It's okay. It's just ... you know he had to leave home in a hurry himself, don't you? He knows a lot about a lot of things. He's been dodging the Iranian secret service for years.'

'No,' she says, again. 'No, I'm sorry. I shouldn't have told *you*. It was wrong of me. You don't need to get caught up in this.'

'Well, I am, now,' says Vesta. 'Not much we can do about that. We'll have to think. I daresay you're reasonably safe here for the time being. Presumably he's got you paying cash so he doesn't have to make a record, isn't he?'

Collette is not sure who she means for a moment, then realises that she means the Landlord. She nods. 'Yes.'

'Well ...' Vesta sips at her brandy and stares at the door. 'For what it's worth, I think you're doing the right thing. By your mum. It's the right thing, poor soul. We'll see you through that, and then you can decide what happens next.'

Chapter Twenty-Four

Down at the bottom of the garden, there's a shed. As far as he knows, no one has been in it for thirty years. It's built of the same concrete sleepers as the railway line – sleepers that were probably originally intended *for* the railway line, for all he knows – strapped together with metal bands, and topped with a roof of corrugated asbestos. He knows it's asbestos, because someone, a long time ago, if the fading of the letters and the advance of the lichen across it are anything to go by, has printed off and laminated a sign that reads DANGER NO ENTRY ASBESTOS and thumbtacked it to the door. It works beautifully. None of the other tenants, not even Vesta, ventures more than halfway down the long garden, as though even looking at the sign will give them fatal lung disease. So only the Lover knows that, behind it, the fence has long since disintegrated and there is a straight path into no man's land.

It's not a big patch of land. Too small to be built on or, property being what it is in London, someone would have slapped in a block of flats at some point and called it Northbourne View or Park Vista, despite the fact that its outlook would be of the railway at the bottom of the embankment, and the line of scrubby sycamores that mark the edge of the common on the other side. There are fifteen feet between the bottom of the garden and the bindweed-twined chain link that demarcates railway property, and this patch of lost land runs the length of Beulah Grove, home to brambles and buddleia and ragwort and a family of urban foxes. It's his own secret garden, his private domain.

He likes to come here as dawn is breaking and the blackbirds are starting up their greeting to the day. At this time of year, daylight begins in earnest by five o'clock, when his neighbours are still safely tucked up in their beds and he can be fairly certain that he will not be overlooked. So he risks carrying a load that in normal circumstances would be foolhardy: Alice, jointed and stuffed into two tote bags, the longest pieces her femurs, the bulkiest her skull. She chinks as he walks: her bones, stripped bare, ringing out like china in the cool, damp air.

Someone will hear me, he thinks; someone *has* to hear me. They've all got their windows open in this heat, and God knows I've not been sleeping deeply myself. He puts the bags down to give himself two hands to lift the gate into the side-return. Raises it on its hinges to stop the scraping sound that will give his presence away, and is surprised to find that it has been freshly oiled and opens with the merest whisper. Funny, he thinks. Of all the bits of maintenance that need doing around here, you wouldn't have thought he would have started with *that*. He picks up the bags again and sets off, on tiptoe, across the grass.

There's been a heavy dew, and the lawn is wet. It soaks his shoes, weighs down the bottoms of his trousers. Beyond Vesta Collins's little patch, the grass is long and unkempt and trips him up a couple of times with grasping tentacles. The shed, with its blank windows, overlooks his approach. He wonders occasionally what lives in there, whether even the Landlord knows. From the look of the notice, and the rust on the padlock that holds the painted steel door shut, it's been closed for decades. There could be anything in there. Junk furniture, a workshop – dead bodies?

His sledgehammer is still there, leaning against the rear wall of the shed, its head shiny with newness. He tucks it awkwardly under his arm, and ducks through the gap in the fence then breathes deep and releases his tension. No one can see him, now. The garden fences are eight feet high, the bindweed so thick that barely a gap shows through. At one end, the blank back wall of the post office, at the other, a small office block that hasn't been tenanted since the recession hit. For now, he is safe.

There's a path, of sorts, worn by animals through the middle of the maze of weeds. He turns to his right and walks thirty feet up, to the bottom of the garden of number twenty-seven. The house is empty at the moment, covered in scaffolding and plastic sheeting as the new owners – well, their team of Slovak builders – gut and renovate. Four months ago, the builders, like many before them, used the strip as a dump rather than pay for a skip, flinging joists and broken bricks and bits of crazy paving over the fence. It's perfect for a demolition of his own.

He opens and upends the bags. Alice rattles out, rustles and clatters into a pile on the rubble. The Lover looks down at the bones, and marvels at the way he no longer associates these jigsaw pieces, these bleached lumps of calcium and carbon, with the girl who stirred his passion. She's just rubbish, now, is Alice. But still identifiable, in her current state, as what once she was – once-human. Foxes and dogs and insects make short work of the soft stuff – the age-old recycling of Mother Nature – but bones are bones are bones, all the marrow boiled out of them.

The skull grins up at him, sightlessly. A few scraps of leather still cling to the cheeks, a lock or two of hair to the fontanelles. Though it's unlikely that anyone will be along here before the brambles have piled high over the top of them, it's best, he thinks, to make sure that, if they do, all they'll see is chunks of something else hard among the scraps of concrete, the brown-and-orange tiles, the avocado bathroom suite.

He raises the sledgehammer above his head and brings it down.

Chapter Twenty-Five

I can fly, Cher thinks, as she turns into the alley and speeds through the night, as she hears his panting imprecations drop further into the darkness. I'm so fast, it's like I've got wings on my feet. I swear, if I went any faster, I could actually take off and soar through the air like a bird.

Her foot lands on broken glass, and she yelps with pain. She staggers sideways and twists her ankle, lands heavily against the wall, cracks her head on black bricks. No, she thinks, no, no, no! She hears him turn into the alleyway, pushes herself upright and tries to hop-limp away from him. Oh, God, oh God. Why didn't I check? I've got careless. I should have checked.

The glass is embedded in her sole. She tries to balance on the ball of the foot, but the ankle is weak and lets her down. She manages another four, five limping steps before he's on her, catches her with a punch to the back of her skull. She goes face down among the weeds and the fag butts.

He's on top of her before she hits the ground. Knees clamped either side of her hips, stale sweat rising from his leather coat. 'Fucking little—' he pants. 'You fucking little ...'

He punches her again and snatches his wallet back. Clamps her wrists together with his spare hand as he tucks it into his back pocket. Then he flips her over beneath him and sits on her pubic bone, grinds her buttocks into the grit. He's huge. She'd thought it would be an advantage, that he'd be slow on his feet, but he's clearly fit beneath his bulk, like a rugby player. Oh, God, I'm in trouble now. I'm in so much trouble.

He slaps her, open hand and open arm, once, twice across her face. Rips the wig from her head, hairclips tearing through the hair beneath, and slings it into a drain three feet away. Then he clamps her jaw between meaty fingers, squeezes her lips together like a tweety-bird and spits, full on, into her face. 'Don't you move. Don't you fucking *move*, you little shit. Don't fucking move or I'll fucking *do* you.'

She lies still, pupils huge in the dark, and looks him in the face. A bald-man's crop, rolls of fat on the back of his neck like a Charolais bull, thick two-inch sideburns. Flecks of spittle at the corners of the mouth. Three-day stubble that smells of fried onions and stale beer. Eyes made of pure contempt. He can do whatever he wants, she thinks. I'd better let him before he gets angry enough to kill me.

When he's done, he gives her a couple of kicks in the stomach for good measure, throws her sideways against the wall like a piece of litter and swaggers off towards the light, buttoning his trousers. Cher curls up, pulls her knees to her chest and gingerly closes her bruised thighs. Her knees and ankle and foot throb; pulse with the beating of her heart. Her head is splitting where he punched her, her lip swelling and one eye closing. She can feel the bruises coming through on her neck; ten spreading marks of squeezing fingertips.

Cher drops her head on to her hand, and falls into the rising dark ...

When she wakes, the streets are silent. No sounds from the station, no swish of distant traffic on the Embankment. But the sky is lighter, and somewhere, on a rooftop, a nightingale is greeting the dawn.

There's been a dew as she slept, and her clothes and hair are damp. Slowly, gingerly, she unfurls herself and sits upright. It hurts. There's not a place that doesn't hurt – sharp pains and scarlet throbbing, and a screech of white light in her head. Dully, she pulls her foot up on to her lap, her swollen privates strangely soothed by the morning air, and examines the underside. The glass is buried deep in her heel, the thick brown glass they use for beer bottles, a shred of a Watneys label still attached. She takes a grip with trembling fingers, and pulls. Lets out a gasp of pain as it comes loose and slides out. Jesus, she thinks, examining it, it's huge. It must have gone right through to the bone.

She wants to sleep again, but knows she mustn't. She needs to get home, hide away, clean up, get over it. Trauma is a luxury for other people. To all intents and purposes, Cher does not exist. She knows this. It's her choice. It's not for ever. A time will come when she can come full out into the world, but that time's not now. She groans as she pushes herself up the wall, limps over to her flip-flops and slips them on. The pain of standing on her bad ankle, on the ball of her foot to avoid dirtying her gaping wound any further than it's already dirty, makes her hiss through her teeth, but she manages it, and at least now she won't fall prey to whatever else is left of the beer bottle. She leans one hand on the wall and looks down at her wig. It lies, half-in, half-out of the drain, matted and ratty, the ends black with dirty water. Not worth the effort of bending to fetch it. She's going to need all the strength she has just to get home.

It takes her twenty minutes to hobble back to her bag, holding on to walls and lamp-posts, stopping every now and then to doze on her feet, like a horse. When she gets there, she is tempted to curl up again behind the gate, where no one will find her, and sleep until the day is full. She lowers herself on to the ground and pinches herself, hard, on the inside of her elbow. You can't sleep here, she tells herself. If he's really hurt you, if you really need help, no one will find you. Not till you start to stink. She peels off her grimy, bloodied whore clothes and drops them on to the ground. She won't be using them again. She doubts she'd want to, but anyway, they're all spoiled.

She switches on her phone to check the time, and is surprised to find that it's gone four o'clock. Her sleep didn't feel like it lasted more than a few minutes. She finds a sachet of wet wipes and passes one over her face, is astonished by the amount of black dirt and rusty blood that comes away. Checks herself in the hand mirror and barely recognises herself. Her right eye is almost completely closed and her mouth is lopsided, her lower lip barely able to obey the request she sends it to close. A trail of dried blood leaks from her right nostril. Gingerly, she dabs at it until it's gone. Her nose itself looks okay; but it aches inside, as though something's bust. Christ, she thinks, I won't get past this in a while. I'll stand out like a sore thumb for weeks.

She pulls on her street gear, feels better for being covered. Picks the last of the hairgrips from her hair and lets it loose. Inches her hurty foot into an Ugg, sucking air sharply between her teeth as she does so, but it feels better once it's there, the ankle supported, at least, and the cut cushioned.

At least he didn't get my bag, she thinks, thankful for small mercies. I've still got my Oyster card.

Cher rolls on to her knees and gets to her feet from a downward-facing dog.

The night bus is full of drunks. Drunks and exhausted night workers slumbering in their hi-viz uniforms. Everyone is sunk into their own exhaustion, staring numbly at spots a few inches from their faces, and she's glad of that. She takes a seat at the back, facing away from the driver, and huddles against the window. The day is already warming up, fingers of pink streaking the sky over the river. London, she thinks. You were going to be the saving of me. Do you remember? I wasn't going to be like the other girls, in and out of foster care and slipping, with each return, further down the road to street corners and late-night beatings and a place on a methadone programme. Oh, God, this hurts. I think I've got some tramadol I found in a bag a few months ago. It's probably still good. At least I'll get some sleep. When I get back.

As they trundle along the Wandsworth Road, up Lavender Hill, she realises that she is beginning to drift off to sleep again. Maybe I've got a concussion, she thinks. I banged my head enough. You're not meant to sleep if you've got a concussion. I must stay awake. I must make myself stay awake till I get home. Vesta will know what to do, when I get home …

She dreams about the attic again. The secret attic under the stairs. This time, it's full of dressmakers' mannequins and brass bedsteads, the mattresses heaped with dustsheets. Something moves, away in the far corner, beneath the eaves, out of her eyeshot. Something big and dark and old. Cher wants to run, but when she turns to get away, she finds that the stairs she came in by have disappeared …

She jumps awake. The bus is empty and the engine is off, and the driver, still locked in his cab, is flicking the lights on and off to attract her attention. Cher sits up gingerly from the bundle she's made of herself in the corner and peers through the window. Her eye has almost closed as she slept and it takes her a moment to recognise the bus stand at the top of Garrett Lane. She's missed her stop and ended up in Tooting. It's an hour's walk to Northbourne, and that's on two good legs. 'Thanks,' she mumbles, though her mouth is so dry the word comes out as a croak, and stumbles off.

The newsagent is opening up at Tooting Bec, the lights coming on as she arrives at the door. She buys a pack of Nurofen and a can of Fanta, the guy behind the counter studiously avoiding her eyes, takes four pills and drains the can to wash them down. She can barely get her mouth to fit round the opening; a dribble of sugary liquid runs down her chin and on to her collar. But she doesn't care any more. Everything hurts: her head, her neck, her stomach, her back – everything. Maybe it would have been better if he'd killed me after all, she thinks. I wouldn't have to live through this, then. It would all be peace and quiet.

She hoists her bag on to her shoulder and sets off for Northbourne. She's shaking and her legs are wobbly. She wonders if she should stop and get something to eat, a Mars Bar or a Snickers or something full of sugar to get her the last mile home, but she doubts she'd be able to chew it – and even if she did she doubts it would stay down.

She sits for a bit at a bus stop halfway to Northbourne, pulls the hood of her jacket over her head and greys out again. Comes to and finds herself inside a small gaggle of people in work clothes, all keeping a polite and frosty distance from the bench. I'm just another Homeless, she thinks, so much nicer when you're talking about me on Facebook than I am in real life. One woman has perched at the far end of the bench, and keeps a tight grip on her briefcase. Cher looks at her phone. Quarter to eight. She's lost another hour. No one meets her eye. Oh, Londoners. You'd step over a corpse in the street rather than cause a scene.

She stands up again as a bus pulls in and her fellow travellers surge silently towards it. Feels the world start to tip and steadies herself against the shelter. When she takes her hand away, she sees that she's left a smudge of blood on the glass panel. She closes her eyes and breathes. Not so far to Northbourne Junction, now. It's just across the Common. Then it's just up to the High Street and home.

The Nurofen doesn't seem to be working. Her head pounds as if there's something in there trying to get out. Her pace slows and slows as she limps up Station Road, weaves her way unsteadily past dog walkers and joggers and working mothers wheeling wailing toddlers to the Little Sunshine nursery. She stops by a waste bin and retches. Nothing comes up, not even the Fanta, but her mouth tastes like old tin cans. She can barely see from her right eye, drops her hoodie further down to hide the Halloween mask that is her face. Someone, she thinks. One of you must wonder. Don't you wonder? No one in Liverpool would walk past someone that looked like me and pretend they haven't seen.

But it's not true, though, is it? If Liverpool was so great, if the chirpy-chappie, bravely suffering people of your hometown were so great, you wouldn't be in London. It's England, isn't it? It's people. They'll only help you if they think you matter.

The High Street is still half-closed. Only Greggs and the greasy spoon and the Londis and the greengrocer show signs of life. The new shops – the posh shops – don't open until ten. That's the thing, if you have money, she thinks bitterly. Ladies who lunch do lunch because they're never up for breakfast. She feels tearful, weak, despairing. Can feel the blood seeping down her legs and chafing the skin on her thighs. She's sweating profusely, though she feels so cold she's shivering. She wipes the sweat from her forehead with her sleeve, stumbles blindly on and blunders into sturdy male body.

'Sorry,' she mutters, and tries to dodge sideways. Feels her balance go out from under her again and puts out a hand to catch the wall. 'Sorry.'

'Cher?'

She looks up. It's Thomas Dunbar, Mr Chatty from the top flat: a loaf of bread, a pint of milk and a copy of the *Guardian* under his arm. He's gone as white as a sheet, his mouth open, ready to catch flies, his specs glinting in the early morning sunlight.

'Oh, dear Christ, Cher,' he says, and catches her by the arm as she begins to wobble. 'What's happened? What the hell's happened to you?'

Chapter Twenty-Six

There's a tap on the door. In the bed, Cher shifts and mutters, but doesn't wake. Vesta puts her book down on the duvet and tiptoes across to open up.

It's Thomas. He starts to speak and Vesta hushes him with a finger to her lips. Puts the door on the latch and steps out on to the landing, pulling it to behind her.

'How is she?'

'Asleep. Finally. Didn't want to wake her.'

'No,' he says.

'Couldn't let her drop off properly. Not while we had to check her for concussion. Collette's coming back up in a bit. She was up all night, poor girl. Didn't get a wink.'

'Right,' he says.

'So ...' she begins.

'I understand,' he says. 'But I brought some stuff.'

'Stuff?'

Thomas holds out a pink-and-white tube of cream. 'It's arnica. For bruises. It's not new. I've used it. Sorry.'

She takes it and tries to read the back, but her specs are in the bedroom by her book, and she's reduced to hopeless squinting. 'It's herbal,' he says. 'You just rub it in. It does help. I know you probably think it's woo-woo, but it helps.'

'Okay,' she says, doubtfully, surprised that this clipped little man would be dabbling in the world of woo-woo.

'And I got some vitamin C. It's meant to help, too. I don't know if it does, but it can't do any harm, can it?'

Vesta gives him an encouraging smile. 'I should think it'll do her the world of good. Easier than making her eat a vegetable, anyway, eh?'

He laughs, more explosively than she expected. 'I should say so. Is she ...' His face changes, goes suddenly rusty, like he's been left out in the rain. She realises that he's on the edge of tears. 'Vesta, is she okay?'

Well, well, she thinks. You never know with people. It must have been a horrible shock for him, finding her like that. She gives his arm a tentative rub, then finds herself overtaken by the urge to give him a hug. His body is stiff against hers, as though the show of affection has come as a shock. It takes him a full five seconds to respond, then he wraps his arms around her like a teenager at a dance and practically crushes the breath from her. Vesta is suddenly filled with a powerful urge to fight him off. It feels so wrong, squashed against his body like this, smelling his nervous sweat. 'It's all right, lovey,' she sputters. 'It's okay. You did brilliantly. She owes you, she really does.'

He lets her go, and seems to stagger slightly as he goes to lean against the banister. 'She was just so ... oh, my God, who would do something like that? She's only a kid. I thought she was going to die. I honestly thought I wasn't going to get her home and she was going to just … I thought she was going to die right there on the street, in my arms.'

'I know,' she says. 'Poor you – it must've been horrible.'

He snatches his specs off and polishes them ferociously with the tail of his shirt. Without the shading lenses, his eyes are huge, pale blue, like the eyes of a bush baby. 'She's only a kid,' he says, again. 'Can I …?'

'Not right now, Thomas. She's sleeping. Best to leave her. I'm sure she'll want to see you later.'

'I think – I should have taken her to casualty. I just wasn't thinking. I should have.'

Again, she rubs his arm. She needs to calm him down. There can be no hospitals for Cher. No GPs, no crime reports. 'No. You did the right thing. You did. She doesn't want the hospital. You can't *make* her if she doesn't want it.'

'But that's crazy, Vesta. She shouldn't be … I mean, what if there's some internal damage? She could be bleeding inside, and …'

'Well, we'll have to cross that bridge when we come to it,' she says, more matter-of-factly than she feels. She's worried about the big nasty bruise on the girl's stomach herself. It doesn't *feel* hard to the touch, but then, she couldn't touch it very firmly, with Cher howling and fighting her off. It might have to be the hospital, whether Cher likes it or not.

'And she was filthy. Covered in dirt. And all those cuts …'

'I know. I know. We washed her, gave her a bath, and we've put antiseptic everywhere we could get to, Thomas. Please, don't worry. We've got it as under control as we can.'

There's a hesitation. She can tell that he wants to ask about the blood on her leggings, doesn't know if he can. Despite the fact that this is the person who carried her home, who stroked her hair off

her face as though she was a toddler, Vesta feels as though con-
firming his fears would be some sort of betrayal. She puts him off.
'She's sleeping. No better medicine. And she's got the medicines
Hossein got for her – penicillin and enough tramadol to knock
out a horse. Thank God for the immigrant community, eh?'

I wish I could help,' he says. 'Isn't there anything I can do?
Can't I help?'

'You *are* helping. You *have* helped. She was just lucky she
bumped into you. I'm not sure she'd have made it home if she
hadn't. Go on. I've got to get back. I don't want to leave her
alone for too long.'

'Okay,' he says, doubtfully. 'You'll call me if—'

'Won't need to,' she says firmly. 'You can come down and see
her when she's awake.'

'Would she like something to read, perhaps? She's going to be
in bed a while, I should think. I've got some old *Spectators* and
New Statesmen. I know they're probably not ...'

She fights an urge to laugh out loud. Oh, bless you, Thomas.
You don't have the faintest idea, do you? 'I don't think she'll be
up to reading for a while,' she replies soothingly. 'But it's a kind
thought. I should get back to her now, though. Sorry. And thank
you.'

She leaves him standing on the landing and re-renters the
bedroom. The air in here is acrid with sickness, overlaid with
Dettol. In the bed, the diminutive figure lies on its side, hair plas-
tered to the pillow, the cat wrapped in her sleeping arms. He
hasn't left her side, that cat, since Thomas brought her home.
Sits and lies beside her all the time, emitting a loud rattling purr,
as though he thinks that this will somehow help her heal. Vesta
tries to creep across the room quietly, but Cher hears her and
jumps awake with a gasp.

'It's okay, Cher,' says Vesta. 'It's okay. It's just me. You're all right.'

The girl groans as she shifts in the bed, and the cat moves a couple of paces away and squats, glaring evilly. Vesta goes to shoo him off, but Cher grabs him by the scruff and squashes him to her chest. Vesta leaves it. He must be all over germs, that cat, but Cher loves him and it's pretty clear that the feeling is, as far as cats go, mutual. God knows, Cher's not had many things to love in her life. Why deprive her of this one?

And the girl needs all the help she can get. Vesta's stomach churns as she sees the mess this man has made of her face, of the mouth that gingerly presses itself to the sensitive patch behind Psycho's ear. Such a pretty face. She could probably have done with stitches in that lip, but what can I do? I'm not a nurse. I'm just a first-aider. How am I meant to know if that's a straight-forward black eye, or if something's actually broken in there?

Cher's face looks like a muddy football, half-deflated. Her bruises are turning black, and the left side of her face has swollen so badly it's hard to imagine that it can ever go back to anything resembling its original shape. Her right eye is squeezed shut, just the tips of eyelashes full of gunk poking out from the slit. Her mouth, lopsided, hangs open, a great chasm down the centre of her lower lip.

'What time is it?'

'Going on four.'

'Have I been asleep?'

'Yes,' says Vesta. 'You dropped off a couple of hours ago.'

She takes the water glass from the bedside table and holds it to the girl's mouth, waits patiently as she sips. 'How are you feeling?'

Cher drains the glass and collapses back against her pillow. A single pillow in a sickbed – I must bring some up, later. So she can sit up, at least. Poor little kid, I'll bring her some more pillows and cushions when I come back up. Pity she hasn't got a telly. She'll be bored to tears in a bit.

Cher feels around the inside of her mouth with her tongue, exploring. 'I think I cracked a tooth.'

'I'm not surprised. How's the pain?'

Cher pulls a face, and a single tear forces itself out from her closed eye.

'Your tummy?'

'No, I think that's just a bruise. My ribs hurt really bad. He got me there more than in the soft bits.'

'You can have another pill, if you like.'

'Yeah,' says Cher, and her voice goes small. 'Yeah, that would be nice.'

Vesta fetches the tramadol and the penicillin, refills the glass. 'At least you didn't turn out to be allergic to that. You'd've *had* to go to the hospital, if that had happened.'

'Who says I never get a break?' says Cher, and coughs. Vesta puts a hand behind her head, supports it as the girl drinks once again to wash down the pills. Under her hand, Vesta feels a lump the size of an egg. Oh, God, what if it's fractured? What if her brain's leaking out and I've no idea? We should have taken her to A&E. I'll never forgive myself if something happens.

'There,' she says, trying to sound more confident than she feels, 'there. You'll soon be feeling better, I promise.'

Cher allows a small sob to escape. She's been so tough, but she must be worn out. Vesta hurriedly puts the glass down, and takes her hand in both of her own. Strokes the back of it, feels the rough scabs on the grazed knuckles. 'Oh, love,' she says. 'Oh, lovey. You'll be all right. Just you see.'

The sides of the girl's mouth turn down and a whimper breaks from her lips. 'I don't know what to do, Vesta! I don't know what to do!'

'Shhh,' she soothes. 'Shhh. You just concentrate on getting better.'

Cher's face is wet. The salt must sting her grazes. Vesta pulls a hankie from the box and dabs, gently, around the cuts and the bruises, tries to get it all up.

'He'll kick me out,' says Cher. 'I know he will.'

'What? Kick you out for being ill? Don't be ridiculous.'

'But I won't make the rent. I don't know how I'm going to ...'

'Well, he can bloody well wait.'

That bastard, she thinks. Socking the rent up like that, just because he knows he can get away with it. I'd like to show him what he's done, driving her out to take risks like that. I'd like to rub his bloody nose in it. I've got a good mind to go over there and give him a piece of my mind. Lecherous old stinky creep, picking on young girls and probably getting off on it as well.

'You've not to worry about that.' She is surprised by how calm her voice sounds when it comes out, given the spitting rage inside. 'We'll sort it out. *I'll* sort it out. He doesn't want to mess with me.'

Cher moans and closes her other eye, shifts on to her side, trying to find a comfortable position. There are cuts all over her buttocks – Vesta and Collette had to pick bits of glass out last night, while she was still warm and sedated from the bath. There's barely a position she can lie in and be comfortable.

Vesta's heart wrenches in her chest. She wants to cry. She may be old, but she remembers how it was to be young, in the sixties,

191

when everything was fresh, when life promised exploration and adventure and nothing could go wrong. It's all spoiled now, she thinks, right from the start, for Cher. She never stood a chance. No one's looked after her, all her life. For girls like Cher, things like this are just part of the general beastliness.

She reaches out and smooths the girl's hair away from her face. It's crunchy under her fingers, the texture of rough wool. I don't even know which of your parents gave you that hair, she thinks. Which one was black and which one was white. Could have been neither of them, for all I know. I know your nanna was white, because I've seen the photo, but I've no idea whose mum she was. Oh, it shouldn't be like this. Not for you, not for anybody. It's just not fair.

Another tap at the door. Cher raises her head, then drops it back on the pillow as though the effort is just too much. 'Who is it?' calls Vesta.

'Collette.'

Vesta is relieved. She's been on watch since eight this morning, and her back and hips are aching from sitting in the battered chair. She limps over to the door and lets her in.

'All right?'

'Yes,' says Vesta, and turns to look over her shoulder. 'Aren't we, love?' she asks, encouragingly.

Cher doesn't reply; just lies on her side and stares at the bedside table.

'She's just had her pills,' she tells Collette. 'And she's had a little sleep. Hopefully she'll drop off again soon.'

'And how does she seem?'

'In a lot of pain. But I think it's okay. I don't think anything's broken. Not badly, anyway.'

Apart from her skin, and her heart, and her spirit, she thinks.

But all those things can mend. Scars, yes, but they'll mend, if she lets them.

Collette advances into the room. She's got a bunch of flowers – carnations, cheap things that Vesta associates with graveyards – and a bag of tins and packets. 'Soup,' she says. 'I thought soup would be good. And I got some bread. And some grapes. You should eat something, Cher.'

'Not hungry,' says Cher.

'Well, maybe later,' she says. 'I got Ribena, as well. Everyone likes Ribena, right?'

Cher looks up, her eyes full of tears again. 'Yeah. I like Ribena.'

Collette grins. Gosh, she's lovely when she smiles, thinks Vesta. All that pinchedness drops away and she's just – pretty. She goes over to the sink and fills the pint glass. Puts the flowers in it and makes a show of trying to arrange them. 'Hossein sent these,' she says.

'There, you see?' says Vesta, trying to jolly the atmosphere up. 'Isn't that nice? Everyone's done their best, haven't they?'

'Big whoop,' says Cher, and closes her eye.

Vesta closes the door and lets her face drop. The strain of keeping up a good front, of projecting reassurance for all these hours, has drained her. That bloody man, she thinks. I'm going to have a rest for a couple of hours, but then I'm right round there. I can't believe he's got the gall. Utter bastard. I'm going to go round there and tell him. Just because they've done away with tenant rights doesn't mean he can just *bully* people. I've had enough. Really, I've had enough.

She's so stiff she has to hold on to the banisters all the way down the stairs, take them one at a time with her right foot first.

She feels old today, and hates it when she's forced to remember that nearly seventy *is* old. She has always taken such pride in staying young, in fighting all those generational attitudes when they've tried to creep up on her, and the thought that in the end it's all inevitable fills her with dread. She wishes she'd remembered to neck one of Cher's tramadol while she was up there, but there's plenty of ibuprofen in the flat. A couple of those, a cup of tea and a lie-down, and I'll be right round there, she thinks. I'll bloody well tell him he can't bully people.

The stink hits her the moment she opens the flat door. Like the rat – rotten and foetid and old – but far, far worse. It's a thick, viscous smell, and it's huge.

'Oh, God,' says Vesta. What now? Haven't I had enough already? Really, today, over the last few weeks? Haven't I?

She turns on the light and goes in, covering her face with the sleeve of her cardy. It's sewage. She knows it is. It's not hard to tell the smell of shit and fat and urine, even if it's not a stench you smell every day.

The carpet is damp and sludgy beneath her feet. Vesta gags, and forges forward. It's the drains. Those bloody drains she's been asking him and asking him to sort out. Something has gone terribly wrong, and now it's all over her kitchen.

Chapter Twenty-Seven

'I told you. I *told* you! How many times have I asked you to sort it out? And now look!'

The Landlord sits up and puts on his specs.

'Who is this?'

'Don't pretend you don't know who this is. It's Vesta Collins! And my bathroom's all over shit! I *told* you that you needed to do something about those drains!'

'Calm down, dear,' he says, and hears a shriek of rage.

'Don't tell me to calm down! Don't you *dare* tell me to calm down! And don't bloody call me *dear*. I am not your dear.'

Someone's set fire to her bra, he thinks. I'm taking that phone out of the hall, first chance I get. I'm not paying line rental to have her shout at me.

'You're a lazy, greedy little man, Roy Preece! You were like that when you were a kiddy, and you're worse now! My flat's ruined! It's ruined! There's sewage all over the bathroom, and it's coming out into the kitchen, and it's *all your fault*!'

'Well, I don't know how you work that out,' he says, sulkily.

'Because you've stalled and stalled on getting the drain people out, and now every time someone flushes upstairs, or uses the water, there's more sewage coming out of my loo! You need to get Dyno-Rod, and you need to get them now. Do you hear me?'

Like that's going to happen. I'm not made of money, even if she thinks I am.

'I'll come over and have a look in a bit,' he says.

'No! No! No! You need to get it sorted out now! Hossein's been up to his shoulder in kaka for the last hour, and he's got nowhere. There's some sort of fatty stuff clogging it all up. It needs a professional with a bunch of rods, not you and a bottle of bleach!'

'I said,' he repeats, 'that I'll come in a bit.'

'And what are we meant to do in the meantime? *No one* can use the bathrooms without it all coming straight back out again. And I can't use my flat. It's unusable. I can't wash, and I can't cook. If I try and make anything to eat in here, I'll probably die.'

And wouldn't that be a tragedy, you horrible old bat, he thinks. You've been around quite long enough, in my opinion.

'I swear, this is your last chance,' she says. 'If you don't get this sorted out, I'm calling the council tomorrow. Then you'll not just be looking at the drains, you'll be having to replace all those manky water heaters, and probably putting in heating, as well, and the fire provisions. And doing something about the door locks, and dealing with the damp down here, and all the other things I've let you get away with. I've had it up to here with it. This is the final blimmin' straw. I'm going to stay in a hotel till it's sorted out, and you're footing the bill.'

'Now, hang *on*! Nobody said anything about hotels.'

'Well, what do you want me to do? You want me to report you? Do you? I'm sure they'd be interested. Rats and sewage and that poor kid up in her room, all covered in cuts because of you.'

'You what?'

'Oh, yeah. Don't think I don't know about you and your random rent rises.'

Cher Farrell. Something to do with Cher Farrell. 'What are you on about now?'

'And she can't even wash, for God's sake. It's disgusting! I've a mind to report you anyway, greedy-guts. I suppose you think you can get her to . . . to *whatever*. You disgust me, Roy Preece. And I'm not taking any more of it. I'm living in a slum.'

'Well, you get what you pay for,' he replies, triumphantly. 'You wouldn't even *get* a slum for the rent you pay me. You could always move somewhere else, if you don't like it. Be my guest. Because I'll come in my own good time.'

Vesta goes silent. When she speaks, she seems to have regained her control, as though someone's thrown a switch.

'Would you care to repeat that?'

'I said,' he says, slowly, so she can't mishear, 'that I'll come in my own good time.'

'So you're refusing to make the property habitable?'

'I didn't say that. I said you'd have to wait until I can get there.'

'I don't, you know. Shall I call out Dyno-Rod myself? I could do that, and give you the bill. Only I don't have any money.'

Well why don't you pay them out of all the cash you've saved by paying me a peppercorn rent all these years, he thinks. Christ, why can't you just *die*?

'Oh, just go to your hotel,' he snaps. 'Whatever. Who cares what you do, anyway?'

'I'm sure the council will care.'

'You seem to think the council has magical powers,' he says. 'It's a local council, not the United Bloody Federation of Planets.'

'Don't you *dare* swear at me! If you *want* to go on the bad landlord register—'

'There's no such thing,' he snaps, and hangs up.

He takes his specs off and polishes them with the hem of his T-shirt. Bloody Vesta Collins. I'm forty-six years old and she's still talking to me like she did when I was twelve. Busybodying about, telling me what to do and forgetting whose house it *is*.

I wish she'd bloody die, he thinks. She's old enough, for God's sake. She's been retired and hanging about the place all day for bloody ever. Never been anywhere, never done anything, just sat there in my basement wagging her finger. There's no use for her. Bloody old woman and her sensible shoes and antimacassars. Why can't she just take the eight grand and bugger off? Nobody wants her. It's not like she's got any reason for staying round here. No family, no kids, no job. Nothing. It's just pure selfishness.

He hauls himself off the couch and groans as he does so. His weight is really getting to him, these days. He hasn't been near a doctor or a set of scales in years. The last time he did, he had passed the twenty stone mark and he knows that nothing has come off since. His arches fell years ago, and his knees seem to bend and unbend more slowly with each passing month. I'll be on a stick soon, he thinks, and I'll *still* be subsidising that old bag to go on her holidays in Ilfracombe. Says she doesn't have the money for a plumber, but she's never short of cash for a wash-and-set on a Wednesday, is she?

The old bitch has given him indigestion. He stomps through to the bathroom and swigs a tablespoon of Gaviscon straight from the bottle, waits for the advertised cooling that never comes, takes another swig and lets out a burp. Right, he thinks. I suppose I'd better call Dyno-Rod. I don't want her calling the council on me.

He goes to the computer to look up the number, Vesta nagging at the back of his mind. She doesn't seem to be able to take a hint, he thinks. I've given her enough, over the last couple of years. The cockroaches and the leaking bathtub upstairs, the burglary, the Weedol in the herbery ... that rat was a stroke of genius. Why on earth does she stay? I wouldn't. I'd've been gone months ago. She's stubborn, just bloody stubborn. Looks like I'm going to have to step up my game before I end up having to lay out a grand on a new boiler for the old bitch.

I wish she'd just bloody die and get out of my hair, he thinks again as he picks up the phone to dial, then his finger stills over the keypad. The water heater, he thinks. Bloody ancient. The Corgi man said as much the last time he was in for servicing. Said it wasn't far off failing its MOT completely.

Maybe, he thinks, I can help it on its way.

Chapter Twenty-Eight

Vesta doesn't go to a hotel. She can't bear to not know what's happening to her home, can't leave Cher, can't face the thought of not having her things around her. It's a miserable evening spent moving as many of her belongings as aren't soiled to the front room and proofing the door with blankets against the stench. But still the smell elbows its way through. In the toilet, the lavatory overflows with its backed-up load and the floor is an inch deep in filth. Even the bath has regurgitated, and lies half full with stagnant sludge. No point in trying to clear it up. While the drains are still blocked, any attempts to deal with the results will be rendered pointless the moment someone upstairs forgets themselves and flushes their cistern. It would be like cleaning the Augean stables. Literally.

She eats with Cher: feeds her Heinz tomato soup and a soft white bread roll, spoon by spoon, crumb by crumb, letting her suck her way to nutriment through swollen lips, then comes down to her stinky basement and crawls, exhausted, into the makeshift bed she's made on the settee. She leaves the front window open, to try to get some clean air into the room, and falls, despite the unfamiliar sounds out in the street, into an uncomfortable doze some time before midnight.

She dreams that she's up in Cher's room and they have barricaded the door with the bed. Someone is trying to get in. The door handle rattles in its socket and fingernails scratch, scratch, scratch at the panels. And they can hear breathing. Breathing, breathing, breathing.

And then, in the dark, something tells her that the sounds are real.

Wakefulness runs through her like cold water. She's lying on her back, knees drawn up under her blanket, scanning the night with her fading ears. She looks around, wildly, can't place where she is for a moment before she remembers what has happened.

It's all right, she thinks, and settles back against the cushion. Just a sound in the street and a silly dream, someone passing by. You're not used to it, you've been sleeping in the same bedroom for so long you're bound to—

A sound from the back of the flat. Unmistakable. The sound of her back door opening.

No. No, no, no. It's just your mind. Just—

A floorboard creaks in the kitchen. Someone is coming in.

Vesta's body defaults into foetal position on the cushions. She pulls the blanket uselessly over her face, as though it will protect her. Oh, no. Oh, no, no. What do I do? I can't get out. He's in there between the outside and me. I'm old and stiff. If I try to run up the stairs, he'll catch me while I'm still trying to get the door unlocked ...

Slowly, slowly, she works her way off the couch and creeps to the door. Maybe, at least, I can hold it shut. If he comes this way I'll sit against it, push with all my weight, and maybe he won't be able to ...

She presses an ear against the door, holds her breath. She's wearing nothing but a nightie, her dressing gown still hanging on the back of the bedroom door, her clothes lost in the darkness. Maybe if I turn the light on, make a noise? Maybe he'll go away, if he knows I'm here?

And maybe he'll come looking for me.

He's in the kitchen, but the lights are off. She's emptied the lower cupboards, piled pans and serving dishes and cake tins on the surfaces in case the flood should worsen. It's crowded and chaotic in there, hard to navigate, especially in the dark. She hears some extremity of him catch something, hears it fall to the floor with a metallic clatter that seems to go on for ever and ever.

Silence. Oh, God, he's listening.

Vesta freezes. Holds her breath, hears the pulse race in her ears. Shut up, shut *up*. I can't hear anything. I don't know where he is.

In the house, nothing moves. She doesn't even know if Collette is in, but there's no sound from upstairs. From the window a slight draught of air suggests that it's late. There's no one to hear me, she thinks. No one's awake. Oh, God, why did I put those bars on the window? I thought they would keep people out. I never thought that they would keep me in.

The intruder moves again, more boldly. He must have decided that no one has heard him. He thinks no one's going to come. Just like that time before. No one came then. Why would they now?

He's moving away, towards the back of the house.

What's he doing? There's only the bathroom back there. There's nothing there.

And once he's found that out, he'll come this way.

Suddenly, as the first wave of panic dies back, she feels a surge of defiance. Hold on, she thinks. This is my *home*. It's the same man who broke in before. Come back for more. Come back to get more stuff off the little old lady. From my *house*.

Well, he's not bloody going to. If he thinks he can just carry on trying to scare me, he can damn well think again. My mum and dad went through the Blitz in this house. I lived here when it was nothing but junkies and dealers up this way, when half the houses were squats – and no one dared try coming in here. What's happened to you, Vesta? Where's your backbone?

She casts about for a weapon with which to defend herself. The fire irons, bright polished brass, still live by the fireplace even though it was converted to gas in the 1960s. I'll give the bugger a clout, she thinks, and send him on his way. Use the same poker he used to smash my mother's statues with. That's what I'll do. There're enough victim women in this house without me adding to it. I'll give him a thick ear and a nasty fright, and he won't *dare* try it again.

But despite her defiant thoughts, she lacks the courage to cross the room and leave the door unguarded. She has visions of him coming through as she bends in to the fireplace, of being on her before she can straighten up. She leans against the door and scans the stuff she's brought through, looking for something closer to hand. Her eyes fall on the iron, sitting now on the gate-leg table, heavy, old-fashioned, perfect.

She snatches it up, wraps the flex round her hand and listens again at the door. Yes, he's still out back, in the bathroom. She can hear him moving about in there, a clink of metal on metal that she cannot place. She comes out into the sweaty corridor, moves stealthily up towards him.

It stinks, now the doors are open. Forty degrees of heat and standing sewage don't make happy bedfellows. She'd be throwing up if the intervening hours hadn't hardened her stomach. I bloody hate you, Roy Preece, she thinks. First thing tomorrow, if the drain people aren't here by eight o'clock, I'm going straight round to yours and I'm going to hammer your door down till you bloody well come here and fix it.

More strange sounds. She sees now that he has a torch, and that he's rested it on the sink to light whatever it is he is doing in the back of the room. All there is there is the old water heater, big and chunky and forty years old, hanging off the outside wall so its exhaust pipe has somewhere to vent. What's he doing? What on earth is he doing?

Vesta creeps barefoot into the kitchen, recoils at the feel of greasy muck beneath her soles. She treads on something semi-solid, has to bite back a moan of disgust as it squidges up between her toes. It's slippery underfoot, like wearing leather soles on ice. Now that she's near him, can see the vague, gigantic shape of him in the darkness, she feels less certain. Grips the handle of the iron tighter and holds it in front of herself like a shield. From the dim light that illuminates the room, she can see that the man is huge: that he fills the space as though it were a cupboard. He's got a bag of stuff at his feet, and something that looks like a wrench in his hand. And here I am, she thinks, in nothing but a nightie, thinking I'm going to see him off.

For a moment, she considers turning back. I could still make it, if I'm quiet, she thinks. Go out through that open kitchen door and nip out through the garden. Go round the front and knock up the others and ... and get them to help. God's sake, Vesta, you're sixty-nine, not thirty-nine.

Then he turns to get something from his bag, and catches sight of the white cotton that covers her thighs.

Time slows to a crawl. Vesta feels herself leave her body for a moment, sees herself from behind, a frail elderly woman quailing as the giant unfurls itself in the gloom. Sees herself dying, here among the sewage, being found tomorrow morning, grey and gone and rotting.

She lunges, swings the iron at the end of her arm like a mace, and feels it connect. Hears an 'oof' from the burglar and is surprised by how suddenly her forward motion is halted by the solidness of his skull.

Her feet go out from under her. She flies through the air like a cartoon character, arms flailing, and hits the back of her head.

The world goes black.

Chapter Twenty-Nine

Collette wakes to the sound of wailing. A woman's voice, high with panic, calling, 'No! No! Oh, God, no, no, no, wake up! Oh, God, wake up! Help! Please! Somebody help me!'

Vesta. She's out of her bed in her top and leggings – her escape clothes – before she is really awake. She has to stop for a second and rest a hand against the wall as the blood rushes to her head and Hossein's footsteps thunder across her ceiling. Then she slips her feet into her Keds and meets him at the bottom of the stairs.

Hossein's face is still slack with sleep, his black hair sticking up in tufts. 'What's going on?' he asks.

'I don't know.'

'Is it Vesta?'

'I think so.'

'I heard someone shouting. Is everyone okay?'

They jump. Thomas has followed Hossein down the stairs so silently that neither of them had known he was there. He looks exactly as he always looks – checked lawn shirt, tan slacks, slightly tinted specs – as though he merely goes into suspended animation at night rather than sleeping. 'Is someone hurt?'

Hossein frowns and says something in Farsi. Strides past him and bangs on Vesta's door with the flat of his hand. 'Vesta? Are you okay? Vesta?'

Whether she's okay or not, she doesn't hear him. Just keens into the night, 'Oh, God, oh somebody help me! Wake up! Wake up! I can't lift him! Wake up!'

Collette looks over her shoulder, expects the elusive Gerard Bright to put his head out of the door and stare at them with those red-rimmed eyes of his. But the door stays closed. The phone is off the hook, she notices, the receiver dangling by its cord. Funny, she thinks. How did that happen?

They stare at each other in the dimness of the hallway. Thomas tries the door handle, impotently, as though he thinks it will have magically become one that turns. 'Back door?'

Hossein shakes his head. 'It will be worse. I reinforced the frame after the burglary.'

He raises his hand and bangs again. 'Vesta!' Launches himself bodily at the door and bounces off it, clutching his shoulder. Tries again.

'Has anybody got a key?' asks Thomas.

Hossein gives him the sort of wide-eyed head waggle you see in nightclubs just before trouble kicks off. 'Has anybody got a key to yours?'

'Fuck's sake,' says Collette. She pushes past Thomas, looks at the door, then stands on one foot and kicks out at the lock with the other. Hossein hears something splinter. Collette kicks again.

She's half my size, thinks Hossein. This is shaming. 'Hold on,' he says, and takes her place. Copies her with his big bare foot, all his strength behind him. The lock gives under his third kick, and the door flies back and bangs against the wall.

Collette is past him and halfway down the stairs before he's regained his balance. 'Vesta?' she calls. 'Vesta, where are you?'

Hossein pauses to switch on the light. Collette is at the bottom of the stairs, looking wildly about her. The smell hits them like a steam train. Faeces and urine and … something dead. Sweet and dead, like it's been that way a while. Hossein walks past her and she follows him towards the back of the house, where Vesta's voice comes from.

She's in the bathroom, crumpled on the floor, with what looks like a steam iron sticking out obscenely from between her thighs. She's brown and green with filth, her hair matted down with something unspeakable. Her eyes plead wildly. 'Help me,' she says again. 'Oh, God, I can't move him. He's too heavy. I can't – he'll drown.'

Behind her, in the gloom of the unlit bathroom, the top of a pair of gigantic buttocks moons at them over the waistband of a pair of drooping sweat pants. The owner is on his knees, bent forward in prayer position, face down in the overflowing toilet pan. He isn't moving.

'I hit him,' sobs Vesta. 'I hit him! I didn't know it was him. How could I know it was him? It's the middle of the night. What's he doing here? He shouldn't be here! And then I slipped. In this … this … it's … slippy, and I banged my head, and when I came round, he was … oh, God, I've killed him! I tried to get him out. I *tried*. But I can't shift him. Oh, God, help him! Somebody! Help him!'

'Shit,' says Hossein.

Never a truer word. 'You can say that again,' says Collette.

Vesta tugs hopelessly at the back of the man's marquee of a

T-shirt. It stretches and compresses the flesh within so that the dimpled buttocks seem to swell and grow. The body bumps slightly and the head bobs in the toilet pan.

'Is that the Landlord?' asks Collette.

'I think so,' says Thomas. 'It looks like him.'

They've all followed that backside up a set of stairs at some point in their lives. It's not a memory you easily forget.

'What's he doing here?' asks Thomas.

Vesta looks up at them in astonishment. Tears have etched pink streaks through her green-brown facemask and her eyes shine white in the half-light. 'Don't just ... Help me, for God's sake!'

Thomas looks at Hossein, who looks at Collette. Collette looks back at Thomas and folds her arms across her body. Jigs uneasily from foot to foot. There's no way she wants to touch him. What if someone decides he needs mouth-to-mouth?

'How long has he been like that?' asks Thomas, echoing her thoughts.

'I don't know. I don't *know*!'

'Well, how long were you out for?'

Vesta suddenly shows a flash of her old self. Rolls her eyes and tuts. 'Well, if I knew *that*, I wouldn't have been unconscious, would I?'

'Sorry,' says Thomas. 'It's just – well, it makes a difference. To, you know, whether it's worth ...'

The man in the toilet shows no signs of stirring. His face is buried to the ears in effluent and his arms are slack, his fingers trailing across the lino like sausages. The pants have ridden down in the front and Collette can glimpse an apron of fat that extends halfway down his thighs.

'I'm sorry,' she says, 'but what do you expect us to do?'

'Get him out. Help him – something.'

'I think he's dead already,' says Hossein, succinctly.

'We should get him out, though.' Collette looks at him, pleadingly. When I say we, she thinks, I mean you men. I'm all for the gender division of labour, in this instance. 'We should. In case.'

'What's he doing here?' asks Hossein. 'It's two in the morning.'

'Drowning,' says Vesta. 'Can we talk about this later?'

'Yes,' says Hossein. Takes a deep breath and offers her a hand to get up off the floor. She slips, twice, on her bare soles as she rises; props herself against the wall. In her nightie she looks small and frail, that strange warrior queen quality to her features stripped away, and every second of her almost-seventy years is etched across her face. Hossein puts his fists on his hips and stares at the body. It really is huge. It looks like a narwhal has climbed out through the drains and fainted.

'What the fook's going on here?' says a voice. Cher, black eye and split lip, stands in the kitchen in leggings and a pink Hello Kitty T-shirt, her forehead creased in confusion, a hand on the door-jamb propping her up as she holds her injured ankle off the floor.

Vesta starts to weep. 'I thought it was a burglar. How was I to know it was him? What was he doing here at this time of night?'

Collette overcomes her horror of the dirt and goes over to put an arm round Vesta's shoulders. Under her nightie, she's all skin and bone, and shivering as though the temperature has suddenly dropped. Poor Vesta, she thinks, I can't imagine how this must feel.

'I don't know,' says Hossein, and nudges the tool bag with his foot. The bottom cover of the water heater has been removed, and propped in the bath. 'But I don't think it was a social call.'

'He's all over shite,' says Cher.

'Thanks for pointing that out,' says Hossein.

'How did he end up like that?'

'I hit him with a steam iron,' says Vesta. 'I thought he was a burglar.'

'C'mon,' says Thomas. 'We have to get him out.'

Hossein pulls a face that says that he would rather be back in Evin prison than here, and steps forward to give him a hand. Gingerly, they each hook a hand into an armpit, and heave. The liquid in the toilet pan slurps, sucks like quicksand, then lets go with a sulphurous belch. The Landlord flips free, lurches out of their grip and lands face up in the doorway.

His eyes and mouth are open and his skin is blue.

'Oh, God,' says Cher. 'Oh God, oh God, oh God.'

They gather round the corpse in silence. He lies propped against the wall tiles, and drips. Sewage runs slowly from his mouth and nose; green-brown drool, like a zombie's. He's lost his spectacles. They must be down there in the toilet bowl, but no one volunteers to retrieve them. The fact that his eyes have been open since they pulled him out makes it clear that he will have no further use for them.

'I guess there's no point in trying CPR, then,' says Collette.

'No,' says Thomas. 'I'd say he's been dead for a while. You must've been out for a bit, Vesta. Do you feel okay?'

'How do you think I feel?'

Cher stands by the cooker and absently fingers the lump on her own skull. 'What do we do now?' she asks.

Chapter Thirty

The silence seems to last for hours. Five people, gathered round a corpse, and suddenly no one wants to meet anyone's eye. Even Vesta hangs her head. She feels sick: from the bang on the head, from the shock, from the wallowing in stuff that should be safely underground, from the sudden lurching change to her world. She rubs at her arms and sees that all it does is spread the slime. Grabs the kitchen paper and wipes hopelessly at her face. It will never come off. It's her Lady Macbeth stain.

She looks under her lashes at the others. Collette has moved away, and is gnawing at a hangnail by the cooker. Probably shouldn't be doing that, thinks Vesta, but doesn't point it out. Hossein looks pensive in his red T-shirt, his old-fashioned striped pyjama bottoms with the cord tie. Cher huddles by the sink, looking terrified. Thomas stands in the doorway looking … what? Goodness me, she thinks, amazed. He looks intrigued. As if this is some sort of psychology experiment and he's running it.

They're going to put me in prison. I've killed someone and I'm going to jail. So this is how it ends: he always wanted me out of here and now he's got his wish. He'll be sick as a dog that he never got to benefit.

She looks round her devastated home. Mum would turn in her grave. She was always so houseproud, and I've tried my best to keep it the way she'd like it, always felt bad that I lacked her application and her eye, but now look. It's all completely spoiled. She would cry and cry, if she knew. Every day, she washed these floors. She couldn't abide dirt, and God knows the world was dirtier when I was a child than it is now.

Thomas speaks. 'Do you want to call an ambulance?'

'Don't think that'll do much good,' says Cher. 'He's dead, isn't he?'

'Yes, but there are ways that things are done,' he says, 'and that would be the normal way.'

Hossein leaves the room and comes back a few seconds later with Vesta's old quilted dressing gown. He holds it out for her and she shrugs herself into it distractedly, stands by the Landlord's swollen feet and hugs the collar round her neck. 'I don't know what to do,' she says again. 'I don't. I didn't *mean* to kill him.'

'I'm sure they'll understand that,' says Collette. 'It was an accident. How were you to know he'd let himself into your flat in the middle of the night?'

'I don't know,' says Thomas. 'With that great big dent in his head.'

Vesta bursts into tears. She's been numb with shock for the past few minutes, but now emotion floods her, chills her. 'I can't! I can't go to prison. I didn't know ... he was creeping around in my bathroom. He could have been *anybody*.'

'You should be okay,' says Thomas. 'People do get sent to prison, but it's usually for guns ...'

'You're not helping much, Thomas,' says Hossein.

'I'm just telling the truth,' he says. 'We need to be realistic, here.'

She sees herself in a grey uniform, carrying a divided tray of textureless taupe foodstuffs through a room full of glaring women. Feels cinderblock walls close in, suffocates in the confines of a bunk bed. 'I can't. I just can't go to prison. I'd *die* in prison. I've never been in trouble in my life.'

Collette speaks up. 'And they'll want to question all of us.'

The room falls quiet again.

Oh, God, thinks Vesta. What have I done?

'Fuck,' says Cher. 'Then I'm screwed.'

Thomas's curious expression deepens. 'Why would that be, Cher?'

''Cause I'm only fifteen, you stupid dick,' she snaps.

'Language, Cher,' says Vesta automatically, without the help of her brain.

Collette's mouth falls open.

'You're fifteen?'

'Are *you* thick, as well?'

Collette's head is full of bees. She can barely hear her neighbours over the sound of buzzing. I have to get out of here, she thinks. There's going to be police swarming all over the place, and once there's been police, sure as night follows day there's going to be press, especially with the way he's died. It's the sort of story the papers eat for breakfast. If the police don't put two and two together, it's only a matter of days before Tony does. Just one careless moment, a photographer waiting outside when I come out to put the bins out, and I'm toast. But what do I do? What do I do about Janine? I can't leave London now. I can't leave her. She's dying. I'll feel guilty for the rest of my life ...

'But ...' she says, the protest only very loosely applied to Cher. The girl takes it as a reaction to her revelation, and glares at her. Of course she's fifteen, thinks Collette. An attitude like that, she couldn't be anything else. Why on earth didn't I see it?

'Ever been in a care home?' asks Cher.

'I ... well, yes, as it goes.'

'Well, then,' Cher begins, then looks annoyed, as though Collette has stolen her thunder. She hobbles away and fishes a pack of Marlboro from the back of her leggings. Stands in the garden door and lights one with the little Bic tucked beneath the cellophane. 'And the first person who tells me I'm too young to smoke gets this in their eye,' she says. Her hand is trembling.

'Roy Preece,' says Thomas, gazing down at the Landlord. 'What d'you suppose he was doing?'

'He wanted me out,' says Vesta. 'He's been trying to get me out for years.'

'Well, it looks to me as if he was doing something with your boiler,' says Thomas.

'At two in the morning?'

'I didn't say he was doing anything good, did I?'

'He thought I was wasn't here,' says Vesta. 'That's it! I told him I was going to stay in a hotel because of the drains. This afternoon. He must've thought I wasn't going to be here. Like with the burglary. And that time when my garden got vandalised. He knew I was away, every time.'

Hossein frowns and walks away into the bathroom. They stand in silence and listen to him moving things around, the clang of metal on enamel as he shifts the boiler cover.

'I can't be here,' says Collette. 'If there's going to be police. I'll have to go, tonight. I'm sorry. I'm sorry, Vesta, but I have to get out of here. I'd help, you know I'd help, but ...'

'I know. I understand.' Despite her dirty face, the old dressing gown and the tangled hair, Vesta, with her noble bone structure, looks suddenly dignified in the wreck of her kitchen. She stands up straight and pulls her collar tight, stares off into the distance. Resigned, thinks Collette. She looks resigned. Like she's given up already. 'It's my mess to sort out. It's wrong to drag any of you into it.'

'We're in it already,' says Thomas. 'You know that, don't you?'

'Yes,' she says, and stops to bite back a surge of tears. 'Yes, I know that, and I'm sorry.'

Thomas sighs, and comes over to stand by her. He rubs her arm, awkwardly. He doesn't look as if the gesture comes naturally to him. He looks, thinks Collette, like someone who's acting out sympathy based on things they've seen on telly. I hope he doesn't hug her. She might scream. 'Poor Vesta,' he says. 'This wasn't your fault, you know.'

'I thought he was a burglar,' Vesta says, again. The phrase is coming automatically now, as though she's rehearsing her statement.

'Does he have any family?' Thomas asks, gently.

She shakes her head. 'No. Three sisters, there were, and they managed to produce one child between them. I suppose it explains a lot, really, if you think about it. Why he was like he was. Terribly spoilt, when he was a child. Always stuffing his face with chocolate. God knows how much pocket money he got; he always had a comic or a gadget or some trendy toy when you saw him. But his mum wouldn't let him play with the other kids. She thought they were dirty so I don't think he had any friends. He'd come here after school and hit a ball round the garden with his cricket bat, all by himself. Always smashing my herbaceous border. His aunties lived here, back then, in the upstairs. Never saw them have a visitor, either, apart from Roy and his mother. It's not normal, is it?'

No one seems to know what to say to this. They murmur in agreement. As an epitaph, it's not much, thinks Collette. Roy Preece: he ate a lot of chocolate and read the *Beano*. I wonder what mine will be? I wonder if I'll get an epitaph at all? You tend to only get an epitaph if there's a body to bury.

Hossein appears in the doorway. 'Vesta? Do you recognise this?'

He holds out a man's T-shirt, white-gone-grey and marked with grease. Vesta looks at it as though it's a hundred yards away, then shakes her head.

'Only it was in the ...' He loses his vocabulary, blinks and pulls a face as he tries to find the word, '... hole. You know. In the wall. Sort of tubey thing that lets the gas out.'

'The vent?' asks Collette.

'Yes. The vent.'

'Of the *boiler*?' asks Thomas.

'Yes.'

'You don't want to do that,' Thomas says to Vesta, who's slow on the uptake. 'Might as well lock yourself in the garage with the car engine running.'

'I want a drink,' says Vesta, and bursts into tears.

Chapter Thirty-One

As they come down the front steps, Cher lets out a hiss of pain, and Collette, remembering, grabs her by the arm. 'How are you feeling?' she whispers.

Cher hops her way down the steps with a grimace and, when she reaches the bottom, whispers, 'Like I've been beaten up, thankth for athking.'

She's deliberately lisping to stop the sound from carrying on the still night air. It's an old trick that passed from kid to kid in the care homes, along with skills like lock picking and uses for aerosols. But they both glance nervously to their left, up at the front windows, as though they expect to see that the man who didn't come to his door when they were shouting outside Vesta's will be looking out from between his curtains. But Gerard Bright's sashes are down and the glass is dark. He must be out. There's been no music from his flat all day, now Collette thinks of it. Maybe he's away. Perhaps the universe is cutting them a break after all.

Beulah Grove is dark. Despite the open windows that show on all the upper floors in the street it seems that Vesta's cries for help have gone unheeded beyond number twenty-three. But everyone knows that, in London, only the threat of theft will fling a householder from their sleep.

'I can do thith by mythelf,' whispers Collette. Cher glances at her sideways.

'No,' she replies. 'It's easier with two of us, and I know where they are. You don't want to be blundering around there in the dark.'

'Okay. Thanks.'

Cher's ankle is really hurting, now. Lying in her bed, she'd begun to think that it was improving, but now she's limping along the street it feels loose and hot and unsteady, as though something's ripped inside. I won't be running for a while, that's for sure, she thinks, and feels a little moment of relief at the thought that her rinsing days are over. It's a stupid way to make a living, actually more dangerous than straight honest whoring. As she's found to her cost, an angry, ripped-off client is the worst client of all. Each step she takes jars through her body from foot to neck. Can't afford to make a fuss, she thinks, and grits her aching teeth. Got to just get on with it.

'Are you feeling any better?' asks Collette. 'Are the antibiotics doing their stuff?'

'Hope so,' she replies grimly, blanks out the worst-case scenarios. Even Cher knows that antibiotics don't work against viruses. There's an ache low in her tummy, but she doesn't mind that; assumes it's evidence that the Levonelle morning-after pill Collette got from the chemist's yesterday morning is working. 'Headache's gone, anyway. So that's good.'

'Good,' says Collette.

'Sorry I didn't tell you,' says Cher. 'You just … you don't know who you can trust, around here.'

'I know. It's okay. I've not exactly been shouting my own business from the rooftops, have I?'

They reach the scruffy front garden of number twenty-seven. It's full of rubble, the stump of the tree that used to lever up the slabs of the pavement in front raw where it's been cut off and painted over with poison. The windows gape, glassless, at them, still framed by scaffolding. The new owners seem to have knocked out every wall on the upper ground floor. Cher doesn't know much about how these things are done, but it seems to her that the whole place must be ready to fall down.

She leads the way into the side-return, stepping carefully round discarded cement buckets and piles of old bricks. At the far end, bright blue even in the darkness, a folded length of damp-proof membrane lies propped against the closed door. Cher noticed it a few days ago as she was passing, remembered it because she was surprised some pikey hadn't been past and lifted it. Maybe it's just leftovers and the builders don't care, but it's perfect for their purpose.

She points. Collette nods and goes to scoop it up. 'Gosh, it's heavy,' she whispers.

'Gonna need to be,' replies Cher. 'The Landlord's no Tinker-bell.'

She grabs one end as they emerge from the alley, and they start to make their way back. 'I still don't understand about the T-shirt,' says Cher.

'Ugh,' says Collette. 'Carbon monoxide.'

'You what?'

'Gas.'

'From the boiler? She'd've smelled that, wouldn't she?'

'No. It's a by-product of burning stuff. That's why those sorts of things are always on an outside wall. So they can have a vent to let it out. You know there's always a British family that dies in a holiday rental in Cyprus every year? It's that. You can't smell it, you can't see it. And if you don't let it out, it builds up and kills you. But you're asleep by that point, because it knocks you out. You never know anything about it. You know. Like those people with the cars and the hosepipes.'

'So he was ...?'

'Yes. Looks like it. Hard to think he was doing anything else. Another old lady dead in her bath.'

'Christ,' says Cher. They pause at the edge of the pavement and look up and down the road. They only have to cover a short distance, but being spotted now could be their undoing. The street remains quiet. Not a light in a window, not a curtain moving. Three o'clock, the dead zone. They set off for number twenty-three. 'Fucker,' she says. 'I'm glad he's dead.'

Collette doesn't speak. She's not so sure, but then, she doesn't have as much history with the Landlord as the rest of them. Cher's injuries are still fresh, on her body and in her mind, and it's clear that she sees Vesta as some sort of granny figure. She's entitled to feel some rage.

They hurry past number twenty-five and into their own alley-way. Once they get behind the gate, they let go of the plastic and take a moment to breathe. 'So how long were you in care?' asks Cher.

'Oh, on and off, you know. Just a few weeks at a time. The longest was maybe a couple of months. My mum wasn't a great coper, you know? Sometimes it just all got too much and she'd check me in,'

'Yeah, I know,' says Cher, but she feels disappointed. She's never known a living adult who's had her experiences. Had hoped that she'd finally found one.

'It's shit, though, isn't it? I was scared stupid all the time. How about you?'

'Since I was twelve.'

'Wow,' says Collette. 'How about your family?'

'My mum's dead,' says Cher. 'When I was nine. I lived with my nanna and that was okay. She was nice.'

'And your dad?'

The sort of question Vesta asks. Cher doesn't mind it from her. She comes from a world where people know their dads. She reminds Cher of Nanna, all kindness and cake and the confusion of the honest. Collette has seemed like she's from a wider world. Maybe not. Cher shrugs. 'Who knows?'

Collette gives her a sympathetic look. She had so many dads and uncles growing up that she forgets that some people have none at all. 'I'm sorry,' she says, lamely. 'It's tough.'

Cher feels a surprising surge of rage. Great, she thinks. Fucking sympathy. That's all I need. She picks up her end of the sheeting. 'Come on,' she says. 'We haven't got all night.'

In the area outside Vesta's kitchen, Hossein has done what he can with a broom to clear away the worst of the slurry. He and Thomas stand in the doorway, looking out for their arrival, and wait as they manhandle their burden down the steps and dump it on the concrete. 'Oh, that's good,' says Thomas. 'Very good.'

'Damp proofing,' says Collette.

So it won't be permeable, then.

They unfold it and lay it out. Even doubled over, it covers most of the flagstones. Collette checks her watch. It's taken less than an hour for them all to turn from victims and rescuers into conspirators. 'I've got the shed open,' says Hossein. 'That lock didn't take more than a couple of bashes with a brick. It must've been there for decades.'

'It has,' says Thomas. 'Vesta says she doesn't remember it ever being open.'

'What's in there?'

'Nothing much. A rusted up old lawnmower and some plant pots. And an armchair that looks like it's been mouse metropolis for many generations. With an ashtray.'

'Where *is* Vesta?' asks Collette.

'Sitting down.'

'I'll go and check on her.'

The men stand around the plastic sheeting, hands on hips. 'Right,' says Thomas, 'we'd better get on with it, then.'

While the women have been on their foraging mission, they have levered the Landlord into the bath and washed him down with the shower hose. The operation has only been a partial success, as the bath is draining so slowly that he wallows in four inches of filthy water, but his face and torso, stripped of its covering, are relatively clean. He gapes at the ceiling, his arm flopping down the side as though it's been stripped of its bones. He's pale, like a mushroom grown in a cellar, the skin below his collar line near-white and spongy. A bluebottle, awoken from its slumbers, buzzes lazily over his head, looking for an orifice to enter. Hossein bats it away.

From the front room, Cher can hear the murmur of voices. She follows the sound. Some part of her feels that moving the body is somehow man's work. She's surprised by how sanguine everyone seems to be now the decision is made. The Landlord is no longer the Landlord: already he's a bulky object that needs moving, a problem that needs to be got under control before the dawn brings out the neighbours, what passed for his soul long passed from his body. But she no more wants to lay hands on that mozzarella flesh in death than she did in life, and the sight of it makes her skin crawl.

In her front room, surrounded by the piled-up mementos of her life, Vesta sits on the edge of her settee, stiff and pale. One hand holds a glass of brandy, the other sits loosely in Collette's as she stares at the air. Collette is speaking, and Cher pauses in the doorway, unsure if she should interrupt.

'... look after you, Vesta. It wasn't your fault. You'll be okay, I swear. We're going to clear this up and nobody will be any the wiser.'

'You're very kind,' says Vesta, distantly, like the Queen receiving her thirtieth bunch of daffs of the day. 'You're all very kind.'

Are we, though, thinks Cher. Is it really because we care about Vesta, or because we don't want people up in our own business? The only person here I can think of who doesn't have a reason to cover this up is Thomas, and God knows what *he's* hiding while he plays good neighbour. I love Vesta. She's been like a nan to me, but if I thought she was going to get me taken back into care I'd drop her and run in a heartbeat. And that one, there: the fact that she's on the run from someone, somewhere, that she's hiding – it couldn't be more obvious, now I see it, than if she was wearing an orange jumpsuit. And Hossein's still months off getting his asylum application waved through, and God knows the *Daily Mail's* on the hunt for foreign trouble-makers. We're all out to protect ourselves, in the end. None of it's really about Vesta.

Vesta buries her nose in her drink and swallows an inch down in a single go. Behind her, Cher can hear grunts of exertion. 'Go left,' says Hossein. 'No, my left. It's caught on the cooker. No, no, go back, then *lift* it.' She steps into the room.

Vesta and Collette look up like kids caught stealing sweets. Their faces relax when they see that it's her. 'How are you doing, Vesta?' she asks.

Vesta pulls a face that's somewhere between tears and laughter. 'Oh, you know, dear, I've been better.'

'They're moving him now,' she says. 'He'll be out of here in no time.'

'You're so kind,' says Vesta, automatically. 'You're all so kind. I should be helping, really. I shouldn't leave other people to clean up my mess.'

'It's okay, Vesta,' says Collette. 'They're big strong boys.'

'But really,' says Vesta, and makes a move as if to stand up. 'I've never asked anyone to do my dirty work in my life. I'm not starting now.'

Collette puts a strong arm on her shoulder, and holds her down. This is so weird, thinks Cher. Tomorrow – later today – I'll wake up and I'll think it's all been a dream. Roy Preece dead on the bathroom floor. It feels like a dream already.

'Maybe you should come up and stay in mine, tonight,' says Collette.

'Oh, no, I couldn't,' says Vesta, still talking on autopilot, clinging to an independence that has vanished. 'I wouldn't want to intrude.'

Collette looks sharply up at Cher and gestures her away with her free hand. Leave me to it, the look says. You're not helping. It's all I can do to keep her under control.

'It's not an intrusion, Vesta,' she says as Cher goes back to the men.

They've got him out on to the plastic. He lies on his side, blubber spreading across the ground like melted candlewax. Sweat drips from their faces and their shirts cling to their chests. Somewhere out in the dark, over near the railway, a fox barks. Out on the road, the sound of a car engine. There are people, thinks Cher. In London there are people all the time, even in the dead of night. Maybe that man in Flat One is lying there, listening to his heartbeat, wondering what we were doing breaking down Vesta's door. Maybe he isn't out at all, maybe he's just too scared to admit that he's in. She glances at the old sunburst clock on the kitchen wall, a spidery hand ticking off the seconds. Nearly half past three. An hour, maybe less, until daylight. At this time of year people get up to get in a morning's fishing at the pond on Northbourne Common before they start their day's work. Children, overheated in their stuffy bedrooms, will catch sight of the dawn and want attention.

Beyond the stink of the sewage, the hot scent of masculine sweat, she can smell the familiar honk of Landlord. That mix of fungus and must and three-day-old curry, the cheesy tang of desultory washing that has filled her room, and her worries, for months on end. I thought that was the worst smell in the world, she thinks, but he'll soon smell a whole lot worse than that, and has to bite back a bark of hysterical laughter. My God, I'm fifteen, she thinks. I'm meant to be rowing with my mam and saving up for One Direction tickets. I'm meant to be choosing my GCSEs.

Thomas looks up at the sky. He looks curiously vital in his tinted specs, as though he's on the adventure of a lifetime. But thank God for him, thinks Cher. He's the only person who seems prepared to take charge around here. 'Come on,' he says, like a general urging his troops over the top. 'One last push, and we're done. Cher, do you think you can manage a corner?'

Cher gulps. Yes, with my sprained ankle and my bruised ribs

and my face that'll split open if I strain, sure. Any time. She bends, obediently, and takes hold of the plastic. Got to find a way. Get through tonight, take some pills, get some sleep. How can it get worse, anyway?

Thomas bends, and rolls the Landlord on to his back. A long, dank strand of comb-over has come loose and wraps itself around the puffy neck. Thomas picks it up between his fingers and strokes it back into place, the gesture almost tender, the first moment of care anyone has shown for Roy Preece's dignity. No funeral-parlour niceties for him. No embalming fluid or lilies, no church candles discreetly burning to cover the smell of formaldehyde.

Cher remembers her nanna, in her coffin with its polyester-satin lining, her best shirt dress buttoned up to the neck and her mouth turned up at the corners, the marks on her face miraculously disguised by the skill of the cosmetician. And Cher standing there, flanked by two social workers as though she might make a break for it, and all the old people popping in and telling her how her nanna used to talk about her all the time at the pensioners' club, sucking their Werther's Originals and treating it like a day trip. Suddenly, she wants to cry, to howl at the moon, *My nanna's dead and there's nobody left to love me.* She bites fiercely at her lower lip and forces her face to imitate the frozen impassivity she sees around her. Only kids cry, she thinks. Only stupid little kids. You're with the grown-ups, now.

Thomas takes hold of a corner of the sheet and pulls it across the Landlord's body to hide the slack, staring face. The action seems to spur them all into life. They leap forward and pull it fully across, tuck it in like a sleeping bag. Thomas and Hossein take the other side and pull it back towards her, and suddenly he's not the Landlord any more. He's no longer leering Roy

Preece with his roguish lip twitches and his way of hitching his trousers up that seemed at once both pathetic and obscene. Now he's just a hulking bundle of dirty blue plastic, a nuisance in the garden, a problem to be solved.

'He's still filthy,' says Hossein, tiredness making his accent stronger so the word comes out as *feelthy*. 'We can't put him back like that.'

Thomas rubs his hands together, almost gleefully. 'I'll get up to the tool hire place tomorrow,' he says, 'and hire a power jet. Once we've got these drains unblocked, we can get it all cleared up. We can just turn the hose on the lot of it, give him a change of clothes and no one will be any the wiser. Come on. Time's wasting.'

Hossein looks doubtful, but takes his corner. 'Remember to bend at the knees,' says Thomas. 'The last thing we need is someone putting their back out.'

They shuffle around the corpse, trying to work out the best way to carry it. Settle, in the end, for Thomas taking the feet and Hossein and Cher sharing the top end. Thomas counts down: three ... two ... one ... and they straighten up together. Cher gasps at the sheer weight of him, at the pain shooting up through her foot. He's a forklift truck, a reinforced ambulance, a supersized operating table. He's not a man, she thinks, and feels her junk-fed muscles strain under her share, the sweat spring to her scalp like someone's turned on a tap. There's something else in there, there's got to be. A whale. A load of cement. But she sees a jellyfish hand creep out from the fold in the plastic, and knows it isn't true.

It seems to take an hour to get up the steps to the garden. Though they strain at the plastic, they can't stop the heavy middle section from drooping, and it catches on each edge as they pass it. Her teeth grind against each other as she struggles to control the pain, and a protest from her cracked tooth at least distracts her from the howls of rage coming from her leg. They stop three times and rest their package on the bricks while they pant and flex their backs. She understands now what they mean by the phrase dead weight. Even Roy Preece can't have been this heavy when he was breathing. She greys out a couple of times, aware of nothing but the deep crimson agony in the central core of her being, but eventually, though she has long since lost track of her surroundings, she realises that her flip-flops are on soft cool grass, and they are out in the open.

'Keep going,' Thomas urges, his whisper urgent. There's no chance of secrecy now, of pretending they're not there. A casual insomniac glancing out through their curtains will know exactly what they're doing. 'Hurry. Not much further. Come on.'

She limps forward. Her foot seems to have given up, decided that complaining is pointless, died down to a deep pulsating ache that she knows promises trouble for tomorrow. They're able to let out a bit of slack in their screaming arms now they're on the flat. They shuffle awkwardly between Vesta's pots, then hobble crabwise across the uncut grass, feet catching, balance uncertain. What must we look like, she wonders, out here in the dark. But she knows the answer, and doesn't ask the question again.

The shed approaches. Twenty feet ... ten ... five ... She can hear her pulse in her ears, feels sure that the veins are sticking out of her skin like tree roots. Tendons stand out like hawsers in Hossein's neck. Thomas looks like he's going to burst. They reach the open door, and relief floods through her. Thomas backs in to the darkness. We're nearly there. We're nearly—

He sticks. The door's too narrow. Roy's life of chocolate and sausage rolls and late-night pizza has rendered him too wide to fit.

'Shit,' hisses Cher, and drops her corner. There's a noise inside the shed – a tumbling, thumping noise – and she realises that Thomas, caught unawares by the sudden halt, has lost his grip and fallen over.

'No,' says Cher. 'Not now, *fuck's sake.*'

She hears him grunt and pull himself up, then the pulling starts from the other side again. Cher and Hossein brace themselves, and push. Their burden just bunches up against the frame, gets thicker, lodges the wood more deeply into itself.

'Stop.' Thomas's voice sounds horribly loud on the night air. They suck their breath in and halt. Wait for the sound of sirens. Someone must have heard them by now. Come to their bedroom window to see what the neighbours are up to. She stares around, looks up at the Poshes' hundred-pound roller blinds, but nothing stirs in the gardens, no faces appear at the windows.

He speaks again, *sotto voce.* 'Turn him on his side.'

Don't see how that will help, thinks Cher, but they obey. The body still sticks, like a cork in a bottle. But it's soft tissue, without the underlying hardness of hip bones.

'Tuck him in,' comes the voice.

'*What?*'

'Tuck him in. Go on.'

Oh, God. She looks at Hossein and he looks back. He's on the far side from the pendulous stomach. He can reach across and pull, but it's going to be her job to tuck. She gulps. I'm fifteen, she thinks again. It's all downhill from here.

He's over halfway in, his stomach forced up towards his nipples by the pressure of the door frame. Cher balls her hands into fists, closes her eyes and presses. She's never kneaded bread, but she thinks it might be a similar sensation.

Chapter Thirty-Two

The Poshes next door are throwing a party. At two o'clock in the afternoon, while Hossein is flushing out the drains with the power jet that Thomas, true to his word, hired from HSS, the sound of plummy merriment begins to float over the fence, and the air fills with a tantalising scent of a Saturday barbecue. The street fills up with SUVs, and Thomas's rusty old Honda stands out like a bungalow in an executive development.

Hossein can't believe that anyone would want to eat among the stench his labours are producing. But the English, he finds, are an odd race, prepared to put up with just about anything rather than engage with a stranger. It was one of many things about this grim grey city that depressed and confused him when he first came here. It took him a long time to learn not to take it personally. But he's used to it now, and he can see its advantages. Certainly, it gives him some confidence that their plans for Roy Preece's remains could see success, at least for a while. The Landlord's neighbours will probably tut and spray Febreze around for months to avoid ringing on his doorbell and potentially having to deal with rudeness.

He bends back to his work. Everything they plan to do depends, ultimately, on getting these drains to work. They need to clean Roy up, get him pristine for his clean clothes, make sure he doesn't contaminate his final destination. And the only way they can do that is by making sure that the place where they wash him is itself clean. And after that, if they are to carry on living here, business as usual but no rent to pay while, one by one they gradually melt away among the teeming masses ...

Hossein is an economist by training, a troublemaker by reputation. He's always prided himself on his competence. But sitting at a computer and marching with the Green Movement have done little to prepare him for the competencies he's had to learn since he came to London. With a landlord like Roy, whose combination of meanness and inertia have meant that no repairs would get done unless one did them oneself, he's had to become a carpenter-plumber-locksmith-glazier just to survive. And now, it seems, he is a drain clearance specialist.

He wonders what Roshana would make of him now, squatting over a manhole with a hose in his hand, waiting for some sign that something might happen. She used to tease him about the way he rolled up his sleeves and assumed an air of manly competence, which was pretty well non-existent. There were times he resented it – but he would give anything to have it back now. Her beautiful hands, her swift rejoinders, her courage, the way she railed against restriction. He tries not to think too much about her, for when he does, he feels as though the loneliness will overwhelm him.

He would be the first to admit that drains are not his area of expertise, but even so this blockage seems quite bizarre. The stuff he saw when he opened the manhole cover seemed to be at odds with the pool of blackened sewage he had been expecting.

Sure, there's sewage there, but it's greasy, as though it's been mixed with a gallon or two of cooking oil, and the greater part of the chamber seems to be stiff with something that looks unpleasantly like lard. Though there are six people living in this house, all cooking in their tiny kitchens, he finds it hard to believe that even all that could produce this much fat. I must talk to them all, once it's clear, he thinks. They probably don't know about fat: the way it hardens and turns to something that almost looks like stone once it's coating the walls of a sewer. He only knows himself because he went down, as a cub reporter, into the bowels of the city with a team of sewer workers to see for himself, watched them scrape the stuff off the walls like barnacles off the underside of a boat.

'That's weird.'

He looks up and finds Collette standing in the kitchen doorway.

'It looks strange to you?'

'Yeah,' says Collette. 'Is that fat? It looks like fat.'

'I think so.'

'Is it moving?'

'I don't know. It doesn't feel like it.'

'Careful, you don't want to get a blowback.'

'Thanks,' he replies sarcastically. 'I'll do my best.'

A burst of laughter from next door; men and women together, talking in confident, ringing tones. The expensively educated in this country seem to have different voices, he's noticed. Not just the accent: the actual tone. It's as though money gives you extra lung power, the women's voices deeper, the men sounding as though their throats begin somewhere deep in their abdomens.

'Sounds like *someone's* having a good time, anyway,' says Collette.

Hossein looks at her. He knows they're thinking the same thing. This wasn't an event they had factored into the plan.

'It's okay,' says Collette, uncertainly. 'They'll be done by teatime.'

'Here's hoping,' says Hossein, and bends back to his work.

Deep beneath the earth, something gives. He feels it through his hands: a jerk in the hose, then a slight softening of its rigid hardness. The visible part of the chamber empties, suddenly and swiftly, as though a giant mouth had sucked on the other end. Around the sides, the fat still clings, greyish-white and granular.

'Yes!' says Collette. 'Is that it?'

'Looks like it,' says Hossein.

'Thank Christ for that.'

'I think I'll keep this thing running for a bit,' says Hossein. 'If this stuff's all the way down to the sewer, I think we need to get as much of it off the sides as we can.'

'What *is* that?' She comes over and squats beside him, looks disgustedly down at the sludge. He's suddenly, acutely aware of her proximity, the soft roundness of her bare shoulder in her sundress, the smooth curve of her neck, the golden curls tumbling around her ears. She smells good: like freshly ironed linen and baking bread. He feels himself blush, and turns his gaze studiously back to the drain. 'Where's it come from?'

'I don't know.'

'It doesn't look like anything I've … we should dig it out, you know. We can't just leave it there. It'll just gum everything up again.'

Hossein feels an urge to hurl. The fat looks evil, somehow. Unnatural. And now that the liquid sewage has drained away, he feels even less inclined to touch it. But he knows that Collette is right. There is an old plastic bucket in the corner of the area, covered in paint. If he uses the ladle from Vesta's kitchen, it will probably work as a receptacle. They can dump it at the end of the garden. Dig a hole, if they have the strength left.

'Where's everyone else?' asks Collette.

'Cher's with Vesta in the garden – and I think Gerard Bright is back in his room. I heard him coming in this morning. Thomas, I don't know.'

'How's Vesta doing?'

Hossein shrugs. 'As you would expect, I suppose.'

'Yeah.' She scratches the back of her neck and stares uncomfortably at the drain. 'I'll get the bucket,' she says.

'Oh, no,' says Hossein. 'It's okay. I've got this.'

'Don't be silly,' says Collette, and gives him a sweet, sunshiney smile.

He gives the hose another push, and finds that he can feed another three feet into the drain.

With all the water flying around in the shade, Hossein and Collette have no idea how hot the day has become. Sitting out in the sun is like being *on* a barbecue. The shed must be as hot as an oven inside, its contents baking like a slow pot roast. Vesta and Cher sit on the deckchairs, their backs turned firmly to the light, their eyes closed, in silence. Vesta looks old. It's as though she's aged a decade overnight, deep lines etched around her mouth, her skin grey and toneless, despite the long, long summer.

Cher has covered her eyes with a pair of giant panda sunglasses, but the bruise on her face is still visible around the edges, beginning to turn green as it develops. Her lip has scabbed over and looks worse than it did when Thomas brought her home. She's a skinny little thing; looks like a baby bird in her sprigged cotton sundress, and her platform wedges. Neither of them stirs, but nor are they asleep.

The party is warming up over the fence, in as much as a British middle-class party ever warms up, the sound of glass clinking and confident voices ringing out in the hot air. The women's laughter sounds like church bells. If they knew, thinks Vesta, what's lying there on that concrete floor just yards away from them, they wouldn't sound so sure of their place in the world. It must be great, living in a world where nothing's ever undermined your self-belief. Where pension funds and mortgages figure because you think you're going to live to ninety. Where your prospect for the night involves tipsy, sunburnt sleep and the worst thing that can happen to you is feeling jaded as you start the week, rather than creeping your way through darkened streets with a corpse in the boot of a car.

The sunlight has that strange yellow-gold tinge you only find in cities. Pollution, presumably, but it's a pleasurable thing to look at through half-closed eyes. Vesta turns her head and soaks up the rays. Hears the power jet's engine cut out, and its hum be replaced by the sound of rhythmical scraping. Oh, dear, she thinks. I know I should help him, but I can't do it. People look at me and think I can handle anything, they always have, but they're wrong.

Now the engine sound is gone, she can hear the conversations next door with greater clarity. A woman is telling a long, boring story about a trip to an all-inclusive resort hotel in Thailand. 'Gaad, it was gorgeous. Premium-brand spirits and food all day. We didn't really leave the pool, except to eat. And we had a waterfall in our room! Imagine! Your own waterfall!'

'Did you go on any trips?'

'There was a trip to an elephant sanctuary. We went on that, but we didn't feel like anything much other than sleeping and sunbathing.'

'Well, one works so hard. Sometimes I'd just give anything for a rest.'

'I know. Exactly! And really, when you've got it all laid on like that, there doesn't seem much point bothering with doing the tourist thing, really, does there?'

'Not even shopping?'

'Oh, yes, *obviously* shopping!'

The food smells amazing. Fragrant and clean and fresh, as if it's come straight off the farm. Vesta's mouth waters as gusts of savoury spice wafts over the fence and fill her nostrils. So funny how the world has changed. I grew up on roly-poly pudding, in a world where parsley sauce was regarded as exotic; and horse-radish with your Sunday beef, if you had it. Mum and Dad would practically wrap wet towels round their faces when the Asians moved into the street and the gardens smelled of curry, but it always smelled like adventures to me. I still remember the first time I tasted jerk chicken. I thought I'd gone to heaven. So funny. Once upon a time, smells like those coming over the fence right now were smells you only smelled on the bottom rungs of society. And now they've brought it all back here with them and their giant people carriers. They could no more cook without garlic than they could without salt.

I wonder, she thinks, how I shall see this day, when I look back on it? The surreality of it, the enforced inaction, all of us waiting for darkness to fall. Is this how everyone feels, when they've killed someone? Not jittery, not afraid, not sorrowful, but numb?

*

In his attic eyrie, Thomas stands by the window and watches the *va-et-vient* below. Next door is having a party, and he has a great view from his attic dormer: children dressed in the sort of cotton pinafores and coloured dungarees you see in the catalogues that fall out of the *Sunday Times* stomp around in an inflatable paddling pool and bounce in a netted trampoline while adults stand about pouring white wine from a collection of bottles stored in an old enamel washtub full of ice. Every person in the garden has a cardigan tied round their shoulders, as though they've been handed it like a name badge as they came through the door. It's a form of uniform, of course, no less recognisable than baseball caps or hoodies. It lets them know who to smile at in the street, who to ask for directions, who to cross the road to get away from. Half a dozen identical cocker spaniels pant in the shade of a pear tree.

He feels surprisingly relieved at the way things have turned out. There's a tension about what they have to do tonight, but, if all goes well, Vesta Collins has done him a favour. The others may be confused by the blockage in the drains, but he knew what it was the moment he set eyes on it. And if the Landlord had done as the silly old woman kept asking, and called a professional cleaning outfit, they would likely have guessed what it was as well. It wouldn't be the first time in London's recent history, after all, that drains got blocked by subcutaneous fat.

I've been careless, he thinks. Stupidly, arrogantly careless, thinking that because my natron did such a good job of dissolving the stuff that it would carry it all the way to the sewers. Thinking that, because nowadays you can buy a blender for less than the price of a curry, you could just pour those entrails down the toilet, cup by cup. Sixty per cent of the brain alone is made of fat. Where did I think it was going to go?

He needs a new plan – this much is evident. When he realised that Roy Preece was dead and police would soon be swarming over the house, he'd nearly died of fright. If he'd had less presence of mind, if he'd been less able to think on the spot and see his way forward, he would have bolted from that kitchen, from that frightful body and the idiot neighbours lolling about waiting for someone to tell them what to do, fled upstairs and tried to hide his girls. Now Alice is gone, there is room in the bed for both of them, and that's good, but the flat is full of equipment for which he's never bothered to work out proper storage places, and even he, inured as he is to the smell by living in such proximity with it, knows that the place still carries olfactory reminders of Nikki's dissolution in its very fabric. I can't leave myself vulnerable like this, he thinks. I've been a fool.

He stands on tiptoe and leans from the window to snatch a view of the patio. The Iranian man, Hossein, seems to be finished with the power jet, and is scooping the remaining contents of the drain trap into a bucket. He has found a piece of cloth and tied it round his face like a bandit in a cowboy movie. His movements are deliberate, methodical. From what Thomas knows of his history, he's a man well versed in keeping secrets when secrets need to be kept. Thomas does a web search on all of his neighbours as they move in, just to be sure, and is rarely surprised by what he finds. But Hossein Zanjani is clearly not a popular man, at least with the current regime in Iran. Unpopular enough, indeed, to have his own listing on the Amnesty website. He's not worried that this will jeopardise his asylum application: he just doesn't want the people with knives, or guns, or poison umbrellas, or whatever's fashionable with the mullahs this year, to know where to track him down. He's interesting, thinks Thomas, a man of principle. In other circumstances, he would probably never have gone along with this, but even a popular hero can be turned when he's staring down the barrel of an AK47.

A house like number twenty-three doesn't militate a high web presence. As far as he knows, he's the only person who's ever lived here who owned a computer, though the fact that Hossein seems to write quite regularly for a number of political websites suggests that he must, at the very least, have access to one. Gerard Bright turns up briefly as the star of a few slow-season comic newspaper stories – nothing like a private school music teacher cocking up to make a few gloating headlines in the quality press – but otherwise his viola and he just feature in a few concert programmes so amateur that the organisers never got round to taking them off the web afterwards. In fact, it seems as though he's playing in a series of low-rent chamber concerts in local venues across the south-east this week, as luck would have it, the last one tonight. God knows what would have happened if he'd been here last night, or if he were here tonight. A whole new outcome flashes briefly across Thomas's imagination. He dismisses them, hastily. Can't think about that, he thinks. I have too much to do, too much to organise.

There are few mentions of Vesta Collins, but she pops up in the *Northbourne Advertiser* at every jubilee, smiling gamely in a party hat. He was surprised to find no signs at all of Cher or Collette, but he's tracked down Cher, now, or at least the tragic little FIND CHERYL FARRELL Facebook page, set up by social services, that seems to have been the only effort anyone's made to find her. The page is almost eighteen months old and the sulky twelve-year-old (clearly the most recent photo anybody's bothered to take) face that stares out from it in school uniform is barely recognisable. Cheryl Farrell was a thickset black kid with frizzy black hair rubber-banded into two bunches like horns on the top of her head. She looks nothing like the leggy, brown-skinned girl with the corkscrew curls who's slumped on a deckchair in the garden.

He feels that he knows them all better after their shared experiences. He's certain, now, rather than suspecting, that Collette is on the run from someone, and that all of them are ready to be told what to do, as long as it keeps them off the radar. He watched their faces as he spoke last night, saw the ill-masked gratitude on each of them as he took control, and he knows that they will do anything he wants. I'm their friend now, he thinks. They used to avoid me when they saw me, find reasons why they had to be elsewhere. But now I'm their saviour. After tonight, when it's all over and everybody's home and safe and they're counting their blessings, I'll be one of them. I'll be included. The dad of the house, where Vesta is the gran.

I've had a lucky escape, really. They're never going to speak, never going to tell. They'll clear it all away, and I'll be more careful, safe again to be with my girls.

He turns back into the room, feeling light-hearted for the first time in what feels like years. He has things to sort out – not least how to dispose of the contents of the freezer, now the blender's out of the question – but he feels he's been given his life back once more.

The girls sit side by side on his little sofa, a man-sized gap between them. Nikki's come out beautifully from her forty days of sleep. A little wrinkled, and her mouth slightly further open than we would ideally like, but otherwise she's perfect. They sit together peacefully, wide eyes and curled hair and shiny painted nails, and wait for him. He checks his watch: it's four o'clock, the party's in full swing and everything downstairs is under control. Tonight, once it's dark and the guests have gone and the lights are out and the trains are no longer running, there will be work to do, but for now a lazy afternoon rolls itself out before him.

He lowers himself gently on to the sofa between his lovelies, and slips a hand into one of each of theirs. Rests his head against the cushions and looks from one to the other, captivated by their quiet beauty. It's shaping up to be a wonderful summer.

Chapter Thirty-Three

When they open the boot, the smell – shit and Camembert and nail-varnish remover and toasted durian – explodes from the confined space as though it's alive. It wraps itself round them like a fog, makes them gasp and choke, hands over their mouths to force the sounds back in. Collette's eyes blur with tears. She looks wildly round, sees that they are pouring down Hossein's face, too. Thomas has taken his glasses off, is polishing them, ferociously, on the hem of his shirt. Only Cher remains impassive. Just stands there with something akin to a sneer on her face. She jerks her head impatiently, steps forward and takes hold of the plastic sheet.

He's crammed into the small space like batter. This afternoon he was rigid with rigor, but twelve more hours of sweaty heat in the airless shed, and it has passed. He slid in bonelessly, and settled like cake mix into a tin.

But getting him out is like wrestling jelly. Limbs and hair and belly, great slabs of thigh and lolling head sliding about in the confines of the boot, refuse to afford them any traction. They struggle for a minute, silent for fear of waking the neighbours, elbowing each other and tying their arms in knots like the Keystone Cops, but the Landlord is stuck fast.

Thomas lets out a tiny hiss, grips Collette by the upper arm. He shakes his head and gestures to her to move back. She obeys, meekly. She's amazed and relieved by the way Thomas has taken on authority, delegated tasks – just known what to do while the rest of them were floundering in panic. She taps Cher on the elbow, jerks her thumb towards her chest to tell her to move.

Thomas stands with one hand on the boot lid, looking down at the body as though it were a logic puzzle. Then, with a single, smooth movement, he lays his hands on one corner of sheeting and hauls upwards. Like an extra in *The Walking Dead*, Roy sits up in his plastic wrapping, turns and flops over the lip of the boot, like a jack-in-a-box. Slowly at first, then faster, as his centre of gravity shifts, he slithers over the lip and on to the tarmac, like a great blue maggot.

They bump him down the steps, each crackle of plastic and scrape of a sole jerking them to a silent stop. We've come so far, now, thinks Collette. Please God don't let us get caught now. There's nothing we can do but go forward. She wishes they could hurry, but they can't afford to get careless. Four people and a stinking corpse: there's no way you can talk yourself out of that one. By the door, Thomas shuttles through the bunch of keys they fished from Roy's damp pocket, looking for the one that opens it. Collette climbs back up a couple of steps and scans the street. Any moment now it's going to fill with a posse of torch-bearing householders, she knows it. A light will come on, then another light, then a voice will ask what they're doing, and ...

And then the door is open. Thomas bends and starts to drag

Roy through. Collette rushes down the steps and joins the others.

It's a night of smells. She can feel that they've come straight into a room; a stuffy, hard-surfaced room that smells of frying and onions and sweat and stale alcohol, just like the Landlord himself before other, stronger, smells took over. Laminate floor beneath her feet, some sort of storage unit to her right; nothing that soaks up sound anywhere near, just the dull echo of their panicked breathing, the shuffle of their feet.

The weight dragging on her shoulders gets suddenly heavier, and she realises that Thomas has dropped his share of the burden. She does the same, hears the Landlord's skull crack against the floor. The door closes.

'Where's the lights?' hisses Cher.

'Hang on.' He's speaking normally now, confident that they're not overheard. She hears him feel his way across the room to the window, and they are plunged in darkness as a blind is drawn down.

A hand slips into hers and squeezes. Over the smell of the room and the smell of the dead man, she catches a slight whiff off the clean, sandalwood scent of Hossein. He doesn't say a word, but she feels comforted, suddenly safer. She waits, calmer now, as Thomas works his way back to the door and feels around for the light switch.

He hits it, and they are bathed in light so bright that her hands fly to her eyes. When she opens them, she sees her three companions blinking, their features washed out, pale with fear and tiredness, eyes wild as they check out their surroundings. Cher still holds on to her corner of the plastic. Lets go as she realises that she is the only one. She looks around her, at the lair of her tormentor, and voices her judgement.

'Fucking hell. What a shithole.'

Collette looks around. It's quite a large room, the width of the building and probably half its depth. Walls that were probably once magnolia, favourite choice of property developers everywhere, but which have started to turn sepia with age, greasy black marks all around the light switches where he's groped around in the dark and never used a wet wipe.

A featureless, joyless room. She guesses, from the lack of embellishment, that it was converted at the height of the 1980s extra-dry Chardonnay boom, when everyone liked to think that they craved a minimalist lifestyle and forgot that they would need storage to achieve it. It's a bachelor pad, she thinks: a real one, not the style palaces you're supposed to imagine when you hear the phrase. A place that's lived in by a man who's never bothered to make it attractive, because that's what *women* do. He's just bought things as he's gone along and dumped the old ones in the corner.

There's barely a thing in here that a normal person would call furniture. Her small bedsit is opulent by comparison. How long's he lived here? she wonders. It could be any time at all, but judging by that pile of stereo equipment over where the fireplace must have been once, it's decades. He's bought stuff and put it down, and never thought about finding something to put it on.

In front of her stands a sofa. Tubular legs and black leather, the chrome chipped and smeared and the cushions sagging deep in the middle, the imprint of ten thousand nights watching one or other of the three televisions that sit opposite, wired up, it seems, to a DVD player, a video player and a Sky box. Why a man would need more than one telly, she'll never know, but she's not a man. Between them, with just a foot-wide gap from the sofa so that no one on it would have to stretch to reach it, there's a black-painted MDF coffee table with a smoked glass surface. Yes, the 1980s, she thinks. He bought the flat off the developer, went to MFI and got some man-stuff, and hasn't done a thing since. The walls are lined with a hotchpotch of storage: metal shelves of the sort you find in a garage and those dark-veneer dressers that were all the rage before IKEA invaded with its palette of birch. A few cushions that he's used for comfort rather than decoration on the sofa, and a polyester blanket, also in black. In the gaping space where a table should be, an exercise bike and what looks like it might once have been a rowing machine; souvenirs of moments long ago when Roy Preece thought he'd get fit and find a wife, but has long since adapted into laundry storage. On the shelving, row upon row of media. Videos, furthest away, then piles and piles of DVDs, no pretence of order or caring how they look. Most of the cases are blank, but she can see from the glimpsed covers of the few pre-printed ones that the Landlord hasn't been watching chick-flicks as he's lain on that sofa. She can see cocks and breasts and buttocks from where she stands. Mostly breasts.

Hossein takes them in with a look of elegant disgust. Looks down at the coffee table. It's strewn with the litter of a bachelor's neglectful existence: aluminium takeaway cartons with traces of curry still clinging to the sides, a half-eaten kebab in its polystyrene box, screwed-up chip paper, a scatter of cardboard boxes, a collection of remote controls, an Android tablet in silver chrome, a bottle of baby lotion, a box of Kleenex. Poking out from beneath, she sees a bin liner, half-full with more of the same. He looks politely away, as though doing so will somehow spare the dead man his shame.

Cher voices what they're all thinking. 'Eugh,' she says. She looks down at the shrouded form at her feet and pulls a face.

Don't, thinks Collette. Don't say it. We're all thinking about it already. We don't need to talk about it.

'Three tellies,' Cher says. 'What the hell did he want with three tellies?'

'I don't know,' says Collette.

'You don't think he used to watch 'em all at once, do you? Eugh, *God*.'

'That's enough, Cher,' she says, firmly. She really doesn't want to think about it.

Cher looks thoughtful. 'I don't suppose ...' she begins.

Collette knows where this is going. 'No. We're not taking anything.'

'But I *need* a telly,' says Cher. 'You *know* I need a telly.'

'I said no,' Collette says, and she suddenly thinks, oh, God, I sound like her mum. She'll be telling me she's sorry she was born in a minute.

'But—'

'No, Cher,' says Hossein. 'I'm sorry. No. It's not going to happen.'

Cher looks thunderous. Looking at her now, Collette can totally believe that she's fifteen. Her veneer of worldliness is paper-thin when it comes down to it. She's in the middle of committing a crime, and she's practically thinking about nail varnish and mascara. 'Right,' she says, in that you'll-be-sorry voice she remember from her own teens. She chucks her chin in the air and pulls a face. 'Come on, then. We haven't got all *night*.'

Before anyone else can move, she strides over to the body and yanks on the loose end of the plastic wrapper. The Landlord rolls out like a genie from a carpet, bumps up on his side against the wall, comes to rest staring at their feet. His eyes have clouded over and his skin, scrubbed clean with the power jet before they put him in the car, has begun to turn grey.

Cher starts to fold up the plastic, all business now she's starting to feel safe. 'Come on, then,' she says, and starts towards the door.

'Hang on,' says Thomas.

Cher stops. 'What?'

'We can't leave him like that,' he says.

Cher puts her hands on her hips. 'It's a bit late to come over all respect-for-the-dead,' she says. 'We had to squash him down to get him into that boot.'

'No,' says Thomas, 'it's not that. Look at him.'

For a moment, they all look. A blubbering whale of a man lying against a skirting board, his eight chins dipping into the neck of the green T-shirt Thomas had gone and bought him. A swollen tongue protrudes from slack white lips and his feet and shins are covered in rough, flaking skin where his circulation had begun to fail.

'What?' asks Cher.

'Look at his colour.'

They look. Grey-white on the front and then, they notice, red on the back. From what they can see of his skin, where cloth has rucked up and flesh has burst out, Roy's gone two-tone. He's turned into a Battenberg: all spongy-pale on one side and pinky-purple on the other. He looks like someone's stood over him with a rolling pin and tenderised him from top to bottom.

Cher shakes her head and frowns. 'What the fuck is that?'

Hossein clears his throat. 'Livor mortis,' he says.

'Liver what?'

'Livor mortis,' he says. 'It's when the blood settles after death.

It doesn't stay in the veins, it … comes out. It makes the flesh turn that colour, where it settles.'

'Christ,' says Cher, 'how the fuck do you know a word like that?'

'It's Latin,' says Hossein. 'It's the same in any language.'

'Okay,' says Cher. 'So what do you want me to do? Get out my make-up?'

Hossein shakes his head. 'Thomas's right. We can't leave him like that.'

'Go on then, professor. Why not?'

'When they find him—'

'*If* they find him.'

'They *will* find him eventually, Cher,' he says. 'And when they do, they'll know he's been moved.'

'How?'

'Blood follows gravity,' he says.

'You're in Britain now,' she says. She always gets rude when she's feeling ignorant. It's a defence system she learned long ago. 'Speak English.'

'Wherever is the lowest bit, that's where the blood goes. When you die. It doesn't just stay where it was.'

'Oh,' she says.

'So they're going to know he was on his back,' he says. 'So they'll know someone moved him.'

'So what? They're not going to be thinking it was a heart attack with that dent in his head, are they?'

'No, they're right,' says Collette. 'If we leave him like that, they'll know it wasn't a burglar. They'll know he didn't die here.'

'They'll know he didn't die here anyway, won't they?'

'Why?' asks Thomas.

'*Doh*. No blood.'

'Skin's not broken on his head,' says Thomas. 'Did you notice him bleeding at Vesta's?'

'No.'

'Well, then.'

'Come on, then,' says Collette. 'Let's roll him over.'

Chapter Thirty-Four

Sunday. Vesta has always liked Sundays. She likes the way the road is quiet, the way the house tends to start its life and noise mid-morning. Her Sunday routine is always the same: a lie-in till nine o'clock, a nice breakfast of poached eggs on Marmite toast followed by Sung Eucharist at All Saints church on Norwood Road, a glass of sherry at the social in the vestry, then a quick diversion into Morrisons on the way home to see what's in the reduced fridge. By two o'clock, they've often decided that the Sunday-lunch crowd has passed and have reduced the few remaining joints to half price. It's one of the nice things about nowadays – that joints come in all sizes, including spinster-size. She likes to spend Sunday afternoons pottering about the kitchen, doing a bit of baking, making sure everything's in shape for the coming week and looking forward to her dinner.

This Sunday, she wakes at six and smells the drains – Hossein has cleared them, but it will take time before the lingering aroma disperses – and it all comes crashing down on her head. Two nights ago, I killed a man, she thinks. I can't go to church in a state of sin. I can't mix with those good people, take the host, laugh over the cheese straws any more. It's all over. Everything I knew before has gone.

She lies on her back in her single bed and stares dry-eyed at the ceiling. This ceiling, the cracks slowly growing across it, has been the first sight to greet her each day for the best part of the last thirty years. It has been her safety and her contentment. Not a big life, but a good one, with all the never marrying and the no kids and the moments of loneliness. It's been a better life than many, and I've lived it as well as I could. And now it's gone. For ever.

I shall never feel happy here again, she thinks. I've lived here all my life, and now my home is gone.

She sits up and pulls on her dressing gown. Might as well get up, she thinks. No point lying here. That's not going to get any parsnips buttered.

The sound of the phrase in her head causes her a sudden wrench of sadness. It's one of her mother's phrases, the slightly skewed clichés that have slid into her own vocabulary without her even really noticing. Needs must when the devil dances. Where there's muck there's muck. Don't listen to him; he's the devil's apricot. Whenever she says them, even in her own head, she hears them in her mother's voice, and she's right back, just for a moment, in the room with her. Her lovely mother. Her churchgoing, house-proud, lovely mother, flowered apron and steel-grey hair. She would be so ashamed of me, she thinks. So ashamed of what has happened in her home.

And then the tears come.

Collette can't sleep. She has to go and see Janine as usual today, keep up the routine, behave, as they have all agreed, exactly as they normally would. And she hopes that one day, if she goes often enough, Janine will remember her. But today will exhaust her. She's been awake all night, and barely slept yesterday, and she feels as though the calcium has been sucked from her bones; that the slightest jar will make her simply shatter.

I should go, she thinks. I should just pack up and go. It's not like she even knows who I am, like it makes the slightest difference to her that I'm here. All I'm doing is turning myself into a sitting duck. But, oh, God, if I could talk to her one more time. If I could just see her eyes light up when she sees me, know that she remembers who I am. She wasn't a bad mum, she really wasn't. She didn't mean to be. I've spent so much of my life blaming her, but there were good times, too. In between the uncles and the new dads and the 'he took your lunch money', there was us, and we loved each other. It's not her fault that I got ideas above my station, decided to shortcut my way to a decent income. And now I've been gone three years. I abandoned her when she really needed me, and I can't leave her to die alone.

She remembers a good time, back when she was Lisa, and small: when they went to Margate on holiday: one of those cut-price deals from one of the newspapers. Janine went to the library and snipped the coupon every day for three weeks, and they had a chalet in a holiday park. And it was sunburnt shoulders and Janine sitting with the other mums as she went on the slides and the roundabouts, and teaching her to swim in the great big communal pool, and she remembers watching her mum stand up and sing 'Stand By Your Man' at the talent competition, and she got every single note bang on, and she looked so golden and glittery and Lisa felt so proud she could have exploded. I can't leave her, she thinks. I can't. No one should die alone. And if I'm not going to leave, where would I go other than here? Where else would I find, where nobody wants to know who I am, where nobody's writing me down and making a record?

But they'll find you. You're mad, being in London, even for a short while. If Tony doesn't find you, DI Cheyne will, and that's pretty much the same thing, just more circuitous. He wants me because he knows *she* wants me, and *she* wants me because she thinks I'm the way to send him down, but either way, I'm fucked. You just have to look at News International to know how leaky the Met is. And once he knows I've dobbed him in, no amount of witness protection will keep me safe. I need to leave. I have to. It's the only way I'll stay alive.

But Janine, she thinks. I can't leave her. I can't leave my mother till she's gone.

Hossein lies pinned to his bed and weeps for his dead wife. It's nearly five years since she went out to her women's group meeting and never came home, and each day, still, he wakes and weeps when he finds she isn't there. The basic story is no mystery to him: it will have been the Secret Police that took her and the Secret Police that never sent her back. The rest of it he will never know, and the pain of that is often more than he feels he can bear.

He speaks to her, sometimes, in his empty room, as though doing so will somehow bring her back. He says her name: '*Roshana, Roshana, Roshana*', like a magical incantation. And when the room stays silent, when no soft voice speaks in return, he bends double with pain in his bed, grinds the heels of his hands into his eyes and sobs for the lost past.

I had rather, he says to her ghost, I had rather it had been me. I had rather we went together, that I had followed you. If I'd known how it felt without you, I would have died in your place, my love. I'm sorry. I'm sorry. I loved you so much, and I couldn't protect you. My brave, my beautiful. My Roshana.

It's been over a year since he moved here from the asylum centre, and it's better, it's undoubtedly better, but the room is cheerless and he has never found the will to improve it. He thinks of their flat in Tehran, the family things, the rugs and pottery, the roses she grew on the balcony, high above the trees on Khorasan, and wonders what she would think of these sad cream walls, the dark blue bedclothes, the two pots that constitute his kitchen.

Two photos are all he has left: two photos from a life built together; all that managed to make it to the end of his journey. A formal shot of their wedding day, the two of them so young, side by side on an ornate throne, their hands entwined, as they waited to take their place at the sofreh-ye aghd and begin their feast. The other, his favourite shot of her, is wrinkled from travelling all the way here next to his heart. In it she leans, in western clothes – palazzo pants and a crisp white blouse with a frilled lace collar that stood up all the way to her earlobes – on a white balustrade by the Caspian Sea, a stiff breeze blowing her thick hair into her eyes as she turns and smiles at him. Roshana, free of the *chador*, is taking the risk of being observed to feel the air on her skin, her soft brown lips, her strong features, her elegant hands. The gold earrings she wears in it, her wedding ring, all gone and nothing left. He's carefully framed the pictures, preserved them from harm, and still, four years on, he cannot look at them without a wrench in his heart.

I must live, he thinks. There is no alternative. I won't be here, trapped in this waiting limbo, for ever. One day my application will reach the top of the pile. Day by day that day moves closer, but then what shall I do? What is there for me? No book I write, no speech I make, no plans, journeys, demonstrations will ever bring you back. If we'd had a child, Roshana … They say the pain fades with time, but time does nothing but make the ache sink deeper. I miss you. Oh, I miss you. If you were here with me …

Cher can sleep anywhere; it's a skill she's had to learn. She came home soon after dawn, climbed under her single sheet in the morning coolness and dropped off immediately, and the cat slunk in to join her as she slept. She sleeps, and sleep heals, but in sleep they also come back. You can escape anything, she has found, except when you're dreaming.

She mutters in her sleep. Her frozen muscles strain to run, strain to fight. Sometimes, when she wakes in the early afternoon, she is sore and aching, as though she's run a marathon.

A slight breeze stirs her thin curtains and cools her boiling forehead. Inside her head, she's back in the attic. She's found her way into the Landlord's cupboard again, and climbed those stairs, and she's in among the dust-motes and the shrouded furniture. Only this time, her nanna's furniture is there. She can see the old familiar shapes, and wants to weep: the Welsh dresser with its display of mismatched china, cast-offs of dinner services that have passed out of Big House fashion, the squashy settee with the shiny flowered fabric that Nanna kept for best. The little varnished pine table that sat against the wall in the kitchen, where Cher ate every meal, the wall clock with the painted convolvulus on the face behind the hands. The Venus bird bath from her nanna's bungalow garden, the goddess cradling a conch shell in her arms rather than stepping half naked from it, the collection of whimsical pigs that cluttered every surface.

And Cher is hiding, under a dust sheet under a table, because she's heard her father's tread on the stairs and it's where her nanna's told her to hide. Don't come out, she's said. Don't come out for anything. I've called the police and they're on their way. Just don't come out.

Cher lied to Collette on Friday night. She does know who her father is. And she knows where he is, as well. He's in jail for killing her nanna.

Oh, no, she mouths silently into her stuffy bedroom. Oh, no, no, no. Not again. Not Nanna. Oh, save me. Her hands creep up to cover her face and, in her sleep, she rocks.

They don't even bother to talk, in her dreams, now. When Cher was twelve, there was plenty of talk. There was shouting from her father and pleading from her nanna. There was his name, over and over again. Danny. Oh, Danny, don't do this. Come back when you've not been drinking and maybe then you can see her. But in the years that have passed, each time she relives it, the overture gets shorter. Now it goes straight to the main event. Her nanna's black shoes, the little heel, the crossbar strap, and his trainers, grey from the rain outside, striding across the parched floorboards to stand in front of her.

And then the noises. The dull, hard crack of fist on face. And over and over, her nanna's heels raised off the ground, kicking helplessly as he holds her like a punchbag. Her nanna saying his name over and over *Danny, oh, Danny, no Danny, Danny please*. Cher pokes her fingers all the way into her ear canals, but still she hears when the punches turn crunchy, and when they turn pulpy. And then the feet stop kicking, and she sees the ankles crumple as he drops her. Her nanna slides down on to the kitchen floor, and her face hits it with a wet slap because her arms have no strength to break the fall. And she's not her nanna any more. She's a weird mask of blood and broken bone, and all her teeth are gone. But still, as he pulls his foot back to kick – the trainers spattered red now, blood soaked deep into the laces – she raises a finger to her broken lips and gazes at her with her broken eyes.

And her dad's voice. Calm as a tea party. 'You can come out now, Cheryl,' he says. 'Daddy's here.'

Under her sheet, Cher claws at the air and mouths a silent scream. And then the dream passes and she curls around her cat.

It's so strange, thinks Thomas, how a single experience can change the way you feel about someone for ever. Five days ago, she was just the stupid little girl downstairs. Loud-voiced, tactless, a bit tarty, always in trouble – and now he sees her. *Really* sees her, for the first time.

She's like me, he thinks. She was the only one among them who really stayed calm. I can't believe she's so young. So young, and unprotected, and she handled herself like a queen. Even when I found her broken in the street, there wasn't a tear. Not a moment's hesitation, not a sign of fear. She just did what needed to be done, and she did it well.

He sits in his armchair and drinks his coffee. He used to enjoy Sundays more, when he knew that there was a Citizen's Advice day coming up next day. But now it's just another day among the others in a life spent waiting for the two days when he has a function in the world. These budget cuts haven't only sliced away protection for the vulnerable: they've sliced away his own sense of self. That's all he's ever wanted to be: a good neighbour, a helpful friend, a citizen who makes a contribution. I've certainly done the first this weekend, he thinks, and the second. Please, God, let me make it a hat-trick this week.

She's pretty, he thinks. When she's not done up in those bright fake colours the young are so keen on these days. When her hair's just loosely piled on her head and she's forgotten about make-up, she's a real natural beauty. That lovely skin: so smooth, so flawless – well, it was, and I'm sure it will be again, when it's healed – apart from the little smattering of freckles across her snubbed little nose. It's the perfect shade of tawny. How lucky, he thinks. She's not had much of a start in life, but at least she's got looks.

It's another golden, twinkly day, a welcome breeze stirring the leaves of the shady chestnut tree. His girls face him on the sofa, both dressed in green. A good summer colour: dignified, sophisticated. Nikki's dress is a vibrant lime. An unlikely choice on a redhead, but it really works; brings out her golden highlights and makes her eyes shine. Marianne's back in her olive silk, his favourite dress of all. She looks so elegant when she wears it. So calm and poised, so ...

... dry.

Thomas sits forward and two lines appear between his eyebrows. He's been too busy to give the girls their full share of attention this weekend, but Marianne is looking distinctly desiccated. The skin over the décolletage, where the elegant bones have always given her supermodel status in his eyes, looks distinctly flaky. He puts his coffee down and goes over to look more closely. Marianne gazes placidly at him as he bends to study her breastbone. Yes. He can't remember when he last looked this carefully, but the skin is rougher than it used to be. It's scaly, like a snake beginning to shed its skin.

Chapter Thirty-Five

She always holds it together when she's in the room, and when she's coming out past that sour-faced bitch on the reception desk, with her judgements and her pointed stapling, and maybe her careless way with a phone number, but seeing Janine wrings tears from her every day. The empty face, the faded skin, the oxygen tube clamped to her face and taped there to stop her wandering mad hand from ripping it out. God knows, Janine, I've resented you, but I've never wanted to see you like this.

When she steps into the sunlight, she wants to scream at the sky. That's my mum. My mum. The party girl. The good time had by all. How can she be like this? How can it have happened? Oh, God, how can she not know me?

She wants to break things and rip her hair out, but each day she straps on her dignity as the tears stream down her face and she walks away from those cold receptionist eyes. Don't look back. Don't look. Just keep walking. One foot in front of the other. Steady as she goes. Willowherb and ragged robin, the edge of the road crumbled away into chalky soil. Keep walking. Just keep walking. She pulls her sunglasses from her bag and clamps them to her eyes. She's never wanted strangers to see her crying.

Janine is dying. They've told her as much. Every day, that heart beats less and the lungs fill up a little more. And she won't let me hold her hand. I see her fingers plucking, plucking, plucking at the tan plastic cover on her chair, and when I reach out to soothe it, she snatches it away, looks accusingly at me like I'm trying to hurt her. She hardly speaks any more. Just random mumbled syllables, mostly, her brain cells dying, dying away for lack of air. I want her to die, she thinks, but I don't want to lose her. Not like this. Not when I'm not allowed to say goodbye. Not when …

Malik is standing outside the Costcutter on Christchurch Road.

She's so wrapped up in her thoughts that she doesn't see him until she is almost upon him. Then something about his bearing – the slim Armani-clad body that she knows from experience is made of solid muscle – suddenly catches her eye, and she dives into the Venus bar and hides herself behind a potted palm.

Her heart hammers, and she hears the sound of the sea. Somewhere, a long way away, a clatter of glassware coming out of a dishwasher, a voice asking in a pointed manner if it can help. She turns and waves at the barman, and he shakes his head and turns away, rubbing at a wine glass with a cloth.

Collette creeps forward to the folding door. She's not even sure if it *is* him. His hair is different. When she last saw him, he had a buzz-cut. Now it's long enough to curl over his collar, swept back from his face with some product that glistens.

Yes, it's him, all right. She shivers, despite the heat of the day. What's he doing here? What the hell is he doing here?

Malik seems to be watching the road from behind his sunglasses, scanning it up and down with those laser-beam eyes.

The underground is a hundred yards away, but it might as well be a mile. She can't walk past him. She's changed, but not so much he won't recognise her if she's who he's looking for.

It might not be, Collette. It could be coincidence. London's full of Turks; there's practically one on every street corner. You don't even know if he *works* for Tony any more. For all you know, you're standing in his bar.

Yeah, she thinks. Want to test that theory?

'Can I help you?' the barman asks again. He's going to throw me out in a minute, she thinks. Walks across the wooden floor and buys a glass of Sauvignon. It's early to be drinking. The place is empty apart from two thirty-something women eating panini and wearing sunglasses. The barman silently pours her drink out, slides it across the counter.

'Meeting someone?'

'No,' she says. 'Avoiding someone.'

'Ah,' he says, and goes back to polishing his glasses. He's not interested. She's just another lush finding an excuse to start her day.

She walks back to the doorway. He's still there, still outside Costcutter, hands crossed over his crotch like a footballer waiting for a penalty, still looking. He scans the road like a Terminator: a slow 180-degree sweep up, down, up, down, the whole movement taking maybe ten seconds.

Look, the whole place is full of people, she thinks. What can he do?

Follow you.

She has to go. She knows that. It's only a matter of time before he changes his vantage point – he's not standing on the route from Sunnyvale to Collier's Wood underground for nothing. He's not waiting for a girlfriend.

Her hair has grown, and grown out, since they last saw each other, and she's stopped straightening it and let the natural curl come in. And she's put on weight. When you ran a bar full of twenty-year-old girls who took their clothes off for a living, keeping yourself awake on coffee and the odd line like everyone else, your natural weight quickly became whippet-like, but it was never a weight that she could have maintained while eating. She's gone up two full dress sizes since she left, though that still only makes her a twelve. And she's wearing flat sandals – he's never seen her in anything other than towering heels. From the back, she reassures herself, I look like a completely different person.

She counts as she watches his scanning technique. Yes, ten seconds. If she leaves as he reaches the apogee of his turning arc, she can get twenty, thirty feet down the road before his eyes hit her back. Far enough that he won't know her. Far enough that she'll just be another girl in the street. She walks down to the far side of the restaurant's bistro folding doors, puts her wine down untouched on a table, waits, counts and exits.

Don't show fear. They operate on fear. Just keep walking, normal pace, and don't look back. He's not going to try anything now, even if he does see you. Stay where there are people and you'll be safe. It's when they find out where you live that you're really in trouble.

She tells herself these things, but she only half believes them. She strides out along Christchurch Road, her footsteps unnaturally loud in her ears, as though she were in an echo chamber. Breathe. Breathe, Collette. They want you to be afraid. You get afraid, you get disorientated. You get disorientated, you make mistakes.

She hears his feet turn on the pavement and start to follow …

*

Drawn up by the mouth of Christchurch Close is a shiny black Beemer. Tinted windows, chrome accessories, undoubtedly this year's model. Totally Tony. She can see someone in the driver's seat, a darker shadow behind the dark glass. Unless Tony's had a change of staff, it's most likely the Albanian, Burim. Rough manners, an attitude that says he will settle any disagreement with a knife. Malik's number two, but never backward in coming forward.

They could take me now, she thinks. The two of them. Take a chance on it and flip me into that car in broad daylight. Where is he? Where's Malik? I wish I could risk a quick look; see how much he's caught up. He sounds so close. His heels click and scrape on the surface. Segs. She remembers that he always hammered metal segs into his shoes the moment he bought them. He said they made them wear better. It was only later that she realised that they also inflicted more damage if he felt a need to stamp.

She can't tell if the figure in the car has seen her. She dips her head and crosses the road. If Burim wants to get her, she's going to make him leave the car and give her warning. No silent electric slide of the window and a steel-hard hand shooting out to grab her wrist for him. She lifts her bag off her shoulder and puts it over her head so that the strap crosses her body. If she's going to have to fight, or run, she needs both hands free.

The sunshine is so bright that, even through her shades, it hurts her eyes. Step, breathe, step, breathe.

Away from the shops around the tube, there are fewer people on the pavement, but the road is filled with the blessed hum of noonday traffic. If they try to take her, they will be seen. She reaches the far-side pavement and stops to choose her direction. Go on to the bus stop, or go back? You might get past him, or he might just turn around and follow you down the escalator. These suburban stations are all but empty at this time of day. You'll be most likely alone on the platform with him, nothing but air between you and the track.

Okay. The bus. I'll take the bus.

They can follow the bus. I can take it to Tooting. It's always busy there, because of the hospital, and the market and the shops. Go to Tooting, get on the tube. If you cut through Sainsbury's, come out the back way, you might get there before he realises where you've gone.

She scans her possible routes home in her head. Maybe I should go into town. Victoria, Waterloo – they're both busy. Lots of places where buses and cabs can go and cars are forbidden. If I go up to one of those ... then back down to Clapham Junction. Busiest station in the country. When a train lets out there, that long, long tunnel beneath the tracks is like *28 Days Later*. If Malik's following, I can change to another platform before he's even seen where I've gone. Hide in one of the shops. Go out the exit where the cars drop off: most people don't even seem to notice it's there as they rush up towards the main barriers. Yes. Clapham Junction. If I'm lucky, I can get the Northbourne train first time.

And if you're not, you'll lead him straight to your front door.

Ahead, she sees a bus approaching. The stop is a hundred yards away, no distance at all. The display on the front says it's going to Wimbledon, but it's single-storey, which suggests that it might well take a long route to get there. But it's a bus, and that's people, and people are safety for now. Wimbledon's always busy, around the station. If he follows her now, she can lose him there.

Without looking over her shoulder, Collette takes to her heels and sprints.

Chapter Thirty-Six

'Excuse me!'

In another life, this woman would have run the WAAF. She has a natural built-in foghorn, a height and stature you only get from generations of plentiful meat. Thomas sits up to attention as she marches towards him wheeling her three-wheeled lightweight buggy, an OshKosh toddler straining to keep up without dropping its Peppa Pig. She gets within talking distance, but her tone stays the same, as though they are communicating across a playing field. She's got a touch of sunburn. That high medieval forehead, made higher by the sort of Alice band he hasn't seen since the 1980s, will be peeling later. 'Do you mind not feeding my dog?' she shouts.

He adopts his harmless smile and blinks at her, myopically. Chucks his new black spaniel friend behind the ear and lets it go. 'Molly!' she shouts. The dog, ignoring her, circles the bench on which Thomas sits a single time, sniffing the ground in the hope that he might have dropped a titbit, then comes back and sits at his feet, gazing up, expectantly.

'I'm sorry,' says Thomas. He puts his hands pointedly in his lap and says to the woman, 'It's just a bit of kidney. Nothing harmful.'

'*Molly!*' she shouts again. The dog ignores her. Its eyes plead until he sees the whites at their edges. 'Yes, but she's on an all-*natural* diet, you see,' she informs him, staying ten feet away, as though she is nervous of getting closer.

The common is full of sunbathers and picnickers and joggers and drinkers, the way it has been all summer long. On a day like this, when a twenty-foot gap from your nearest neighbour feels like luxury, she stands no chance at all of coming to harm unless she eats a hotdog from the unlicensed wheelie-cart, but there's a type of woman who revels in their sense of vulnerability, he's noticed. Somehow the thought that someone could want to harm them makes them feel special.

'Nothing more natural than a nice bit of kidney,' he says, and smiles his most endearing smile.

The toddler starts to approach and she yanks on its harness reins and hauls it backwards, presses it, unwillingly, against her thighs.

'It's not preserved or anything,' he says. 'It's just kidney. I'm clearing out the freezer. Didn't want it to go to waste.'

The woman snorts. 'Molly eats chicken breast and rice and vegetables,' she says. 'Not *offal*.'

'No dairy?' he teases, and she looks horrified. Then he sees her suspect that he might be taking the mick, and looks affronted.

'Anyway, please don't feed her,' she says again, trying to wrest back the control. Hello, Narcissistic Personality Disorder, he thinks. Even your *dog* is special. 'Would *you* like someone else feeding *your* dog?'

Thomas considers the question, thinks that he probably

wouldn't mind that much, then thinks that this might well be the wrong answer, so settles for apologising again. 'She's a lovely dog,' he tells her. 'Ever so friendly.'

She accepts the compliment without much grace. 'Come *on*, Molly!'

Thomas shoos the dog away, and it sulks over until it is close enough for her to clip its lead to its collar. She jerks the lead a couple of times, irritably, then starts to walk off towards Station Road. The toddler stays for a moment, chewing Peppa Pig's crusty ear and staring at him. He can't tell if it's a boy or a girl, but doesn't suppose it matters either way. It will quickly learn to be whatever Mama wants it to be, if it has any sense of self-preservation. He gives it a four-finger wave and it turns on its heels as its mother gives another tug on its reins.

Thomas sits back and extends his arms along the back of bench. Turns his face to the azure sky and enjoys the late afternoon. Never mind. There'll be another one along in a moment. It's Northbourne Common. All the dogs of Northbourne have come to love Thomas over the past few days. He's the man with the treats. The special titbits, carefully selected from the choicest of cuts. He can't believe he didn't think of this before.

As he has predicted, he doesn't have to wait long. The postwork *passeggiata* is in full swing and the park is a sea of dogs. He tosses a sliver of heart in the path of a Jack Russell, a choice slice of liver beneath the questing nose of a Weimeraner.

The Egyptians believed that the dead needed their internal organs with them, if they were to survive the afterlife. Once they were removed from the bodies, they were stored in canopic jars, preserved in herbs and honey and sealed with resin, and stored close at hand for when they were needed. Thomas is a man of the age of science. He knows that his girls are going nowhere.

And the Ancient Egyptians didn't have blenders, or refrigerators with freezer compartments.

At first, he thought that this new method of disposal might be a nuisance – the weekly defrost-and-blend ritual had seemed so *convenient*. But he's discovered that it's quite the opposite. He really enjoys his sojourns in the park. It gets him out of the house, into the fresh air, provides a seemingly endless opportunity for social moments. The flat has been feeling oppressively small for the past few days, especially now he's started to fall out of love with Marianne. He doesn't like the sense of reproach about her peeling skin. Feels like he's being judged and found wanting. It's not *my* fault, he thinks, resentfully. It's this bloody weather. Drying everything out. Just look at the lawns in this park: it's like the Gobi desert.

His hand brushes a hard edge of cold metal and he looks to see what it is. It's a little plaque, brass, screwed firmly to the cross-strut. 'In loving memory of John and Lizzie Brewer,' it reads. '1922–96, 1924–2005. They loved this park.'

That's sweet, he thinks, running his finger over the lettering, while at the same moment a suffocating feeling of melancholy washes through him. That was all I ever wanted, he thinks, a bit of love, a bit of lifelong companionship. It can't be that hard. You just have to look at all the nonentities strolling hand-in-hand to see that. Why did it never happen to *me*? Every bench in this park has a plaque like that, put up by their children, mostly, or their widows or the friends who mourn them. Who's going to do that for me?

He shakes his head like the dogs he's been feeding, to shrug off the mood. Gets up and goes for a stroll past the bandstand, to leave it behind. There's a coffee stand there, and its owners have erected a small collection of tin tables and chairs in among the benches. It's where a lot of park regulars go, to meet and greet and pass the time of day. Thomas doesn't count as a regular, yet; he's only been coming here a few days. But he has hopes. One day, he's sure, someone will smile in recognition and give him the friendly nod.

A pair of dog walkers chats at the coffee stand, adding sweetener to their drinks, while their charges – three Scotties, a Pom, two pugs and a Dalmatian – mill about at the extreme end of multi-leads and sniff about at the base of a waste-bin. A perfect opportunity, right there. He potters over and empties the remainder of his bag in among them, enjoys the pleasure with which they wolf down the unexpected goodies, the shining eyes that turn towards him in search of more.

He squats down and scratches behind the Pom's neck ruff. It licks its lips and gives him a huge, foxy grin and he rewards it with a final piece of well-chopped tripe. It snarfs it up with a tail-wag so violent it almost loses it feet, and pants hopefully at him as he stands up once more. Thomas likes dogs. So trusting, so loyal. He sometimes thinks that, had he had another life – one where landlords allowed pets, for instance – he might not have had need of his girlfriends at all.

'Sorry, poppet,' he tells the friendly Pom. 'That's the lot for today. See you tomorrow, maybe?'

He walks back through the sunshine on the path to home. He feels no great need to dawdle. He'll be taking a walk every day this week. The freezer compartment is full to bursting, and he suspects that he might soon need to free up some room.

Chapter Thirty-Seven

She thinks it through and decides to go in the daytime. A teenager carrying a television through the streets in the dark is asking for a stop-and-search, whereas you can walk around with pretty much anything while the shops are open. She once carted a bike, with its lock still on, all the way from Twickenham to Kingston, and nobody even batted an eyelid. For sure, a casual-looking girl with no obvious signs of drug abuse carting a flat-screen under her arm will be fine.

Cher's thought and thought about that telly. She's never had a television of her own, never even had control of a remote. And God knows she's longed for one. A telly will make all the difference to her life, and the Landlord has three that he no longer needs. And besides, he owes her that much. That's what she figures.

She passes a couple of people in the street and smiles boldly at them. The trick is to always look like you belong; like you have a right to be wherever you are at the time. Look shifty, and people will assume that you *are* shifty. Fix them with a smile and cry out 'good morning', and nine times out of ten, in a city like this, they will shrug themselves into their imaginary coats and hurry by, mumbling an embarrassed greeting in return. The rest are either up to something shifty themselves, or they're a bit mad, so they don't really count.

She strides confidently to the Landlord's basement stairs and skips down them, pulling on her gloves. Fishes from her pocket the bunch of keys she lifted off Thomas in the car when they were on the way home, and leafs through them. She identifies them in no time. Can't believe it took Thomas so long, though she supposes it *was* dark when he was looking. They stand out from the Beulah keys because they're new, and shiny, and have more than three levers to them. She undoes the mortise, then turns the Yale and steps cheerfully inside.

In an instant she is gagging. She had remembered the smell from the boot, and had expected to have to make an adjustment, but eight days has magnified it so much that it takes her breath away completely. Her throat closes up and she feels her gorge rise. She's never smelled anything like this. The smell of ripe shit in Vesta's bathroom is like flowers in comparison. Her lungs don't seem to want to take this fetid air into themselves. They rebel each time she tries to breathe, let only tiny sips of it through before her epiglottis clamps down and everything stops.

How can the neighbours not smell this, she thinks. It's not possible. Maybe it's … God, I've never smelled anything like this. Nothing close to it. Maybe they just don't know what it is?

She switches the light on. Lets out a huge bronchial cough, the sort that can turn too easily into the gag reflex. But once it's out, she finds that she is able to breathe. Not normally, not by a long chalk, and she has to keep her lips clamped firmly closed, but enough that she doesn't have to flee the room.

The Landlord has been leaking. The floor is sticky with fluids.

They have spread outwards across the beech-look laminate by several feet, have stained the wall against which his right arm presses. Now the first wave of nausea has passed, she's interested. He's not her first corpse. But her mum and her nanna were freshly dead when she saw them, and she didn't have a lot of time to study them before they were swept up by forensics and taken away for autopsy, then given the old cosmetic beautification by an undertaker. By the time they were buried, they looked like waxworks. Overpainted, their features sewn up with clever threadwork into Mona Lisa smiles.

The Landlord doesn't look like that. Eight days has not been kind. His huge belly has swollen to the size of a Space Hopper and all his limbs have bloated. How it's not split open, she has no idea. It can only be a matter of time. In the places where, when she last saw him, his skin was grey-white, it is greenish, now, and mottled like a marble floor, the occasional patch of livid crimson breaking through where his skin seems to have started to literally slide off the fat beneath. The parts that were purple are lustreless ebony black. His T-shirt, stretched so tight that the seams are beginning to split, seems to be undulating. For a moment she thinks it must be some kind of optical illusion, until she notices something small and white, the size of a couple of grains of rice, work its way over his swollen lower lip and drop to the floor.

'Fucking 'ell,' says Cher.

She stays and looks for a bit, fascinated. Her body still fights to act out its revulsion, hitting her with sudden, convulsive throat spasms so that she has to keep her hand clamped over her mouth, but her mind is clear, and curious. She's always been inquisitive that way. If she'd learned to read really well and gone to a school where the staff had any ambitions for their students other than keeping them from rioting before playtime, she'd have been being encouraged into the sciences by now. So this is what happens when you get buried, she thinks. I'm bloody well getting cremated.

She spends a few minutes staring at the pullulating cloth, drinking in the detail – the wide-open, grey-misted eyes, like the zombies in *The Walking Dead*, the way that the fluid leakage seems concentrated around the head and, God help us, the flattened buttocks, the fact that the marble patterning – if it were a tattoo, say, or body paint rather than putrefaction – is almost pretty in its delicacy. I won't forget this in a hurry, she thinks. Shame there's no one I can tell about it, really. Probably not ever.

A car door slams in the street and snaps her from her reverie. She remembers the purpose of her visit, looks at her quarry. The big telly, the one she really lusts after, is situated directly over the corpse's head, its cord trailing through a pool of brackish goo. Maybe not, she thinks, and goes round the coffee table to the small screen on the other side.

It's a nice little apparatus, no more than a couple of years old. Silver casing and a Sony logo. Actually, this is better, she thinks. I'll have to move on at some point, when they find him or whatever, and that big thing's not exactly portable, is it? She bends down and unplugs it from the aerial socket, switches off the electricity and takes the plug from the extension adaptor on the floor. Stands on tiptoe to reach over the media cabinet below it and lift it from the wall-bracket on which it perches. It looks quite precarious, and she balances carefully to make sure not to drop it when it comes free.

It doesn't come free. Taken by surprise, Cher wobbles on the balls of her feet and has to grab the telly by its frame to prevent herself overbalancing. She swears under her breath – doing anything lungfully is ill-advised in her current circumstances – and drops down on to her heels, her damaged ankle letting out a shriek that reminds her that she still needs to take care. She bends down to look for a hook, or a latch, or some other piece of Japanese ingenuity that's lending the set stability. What she finds wrings another, louder word from her lips. A screw runs through a hole in the metal bracket, and is firmly embedded in the underside of the machine.

'Fuck,' mutters Cher. Might have known this wasn't going to be that easy, she thinks. Like the universe was ever going to cut me a break.

'You bastard,' she says to the bloated body, and could swear that it releases another gust of swamp gas in response. 'Bet you think you're having the last laugh, don't you?'

She stands up and glares round the room. Enough porn to power the Titanic, but nothing practical anywhere to be seen. The remains of a kebab on the table has gone green and sprouted fur. 'Eugh,' she says to the Landlord, 'you really were a filthy fucker, weren't you? If you'd put as much energy into walking as you did into wanking, you probably wouldn't look like that now.'

The Landlord doesn't answer. She tries the drawers of the media cabinet and finds little other than a bunch of unlabelled DVDs and those bunches of useless wires and plugs that seem to breed secretly in the dark places of every house.

'Bugger,' she mutters. She's going to have to go further into the flat to see if she can find anything to undo the screw with. A knife would probably do it. If he owns a knife. It doesn't look like he ate much that he couldn't eat with his hands.

Even with the bare light bulb on, the hall is dark, and stuffy. The two doors to her left and the one at the end of the hall –

hollow, unpanelled doors, seen-better-days white gloss paint, those old-people half-moon pull handles – are closed, and neither light nor air seep through. More of the same boring laminate, no embellishments other than a row of half full recycling boxes and a couple of grubby coats on hooks. A joyless sort of place, she thinks, as she walks up it to what she assumes will be the kitchen. Not exactly living for pleasure, was he? Apart from eating kebabs and fingering his privates.

She has all sorts of plans for the things she'll do with her home, when she gets on her feet at last, based on things she's seen through windows, or in the pages of magazines. If your life is made up of necessities, your head is filled with all the pretty shiny things that would make it complete. Pink paper lampshades. A collection of paper fans, opened out and pinned to the wall. Sari fabric draped round curtain poles. Floor cushions. A Tiffany lamp. One of those make-up chests that looks like a steamer trunk. A collection of slogan mugs hanging from hooks under a shelf full of tea caddies. A wall motto, spelled out in big gold letters. She's not sure what it will read, but she likes the look of them. A fake fur bedspread. Nothing slaggy, like animal print. Classy. Wolfskin. Or mink, maybe.

She finds it hard to imagine how someone with the sort of money the Landlord has – had – could live in a place that looks like a storage unit. Even with Vesta paying practically squat, he must have been taking in over a grand a week, and a lot of it – hers and Collette's, anyway – cash-in-hand, as well, so no tax. Cher can totally see why someone blessed with what she regards as footballer levels of wealth would fill their house with high-spec electronics, so she's not surprised by the televisions, but the rest of the flat, its sparse furnishings, its piles of redundant stuff that suggest that he was simply too lazy to take them to the dump, is a disappointment. She'd sort of imagined him sitting on a gold sofa, wearing a gold lamé tracksuit and fingering his gold pendant chains as he watched *Dallas* on a gold TV and sent texts from a mobile encrusted with Swarovski crystals. Instead it's chocolate milk bottles in plastic recycling boxes and a small collection of offcuts of timber stored along the hall wainscot.

The kitchen is a galley, lined on both sides with cabinets in the nineties Spaceship Interior style. Scratched stainless steel surfaces, chrome door handles, lino that's done up to look like those steel plates you find on walkways. I'd never have that, thinks Cher. Why would you have that? You'd never keep it clean, all those bobbles. Nobody would have a kitchen that looked like this if they meant to cook here. It's the kitchen of someone who lives on takeout.

Nonetheless, there are greasy plates piled up by the sink, and a rancid waste bin. She goes through the cupboards and drawers at lightning speed. Plates. Pint glasses. Cutlery: but the knife blades are thick, like kids' school knives. She doubts they'll fit in a screw head. Well, he must have a screwdriver somewhere, she thinks, or how did he screw it in in the first place?

She carries on. A bunch of pans that look inherited – pitted exteriors, handles with melt marks and scratches – and unused. A drawerful of spatulas. A cupboard so full of gas bills and council tax reminders that she has difficulty getting it closed again once it's open. A collection of tea towels that have the eerie look of souvenirs about them. Inherited again, she thinks. Like the apron and oven gloves that hang on the end wall. A cork pinboard to which two dozen delivery menus and a couple of minicab cards are fixed with drawing pins. Cleaning stuff. She raises her eyebrows at this. She's not seen much evidence that he uses it. A bucket with a grey old rag hanging over the edge. A pressure cooker. A slow cooker full of Tupperware lids. A toasted sandwich maker.

Nothing tool-like; nothing that will help her. She goes back down the hall, pokes her head into the bathroom. Mildew along the border of a glass shower screen, a hair attached to a bar of soap, a cardboard box on the toilet cistern stuffed with chemist drugs: laxatives, Immodium, Boots Soothing Heartburn Relief pills, cough mixture, Bonjela. She doesn't bother with more than a cursory look. No one keeps tools in the bathroom unless they've been doing work in there.

A flash of memory. The tool kit on Vesta's bathroom floor.

'Oh, shit,' she says, out loud. Her voice echoes off the tiled walls, mocks her. They took the kit down to the building site when they dropped off the remains of the damp proofing. Some Slovak will have most of it strapped round his waist by now.

She comes out of the bathroom, disconsolate. She's about to go back to the kitchen and try one of the knives when she notices the cupboard. It's a big cupboard that fills the space where the stairs up to the ground floor used to be. For some reason, she's taken the narrowness of the hall, the jink at the end, for granted, maybe because Vesta's basement hall is nar-rower, if anything. Ah, now, there you go, she thinks. I should've thought that even someone like him would have a Hoover hidden away somewhere.

It takes her a moment to work out how to open the door, picking at its seam with her fingernail, until she tries pushing on it, and it swings open. It's big enough and deep enough to house a cloakroom, if he had wanted one, though someone his size wouldn't have used it with any great ease. Instead, it's filled with more of the sort of junk that lies about the living room: arm and leg weights, an ironing board, an old record player and a box of vinyl records, the vacuum cleaner, an old fold-up director's chair. A series of narrow shelves on the wall just inside the door houses boxes of bits and bobs: light bulbs, screws, nails, super-glue, fuses, batteries: and on the floor, in the back, another toolkit box.

'Aha!' she cries, triumphantly. Dives on it joyfully, drags it into the light. It has one of those lids that split in two, and beneath that a plastic tray with more of the same crap as on the shelves in its little divided sections. She lifts it out and puts it on the floor, expecting to find the tools in the void beneath. Looks back in – and takes a huge, gasping breath.

It's not tools. It's money. Lots and lots of money. Ten and twenty and fifty pound notes, stacked neatly by denomination. Cher stares at it and her pupils expand. Cash that nearly fills the box. There must be thousands and thousands, here in the cup-board.

'Fuckin' Ada,' she says.

She can hardly bear to touch it, in case it vanishes like some fairy glimmer under her hand. Then she does, and feels that it is real, and sighs in astonishment. Looks guiltily over her shoulder, suddenly expecting someone to come in and find her here, and touches it again.

She sits down heavily on the hard, cold floor. She knows beyond doubt now what they mean by a rush of blood to the head. It really is thousands, she thinks. Thousands and thou-sands. That's why this flat is such a shithole, why everything looks like it's on the edge of falling apart: he's been socking the rent money away under the stairs.

She picks up a bundle of fifty pound notes. A generous handful, maybe three inches thick. Looks at it the way an ento-mologist would look at some insect species they'd heard about but never seen. The notes are real, all right. She has no idea how much money she holds in her hand, but she suspects that it might be more than has passed through them in the whole of her life to this moment. Lovely mellow reds, the queen serene and smug on one side, blokes in wigs on the other. Paper quality that feels like luxury itself.

I can't, she thinks. I can't. I mustn't. Oh, God, the things I could do with this. The things we could *all* do. But I can't. It would tip us over. What we've done already is wrong. I know that. But it's a wrong I can live with. It's a wrong that stopped a load of other wrongs. But this?

She fans the notes out, puts them to her face and sniffs them. They smell like – money. Wonderful money. Wonderful, wonderful money, root of all freedom. The only people who really believe the 'money doesn't buy you happiness' line are the ones who've never had to live without it.

Through the open door to the living room, she can see the melting corpse on the floor. A miserable life, a miserable death. No one to mourn him, no one to care. Died because he was greedy, in the end. Because his love for this stuff made him think an old lady's life didn't matter. And he didn't even get to spend it. Didn't enjoy his life. Just stashed it in a box and lived on his settee, watching other people live their lives on his TV screens.

Reluctantly, she puts the notes back on top of the pile. Strokes them, as though they were alive. They're someone else's, she thinks. Not mine. I'm not that person. If I take them, I'm all the things I ran away to stop myself becoming. Doing the things I do to keep the wolf from the door is one thing. I'd be doing this to chase down luxury. I'd be stepping over the line.

She can't stop herself from creaming half a dozen notes off the top. She's not a saint. Tucks them into her bra and feels better. Call it a rent rebate, she thinks. That's a couple of weeks' fags and groceries, some shoes and a good winter coat – compensation for the time I couldn't work.

She puts the tray back in and closes the lid. Pushes the toolbox back into the back of the cupboard. Someone will find it one day. Maybe they'll be honest, maybe they won't. But they won't be me.

She's been here long enough. If she doesn't get on with it, it will be rush hour by the time she gets back to Northbourne High Street, and she knows that, strangely enough, you sometimes stand out more in a crowd. People are more on their guard, more aware of potential threats, and the differences become more obvious. She closes the cupboard door and returns to the living room.

The TV taunts her, smug on its single screw. Ach, fuck it, thinks Cher. I may be doing the right thing, but I'm not *that* much of a bloody saint. She puts her hands on either side of the casing, braces one foot against the wall and rocks. After a couple of seconds, the rawlplugs in the wall give way and the TV comes with her, stand, plaster and all.

Chapter Thirty-Eight

He doesn't like to waste things, so he folds his Ziploc up into quarters and tucks it into his trouser pocket. The dogs on the common have benefitted from his presence earlier than usual today. It's always good to mix things up a bit, inject a bit of variety into one's life. And besides, Marianne is starting to get on his nerves. Having to look at that peeling décolletage is like living with a nag.

It's Wednesday, and his short working week is already over, at least until his half-day Friday. When he was working full time, he often bemoaned how few hours he seemed to have for himself. But now he has all the time in the world for galleries and museums, the cinema, for just sitting at a pavement table and watching the world go by, and he doesn't have the money to enjoy them. He can't even keep himself amused for long on the internet, because top-ups for his dongle seem to be getting more expensive by the day. Life on part-time wages involves a lot of television, a lot of supermarket cider and very few nights out. Not that his social life has ever been a whirl. Thomas has never understood why, but he seems to make people uncomfortable.

Even when the CAB was fully open, his colleagues often forgot to ask him when they were planning their after-work drinks, and after a few council meetings the furniture cooperative people could barely meet his eye when he talked.

Today he feels like a treat. His finances, after all, have eased a lot now the Landlord's dead and no one will be collecting rent for a while. The lunchtime rush is over, and Brasserie Julien will have finished its must-eat period. He fancies a cappuccino, lots of froth, chocolate on top, and a sit among the baby buggies. It's another bright day, and it'll be nice to watch the girls – so unself-conscious as they stroll the pavements in their thin summer dresses – from the shade of the brasserie's awning, the spillover of their air-conditioning cooling him from the open windows. After, he'll do a little food shop, pick up a four-pack and spend some quality time on the sofa with Nikki.

The High Street is its lackadaisical mid-afternoon self. It has its waves of busy – first thing in the morning and around the rush-hour – but the rest of the time you can see that London is still feeling the triple dip. People just don't go out to wander shops, even to browse, the way they used to. Too much danger that one might end up buying something. That's why Thomas stays at home. Art galleries are still mostly free to get in to, but a small bottle of water from one of their cafés quickly compensates for that. The brasserie seems to be the only business that does okay all day. It doesn't even bother to open until eleven, but it does a moderate-to-good trade from then right through to closing time, catering as it does for each market that washes through: the mummies coming home from the gym, the lunch crowd, the idle time-fillers like himself, the post-work drinkers and the embarrassed first-daters, all looking for somewhere to meet that doesn't have an edge of scary like most of the local pubs.

He's disappointed to see that all of the pavement tables are taken. One, though, at the end by the bookies, has only one occupant. A studious-looking woman, late twenties, he thinks, who's reading a Kindle with the sort of fierce concentration that suggests that she's not reading it at all. Stood up, he thinks, or filling time before a meeting. Whatever, she doesn't look like she'll be there long.

He goes up and asks if she minds sharing. She looks up and he sees that she's rather pretty: pixie haircut, overlarge eyes, a small but full-lipped mouth, a cute little pointed chin. If it weren't for the specs and the wrap dress, a cami underneath to cover the worst of her cleavage, she would look rather like a Manga character. I would dress her, he thinks, indulging an idle fantasy as he often does about women he encounters in the street, in a bustier and Capri pants. She has small breasts and what looks like a narrow waist under that blouse. Something to pull her in and hoist her up would be perfect.

He sees her consider him. 'I'm sort of waiting for someone,' she says.

'Okay. How about I move if – when – they come along? I so want to be outside today.'

She shrugs. 'Sure,' she says, and turns her chair side-on to the table to signify that she's not into conversing and looks back down at her screen.

He sits, waves at the waiter, who gestures back that he will be along in a minute. Thomas turns his own chair towards the street and crosses one knee over the other, mirroring her body language as in all the best NLP manuals. 'Beautiful day,' he says.

'Mmm,' she says, and doesn't look up from her reader.

'Sorry,' he says. 'Silly. Every day's a beautiful day at the moment.'

'Yes,' she says, and clicks the clicker to turn the page. Clicks the page-back button a second later. Thomas looks out at the street. Not a particularly endearing sight. They're opposite the Post Office sorting depot whose back wall faces out over the railway embankment's no man's land. It's square, yellow-bricked, featureless, with a wheelchair ramp up to the red metal doors where the undelivered parcel window lives. A woman walks past in a green jersey tunic and black leggings, gladiator sandals on her feet and a rough bun on her head. Leggings, he thinks, are the devil's work. Women think they hold them in, but they really don't. If anything, they *emphasise*.

He turns back to his companion. 'Good book?'

She looks up. 'Look,' she says, 'I'm sorry. I wouldn't have said you could sit down if I'd known you were going to try to talk to me. Sorry. But I'm not looking for friends.'

Thomas feels the blood rush to his cheeks as she looks down once again, pointedly, at her book. 'Sorry,' he says, plaintively. 'Only being friendly.'

She rolls her eyes and purses her lips. Picks up her coffee without taking her eyes from the reader and takes a sip. Plugs in her iPod earphones as a final dismissal.

Embarrassed, he gets up and leaves. He knows when he's not wanted. Well, actually, of course, he often doesn't. This is one of his problems. He grew up thinking that it was all about the men, that the women were just waiting to be chosen, and that all the men had to do was choose. It's been a terrible disappointment to discover that the rules are more complicated. He hurries off up the street once he's got a few paces from the table, keen to put space between himself and his humiliation. Reaches the Sunrise Café and sees that it's still open. Oh, well, he thinks. They probably do cappuccino too. Everywhere does, these days. And one of those Portuguese custard tarts. They're always good.

'Piss off,' says a voice beside him.

Thomas looks round, surprised. It seems such a random thing to have said. He sees a man, donkey jacket on despite the heat and combat trousers, glaring at a mousy woman in a loose tweed skirt, a formal white blouse and a lilac cardy. She's clutching a sheaf of leaflets, one sheet frozen in the air between them where she's clearly tried to hand him one.

'Sorry,' she says.

'You're allowed your beliefs,' he says, 'but stop trying to shove them down other people's throats.'

'I wasn't!' she protests. She has a Princess Diana haircut, circa New England Kindergarten, and a little crucifix on a chain round her neck. Lovely blue eyes, though, and a neck like a swan's. He peers to see what the leaflet says and catches a glimpse of a big black THE GOOD NEWS and a hand-drawn, childish cross. 'I was just—'

'Trying to talk to me about God. Yes. I know. And I don't care.'

'But I just—' she says.

'You people make me sick,' says the man, and knocks the leaflets from her hand. They cascade to the pavement.

Thomas sees his chance. Leaps across the gap between them and is sweeping them up in a moment, as the assailant is still making his way past to storm off up the street.

'Sorry, sorry,' says the woman. How the British love to apologise. 'Thank you. Sorry. Thank you.'

She has a high-pitched, schoolmistressy voice. A voice that's far older than she is. And beautiful skin. White as snow and faultless. Hypoallergenic soap and cold cream, he thinks. None of your modern cosmetic products. You only get that beautiful English Rose complexion from cold cream. Lovely skin. The sort of skin you want to touch, because you know it's not often been touched before.

'No, no,' he says. 'I'm sorry. There was no need for him to go all Dawkins on you like that. Totally unnecessary.'

He manages to collect the leaflets together, taps them back into shape. Yes, they're Christian leaflets. They have the name of the local evangelical church across the bottom. He occasionally sees them coming out of their barn-like building on a Sunday, pink-faced and pleased with themselves, the men in grey suits and V-necked sweaters, the woman dressed almost exactly as this one is now. He holds them out to her and she takes them with a grateful, bashful smile. 'You have to expect that sort of thing,' she says. 'Some people just don't want to hear the Word.'

'What "word" is that?' he asks, though he knows, and he sees hope spring into her eyes. She's clearly not been having much luck today, judging from the quantity of leaflets she still has left.

'I'm spreading the Word,' she says, emphasising the Word as though it's significant for its very existence, 'about our church.'

Thomas feigns interested surprise. 'A church? Well!'

'I don't suppose ... do you *have* a church already?'

He can feel little prickles of excitement under his clothes. Such beautiful skin. If I had her alone, I could touch it. 'Well, I ...'

'I don't suppose you even live around here,' she says, and looks disconsolate. It clearly doesn't occur to her that anyone who doesn't tell her to piss off might not be interested in God.

'Oh, no! No, I'm just ... it's funny I should bump into you,' he says. 'I've only just moved into the area, and ...'

'Oh! Where from?'

He thinks fast. The first name that comes into his mind pops out. 'Colindale.'

'Colindale! That's a long way!'

And I've never been there. That's why I picked it. No one from Northbourne has been to Colindale. It's at the far end of the Northern Line, and God knows the Northern Line's a hike from here.

'Yes. Yes, it is.'

Her skin is so pale it's almost translucent. It's as though she's never been out in the sun before. I can almost see the blood beneath your skin, he thinks. I can almost see your arteries.

'You must be a bit ...'

'Yes, it's not ... anyway, I've not found a church yet ...'

She looks as pleased as punch. 'So I'm preaching to the converted, then!'

'Hardly,' he says, and sees her look confused. 'Preaching – you weren't preaching. Heavens, what did you think?'

She laughs. Little white pearly teeth. Not rabbity at all, as he'd half-expected. As she does so, she tosses her head back and shows him her long white throat. Beautiful. He feels the prickle of his skin again. And so open. No wedding ring, he notices. No one waiting at home.

Chapter Thirty-Nine

Psycho has caught a beetle, and is torturing it on the lawn. Funny, thinks Hossein, how that cat always looks at his best when he's at his most vicious. He's all sheen and lean, long muscle, stalking the hapless insect on dancer's legs with a tail like a shepherd's crook, glancing up occasionally to check that his audience is still entranced.

'I'm sure that cat used to be called Toby,' he says.

'He did,' says Vesta. 'And before that he's been Snooki, and Bell-end, and all sorts. For a bit he was Mr Skwoodgy.'

'Mr Skwoodgy?'

'I know. I think you can probably guess what *that* lad was like.'

Hossein smiles. For a moment, with his almond eyes and his golden aura, he looks not unlike a cat himself. 'Psycho is better, I think,' he says.

'Yes. It suits him. Mind you, I don't think he cares *what* you call him, as long as you call him for dinner.'

'Talking of dinner,' he says.

'Yes,' says Vesta. 'I should get started, I suppose.'

But she doesn't move. Looks instead at the steps going down to her kitchen with a face full of sadness.

'It's all spoiled, you know, now,' she says.

'Oh, Vesta …'

'I know. I'm sorry. After all the work you've done and all the help, and all of you … the things you've risked for me … but I can't. Every time I'm in there, all I can see is …'

He glances at the fence that divides the garden from the Poshes'. It's not just walls that have ears. It's fences, too. Vesta sees his eyes move, and quietens down. 'Sorry.'

'Don't be; I understand.'

She looks at him with a face that says that no one will ever understand. 'I don't want to be here any more,' she says.

Hossein nods. 'I understand. After Roshana … even though none of it happened there, I couldn't be in the apartment any more. I kept seeing her. Disappearing round corners, standing on the balcony. Sometimes, places … they get poisoned.'

'But I don't know how to leave,' she says.

'You just … leave, Vesta. People do it all the time.'

'"People" aren't nearly seventy. With no money and almost no savings, and the only thing they've got that's of any value at all is a secure tenancy. If it weren't for the secure tenancy, I would have left years ago.'

He's silent for a moment, thinking. 'So in a way, it's been a prison, not a blessing?'

She starts, as though this is the first time she's ever thought of it. 'Well. God … Stupid, isn't it?'

Hossein shrugs. 'Most of us are. It's human nature, to stay. Change frightens us because we don't know what will happen. You see it all the time in countries that are being held hostage as much as people. Most people have to get to a point where they don't have a choice before they'll change something. I read once that we're more afraid of change than we are of death, and I can believe it.'

She looks at him shyly, this man who's crossed the world. 'Where would you be, if you had a choice?'

He sighs. 'I'm tired, Vesta. Tired of being sad, tired of being afraid for the future, tired of waiting to know what's going to happen next. It's not a place I want particularly. It's just peace. Peace and quiet and a tomorrow I can predict. It'll be good when I get my residency and I can go back to work. Work's good for the soul.'

'That's all I've had,' she says. 'At least, that's what I thought I had. And I know what you mean. I've felt sort of ... pointless since I retired.'

'And you? If you had a choice, if you could go anywhere? Be anywhere?'

'Oh, that's easy. Ilfracombe. I'd be off to Ilfracombe like a shot.'

'Vesta? Hello?'

Collette's voice, coming from the flat. They sit forward and peer towards the house. 'In the garden,' calls Vesta.

She appears at the kitchen door: wearing a jacket and jeans, sports bag over her shoulder. 'Your door was open,' she says. 'Sorry.'

'That's okay,' says Vesta. Strangely, her home invasions have made her more, rather than less, careless about security. She no longer feels there's much point, when people seem to come in with such ease anyway. 'What can I do for you?'

She comes up the steps and they see that she's got biker boots on. Full armour, ready for flight. She arrives on the lawn and drops her bag on the straw-dry grass in front of them. Psycho starts at the sound, and shoots off into the bushes.

'I came to say goodbye,' she says, and they see that her eyes are red from crying. 'I'm off.'

'Off?'

Collette nods and looks away. 'Can you say goodbye to Cher for me? I can't find anyone and I want to get moving.'

Hossein jumps to his feet. 'No,' he says. 'You can't!'

Vesta sees the blush that rises to her cheek, the refusal to meet his eye. Oh, look, she really likes him, she thinks. I hadn't realised that he liked her, though. How blind can you be?

'What's wrong, love?'

She hesitates and eyes Hossein, clearly unsure how much to say. Eventually, she just forces a gay little laugh out and goes: 'Oh, nothing. You know me. Always on the move.'

'Where are you going?'

Again, the hesitation. 'Oh, you know,' she says, eventually. 'I thought I'd just go up to Victoria and see what's on offer.'

'You're going *away* away? What about your mum? Collette, has something happened?'

'Oh, look,' says Collette, 'it's not like she's got the first idea who I am. She won't miss me. I'd sort of made my mind up to go when – you know –' she gestures towards the empty shed '– everything happened. But now ... itchy feet, you know? What can you do?'

Something's happened, that much is obvious. Collette looks like she's seen a ghost. Like her ghosts might be catching up with her. 'It's almost dinnertime,' she says. 'Where are you going to go?'

Collette lets out a sigh. 'Transport runs most of the night,' she says. 'Might as well sleep on a bus and get a head start.'

'I thought,' says Hossein, 'we were all going to sit tight for a bit.'

'Yeah, well,' says Collette. 'Nobody actually knows I was here, do they? It won't make a lot of difference if I bugger off again.'

'Collette, has something happened?' asks Vesta. 'Are you okay?'

'No,' says Collette. 'I just fancy a change of scene.'

'Is it your old boss?' asks Hossein. 'Has he found you?' And the bravado goes out of her like the air from a pricked balloon and she turns to Vesta, shocked.

'You told him.'

'Yes. I did.'

'Jesus,' says Collette, and drops down on the grass beside her bag. 'So much for secrets.'

'I told Cher as well,' she says.

'When?'

'Around the time you told me, Collette.'

'*What?* And did you tell anyone else? How about them next door? How about them? The greengrocer, maybe? How about the bloke in Flat One? I'm sure he'd like to know so he can keep his door locked.'

'Sorry,' says Vesta, but she doesn't sound it. 'It's not like either Hossein or Cher is going to go to the police with the info, is it? And frankly, if there was going to be people turning up on the doorstep looking for you, I'd rather people knew what to expect.'

'Fuck,' says Collette, and slumps. 'Well, thanks. Thanks a lot.'

'You're welcome,' says Vesta, and Collette shoots her a look of pure evil.

'I can't believe you did that. What am I? Bambi?'

'Sorry,' says Hossein. 'I shouldn't have shared that I knew. She swore me to secrecy.'

'Yeah,' she sneers. 'Well, secrecy's obviously a big thing around here.'

'Would you like a cup of tea?' asks Vesta.

'No! No, I *don't* want a cup of tea! What's that going to solve?'

A reasonable question. Vesta's been drinking tea every hour of the day since the Landlord died, and she still feels as though her heart's been sprained.

She gets off her deckchair and heads for the house. 'I'll get you one. We could both do with a refresher, anyway.' I'll leave them to it, she thinks. She's cross with me right now. Laying whatever it is she's upset about at my door. If anyone's going to get through to her, Hossein will manage it. He can talk to her through her soft spot the way I just can't.

She steps in through her kitchen door, and her own ghosts swoop back in to haunt her. To all intents and purposes, the kitchen is back to normal. Better than normal, if anything, for Hossein has managed to restart the pilot light on the gas cooker, which went out some time in the 1990s, and has changed the washers on the sink taps so that they no longer drip. But she can hardly bear to be in here. When the bathroom door is open, she keeps having flash memories of the Landlord, squatting face down in the toilet. When the door is closed, she hears someone moving behind it. Using the bathroom is close to agony. She used to love a long bath with a book; now she scuttles through hasty showers, and has to close her eyes and hold her breath when she sits down on that toilet seat.

She puts the kettle on and fills the watering can at the sink, so she can water her herbs while it boils. It's just an excuse to get out of the room. It's unbearable, she thinks. I can do this now, but what happens in the winter?

In the garden she can hear the low murmur of voices. It sounds like Collette has at least calmed down enough to talk.

All my life, she thinks. All my life I've lived here, and now it's spoiled. All the memories – all the Mum making cakes, the laundry days and the pegging out, Dad coming home in his butcher's coat and his straw boater and chasing me round the garden with his cleaver, pretending to be an ogre as I shrieked with half-joy, half-terror, the looking after them as they got ill, the I-love-you deathbeds – all painted over in black by one single moment. I know it's early days. I know I'm still in shock and I'm scared about what will happen next, what will happen when they find him, but I feel as though it will never be the same again. What if I'm eighty-five, all alone here, all these people long gone, and I'm still dashing in and out of the bathroom like the hounds of hell are on my tail?

The kettle clicks off and she goes back inside. It seems darker in here now, she thinks. It was never exactly a bright room, but now it's as if there's a shadow hanging over my shoulder all the time. I want to be gone from here. I want to be gone.

Chapter Forty

Now he's going to come over all paternal, she thinks, plucking at the grass beneath her shin. Vesta's left me alone with him so he can give me some sort of Big Daddy lecture. Because the thing I need right now is a mansplanation of the error of my thinking.

Hossein looks embarrassed.

'I think she wants me to reason with you,' he says.

'Well, I wouldn't bother.'

'No,' says Hossein. 'I don't think I will. You're an adult. I'm sure you know what you're doing.'

She's surprised and, suddenly, a bit hurt. That's nice, she thinks. Glad to know you care.

'It's not like I *want* to go,' she says. 'It's that I don't have a choice.'

The cash, hastily unearthed from its hiding places, is hidden beneath her clothes in the bag, a thousand kept back for speedy access in her shoulder bag. Down to ninety-five thousand now, what with deposits and Janine's latest bill, which came in yesterday. Payable in advance, of course. Still a lot of money, but only a lot of money if you're not waiting to run.

'Have you any thoughts about where you might go?' he asks.

'No. I'll see what's leaving at Victoria coach station.'

'So mostly Eastern Europe, then?'

'Snarky.'

He bobs his head in recognition. 'I think if I were running away, I'd probably want to go somewhere warm.'

'Obviously,' she says. 'That's why you came to Britain.'

'You have a point. I came here because America's further away. And besides, you don't have the continental winters. You have a bit more choice available to you when you have a European passport, though.'

She finally gets over her rage enough to look at him. His face is calm, but friendly. No sign that he wants to tell her what to do, that he's waiting for his opportunity.

'You can borrow my computer, if you like,' he offers, 'to research a destination. It seems a bit random, just going to the bus station.'

'Random is good. Random's great. If I don't know where I'm going to go, it's harder for other people to work it out, isn't it? You've got a computer?'

'Don't tell anyone,' he says, 'or they'll all want a go. It'll turn into a conduit for eBay. But yes. I use it to write, and cause trouble on the internet with my little wireless dongle. Are you going to be okay for money?' he asks.

She deliberately keeps her eyes off her bag. 'Yeah. I'm okay for now.'

'Because, you know, if you need some, I ...'

She gapes. He can't have more than a bean himself. She's been amazed by how open-handed the poor people she's met have been, on her travels. Most of the types she met on the up-and-up seemed to think that helping other people out was a sign of weakness.

'No, Hossein! I wouldn't dream of it. Don't be stupid!'

'Okay.' He hold his hands up. 'Just … you know. So you know.'

'I'm okay,' she says. 'Really. Money's the least of my worries.'

'I'll take you down there, when you're ready, then.'

'Why would you do that?'

He shrugs. 'If you're running away, I'd like to make sure you at least leave safely. I'm assuming you're not really just going on a whim? Nobody goes on a whim without a couple of days' notice.'

'I can't believe she told you.'

'Yeah, I know. I'd be annoyed, too.'

'Christ!' she snaps. 'Don't be so bloody *understanding*!'

'Okay,' says Hossein. 'If you like. So you're just going to leave your mother, then? How is she, anyway?'

She feels like she's been slapped. Gulps. 'I don't have a choice.'

He's going to tell me everybody has a choice now, she thinks, and then I'll have to punch him.

'What happened? Please, can I ask?'

She feels exhausted. Plain worn out. Shakes her head.

'So it is your old boss, isn't it?'

'Yes. No. Oh, God, I don't know. It could have been.'

He waits for her to speak, doesn't prompt her.

'I saw one of his … people. Malik. Yesterday. I think it was him. No, I'm sure it was him.'

'Oh.'

He considers this fact, turns it over in his mind. 'And did he see you?'

Somewhere nearby, a woman screams. A single scream, high-pitched and short. One that sounds like it's been cut off mid-breath. They tense, look up and do a city-person's pantomime scan of the near horizon. With everyone's windows and doors open to the heat, they can't even tell if it's come from somewhere inside a house, or out.

'It's so weird, with all the windows open everywhere,' says Collette. 'You don't have any idea how much noise people make, normally, do you?'

'Yes, God, Saturday night especially,' he says. 'I wonder if people realise how much it sounds as if they're getting attacked when they make noises like that in the street?'

'They don't think about it at all. They're pissed, mostly.'

'Yes. It's so funny, though, isn't it? You read in the papers all the time about how people ignore people screaming for help in this city, but they never seem to put the two things together. We'd be out on the street with baseball bats four or five times on a Saturday night, and this is a quiet road.'

'And the foxes,' says Collette. 'They sound like someone being strangled.'

'Ha. At least they're having fun, though.'

She blows a strand of hair off her face. 'At least someone is.'

'Oh, I know,' he says. Their eyes meet for a brief second, then they both look hurriedly away. Oh, God, she thinks. I think he fancies me, too. Does he know? That I've been having stupid dreams about him, between the dreams of Tony? It's not been *that* obvious, has it? Jesus. It's like being back at school, trying to hide your crush on the football captain in case anyone finds out.

'Anyway,' he says. 'So that's why you're leaving?'

She nods.

'Collette,' he says, and the name sounds like poetry from his mouth. She looks up and sees kindness in his eyes, and wants to wail.

'You'll leave your mother when she's dying because you *think* you saw someone?'

'Don't patronise me,' she says wearily.

'Sorry,' he says.

'I *did* see him. He was as close to me as you are now.'

'Okay.'

One foot wrong, he thinks, and she'll be gone. And I don't want her to go. Not in chaos, with loose ends left dangling that she will never be able to tie up. And because I like her. I really do. She has an attitude, an independence, I admire.

'Maybe I could come with you.'

'Hunh?' She's so caught up in her memory of Malik that for a moment it sounds to her like he's just asked to run away with her.

'To see your mother. I could come with you. Make sure you don't come to any harm. It's not as if I've got anything pressing to do here.'

A hole opens up in the pit of her stomach. No. No, look, if you do that, it will mean I've agreed to stay. And I decided. I already decided. It's stupid. I have to go.

'Collette, it could be a coincidence.'

She shakes her head, vehemently. 'In Collier's Wood? On a Tuesday afternoon? Come on. What are the chances?'

'I don't know. I just ...'

'Hossein,' she says, 'if you were in Tehran and something like this happened to you, what would you think?'

'It's not the same.'

'Christ,' she says, and tosses her head. 'I love the way you think this country is some kind of fucking safe haven. There are bad people here too, you know. Really bad people. They're not the ones in charge so much, but they're still bad people. This isn't some stalker thing, Hossein. It's not – you know – get a restraining order and he'll go away. It's ... he's a bad man. A *really* bad man. People *die* around him, and nobody does anything because they're either too afraid or they belong to him. No. No, I'm not doing it. I'm not. He's enjoying this. He's loving every minute. Every time he calls me on the phone, I can hear it in his voice, how much he's liking it, and every time I change my phone he finds the number again. He doesn't let go. I can't. I can't do it. I can't. I'd give my right arm to be free of this, but I don't think I ever will be.'

Hossein stretches in the sunshine and shows her a sliver of flat brown belly, a neat line of hair pointing down into his crotch. She is suddenly overwhelmed by a wave of lust that almost knocks her sideways. It's the fear, she thinks. Just being made to think about this and I'm all over adrenalin. I'm mistaking adrenalin for arousal. People do it all the time. He looks over her shoulder and smiles at Vesta, coming up the steps with the tea mugs.

'Well, think about it,' he says. 'For your mother.'

'She wasn't a very good mother,' says Collette, doubtfully.

'Still,' says Hossein. 'You'll never have another.'

Chapter Forty-One

His love is forged in tears. They spring from his eyes as they struggle for that one final breath, pour down his cheeks while his hands are still about their necks. As he watches the light die out, the surprise, the fear, the pain melt away into nothingness, he feels his chest tighten as though his heart will break. For a moment, as the tears flood down, he will find it hard to swallow. He will take his hands from them and press them to his face, bend double and let the sorrow out.

'I'm sorry,' he tells her. 'I'm sorry, oh, I'm so sorry.'

I'm out of control, he thinks. I no longer have any control over it – over this – this love. It's got too much for me, now. The loneliness is too extreme. I thought my ladies would heal me. That it would stop this longing, this ache, this empty hole in me if they could never leave.

But it's all backwards, this love of his. It starts the right way, every time. The way it starts for everyone. A chance meeting, a flash of attraction. The thinking about her when she's not there, the slow build of intrigue, the fire of passion. But after that it's all wrong. After the passion comes the mourning, and then the contentment, the relationship, the moments of easy intimacy. And then, creeping over him, day by day, the indifference. He feels nothing for Marianne now. He looks at her and he can barely remember the devotion that filled him just a few weeks ago. She's just another withered, wizened disappointment, and him with the gnawing emptiness that grows and grows each day.

He looks at the God Girl and feels another rush of sorrow. My God, he thinks, I never even found out what your name was. I'm out of control. I am. If I'm going to do this, if I'm going to make these ... *sacrifices* for love, the very least I owe them, the very least I owe *myself*, is the tenderness of anticipation. I've never been one of those people, going out to discotheques in search of thrills, collecting and throwing women away as though they were last night's garbage. When I mate, I want it to be for life. I always have. And now look.

She struggled, far more than Marianne or Nikki did. Not a surprise, really, for his girls before have known him. Have at least known him well enough to have let their guard down, sit down in a chair, be relaxed and unready. The God Girl was torn between the need to evangelise and the awareness that she had come to a flat alone with a stranger. She didn't sit, didn't turn her back on him, but stood against the draining board, her Bible in her hand, and talked about Jesus until he wanted to howl at the moon. In the end he had to ask her to draw a map of where her church was, just to get her to take his eye off him for a moment and turn her back. And when he pounced, she was bending over the table, just feet between her and the door, and she fought and fought. Got off a scream, as well. First time anyone's managed that.

Like riding a bucking bronco, he thinks, remembering her strength. Surprisingly strong, for one so slight. With a plastic bag over her head and both his hands clamped tight to hold it shut, she threw him from side to side as though she were made of springs.

Never gentle, he thinks. It's never gentle. I wish it were. I wish there were some way to help them quietly off to sleep. That their transformation was a moment of quiet blue peace.

Her mouth is open. Thomas wipes his eyes and peels the bag away, gazes into the bloodshot eyes. Hazel, he thinks. That's the colour they should have been, not this gooseberry green that goes so badly with the red of petechial haemorrhaging. Her blue veins, already so close to the surface, have bulged upwards, arterial roadmaps scrawled across her lovely features. Her nose, already a little overlarge for his particular taste, is, he realises, broken.

She's spoiled. Quite spoiled. All that suffering, all that sadness, and he's come out with nothing, just a useless ugly thing, a bonfire Guy, no good to any man.

He drops her to the floor and sits down heavily in his chair, next to her powder-blue leatherette handbag with its spill of spectacles and prayer pamphlets. Puts his face in his hands and begins to sob.

Chapter Forty-Two

This time, she doesn't see him until they're halfway home.

They're strap-hanging on the tube, face-to-face, and Hossein's presence lulls her. More than lulls her. Now she's trusted him with her safety, she feels opened-up to him. She knows it's foolish, knows it's almost wrong, but she wants to look at him all the time and has to drag her gaze away, is intensely aware of his presence, the scent of him nearby. They're bending their heads close together to hear each other's voice over the rattle of the carriage, when the train jerks as it passes over some signals, throwing her back for a moment as the man standing in the doorway to the next carriage slips briefly into the light of the window.

It's Malik. Definitely, really, Malik. No mistakes, no imagining.

Her mouth falls open mid-laugh and the blood drains from her face. She ducks back, out of sight and doesn't know why she does so, for there can be only one reason why he is on this

She turns her back to the doorway. 'Don't look,' she says.

He frowns. 'At what?'

'He's here. In the next carriage.'

Instinctively he starts to turn, then stops himself. 'Are you sure?'

'No, I'm making it up.'

'Don't ...'

She leans her back against the glass barrier. Feels him stand closer, the heat coming off his body. They glance up and down the carriage, look to see who else is with them. Mid-afternoon, this far down the Northern Line, there are only a couple of other passengers: solitary readers, no use in trouble.

'We mustn't get off,' she says. They're almost at Balham, where they should change for the overland. Long, empty outer-suburb platforms and a slow escalator ride to the High Road.

He nods, his eyes wide. Puts a hand out as the train begins to brake and holds on to her arm, protectively. 'It's okay,' he says. 'Just breathe.'

She realises, when he says it, that she has stopped breathing altogether. Takes a huge gasp in and hears it jitter out again. Pull yourself together, Collette. You won't get out of this by stuffing your fists in your mouth and screaming.

'Did you notice what sort of train it was?'

She shakes her head. The branch of the Northern Line the train would take through the centre of town was irrelevant while they were staying south; neither of them looked when they ran on to the platform and threw themselves in through the doors. 'How did we not notice him?' she asks, but she knows why. Hossein has never seen Malik in his life, and she, stupid woman, has been gazing at Hossein.

'It doesn't matter. We know now.'

The train pulls in and he pokes his head out through the open door. 'Western branch,' he says. 'We'll stay on and get off at Waterloo.'

They ride in silence, hold tight to the hanging straps. Collette stares down the carriage, her back rigid as she imagines Malik's eye boring into her shoulders. She hates the readers. Hates them for their absorption, their open body postures, their bags sitting casually on the seat beside them to reserve the space until the carriage fills up. Hates them for the fact that when they get off the train the worst that can happen is a quick and easy mugging.

Hossein's eyes have narrowed, the pupils so wide they look flat and lustreless. He doesn't look afraid, she thinks impatiently. He looks as calm as if this were some awkward social encounter. They pull in to Clapham South, stand aside to let the trickle of passengers on. A couple of backpacks, a tricycle buggy, an art portfolio. She takes the opportunity to turn casually and glance at the door between the carriages. No sign of Malik. Of course not. He's waiting on the platform edge, in case they make a run for it.

The doors close and they move off. The rhythms of the London underground: shrill beeps, a brief flicker of the lights as they pass out of the station, something incomprehensible on the tannoy. The new passengers fan out and settle themselves into the corner seats. Everyone likes a corner seat, where only one person can crowd in next to them.

Clapham Common. A narrow platform between two tracks, nerve-wracking when two trains come in at once. A rush of Hipsters: woollen beanie hats in the height of summer, scraggy stubble, iPads, iPods, iPhones, old document bags that used to hang off newspaper sellers, now sold for fifty pounds in retro clothing stores. Checked shirts, biker boots, cotton dresses over leggings. Strap-hangers, hoping to burn off calories by tensing their abs.

Clapham North. The racial mix begins to change. London likes to think of itself as integrated in a way that American cities are not, but you can still tell the district you're passing beneath by the skin tones that get on the trains. Now the carriage is half-and-half black and white, everyone tensing themselves for when the atmosphere gets harder at Stockwell. Stockwell, Oval, Kennington, Elephant: they've never recovered from their reputation for steaming gangs in the eighties. Houses there long since passed into the millions, but still the people passing beneath edge their bags closer in to their bodies as they leave Clapham, and check that their wallets are in their inside pockets.

I could do with a steaming gang right now, she thinks. A big row of scary teenagers piling through the carriage, causing chaos, making a pitch for Malik's Rolex and distracting him as he takes them down.

They don't come. The train pauses at Kennington and the carriage fills with commuters who tipped off the last train as it headed up towards Bank. She looks at Hossein and sees that he has moved towards the door, ready for the off. She stays where she is. Doesn't want to alert their pursuer that they're ready to move.

'Brown line,' says Hossein, and she nods. North, into the centre of town, where the crowds are. Easier to lose someone in a crowd, to dodge behind a placard, slip into a doorway.

The train pulls in, and they force their way off through a great whaling press of people, out-of-towners in from the country with no comprehension of the etiquette of mass transport, trying to push their way on before those on board have got off, a problem at all the mainline stations. Her bag catches on some-one's walking stick and they curse her as she wrenches herself free, catches a momentary glimpse of Malik, a head's height above the crowd, but agile and charismatic enough that they part before him. I used to enjoy that, she thinks. I used to like the way I could use him as a battering ram in the club. How stupid am I? Then she's away from the snag and hurrying in Hossein's wake.

The crowd goes all the way back into the tunnel. They jostle their way forward, Collette fighting to breathe against the rising panic. If I shouted fire, she thinks, half these people would die in the stampede. They reach the escalator hall, hurry across grey, pitted tiles to the Bakerloo. A train is coming in and they step up their pace, run down the platform to a vacant space and throw themselves through the doors just as they close.

Did he catch us? Did he see where we went? The carriage is rammed; the good people of Surrey heading up to Oxford Street for a bit of lunch and shopping. A French family sits in a neat row, legs crossed at the ankles, and stares at the rumpled scruffi-ness of their English cousins. Some Japanese throw broad, nodding smiles at everyone who brushes against them. Collette and Hossein are forced down the carriage as the doors open at Embankment and the Charing Cross brigade force themselves on board. They're miles from the doors. They'll be the last off at Oxford Circus.

She catches Hossein's eye and he jerks his chin to his left. He's with us, the look says. He's still here. She tips forward beneath the arm of an American frat boy in an ironic Cambridge University T-shirt and verifies the truth. There he is, two doors up, one hand holding the metal bar above his head, a circle of space a foot wide all around him. She swears, inside. Go away, Malik. It's been so long, now. Aren't you tired of it? Don't you wonder if it's time that Tony let it go?

Oxford Circus, and the crowd bursts from the carriage like champagne from a shaken bottle. It swirls around them, a rushing flood of humanity, and carries them towards the exit tunnel whether they wanted to go or not. She feels Hossein's hand slip into hers, gives it a squeeze before a man in a suit barges between them, bellows an excuse-me as though it's a reproach. It's slow. So bloody slow. He could be coming up behind me but I *must not look* she tells herself. The only advantage we've got is that he might not know that we know he's there. She's certain she can hear his heel segs scraping over the floor, knows it's her imagination, but hears it anyway, drowning out a hundred other footfalls.

Tunnel, steps, tunnel, escalator. The stairs on the tube are just steep enough to snatch your breath, not steep enough to take you upwards fast enough. A scrum at the bottom of the escalator, people sighing, checking their watches, edging past each other in the hope of gaining a second's advantage. Practising the London Air Stare that lets them push past strangers by pretending they don't see them. She's got in front of Hossein, steps on to the stairwell, knows from his familiar feel that he's right behind. They tuck in to the right, let the hurriers march past. No point attracting attention by joining them, puffing themselves out now when they might need to run later. She can't stop herself; looks below her.

He's not there. Good God in heaven, he's not there! She feels the tension leave her neck, a rush of painful heat as her muscles relax. Then another as they tighten up again when she spots him ten steps down on the parallel stairs.

Up to the top, Oyster cards out as they approach, a rush through the barriers. For a moment, she's lost, confused, doesn't know which of the hundred exits to head for, then Hossein touches her arm and they hurry, dodging their way round knots of tourists who've stopped to check their guide books, for the nearest. Run up the stairs and turn left towards the Circus.

Even when she lived in London, she rarely came to Oxford Street. It scares her. Whenever she's in these huge, distracted crowds, all she can think of is suicide bombers. It's like that every time. Her mind fills with images of the men in front of them throwing their coats open with a bellowed *allahu akbar*, of light and smoke and body parts. Whenever she's here, she wants to wrap her arms around her head and protect her face from flying glass. They weave their way into the funnels behind the crowd barriers and march smartly down Regent Street.

Again, he takes her hand, and pulls her along like a child. Here, the pavements are wide and the crowds are thinner, but their progress is still painfully slow. Where do we go now? Into Soho? Those mazes of streets where a single turn can leave you suddenly marooned, alone, unseen? The self-regarding streets of Mayfair, where every frontage is a gallery with a ring-and-wait sign on its locked front door? She glances behind her as they pass the old Dickens and Jones building, sees Malik reach the corner of Little Argyle Street. He must know we know, she thinks. Why doesn't he give up? He can't think he's going to do anything here, and we're hardly going to lead him home.

They reach Great Marlborough Street and wheel in, past the florid Tudorbethan frontage of Liberty on the other side of the road. No, this is nuts, she thinks. The road is the one the Londoners take to avoid the tourists on Oxford Street. It's almost empty: a traffic warden and a wino, a skinny lad smoking outside an office three hundred yards away. Crazy. We should stay where the crowds are. She starts to tug him back but Hossein pulls her on. 'It's okay,' he says. 'I know.'

'But—' She's out of breath from hurrying. She's got unfit, living this underground life, hiding indoors.

'It's *okay*, Collette,' he says, and pulls her across the road, guides her past the great shop's doors. Malik must be nearly at the corner now, she thinks. We're sitting ducks. They turn right into the pub-café-tourist trap of Carnaby Street. Five paces down, and he wheels swiftly and shoves them through a well-hidden door, plain and black and unassuming; one she's never noticed whenever she's been up here.

They're in a bazaar. It takes a moment for her eyes to adjust to the drop in light, as he pulls them on. Carpet and gilt and mirrors. Patterns and peacock feathers. They're in Liberty. Come in through a back door she never knew existed. Pretty things. All the pretty, shiny things, assistants eying them as they rush through. They don't look like they belong here. Once, she thinks, they'd have been sidling over with dollar signs for eyes when they saw me coming, but now they're poised to press the silent alarm if my hands leave my sides for a second.

And then they're back out in the sun, and running back to Regent Street. She has no idea where Malik is: whether he's casting round Carnaby or has spotted their U-turn and followed them. They pound up to the main sweep and Hossein sticks a hand in the air for a taxi. Always cabs on Regent Street. But if you're being followed you don't want someone to just jump into the one behind. She throws herself on to the back seat and looks wildly around. No sign. No Malik, no other hard-faced men flagging down black cars. She breathes; lets her head drop back against the headrest.

They pant as the cab swings round and turns up Maddox Street. He's resting his head too, his face drawn, the lines around his beautiful mouth etched deep.

'Well,' she sputters, between breaths, 'for a man who longs for peace and quiet, you certainly like a challenge, don't you?'

He turns, leans across the space between them, and kisses her.

Chapter Forty-Three

And now she's lost, as she knew she would be.

She wakes to the sound of the front door slamming, finds herself in a tumble of limbs and smells his beautiful skin, and wants to cry. I can't. Oh, no, this can't have happened. Not now. Before, or never – but not *now*.

His arms are wrapped round her, one knee between her thighs. Even in the night, in their sleep, they have gravitated towards each other when the heat should have driven them apart. And she feels the bliss of his arm around her shoulder and feels his breath against her hot cheek, and she wants to howl at the moon, to rail at the fates. She's stiff and pleasurably sore from the zeal of their fucking, the hands, tongues, lips, and skin, the words whispered, the laughing, the fingers intertwined, his beautiful, miraculous cock so hard and ardent, and she wants to weep.

I can't be with you, Hossein. I *can't*.

She picks up his hand and kisses the palm, and he opens his eyes. Smiles sleepily at her, his eyes creasing, and presses his lips against her cheek. Rolls over on to her, and her body gives and opens up to him, because she never, she never knew it could be like this. She's not lived in a world where sex and love went hand in hand. And now he's here and he's beautiful and he's perfect, her reward and her salvation – and she *can't* be with him.

He strokes her hair back from her face and lets out a long, contented sigh. Pressed up against him, she can feel his cock begin to stir, and her body heating up in response. 'What time is it?' he asks.

'I don't know.' She turns her head to look for her phone, and he stops her, holds her wrist against the pillow and melts her with his kisses. 'It doesn't matter,' he says. 'I don't really care.'

Just once more, she thinks. Just once more before I tell him: something to remember, something to carry into my solitary old age. Can you live a lifetime on a single memory? I've never fucked someone before where I felt he even noticed, once he got going, that it was *me*, not someone else, in the room.

She frees her wrist and buries her fingers in his hair, and he butts against her palm like an attention-seeking cat. Kisses her wrist, enters her and laughs at the pleasure rush. 'Oh, God, that's the best feeling,' he says.

'I know,' she gasps, and her head fills with liquid gold.

Their other basic needs drive them from the bed eventually. They both want to wash, and she's pleased and relieved that he doesn't suggest that they share a bathroom. She's always been funny about that. Men who wanted to come in when she was naked and vulnerable in the tub: it always seemed like some deliberate gesture of disrespect, some statement of ownership. Instead, Hossein walks up the corridor with her, kisses her a dozen times at the foot of the stairs, strokes her face and promises to return. She goes into the scruffy bathroom, luxuriates in the hot water from the shower hose and thinks about the night before.

She feels strangely detached from the rest of the world, aware of her skin and her pulse and the heat between her thighs in a way she has no recollection of experiencing before. So this is what the fuss is about, she thinks. I thought I was experienced, but all I was was only someone who'd fucked a lot. She wants to run a long, warm bath and reflect on what's passed between them, but she doesn't want to miss it when he comes back, doesn't want to miss a moment. She runs a hand over her throat where he kissed her, and closes her eyes. Oh, God, Hossein. Why did it have to happen now?

Beyond the door, she hears footsteps approach. Someone tries the bathroom door, and she tenses. She's seeing a lurker round every corner, now. Knows she won't feel safe in London again. The footsteps turn and go away, and a door closes. Just Gerard Bright, wanting a leak. Not everyone who tries a door handle wants to do you harm. She heaves herself from the water and wraps herself in Nikki's old pink towel.

Back in her room, she pulls the rumpled bed back together, puts on eggs to hard boil. She doesn't have much food – just the eggs and some bread and cheese, a few ripe plums. For the first time, she digs through the sorry collection of previous tenants' leavings and tries to put together some poor show of hospitality. She has three plates, a couple of bowls, not much else. But she lays her wares out in what she can find and, after thinking for a moment, lays out the bedspread on the floor and puts them there, like a picnic.

He knocks, respectfully, on the door, and she rushes to let him in. He's clean and shaved, his black hair slicked back and smelling of shampoo, his breath of toothpaste. He smiles at her, and she feels a strange liquid sensation in her guts. Suddenly, she feels shy in front of this man who's touched every inch of her, who's been so far inside her she thought they would actually combine. She lets him in and crosses the room in front of him, looking at the floor. Then he comes to her and puts his arms round her, kisses her face, her eyelids, her mouth, and she feels safe, like a child.

'I brought some things,' he says. 'It's not much, but ...'

He hands her a cotton shopping bag with some strange script across the front. Farsi, she assumes, though it could be Arabic for all she knows. Inside are pistachios, halwa, a jar of what looks like home-made amba, little pots of sumac and black paprika, and a container of olives. She smiles at the gift.

'So funny,' she says. 'You say it's not much, but they'd be paying a score for this lot in Clapham. I can't believe you've got amba, just, you know, in your room.'

'You know amba?'

'Of course. I've been a few places in the last few years.'

'Where did you have it?'

'Israel,' she tells him.

Hossein hisses in through this teeth, then laughs. 'I didn't know they had amba in the Great Satan.'

She looks at him suspiciously for a moment, then sees that he is joking. 'Well, I didn't know your lot were so big on Iraqi condiments myself.'

'You have a point,' he says, and sits down cross-legged on the bedspread. She sits beside him, so she can press her upper arm against his, so she doesn't have to look full in his face. She's not ready for that. Not while she's longing to feel his hand caressing her breasts.

He taps an egg on the side of a bowl, rolls it between his

fingers and peels. She takes a small handful of nuts and cracks them open, one by one. They're wonderfully fresh, sweet and salty on her tongue. I can't let this carry on, she thinks. I don't know what he's thinking, but I have to tell him.

'Hossein?'

She closes her eyes for a moment and feels a wrench of sadness.

'We can't do this.'

He sighs and puts his egg down, uneaten. 'I knew you were going to say that.'

'But you understand, don't you? You must see that ...'

'Yeah, I see. But that doesn't mean I think you're right.'

'I can't stay.'

He rubs his face like a kid, looks like he's shut his finger in a door.

'You should, Collette,' he says. 'You really should.'

'Not after yesterday. Come on. You must be able to see that. It's not safe. It's just not safe.'

'He doesn't know where you *are*, Collette. We lost him. Don't you remember?'

'For now. But look, he's got so close, I ...'

'Not so close. He was at the home. He must have been. We just weren't looking. I'm sorry. I should have been a better bodyguard.'

'It's not you. It's not your fault. But you don't understand. Once they've got my scent, it's only a matter of time. They found me in Paris, and Barca, and Tunis, and Prague ... I'm so stupid. I should never have come back.'

'But what about your mother?' he asks. 'Really, Collette. You're going to leave now?'

A tear forces itself from the corner of her eye and runs down the side of her nose. She dashes it away, impatiently. 'She doesn't even know me.'

And now she's crying and she can't stop. Puts her hand across her mouth and looks away from him, and is grateful that he has the sense not to touch her. She doesn't want sympathy. She wants gone.

'I think about it, sometimes,' he says. 'Dying by myself. It's the sort of thing you *do* think about, in a foreign country.'

'I know,' says Collette. 'But most people do, you know, in the end. All the widows and the people by themselves, all the people who have accidents or end up in hospital before anyone can get to them.'

'I was married, you know.'

She throws him a look over her shoulder. 'No. No, I didn't.'

'Roshana.'

'What happened?'

'I don't know. I think she died. I assume she died. She went out one day and never came back. That's what happens. One day she was with me, and the next she was gone.'

'I'm sorry,' she says.

'The awful thing is, I *hope* she was alone. Wherever she was. Because if she wasn't, it's probably worse.'

Now he looks away, and toys with the fringing on the edge of the bedspread, his mouth turned down and his eyes unfocused. That's the thing, she thinks. I know we feel so close, so loved-up right now, but we don't *know* each other. We know nothing about each other. Not really.

'But I wish every day I had been with her,' he says, eventually. 'She was – for a long time I felt like the lights had been turned out.'

'I'm so sorry,' she says.

'And *that's* not *your* fault,' he says. 'But what I'm saying – I don't know what I'm saying, Collette. Just that it's a terrible thing, to die alone.'

'I'd rather die alone later than die now.'

He puts an olive between his beautiful lips and chews contemplatively. 'Okay,' he says. 'It's not like I haven't been there myself. Where do you think you'll go?'

She shakes her head. 'I hear Norway's nice at this time of year.'

'Bloody dark in the winter, though.'

She laughs. He finally reaches out and caresses the back of her neck. 'Last night was ...' he says.

'Oh, don't,' she says. 'Oh, God, it's not like I *want* to go.'

'I know,' he says, and puts his face close to hers. 'And in another world, you know? I get it. Me too. I understand.'

His skin smells of cleanness and sandalwood. She looks down at his lips, half open, ready to kiss her, looks up at the golden eyes and the careworn lines beginning to settle around them. I think this is a good man, she thinks. I think the universe is having a laugh with me, showing me that there is such a thing.

'But not today,' he says. 'Tomorrow I'll help you, if you really mean to leave. And not tonight.'

'No,' she says, and takes his face in her hands. Kneels in front of him like Mary Magdalene. Kisses his mouth, breathes in the wonder of him.

Chapter Forty-Four

His disappointment is almost painful. He's taken her clothes off – the shapeless skirt, the lace-edge shirt, the modest under-garments – and found that it's hopeless. The God Girl has clearly lost half her bodyweight at some point, and lost it fast. If he were to delve into her viscera, he suspects he'd find a gas-tric band, or one of those balloons they inflate inside the stomach. There's very little fat on her, it's true, but her skin looks like a church candle that's been left burning all through Lent. Like an altar cloth thrown down in the vestry, waiting for the laundry bag.

She's hopeless. Useless. Nothing he can do, no ministrations, will ever make her right. She's just an ugly white sack of blub-ber, an insult to his dreams.

It's not even worth preserving her, if all he'll want to do at the end is throw her away. He stands over the bath and glares at her reproachfully. She's going off, rapidly, her buttocks and the backs of her thighs black with congealed blood, her pupils gone white. And she's really starting to smell. He's emptied the super-market of Febreze and scent blocks, and stuck duck tape over the airbricks to stop the smell circulating, but he knows it's only a matter of time before the people downstairs start to wonder where it's coming from. He has to do something with her, this much he knows, but he's not wasting his skills and time on preserving an object so uncomely. Why on earth did you attract my attention, he thinks, if you were going to let me down like this? I'm glad I don't know your name. I don't want to remember you.

Her rigor has passed, and her forearm is flopped down the outside of the bath, the hand and fingertips blackening almost as he watches. He picks up the hand, lets it drop, watches the loose flaps of skin hanging down from her upper arm wobble horribly in the raw light from the bare bulb above their heads. Whatever I do, I'll have to do it soon, he thinks. What a waste of time.

He has no experience of taking a fresh corpse apart, but he knows it's going to be a lot harder than it was with Alice or her predecessors. Fresh, juicy cartilage will be harder to cut through, and it will be nigh on impossible to break up fresh bones with any tools he can reasonably bring into the flat.

'Piss,' he says, out loud. Turns to the basin and splashes cold water on his face, puts his specs back on and looks at himself in the mirror. Such a mild face, a lock of hair falling foppishly loose over his forehead, his chest and shoulders slightly pudgy under his open-necked shirt. No one, he thinks, would think that I have a dead girl in my bathroom. They wouldn't think anything about me, most of them. They'd just look straight through me, not even notice I was there. Which is good, of course, if you're going to be dropping severed limbs in litter bins. But God, what a hassle. Why can't she just magically disappear?

He sighs and gets down on his knees with his carving knife.

The first and obvious step is the same as it's always been. Rationally, he needs to get rid of the messy inside parts, the bits that spread, before he can start to think about dividing up that flappy torso.

So close to her face, he is assailed by a horrible feeling of being watched by those eggshell eyes. He grabs a hand towel from one of the suction hooks on the side of the basin, and throws it over her face, to hide it. Then he bends forward and slices into the distending belly, coughs as a gust of fetid air rushes out. There's no pleasure in this. Other times, he's been carried through the disgust by the pleasure of experimentation and, in latter times, his pride in his work. This is just a nasty, demanding chore, like doing his taxes.

Chapter Forty-Five

They've put her in a side room. Everyone knows what that means. It's a week – only a few days – since she last saw her, and in that time she seems to have halved in size. She lies among her tubes, swamped in a bed that seems to have been brought in from the set of Land of the Giants. Collette hovers in the doorway, the ward doctor close behind. She wants to turn and walk away, stride off up the ugly hospital corridor with its discarded wheelchairs and its sanitiser stations, as though doing so will make the whole thing not exist. If she crosses the threshold, it becomes part of her life.

Oh, I'm sorry, Janine, she silently tells the stranger-mother on the bed. I should have come. Should have taken one more punt that Malik wouldn't be there. If I'd known it was the end I wouldn't have left you all alone. Wouldn't have spent the week holed up with a man, pretending I wasn't going out of fear.

'She's not in any pain,' says the doctor. She's told Collette her name, but that detail has gone through her head like the rushing of wind, as has much of everything else she's said. All she knows is that she will soon no longer be a daughter. 'We're keeping her comfortable.'

She tries to take the first step, but her foot seems to be stuck to the ground. She throws the doctor an appeal for help with her eyes. Push me forward. Carry me over. The doctor stands, efficiently patient. They must be so used to this, she thinks. These wards are full of the old. Really, how they organise things so that the corridors aren't crowded with weeping relatives is a miracle in itself.

'It's okay,' she says, in a voice that manages to inject sympathy and encouragement into the need for action. I must move, thinks Collette. Janine's not the only patient here tonight. All over this hospital there are hundreds of people, and this poor woman's having to reassure thousands of relatives. Go in, Collette. Just do it.

'She's sleeping, at least?' she asks. 'That has to be a good sign, doesn't it?'

The doctor shakes her head. 'No. I'm sorry. She's slipped into a coma, I'm afraid.'

The word hits her like a bucket of water. Coma. One of those words you never want to hear. Coma, carcinoma, myocardial: words that suck your breath away.

'So I'm too late, then,' she says, desolately. I was right not to let him come in with me, she thinks. It's not the place for him, too much to ask. But oh, I'm so alone. I don't know how I'll get through this.

'No. You're not too late. She's still here. She may well know you're here. And sometimes they rally a bit. Come back for a while. It still matters. That you're here.'

She remembers Hossein's words from earlier. I wish I could

have been with her. She needs me to be here, she thinks. Even if she never knows I was.

She crosses the threshold.

Janine is as white as the sheet on which she lies. A morphine drip runs into the back of a veiny hand, and an oxygen mask is clamped to her face. She's all wires and monitors, her life edging away to a ragged beep, beep. The doctor picks up a chair that's pushed back against the radiator, places it by the bed. 'Sit with her, maybe,' she says. 'Hold her hand. She'll like that. There's a call button just here. One of the nurses will keep an eye on you.'

Collette obeys, like a zombie. Reaches for the hand that lies on the blanket and slides it into her own. It's cold. As if she's been out in the snow. She chafes her palm up and down it, like a mother warming a child. Glances up at the clock on the wall. It's nearly ten, already. Three hours gone past since she received the phone call telling her that Janine has been taken to hospital. I should have got here sooner, she thinks. I should have gone down to visit her this morning. Maybe if I'd been, I would have noticed. Could have stopped it before it got this far.

It's not your fault, Collette. She's been ill a long time. Longer than you realised, probably. And how could you risk going back to the nursing home? No chance that you'd escape Malik a third time. But there's no way they can know she's here, she tells herself. They can't be watching the home twenty-four hours a day, can they?

Janine. Here you are, more yourself than you have been since I came back. The frown has gone, the lines of suspicion round the mouth, the angry denial of who and what she is. It's a long time since she watched her mother sleep. The last time was when she was still Lisa, in Lisa's garden, a day not unlike how today has been, all sweaty heat and rising pressure, but with the lulling accompaniments of a padded sunlounger, a gin and tonic and the soothing plash of that stupid slate dolmen water feature she thought was the apotheosis of sophistication, at the time. Ten years ago, maybe, though her mother looks as though thirty have passed. She had blonde hair, then, and her face was plump with creams and camouflage, painted in, contented. How many people only know what a woman really looks like on her deathbed? she wonders. I've been wearing make-up since I was thirteen years old. I don't suppose anyone much has seen me with my natural eyebrows.

Do I want her to wake up? Shake her till she opens her eyes? Maybe I don't. Not if she's going to be that stranger again. The woman who thinks I'm some kind of jailer. Maybe I want her just to slip away. That way I can pretend that she was still here.

She shifts on her chair, feels awkward as she tries to think of something to say. Thinks about how they always start in the movies, can't think of anything better. Clears her throat and starts, if only to drown out the bubbling coming from her mother's lungs. 'Mum? It's me. It's Lisa,' she says, and starts to stroke the hand again.

This is the last time I shall be Lisa, she thinks. After this, Lisa's gone for ever.

'Collette.'

She looks round, realises that she's drifted away as she held her mother's hand, that time has passed in the mist and Vesta is standing in the doorway.

'Hossein told me,' she says. 'Can I come in?'

'Of course,' says Collette, and feels the tears begin to flow.

She lets go of the hand and stands up, and lets Vesta enfold her, hold her, pass her her strength. A kind, kind woman, the help to strangers. Should have been my mum, she thinks. Should have been someone's mother. If you'd been my mother, I would never have had to have left.

'Oh, lovey,' says Vesta, 'it's hard, I know. But I'm here now, and I won't go away.'

A single sob wrenches itself from her chest, and Vesta holds her tighter. Then she lets her go and finds herself a chair.

At two in the morning Collette hears Janine's breathing change. Her mind's been wandering for hours. The effort of maintaining her concentration, of staying in the moment, is too great even when she wants to fix the moment for ever. She hadn't realised that boredom is as much a part of the deathbed experience as grief. The faces of nurses, popping their heads round the door, have come as a welcome distraction.

She's been off in Peckham, back in her childhood, wandering through the rooms and the rows and the boyfriends. Pulling Janine from the settee and supporting her to her bed. Running down to the corner shop for a packet of Rothmans, because kids could still do that errand in those days, and a KitKat for herself from the change. Feeling the burning shame when Janine staggered on her heels and had to hold herself up on the crossing barrier outside the school gates one afternoon, eating fish finger sandwiches in front of the telly. The table where every now and again Janine would insist that they eat together like a proper family, only she never sat down herself, just stalked up and down the carpet and complained about Lisa's cutlery technique. The what-you-looking-at exchanges with the Murphys next door. The way she enjoyed the stupid things Lisa bought her with her salary: the widescreen TV, the halogen cooker, the memory foam mattress.

She hears the change and sits up. Blinks and rubs her eyes. Janine's eyes are flickering, her lips smacking behind the mask. She stares at her intently, squeezes the hand again, to let her know she's here. Is she coming back? Is she?

Vesta sits up and watches, too. Out in the corridor, someone walks past, the swish-swish-swish of orthopaedic soles. Look, she thinks, she's not dying. There's colour in her face, or at least a couple of fever spots on the crowns of her cheeks. You don't get *more* colour when you're dying, do you?

Janine's eyes open. They blink behind her mask and rove over her surroundings, and her breathing becomes more laboured.

'It's okay,' says Collette. 'It's okay, Mum. You're in hospital.'

There doesn't seem to be any power in her hand. It lies in Collette's like a piece of porcelain, cold, unmoving. But slowly her head edges round until her eyes rest upon her face and a burst of mist explodes into the mask.

'Lisa!'

She is cut off by a cough, then another. Feeble, bubbling coughs with no power behind them, her body too weak to allow her to sit forward. Vesta leaps to her feet, all competence where Collette is frozen. She hustles round to the other side of the bed, grabs a cardboard basin, pulls the mask off and slips her arm behind Janine's shoulders. Pulls her gently forward until her mouth hangs over the bowl. Rubs gently at the bony back. A great gob of green-brown phlegm appears at Janine's lips, but the cough is too weak to push it further. Vesta nods at the box of tissues on the bedside table. Collette, unfreezing from her state of shock, grabs them and clears her mother's mouth. Feels tears begin to prick her eyes. She wiped my bum when I was a baby, she thinks. She's been here all my life.

The coughing fit subsides and between them they lower her back on to her pillows, put the mask back in place, endeavour to make her comfortable. Janine gazes at Collette's face while they do it, her eyes wide and adoring. She lies there quietly for a while after she's settled, her mouth half open, her chest moving visibly up and down. Collette wrings out a cloth with water from the jug, and dabs her grey-white forehead. Oh, Janine, she thinks. I love you. Despite it all, I love you.

The heart monitor has slowed. The beats come so far apart, and so unpredictably, that Collette finds it hard to believe that no one has been in to look. But it's what they're expecting, she thinks. Congestive heart failure and pneumonia and a DNR she signed years ago: she's going to slow all the way down until she stops. The thought brings on another surge of sorrow and she busies herself moving back to her chair, picking up the stranded hand and stroking it until she's fought it back again.

'I didn't think you'd come,' whispers Janine, and Collette's heart skips a beat. She leans forward, looks at her mother and sees that her eyes are clear. She knows me, she thinks. She *knows* me.

'I wouldn't stay away,' she replies. 'You knew I'd come back eventually.'

The beginnings of a tired smile play around Janine's lips. 'It's nice,' she says. 'We're back together again.'

Collette forces herself to smile, and squeezes her hand.

'How are you?' asks Janine.

'I'm okay,' she says. 'I'm fine.'

'And Tony? How's Tony?'

She freezes. 'Who?'

'Tony. You know. Handsome Tony, from the club.'

Oh, no, Janine, she thinks. Oh, no, you didn't.

'Such a nice man,' she says. 'Always brought me flowers. Always asking after you. Always losing your phone number, silly goose.'

So now I know, she thinks, and struggles to keep the compassion in her expression. I should have known it all along. Silly woman, always a sucker for a pretty face, and of course, Tony, there to *know* she was losing her marbles when all I thought from miles away was that it was the drink.

The heart monitor goes silent for three whole seconds, the beep cutting into the atmosphere like a harpy's shriek. It's almost the end, she thinks. I won't tell her. Won't run the risk of letting her die upset.

'He's – he's coming in a bit,' she assures her, and feels Vesta shift in her chair. 'He sends his love.'

Janine's eyes begin to droop. I'm losing her, she thinks. I need to say it. I need to say goodbye. Tell her I love her, that I forgive her, that it's okay. I need to do it now. I need ...

'What was that song?' asks Janine. She blinks, slowly. Each time her eyes reopen, the lids take longer to make their journey.

'Which song, Mum?'

'You know. Steve Martin.'

Where does that come from? Steve Martin? On your deathbed?

'I love that song,' she says. 'D'you remember? We used to sing it. When you were little.'

She shakes her head.

'I'd like to hear it,' Janine says. 'It was in *South Pacific*, too. Loved that film. Don't you remember? We used to sing it.'

What song? What song? I don't know what you're talking about, Janine. I'm here and I'd do anything, and you're going to make me let you down when you're dying.

'"Under the Bamboo Tree?"' Vesta is standing back by the drip stand, trying to keep her presence low-key. But she sees Collette struggling and steps in to help.

A tiny up-down on the pillow, and Janine manages a smile.

Collette panics. A faint memory, some vague jumble of notes, but nothing concrete comes to her.

'Shall I start her off?' asks Vesta. 'She's feeling shy.'

'Don't need to be shy with me, Lisa. I'm your mum,' whispers Janine.

Vesta takes a step forward and starts singing. Her singing voice is reedy, cracked: completely different from her mellow speaking tones, as though she doesn't use it often. But the tune is clear, and the words, once she begins, come flooding back to Collette's mind.

'"I like-a you and you like-a me and we like-a both the same",' begins Vesta.

And she's back in Peckham. Four, maybe five years old, before the drink really took Janine over, when she was still pretty and the world was young. They're in the lounge, the TV on in the background, Lisa standing up on the settee and Janine in front of her, holding her upright on the squashy cushions with her hands. And they're singing along with the telly, she remembers it now. *The Man With Two Brains*, Janine's favourite film and, by default, hers. Janine even had an azalea in a pot, and laughed whenever she said the name, though Lisa never understood the joke. And she remembers that this was the song Janine used to sing to her in bed, back when she still sang to her. Her lovely mother: shiny hair and tight sweaters and the scent of Charlie on her collars. She used to sing to me when she tucked me up. I'd forgotten. Through all the years, I have forgotten.

She joins in. '"I like-a say, this very day, I like-a change your na-a-ame".'

'Yes,' says Janine. 'That's it. That's right, my darling.'

And she closes her eyes and never comes back. For the rest of the night, they sit with her, and hold her hands, and sing, until she leaves for good.

Chapter Forty-Six

She'll go, now, thinks Vesta. Poor old Hossein. He'll miss her as much as I will. More, maybe. Being by himself's only something he's had to learn lately.

She feels blank. Dazed. She's desperate for sleep, longs for the narcotic bliss of unconsciousness. Remembers coming home from the all-night vigil over her father's bed, in a car much like this, tired Nigerian driver, air-freshener dangling from the rear-view mirror, LBC on the radio. When her mother passed, she stumbled from the room and lay down in her own bed in the front room and slept until the undertaker knocked on the door. That was in the days when the basement door was still open to the street, before Roy Preece had it shut off, to protect her, he said, from burglars. I want to die at home, she thinks. Just not the home I'm living in.

Collette leans against the window and watches the south London streets go by. The driver has put a CD of mixed soul music into the player and turned it up slightly louder than necessary, a sweet gesture to give them their privacy. She sees him watch her in the mirror as they wait at the traffic lights at

Tooting Bec, the sari shops and sweetshops just opening for morning trade. I need a bacon sandwich, she thinks. Funny how death always seems to make you hungry.

The heatwave finally broke in the night and fat raindrops fall against the windscreen. Vesta cracks her window open and breathes deeply of the fecund, green scent of cracked earth and exhausted foliage. London smells muddy in the rain. Especially after such a long time without it, the coat of smuts and dust that has settled on streets and cars and buildings washing down to grime the pavements. It'll be autumn soon, she thinks. And then another long London winter, the rain and the cold somehow getting through your clothes in a way that country people could never imagine. But Collette will be long gone by then, and Hossein's heart will be broken. I've seen the way he looks at her, when he thinks she's looking away. It's not like he can go too, is it? Not just now, but later. His future's here. He can't spend it on the run.

Collette has been silent since they left the hospital. Dry-eyed. Still in shock, thinks Vesta, even though she's known that this was coming. It's always still a shock. I had eighteen months with Mum, changing her sheets and mopping her brow and cleaning her down with a sponge as she crumbled away into her pillow, but I still didn't expect it when it finally came. Still felt like I was falling off a cliff. I remember: until the funeral, it was like looking at the world from the other side of a wall of glass. Everything – sound, smell, touch – was doughy and dull, as if someone had turned the dials down on my senses. That's how she'll be feeling now. Just – empty.

As they wait to turn right into Tooting Bec Road, she notices a shiny black car, smoked glass windows, two cars back with its indicator on. Why would you want to drive around in something that looks like a hearse? she wonders. There's enough death in the world without reminding yourself of it every second you're on the road. It bounds forward as the lights change, cuts across the oncoming traffic as though the law didn't exist at all, provokes a chorus of blasting horns. Collette seems to jump from her fugue state and stares at the shaking fists of the drivers on the Balham High Road.

'Bloody Mercedes,' says their driver. 'It's always Mercedes, isn't it? They think they own the road.'

Collette's head drops back against the headrest and the life goes out of her eyes. Vesta waits a few seconds, then says: 'You did well tonight, Collette.'

Collette looks at her with watery eyes. 'Thanks.'

'How do you feel?'

She grimaces, shrugs. 'You know,' she says.

Might as well broach the subject, thinks Vesta. 'I'm sorry,' she says. 'About what she said. About Tony. That must have been ... a shock.'

'I might have known,' says Collette. 'I can't believe I didn't work it out. She'd do anything for a man who paid her a bit of attention. I just didn't think he'd find her. Denial, I suppose. That's what they'd say it was.'

'You can't know everything, Collette. That was good of you, though. I admired you. What you did with it.'

'Thanks,' says Collette.

'You mustn't take it to heart. I daresay she didn't know what she was doing.'

'No, I daresay,' says Collette, but there's an ugly edge of bitterness to her voice.

Vesta tries another route to comfort. 'Hossein'll be waiting when we get back. They all will.'

Collette sighs. 'I think I could just do with some sleep.'

'I'm sure. Me too. Some sleep before you start dealing with things.'

Collette's brow puckers, as though it's not occurred to her that there might be things to deal with.

'You'll want to call an undertaker,' she says. 'They gave you some cards, didn't they?'

'Um, I …' she holds her bag out, open, as though this constitutes some kind of answer. 'I don't even know if I'm going to miss her, Vesta.'

Vesta lays a hand over hers. What do you want me to say, lovey? Don't worry, the pain will kick in soon?

'You have to just take this stuff one day at a time,' she says, horribly aware of all the clichés that death forces from one's lips. She has heard so many with-the-angels-now palliatives from well-meaning people over the years that she wants to bring in a law to ban them.

They turn right past the common, and Vesta notices that the Mercedes is still behind them. Maybe it *is* a hearse, she thinks. Or a funeral car. What would someone in a car like that be doing down here in the middle of the day? 'It will kick in sometime, I'm afraid. You can't avoid it. It's just – how it is.'

'Maybe it won't,' says Collette. 'She's been gone a long time already. And so have I. I don't know if there's much point in throwing a funeral, really. It's not like I know who her friends were. Even if she had any. All she ever wanted to talk about was what had happened on *EastEnders*, when I used to go and see her. Or moan on about the council.'

'Oh, Collette,' says Vesta, 'you've *got* to have a funeral.'

A flash of defiance. 'I don't, you know.'

Their driver is agog. She can feel him longing to turn the music down so he can hear properly. Collette's head slumps back against the window, and she stares out once again, her lips pursed. They reach the three-way junction at the bottom of Northbourne Common, and the driver takes the right-hand branch.

Vesta leans forward. 'No, sorry. We need the other road. The one that runs past the station.'

He puts his brakes on, pulls over to the side to prepare for a U-turn. The black Merc glides past them and turns in to a side road fifty yards up on the left. Suddenly, Collette is sitting up, alert, staring after it. Oh, God, it's not, is it, thinks Vesta. I couldn't have been that unobservant, could I?

The driver makes the turn in three moves and heads back towards Station Road. Collette cranes through the rear window. She's grinding her teeth. If it comes out now, thinks Vesta, I don't know what we'll do. Go on to Gatwick?

They get caught at the traffic lights and have to wait a full minute. A small queue builds up behind them: a Fiesta, a Panda and what looks like the Poshes' SUV, though it could be any SUV, really. Featureless, soulless guzzlers of petrol, a mystery in a world that claims to be worried about resources. No black bonnet emerges from the side road, no cashmere overcoats with the collars turned up against the rain.

Collette sits back as they turn the corner. 'I can't go on like this,' she says. 'Jumping at shadows. Hiding every time I see a tinted window.'

'Yes,' says Vesta.

'It's time I moved on,' she says.

'Hossein will be sad. I'll be sad, too, come to that.'

Collette clamps her lips together and stares out of the window again.

'He will, you know,' says Vesta. 'You're the first ... well, I've never seen him interested in anyone ...'

Collette tries to ignore her. 'I don't suppose anybody much wants to stay in that house now,' she says. 'He'll be gone the minute he gets the chance, trust me. But I'm not dragging him into all this. He doesn't deserve that. I was only here because of ...' She has to wait a beat before she carries on. The crying's going to start really soon, now, thinks Vesta. She thinks she's hard as nails, but she'll be in bits by tonight. '... because of her. I'm stupid. I shouldn't have got mixed up with all of you. Christ, what a mess. He deserves better than that. He was fine here, your little cosy family and your cups of tea, before he knew I existed. He'll be fine when I'm gone, too. We're not some Romeo and Juliet. It just ... is. What it is. You'll all be fine. You'll be better off, really. Give it a couple of weeks and you'll all have forgotten I was ever here.'

Vesta raises her eyebrows. 'You think I want to still be here? After ... *that*?'

Collette shuts up.

'Good God. I bloody hate the place. If that ... *bugger* had just given me a bit of cash I'd have been out of there like a shot.'

This seems to come as news to Collette. 'Really?'

Vesta pulls a face at her. This conversation is getting too personal for a public place. 'Yes,' she says.

Collette considers her. 'It's a crappy life, on the road. Really. You don't want to do that.'

'No. No, you're right. I was thinking more about the seaside, myself. Open a café, feed the seagulls. But I've blown that now, haven't I? I'm going to be stuck in that hole in the ground with the damp and the drains and the ... ghosts for the rest of my life.'

Collette's eyes fill with tears. 'My God, Vesta. I'd do *anything*. I'm so tired. I'm *so damn tired*. Sometimes I think I'm so tired I just want to die.'

Chapter Forty-Seven

She will never be quite sure how it happened. Cats are like that. All love-love and climbing up for a cuddle, then one day they're hanging off your face with their claws unsheathed. Maybe he has an infection somewhere that she's not noticed, maybe it's just a bad mood because his usual marauding had been curtailed by the rain, but Psycho, love of her life, suddenly goes from rolling over and showing her his tummy to slashing at her.

One of his claws catches in the skin on the bridge of her nose, half a centimetre from her eye, and suddenly the two of them are struggling, Cher shrieking in pain and rage and the cat, startled, digging the claw in further then thrashing about trying to extract himself. Then he's free, and he's flying across the room under the impetus of her throw and crashing against the wall. He lands on the carpet, stunned, and crouches there, glaring at her in reproach.

Cher slaps a hand up to the cut on her nose. Blood pours out of it, soaking into the corner of her eye, where it stings. 'Fuck,' she says to the cat, then, as the pain kicks in, yells 'FUCK!' Then white-hot rage fills her, and she runs at him, picks him up by the scruff of his neck and slaps his backside with furious passion. Psycho squirms in her grip, but he doesn't fight back. Even as she's beating him, she's thinking oh, God, it was an accident, what am I doing? But the pain is ferocious and she's in the full grip of her animal brain.

She carts him over to the door, opens it and hurls him on to the landing. Later, she will at least be able to comfort herself that she wasn't so out of control that she threw him out of the window. Psycho somersaults through the air and lands on the carpet on all fours. His eyes are huge with hurt. People who don't live with cats don't know this: that if you know them well, their emotions are written large across their faces, if you only care to look. He hangs his head like a beaten dog, and bobs from foot to foot.

'Yeah, *fuck off*!' she bellows. 'I don't want to bloody see you, you *bastard*!'

She slams the door, shaking, and goes to examine her nose in the mirror. The cut is only a few millimetres long – nothing on the injuries from which she's still recovering, but the fact that he's missed her eye by a whisker makes her blood run cold. Imagination overtakes her, makes her jump outside her body and see herself, cat attached to her eyeball, membrane breaking and juicy jelly cascading over her cheek. She shudders and presses her hand to her eyes. Wets a bit of bog paper from the roll she half-inched from a pub a few weeks back, dabs at the cut.

The cat scratches at her door. He doesn't like being excluded, is trying to apologise. 'Piss off,' she calls. God, it's lucky they're all still out at the hospital, she thinks. I'd have scared them half to death with my shouting.

Psycho yowls, and a piteous paw appears in the gap at the

bottom of the door. She's already over the anger, but she can't resist punishing him a little more. He can stay out there till I'm ready. Little sod. She screws her eye shut and sprays a little perfume on the cut. A cut nose is one thing: a septic nose a whole other ballgame.

A few seconds of frantic scrabbling, then it stops. Cher can feel the rejection beaming through the wood. Oh, poor old sod, she thinks. He's my best friend and he didn't mean to do it. She chooses a little round plaster from the box Collette brought up when she was sick, and fixes it over the cut. It's only oozing, now. It felt like it had gone all the way through to the bone at the time, but it's clearly not that serious. She goes and opens the door.

Psycho is sulking. He has retreated to the corner by the Landlord's cupboard, and has hunched himself into a tea cosy, his chin tucked in to his chest and his eyes wet with reproach. 'Oh, sorry, lover,' she says. 'It's all right. I'm not cross any more.'

She goes over to pick him up. He clocks her approach, and shoots off up the landing, towards the bathroom. Christ, *cats*. You can never snub them without getting snubbed right back. 'Oh, come on, Psycho,' she says, trying her reasonable tone, and follows. 'You hurt me too, you know.'

He stops by the bathroom door and stares balefully at her. 'Honestly,' she says. 'If you had the right sort of mouth, you'd be pouting. Come on. Let me make it up to you.'

She tries blinking at him, but he just lashes his tail in return. Now all she wants is to scoop his hard little body up into her arms and kiss the top of his head until he forgives her. She loves that cat. Loves him stupidly. He's the first creature she's ever been able to love without worrying, and she's distressed to think that she might have spoiled it all. 'Oh, Psycho,' she says, and goes to grab him. He slinks backwards, ducks down and slides through her fingers, bolts back up to the other end of the landing. Stops and stares at her by Thomas's door, then pops out a paw and pulls it open. Vanishes up the attic stairs.

Cher hesitates. Thomas is not a hospitable sort of soul, though she feels she knows him better than she did. He has the largest flat of all of them, apart from Vesta, but no one has ever seen inside. There's music coming down the stairs, a sound that surprises her, as she's never heard anything through her ceiling. She can't imagine Roy Preece going to the expense of soundproofing when it got converted, but there you go. Every now and then she's heard some heavy noise, like something being dropped or dragged, but she's never heard music. She'd always assumed he was just a quiet neighbour.

Would he be pissed off? If I just went up? Maybe if I call up the stairs? I can't help it if he's left the door off the latch, can I?

She cracks the door open and pops her head inside. Pale beige carpeting. Very nice. And though the stairs are narrow, it's lovely and bright in here, lit by the stained-glass window that used to illuminate the whole landing. 'Hello?' she calls.

There's another door at the top, just slightly ajar. The Bee Gees. 'Staying Alive', out of *Saturday Night Fever*. Maybe that's why I don't hear it. There's barely a bass line in there, by today's standards. Most of the time it must be drowned out by that classical crap from downstairs, anyway, coming up through my floorboards. Totally not the sort of music I'd expect to be coming out of Thomas's flat. If I'd expected anything, it would be screechy women and violins. I don't suppose he can hear me over it.

She mounts the stairs, her hand pressed against the plywood wall that divides them from the Landlord's cubbyhole. The window is lovely. From the outside it looks dull and dark, but from in here she can see a lovely pattern of flowers in greens and blues and reds. What a waste, she thinks. If I had this window, I'd have glass shelves all the way up, with glass ornaments on them to catch the light. He's just got a couple of coats on hooks on the wall, and a row of boring-looking books on the windowsill.

It doesn't smell too good, either. The cheesy, mushroomy smell that's been getting stronger through the house as the drought went on seems to be concentrated here, and mingles with a heavy honk of chemical flowers. Bloody hell, thinks Cher. Open a window, maybe? She stops halfway up and calls out again, but no one comes.

Bloody cat, she thinks. I should just leave him to choke to death in that pong. He'll come back when he's ready. But she doesn't want to leave him. Not with things so bad between them. He might never come back, if I don't apologise properly, and I'll just die if he doesn't come back. I've got some sardines in tomato sauce down in my room. If I can get him back there, he'll be back up snogging me with fish-breath in no time. She goes on up to the top and pushes open the door.

Sloped ceilings, and a smell so strong it brings her close to retching. She's surprised how much space there is in here under the eaves. It would be a nice flat, if it didn't look so unloved: manky old taupe three-piece, a battered row of kitchen units in green and brown, like her own, plastic all over the carpet as though he doesn't want to dirty it. The cushions on either end of the three-seat settee have brown stains on them. Fake tan, she thinks. How weird. What looks like thigh marks, and the imprint of a bony bum. Like what Adrienne Maloof kept leaving all over people's couches in *The Real Housewives of Beverly Hills*. I wonder if it really comes out with baby wipes? It doesn't look like it would to me. It looks pretty deeply sunk in, like whoever was wearing it sat there for a long, long time.

The music is coming from an old-fashioned record player on the kitchen countertop. One of those box things you find in junk shops, orange and grey, with a tall spindle so you can stack singles on top of each other. She's never seen one working before, and understands now why the music doesn't travel: there are no speakers, just tinny falsetto voices issuing from the front of the player itself.

The track finishes and is replaced by the hiss and crackle of old vinyl. Now, she can hear the sound of water running in the bathroom. Oh, God, how embarrassing. He's taking a shower. I'd better get that damn cat and scoot, before he comes out. Bet he won't want to catch me looking at his cardboard air freshener collection. It's bloody freaky. I know there's a pong in here, but he's got hundreds.

She tips her head to look at them as the first notes of 'How Deep Is Your Love' crackle out, covering her presence again. He's made something of a decorative point of them. They dangle from the roof beam, fixed in with drawing pins through their strings, wafting out mixed smells of pine and rose, freesia and sea breeze that cloy together like syrup, catching at the back of the throat and burning the inside of the nostrils. Cher can feel her chest and neck start to prickle, the first signs of an allergic reaction. She gets like that on buses sometimes, especially when it's wet, when someone sits down next to her in damp cloth that's been washed in that built-in-perfume washing powder. How can he not notice? she wonders. Surely he doesn't think it's a *good* smell?

And then she sees Psycho. He's hopped up on to a table on

the far side of the room and sits among a strange collection of knick-knacks, lashing his tail at her and pretending to be a statue. She gives him a blink, and his green eyes briefly blink back. He raises a paw to his mouth, licks it with a dainty pink tongue and swipes it over his ear. Oh, thank God, he's forgiven me. Better get him down from there before he smashes something, though.

She goes over and whispers to him, and he looks up and gives her a smile. He sits between a pair of sunglasses – Chanel or Chanel knock-off, by the look of the brassy circles on the open arms – and a pendant on a chain, one of those enamelled Chinese fish with the multiple joints, turquoise and red. It's a strange collection of things. A bunch of keys on a chain topped with a small ceramic shoe, a tiny leather-bound Bible, a ball-point pen, clumsily encased in putty that's been inset with shiny beads before it dried: the sort of project a child would do for Mother's Day. A mug tree from whose arms hangs a collection of bracelets.

'Oh, Psycho, I'm sorry,' she says, and puts out a finger for him to butt with his head. Opens her arms to him. Psycho rears on his hind legs, throws himself against her chest and begins to purr. Wriggles upwards so his front paws are on her shoulder as she picks him up, presses his wet black nose into her ear as she hugs him tight. 'Oh, my pussycat,' she says. 'Let's not argue again.'

She's still kissing his head as she turns round to go back the way she came and glances through the open bedroom door. Jumps, because there's someone in there, a skinny woman, all shrivelled skin and staring blue eyes, stock-still on an old dining chair beside the bed. Cher blushes, opens her mouth to apologise, explain herself, then closes it, hard. She feels as though someone's superglued her feet to the floor, wants to back away, turn, run like hell for the stairs – because the woman is Nikki.

Was Nikki. Oh, God.

Nikki dried up, a Nikki made of leather. Her flaming red hair still recognisable, but brushed out, sprayed and curled in a grim, hard facsimile of an Oscar-night 'do'. She's Nikki, but crossed with a Galapagos tortoise, all hard and gnarly and thin, thin, thin. False fingernails, filed sharp and painted scarlet, stuck on to bony fingers, cheekbones to die for. A green shift dress, and feet and ankles, tendons standing out like guy ropes, each bone delineated by the thin, hard skin that adheres to it, all crammed into over-tight, film-star stilettos with winkle-picker toes.

She finds her breath, gulps in acrid air and turns to run for the door.

Thomas stands outside the bathroom, blocking her exit. He's dressed like a surgeon, in a white plastic pinny that's smeared with brown, and holding a small circular saw.

Chapter Forty-Eight

She doesn't hesitate. Throws, because she has nothing else to throw, the cat at him, bolts inside the bedroom and slams the door.

A smaller room, one side cut off to make space for the bathroom next door. Cher leans against the door and holds the handle, looks wildly round for something that will help her, a weapon, something to stop him getting in. There's nothing. A horrid, bare, dry little room with a divan bed and a chest of drawers against the far wall, an eaves cupboard, a miserable flatpack wardrobe. He's coming. *Oh, my God*, he's coming!

Nikki grins at her mirthlessly from her chair. It's only after a couple of seconds that she notices that she has a second companion. Up against the wall next to her, thrown face down on the floor like a doll whose owner has moved on to the next piece of plastic. Dark hair, faded bluish, brittle, the scalp showing through, the skin gone grey and beginning to flake off from the frame. Arms bent as though they've been designed to hold on to the arms of a throne, the fingers clawed. Cher can see up the skirt, see dainty underwear hanging off shrivelled buttocks. She looks like she doesn't weigh a pound, but she's the only thing within reach.

Cher braces her foot against the bottom of the door and stretches. Gets a handhold round the ankle and starts to pull the body towards her. The skin is oily under the touch, not dry, as she'd been expecting. It slips through her grasp and the dry clutching fingers catch on the carpet, hold her there. Cher drops to her haunches, grips the ankle with both hands and hauls, lets out a shriek of effort. Something in the fingers snaps and the body flies free. Lands on top of her dry, dry hair in her open mouth. She throws it against the door and scoots backwards on her bottom, howls out her disgust.

Outside, 'More Than A Woman' starts up on the record player. She barks out a laugh. Did he put this on purposely? Is this his special music for doing whatever he was doing in that bathroom? Is this why those drains got blocked up? He's probably been putting stuff down the bog for months, flushing away the stuff he's taken out of these women, clogging up ... oh, God, Roy Preece drowned in *Nikki*.

The door handle turns and he pushes against it. She sees the door crack open, catch on the corpse behind it. It won't hold for any time at all. He's already bracing, jiggling it back and forth, and she's jumping on the floor.

Cher jumps on to the bed and dives through the open window.

She hits the tiles, and finds herself sliding. Four floors up, and she's heading down, at speed. Months of dust and pollen and traffic smuts that have settled on surfaces in the dry heat have formed a slick in the rain, a slick as unpredictable as ice, and just as deadly. Her cheap flip-flops skate over the surface, her legs wheeling as she hunts for traction. Her right hand, flat on the roof, catches on something that drives itself deep into her palm. She shrieks in pain as she jerks to a halt, feels something snap at the base of her neck, rolls on to her face and digs her knees in to the tiles.

She's two feet from the edge. A mass of blackened leaves in the gutter, and beyond that, somewhere far away, the pavement. Her hand is snagged on a nail: three inches of rusty iron between herself and the long drop. She can hear him in the bedroom, now. Has no idea where she's going to go from here. But she pulls her knees in underneath her and worms her way upwards until her hand is no longer taking her weight. Something's happened to her arm. It seems to have lost all its strength, and there's a grinding, searing pain at the top of her chest, as though two snapped ends of something are rubbing together. A wave of giddiness breaks over her. She shakes her soaking rat-tail hair like a dog and the screech of protest that shoots through her body brings her back to the world.

The nail is deeply embedded in her heartline. Cher kneels up, stares at the ragged tear that starts at her wrist and runs the length of her palm, where it dragged through and formed a brake. It's missed the big vein in her wrist by nothing more than a miracle. There's blood spreading over the lichen on the tiles, but it's spreading, not pumping.

A sound at the window, five feet from her face. She jerks her head up and sees Thomas, leaning on the windowsill, blinking from behind his tinted specs.

'Oh, Cher,' he says.

'Keep the fuck away from me,' she says.

'What are you *doing* here?' he asks.

She doesn't know how to answer. The question is so unexpected, his benign smile so calm, that she's completely thrown.

She looks down at her hand again. Can't stay like this, whatever I do, she thinks. Takes hold of the hand with her left, grits her teeth, counts to three and yanks it upwards before she can lose her nerve. Feels the world swim away from her, gasps, and is free.

She starts to edge away from the window. Her flip-flops slip and slick on the rain, throw her feet out in front of her, and she flails, slides, sees the gutter heading fast towards her, gasps again at the pain. A tile snaps and breaks free, skitters downwards, over the edge. Cher freezes. Counts one, two, three before she hears it shatter on the concrete below.

'You should come in from there,' says Thomas. 'It's not safe.'

'Fuck off!' she snaps. Remembers that she's in the middle of a city, in the late afternoon. Starts yelling. 'Help! Somebody! Help me!'

Come on. Come on. *Somebody's* got to hear me.

Another tile breaks off. The roof is old and decrepit, like everything else about this house.

Thomas puts a finger to his mouth and hushes her. What is *wrong* with this man? He seems to think this is some kind of party game. 'Come on,' he says. 'Come inside.'

Yeah, *right*. So you can turn me into a stick doll. 'Help!' she shouts again. 'Christ, *please*! Somebody help me!'

Thomas shrugs and puts his hands on the windowsill. He's coming out after her.

She kicks off her useless flip-flops and scrambles upwards, tiles flying out from beneath her grip. It's hard going, one-handed, the injured arm flopping like someone's cut its strings, but desperation lends her strength. If he gets to me, I don't stand a chance. He's twice my size, and this hand is useless. Where *is* everybody? Where are they? They can't all be taking a nap and sleeping. Not through this.

She reaches the ridge and straddles it. Peers down into the street, looking for a sign that someone, anyone, has heard her. The Poshes' SUV is gone from the driveway, and all the kids' toys have been taken inside. Don't say they've gone away. That bloody woman.

From up here, Northbourne looks beautiful: all tiles and tree-tops, elegant chimneys whose brickwork embellishments you never see in among the riot of plastic fascias and sandwich boards. Nothing moves in the street below. She can see the roof of the station, but if there's anyone there they're under cover, waiting out the rain. In the far distance, between the tree trunks, she can see a few lonely figures walking on the common. They'll never hear her. And if they look up, all they'll see is leaves.

Thomas stands up. Teeters for a moment as he finds his balance, then folds his arms and grins at her like a death-head.

'Don't come any closer,' says Cher, and can hear how pathetic she sounds. Like some girl in a teen movie who's about to have her head cut off. Oh, fuck, she thinks, but that's what I am. That's exactly what I am. 'I mean it,' she adds, tentatively, but it doesn't sound convincing.

'Cher,' he says, 'you don't have a lot of choice, you know.'

'Get to fuck, you loony bastard.'

To her surprise, he looks hurt. It's as though he doesn't realise that there's anything odd about what she's seen. As though, in his mind, she's the one in the wrong, the interloper.

'I'm going to come up,' he says. 'I think you could do with a hand.'

Cher runs her hands over the tiles. Manages to get her fingers under one and prise it loose. Waves it at him.

'Oh, come on.'

'I will. You come one step closer, and I will.'

He takes a step closer. Cher throws the tile at his head. He ducks sideways and it sails past, misses him by miles. He comes upright, a beatific smile on his face. 'Well,' he says. Looks down at his feet for a moment, then hurls himself up the roof with a speed that shocks her. She only has a moment to throw herself backwards, gripping the roof flashing between her thighs like a circus rider, howling as her dead arm flops back and opens out her collarbone with its weight.

Thomas snatches at thin air where her face used to be and lurches to a stop, his centre of gravity far over the other side of the roof beam. He staggers. Rocks at the hips like a comedy drunk, drops of rainwater flying from his windmilling arms.

She takes the only chance she'll have, and kicks his legs out from under him.

Chapter Forty-Nine

Collette dreams she is on the banks of the Ganges, among the funeral pyres, surrounded by wailing mourners. She has covered herself in ash, matted her hair with mud, and is weeping, weeping, weeping. She picks up a stone and chips at her hairline, feels blood trickle down her forehead, digs cracked fingernails into dirty wrists. All around her, figures in white, blurred by smoke, howl out their sorrow in family groups. I'm the only one who's alone, she thinks. I'm the only one.

A man in a coarse linen *dhoti shalwar* stops to look at her. His feet are bare and he wears big gold rings. 'You're crying, madam,' he says. 'Have you come to the funeral?'

'Yes,' she replies, and the howl in her head grows louder. 'My mother. She's died. I wanted to say goodbye.'

'And which one is she?' he asks, and sweeps an elegant hand across the burning landscape. She follows his gesture with her eyes, and sees a hundred burning ghats placed down the water's edge, black smoke boiling from crimson flames and blotting out the sky. 'I don't know,' she says. 'I don't know which one.'

'Well, you'd better hurry,' he says, 'you don't want to miss it.'

And then she's on her feet, tripping on the hem of her over-long *lehenga choli*, pulling her scarf across her body because she feels wrong, with so much of her torso on show, when people have died. And she's running from pyre to pyre, slipping in mud stamped out by a hundred generations, and weeping, clutching passers-by by the arm and begging: 'I've lost Janine! Which one is Janine? I can't find her! Oh, God, where's Janine?'

And then she's awake, and her grief is choking her. Her throat has closed up and she struggles for a moment to breathe. She breaks through the barrier of tears and inhales. It's not true, she tells herself. It was just a dream. And then she remembers, and it's as if it's happened all over again.

She stares at the ceiling and listens to the insistent shush of the rain through the open window, feels tears prickle in her eyes. This is no good. I can't afford this. I must get up, get on with something. Be busy. She checks the time on her phone. Nearly five. She's been asleep for four hours. Hossein should be home from his Home Office signing-in duties soon. If she lets herself sleep any longer, she'll be awake all night.

She slides out from the bed and runs herself a glass of water. Coppery lukewarm London tap water, but it tastes delicious. She must be dehydrated, not surprisingly. She remembers a couple of plastic cups of tea in the night, Vesta going off to the vending machine in the ground-floor lobby, sugaring them up for energy, but she didn't drink much from either. She runs another glass, drinks half of it down and goes to the window. It's amazing how different the back gardens of Northbourne look in the rain. The greens are greener already, and brickwork she's thought of as faded terracotta turns out to be dark rust now that the dust has washed off it. She pulls the curtain back and watches the world;

wonders at the way people can simply vanish as if they'd never been.

Someone's crying. She thinks they've been crying all along, since she woke. The desolate sobs of someone young, lost, vulnerable.

Collette squints out of the window. The crying sounds as though it's coming from outside, but it's so hard to tell. Though the heat has broken, everyone has left their windows open to let the cool air in. The crying could be coming from anywhere.

Is it Cher? It sounds as if it could be. She leans out of the window and looks up, but the girl's window is firmly closed. As she ducks back in under the sash, she looks down and sees that a number of roof tiles have fallen into the basement area and shattered. Thank God I'm moving on, she thinks. This place will come down round our ears in the winter, if this is what a little shower of rain will do.

The sobbing continues, low, miserable and despairing. The occasional 'ow' breaking in to the rhythm. They sound like they're in trouble, she thinks. It sounds like somebody's hurt.

Am I still dreaming? Am I having one of those dreams where you think you're awake? Am I hearing myself cry in my sleep, and thinking it's coming from outside me? I am so tired. Maybe I've never woken up at all.

She drifts across the room and slips through the door. In the corridor, the faint sound of Gerard Bright's music lulls her, makes her feel safe. If I were awake it would be a hundred decibels louder, she thinks. I'm hearing it through the fog of sleep, registering it because it's there. She stands at the foot of the stairs, looking up, for a long time. All is silent up on the landing: just the ticketty-ticketty-tick of rain on glass. Something's changed about the light up there. Despite the overcast skies, the landing looks brighter that she's ever seen it. She's halfway up the stairs before she sees that it's because Thomas's door stands wide open.

The sound of sobbing has disappeared. She pauses on the landing and listens at Cher's door, but hears no sound within. She taps, calls her name, but hears no response.

Something draws her to Thomas's door. It's so odd to see it open. She's never seen it so before, never even glimpsed in to the stairwell. A terrible smell rolls down the stairs, a smell of rot and chemicals that fills her with dread. And yet she finds herself walking up. This must still be a dream, she thinks, as she runs her hand up the plasterboard wall of the stairwell. In real life this smell would be enough to send me back down the stairs to look for one of the others. So I might as well go with it. At least I *know* it's not real, not like when I was on the banks of the Ganges. That felt so real I thought I was going to die.

She reaches the door at the top of the stairs and finds that it, too, is open. She calls, tentatively, into the room: 'Hello? Thomas? Hello?' And steps inside. Sloped ceilings, a generalised grime, and an extraordinary and pungent collection of cardboard air fresheners drawing-pinned to the sloping ceiling as though they are a decorative flourish, a television on a stand and a record player on which the arm goes back and forth, back and forth, in the centre of an old LP. She goes over and takes it off. Can't bear to watch old things damage themselves.

Cher's black cat shoots out from under the stained and sagging sofa, trots towards her then moves to a gallop as he gets near. 'Hey, Psycho,' she says, and stretches out a hand. He ducks, slips past her legs and hurtles off into the house. She shakes her head. He's never been a friendly cat, though he's devoted to Cher and follows her wherever she goes.

And now she can hear the sobbing again. It's muffled, as if the voice's owner is shut behind a door. She calls out, once more, more loudly this time. Wherever Thomas is, he's not here in among his stinking artefacts. 'Hello?'

The sobbing stops. A shout in response. 'Hello? Hello? Oh my God! Is someone there?'

It's Cher. Somewhere in this flat, sounding weak and scared and desperate. 'Cher?' she calls.

A noise on the sloped ceiling; someone shifting, up on the roof, the sound of a tile loosening itself, sliding over her head and smashing on the flags below. 'Oh, God! Collette! Oh, God, I'm here!'

'Where?'

'On the roof!'

She almost asks what she's doing there, but thinks better of it. '*Where?*'

'*On the roof!* I can't get down. Please. Help!'

She's beginning to realise that she's awake; fully awake and in a place that makes her very uncomfortable. She doesn't want to wait for Thomas to come back – he's not the sort who would take kindly to uninvited guests.

'How did you get up there?'

'Bedroom window. Oh, no, Collette, don't ...'

'Hold on,' she calls, and goes to the bedroom.

No, I *am* dreaming. I must be. That looks like ...

She stops in the doorway and gapes. Her scalp crawls. Oh, my God, those are *women*. One on a chair, an Egyptian queen made of leather, one on the floor behind the door, one arm contorted beneath her and the other thrown full-length over her head, flaking into the carpet like a resident of Pompeii. Bags of salts, bottles of oil, a rail of dresses. What is this? What *is* this?

Cher's voice brings her back to herself. 'Collette? Collette!'

She does as she always does, as she'd trained herself. Thinks: I won't think about this now, I'll think about it later. Action always trumps thinking in an emergency. She steps gingerly over the wizened brown legs of the woman on the floor and climbs on to the bed. Leans her arms along the windowsill and puts her face out into the rain.

Cher is above her, huddled against the chimney, her clothes clinging to her body and her hair poodled around her face. She's shivering, barefoot, only wearing a light top over her jeans and it's soaked through. She's holding her right arm with her left, her hand dangling between her legs, and black circles ring her eyes. Collette looks closer, and sees that her jeans are stained with blood. It drips from the tips of her useless fingers, mingles with the water and trickles away across the roof.

'Are you okay?' she asks, redundantly.

'Peachy,' says Cher, and grinds her teeth.

Her head is fogged with confusion. 'What the hell's going on? What are those ...?' She points back into the room.

'Do you mind if we talk about that later?' says Cher, in a small voice, her tone surprisingly humble. Her body is rattling with cold and shock and she is beginning to sway on her perch. 'I could do with some help. I've done something to my shoulder.'

'How did you – where's Thomas?'

'He ...' Cher shakes her head. 'He's gone.'

'Gone? Gone where?'

'He ...' She seems confused, dazed, rests her head against the brickwork. 'I think I killed the fucker. He was coming after me, so I pushed him.' She jerks her head behind her, then hisses and clutches her shoulder. 'Collette,' she says, 'it's nice to chat and all, but ...'

Collette slaps herself internally to wake herself up. 'Okay. Yes. Hold on.'

She hoists herself on to the window frame, lurches forward, saves herself by grabbing the open pane. Sees the trees on the other side of the road seesaw towards and away from her. 'Careful,' calls Cher.

'Yes, thanks, I'll try.'

There are dead bodies in the bedroom, she thinks. All this time, we've been living downstairs from a bunch of dead bodies. It looks like he's been mummifying them. They can't have got that way naturally, can they? And, oh, God, I hope Vesta doesn't wake up. One more cracked skull outside her bedroom window and I think she'll tip over the edge.

'Oh, Collette?'

'Yes?'

'I'm sorry. About your mum.'

She looks up in surprise. It seems like such a startlingly *normal* thing for someone to say under the circumstances. She's such an odd kid. 'That's okay,' she says, because she can't really work out what the appropriate response would be.

She hooks a leg over the windowsill and lowers herself slowly down. Heights have never been her thing. Looking over edges has always made the inside of her head ring hollow, like a bell, the muscles behind her ears contract. Well, don't *look* down, she tells herself. Just look at where you're treading, and look at Cher. Once you're up there, you'll have no choice but to keep your cool. Just don't think about what you're doing now, or you might not be able to do it at all.

No wonder he was so calm about the Landlord. No wonder he knew so much about what we were doing. He's been doing it for God knows how long. Up here in the roof, all snuggled up with his corpses. Oh, Jesus, this is so *high*. How come it doesn't look this high from the street? Lying on her stomach, she edges along the window frame until there is no more window frame to be had.

She looks up at Cher. The girl's face has a peculiar tinge of green to it and the shaking has stopped. She's going into shock, she thinks. I need to get her inside, get her warmed up. I wonder if that break's cutting off her circulation? I swear I see a lump on her collarbone. It's snapped clean in two. She must be in agony.

'Hold on,' she says. 'Just ... hang on in there, Cher.'

She puts the ball of a foot down on the tiles to slide herself, and it slips out from under her like it's skating on ice. Collette grabs at the window again, pants as panic overtakes her. I'll just ... I'll go back in. I'll go and find someone. Someone else will know what to do. Someone else will know what to do. Hossein. Christ, bloody Gerard Bright, if it comes to it. Anyone. I'm not brave enough. I can't. She hangs her head in through the window, sees the thighs of the girl in the chair, so still, so thin. Oh, that poor child, she thinks. He would have done it to her, too, and we'd never have known. All the people in this house, moving on, the waters closing over their heads, we'd have been sad for a couple of days, we'd've asked each other where she was, and then ... we would have forgotten her. The way everyone who lives here is forgotten, one by one, by the people they've shared their space with. The same all over London, the anonymity we all cherish: it's a sure road to oblivion.

She pulls herself together. No one has ever missed Cher, or mourned her. *She* won't be one of the people who've let her down. She puts her foot on the windowsill, uses the slip of the tiles to slide herself upwards. Gets a foot in the hinge and kicks again. Now her head is five feet from the roof's ridge, her foot a knee-bend from the top of the window frame. She feels her hip shriek with the strain of the angle, flat on her face, all her weight on her torso, and then her foot is there. She steadies, brings her other foot up beside it and bunny-hops to where she can grab the flashing.

Cher looks as if she's fallen asleep. Up here, with no shelter from the wind, the rain gusts horizontally, catches her in the face like birdshot. It's hard to believe that yesterday they were still in a heatwave, for today they are a long way into autumn. Weird little fucked-up island on the edge of the Arctic circle, she thinks, one of the world's largest economies, and we're still prioritising bankers' second houses over kids like this. If she had disappeared, no one apart from us would know, much less care. She's been disappeared for years.

She reaches out and touches the girl's good arm. Cher jumps, opens her eyes and lets out a moan. Now she's close up, Collette can see the damage she's done to herself. Her collarbone jags out beneath her skin, and shades of black and brown and khaki spread across her chest, vanish inside her top. Her hand has been ripped open by something sharp, the cut dirty and wide and still bleeding. She's going to need a hospital, this time. If Collette can get her down off this roof before she dies of the shock, she's going to have to be sucked back into the system. This is beyond any of their abilities.

'Come on,' she says. She's glad that Cher is small and light, at least. If she were even Vesta's size this would be impossible. 'This is going to hurt. I'm sorry. I don't know how to make it *not*.'

Cher laughs, weakly. 'I'll just have to kill you later.' Still got her sarcasm, which has to be a good sign. She lets out a cough, freezes, tries to suppress another.

Collette takes her good hand and helps her inch her way along the flashing. She can hear Cher's teeth grind together with each bump, makes encouraging small talk of courage and the future. A millennium passes as they move, and yet they hear only a single car. Collette is as wet as the girl, now. Her hands are slippery, and she's afraid that she will be unable to keep a grip if she starts to teeter.

Over the window; a few feet that look like a million miles. I can't do this, thinks Collette. We'll start to slide and I won't be able to hold her. A buffet of wind catches them, blows Cher's dripping hair off her face. The green tinge has gone from her skin, but so has the brown. Cher has turned white.

'Be brave, sweetheart,' says Collette, and cups her face in her hands. 'We're going to go down now, okay?'

Cher nods, like an automaton. I don't like how quiet she is, thinks Collette. She should be making noises. And as she thinks it, Cher starts to sway on the roof beam. Back, forth, back, forth. In front of them the open window, behind her, the long drop.

Collette doesn't have time to make a decision. She grabs Cher's legs and pulls. Drags her off the point of the roof just as she slumps and goes limp. Holds her tight in her arms as they slide.

Her jeans snag on the window frame. Cher is on top of her now, her weight carrying them inexorably forward. Her eyes are open, the pupils staring into Collette's. I can't hold her, she thinks. She's going to carry us over. Whatever happens, I can't protect her shoulder. The best I can do is—

They drop through the window and bounce on the bed, and Cher wakes up and starts to scream.

Chapter Fifty

They stand over the body, silent in the rain.

'We don't have a choice,' says Vesta.

'No,' says Hossein.

Thomas has landed head first. Vesta imagines him, sliding down the roof like a thrill-seeker in a water park, his hands star-fished out before him in a hopeless bid to slow himself, his mouth wide in a silent scream. And then the long dive through sodden air; the drawn-out second as the crazy paving rushed up to meet him, and then the blackness. Do you feel these things? Her experience of fear has always been that it lasted for ever. That every microsecond drew itself out, each sensation, movement, sight, smell, and sound was etched on her consciousness in a way that she never experienced in any other state. Is there a moment when you feel your skull shatter? she wonders.

'No,' says Vesta. 'I don't know what made us think we'd get away with it the first time.'

'Maybe they'll think it was him who killed Preece,' says Hossein. 'Have you thought of that?'

'They wouldn't be that stupid. Surely?'

Hossein gives her a look that tells her all she needs to know of what he thinks of police intelligence. 'There are three dead women upstairs,' he says.

She nods, taking his point, then shakes her head, sorrowfully, and stares down at the broken head. Thomas's skull hasn't simply split; it's shattered. The crazy paving is one vast bibimbap of brains and blood and bone and hair. 'That's one big mess,' she says. 'I don't suppose it'll ever come out. It looks like someone's dropped an ostrich egg.'

Hossein looks at her, surprised. 'You're taking this very well,' he says.

She puffs her cheeks and blows out through the sides of her mouth. 'You know what? I think you run out of reactions, after a while. I don't think you could let a bomb off behind me and make me jump.'

Hossein glances at her sideways.

'Don't do the Auntie Vesta needs a lie-down look,' she says. 'I'm old enough to have changed your nappies, and I'm certainly old enough to give you a clout round the ear. Besides. I'm not seeing *you* having the vapours.'

'I don't have anything left to throw up,' says Hossein. 'After what I found in that bathroom.'

'How did he always seem so *cheerful*?' she asks. 'I mean. Wouldn't you, you know, be gibbering if you had a flat full of dead people?'

'I guess that's why none of *us* do,' says Hossein. 'You have to be a particular sort of person, I guess.'

She turns and retreats into her flat, runs the hot water to wash her hands. 'Check your shoes,' she calls. 'I don't want you treading any of that stuff into the carpet.'

They go up to Cher's room together. Music still pours out from behind Gerard Bright's door. He's not heard a thing, thinks Vesta. He probably avoids us because he thinks we're common. Thinks we'll bore him. Boy, is he going to hit a learning curve.

The door is open. They all know there will be no more locking of doors in this house. Cher lies on the bed, the green back in her face, Collette sitting beside her, mopping her brow with a damp flannel.

'How is she?' asks Hossein.

'Thank God for tramadol,' she says. 'I gave her two. I don't know if it's killing the pain, but at least it's making her care less.'

'Do you think that was wise?' asks Vesta.

'How do you mean?'

'I mean, what if it ... if they want to give her something else in the hospital?'

'No!' croaks Cher. 'No fucking hospital.'

'Oh, for God's sake,' says Vesta, 'look at you. Of course you're going to hospital.'

'Don't fucking talk to me like I'm a kid!' she says as snappishly as she can.

'Well, don't behave like one, then.'

The girl's eyes fill with tears. 'Please don't,' she says. 'I can't go back.'

'I'm sorry,' Vesta says, more gently. 'But look at you, Cher. You're broken. This isn't something we can mend with hooky antibiotics and painkillers.'

'It's just a collarbone,' she says, and bites back a squeal of pain as its ends rub together inside. God, the kid's got guts, thinks Hossein. You've got to give her that. But no one whose hand is going that shade of blue is staying out of hospital. Not if they want to live.

'I'm sorry,' says Vesta. 'Really I am, Cher. You gave it the best go you could. We'll do the best we can for you.'

Cher starts to sob.

Hossein touches Collette on the shoulder. She's been silent since they came in, her face hidden by her hair. 'You need to get going if you want to be gone,' he says. 'We need to call sooner than later.'

Collette looks up at them, and they're all surprised to see that her face is as calm as the face of the Madonna. 'I've been thinking,' she says.

Chapter Fifty-One

They go up the stairs, one by one by one. An execution party, sombre, quiet, their subject composed, dignified. It's started to go dark outside, the onset of dusk hastened by the rain. But autumn is coming, the season is changing, and Lisa Dunne is going to die.

What a place to go, she thinks. And what a way. A footnote in history, another of the missing. By Christmas, the first of the cash-in books will hit the shelves. Someone at Sunnyvale will go through Janine's sad little box and find her sad little photo collection, sell them to the *Sun* and have a holiday.

The smell is less than it was when she came up here before. The windows and doors wide open have stirred up a through draught and at least dissipated the syrupy quality the air in here had before. But still, it's a horrid place. She looks about her at the sad, drab evidence of the life lived here and feels a moment's sympathy for Thomas Dunbar. Not a picture on the walls, not a single tiny flourish that suggests that he loved himself. Just the little shrine on the table by the far wall, his collection of memorabilia.

She goes and stands over it, contemplates these trophies of lives lost. There were more than the three we've found today, she thinks. God knows what's happened to the owner of those earrings, the girl who coveted the Louboutins but could only afford the pretend one for her key ring. Do their families know they're missing? Do they still hope they'll come back, one day?

She strokes her watch. The last of Janine. The last good gift – the first, really. Her twenty-first birthday present, and not a branded thing, an antique with a gold link chain and a mother-of-pearl face. Janine must have spent months squirrelling away the cash for it. She remembers the pride on her face when she handed it over, showed her the engraving on the back. Tiny letters, but still clear after sixteen years against her wrist: For Lisa, my love always, Janine.

She unclips the clasp and weighs it in her hand for a moment. A comforting weight, solid; her proof throughout her life that, however flawed, there was once love. The last of Janine – she has nothing else.

She lays it down on the table next to the big, self-important bunch of keys that used to belong to the Landlord. Takes a deep breath and lifts her chin. 'Okay,' she says. 'Let's get this over with.'

They decide that the bathroom is the place for the final act. It seems logical, given the charnel he has made of the surprisingly elegant roll-top bath, that any cutting he has done has been done here. What is left of his last victim is little but bone, the flesh stripped off with obsessive dedication. There's just a leg left uncleaned. It lies pathetically among its deconstructed skeleton, pale meat drained of blood, a rusty stain around the plughole. Whoever she was, she liked shell-pink nail polish. Probably spent a moment admiring it, turning her foot to catch the light, some short time before she encountered the garrulous man with the tinted specs.

Collette is having difficulty controlling her gag reflex. These pathetic remains disgust her. The last thing she wants to do is get down and get closer. And she's frightened. Afraid of pain, afraid of dying. Afraid of what she is asking them to do. She looks over her shoulder and sees that Hossein has turned pale and Vesta looks grim enough to scare the devil. It's not just me, she thinks. Neither of them wants to do it either. But they must. Someone has to do it. It's the only way.

She kneels down and bends her head.

They're both crying. Hossein and Collette are crying. Despite all the things they've done, the things they've seen, over the past few weeks, this final act has brought them close to collapse. Hossein stands over her, paralysed. He's taken the cleaver from Vesta's hand, come boldly forward, determined to carry it through, and now he's by her, can see her face, her neck, her shoulder, he has crumbled. He sways like a kid on the bathroom tiles and squeezes the bridge of his nose as tears slide from his eyes.

'I'm sorry,' he says. 'I can't. I just can't.'

'Please!' she begs. 'Please, Hossein! You have to! Please!'

'I want to. Oh, God, Collette, I can't. I can't . . .'

He shuts up, closes his eyes and deep-breathes. Struggles to compose himself.

'Hossein, just *get on with it*. We can't waste any more time. Cher's downstairs, for God's sake. Do you want her to lose her arm? Just do it. Just – please, Hossein, I can't do this myself.'

He hauls in a huge breath, raises the cleaver and lunges. But it's a half-hearted gesture. He shies away at the last second, buries the blade in the wall.

Collette screams. With rage, with frustration, with terror. She doesn't want this to happen. Each time she thinks it's about to, the blood surges through her veins and it takes every effort of will she has just to keep still. '*Hossein!*'

'Oh, my God,' says Vesta. 'You're torturing her!'

'I'm sorry,' he says again. 'I'm sorry, I'm sorry!'

Vesta lets out an old-lady humph of disapproval.

'Well,' she says. 'I guess it takes a woman to do a man's job.'

She snatches the hatchet from his hand, pushes it out of the way and brings it boldly down.

Collette screams again. Drops to the floor and curls her whole body round her injured hand, clamps her palm over where the fingers are gone, to try to stem the blood. It hurts. She can't believe how much it hurts. It's only two fingers. What's two fingers? How can the pain from two fingers be running through every nerve I've got?

Vesta picks up a towel, wipes her fingerprints from the hatchet handle and drops it in the bath. 'I told you my dad was a butcher, didn't I?' she says.

Epilogue

DI Burke walks her back up to the car park. It's been a long day and he wants a break. He'll probably take the opportunity to slip out to the Cross Keys for a pint before he comes back in to finish off; the girl's been done and processed and her laborious, childish signature scrawled across the bottom of each sheet of her twenty-page statement. No more overtime, on this case. It's open-and-shut, no one to try, everyone slightly resentful because no one's made a glamorous arrest.

'That's the trouble with the serials ...' He voices his thoughts out loud. 'Half the time it ends up with everyone complaining we didn't do our jobs because no one knew it was going on.'

'Oh, I know, Chris,' she says, sympathetically. 'I mean, Christ, even Fred West had the grace not to do himself in until *after* we'd got him. I don't know what we're meant to do, though, short of CCTV in everyone's houses. It's not like anyone who was *living* there noticed.'

'Harr,' he laughs. 'You won't get the *Mail* pointing *that* out.'

'You do wonder, though, don't you? I mean. Sometimes you have to think that people are *deliberately* stupid.'

'No,' says Chris Burke, 'just simple stupid. Let's face it. Any-one over twenty-one living in a place like that isn't going to be at the top of the evolutionary ladder, are they?'

'I thought you said the man on the ground floor used to be a music teacher? That's not exactly stupid, is it?'

'Touch of Asperger's, IMO. Not uncommon, with musi-cians, as it goes. It's where they get the concentration to practise. Not too good at multi-tasking. You obviously don't remember, but he was a big joke in the papers last summer. Got sacked from some private school in Cheam for not noticing that half his kids had climbed out on to the roof while he was doing something with a speaker system. Anyway, he's gone downhill since then. Wife kicked him out and kept the kids. He was out of the house teaching private piano lessons in the afternoons, but he couldn't find another job. I think he just sat there doing the piano hands to classical music CDs all day while he waited for his access visits to roll around and didn't notice what *time* it was, never mind anything else. He hadn't even noticed that the tenant next door had changed from Nichola to Lisa. Thought they were the same person. That she'd dyed her hair.'

'Blimey,' says Merri. 'That *is* unobservant. Still. People forget their babies in cars all the time, I suppose. I'd love to know how he did it, though.'

'Did what?'

'Did the Landlord. Adipose tissue and sewage in the lungs. What's *that* all about?'

'Must've been some sort of revenge thing,' Burke says. 'Maybe he found out about the videos? He certainly wasn't after the money, was he? That toolbox, full of it, just sitting there in the cupboard.'

She considers this and waggles her head. 'True. Maybe. You're sure it *was* him, are you?'

'Preece's DNA's all over his car boot and the telly in Miss Cheryl's room that she says Dunbar gave to her out of Preece's flat has still got the plaster from the sitting-room wall on it. Oh, you don't think *she* did it, do you?'

He reels back in mock horror, and they both laugh, heartily.

'Still,' she says, 'handy for us. Cuts down on a lot of cross-reffing, I should think. And Lisa Dunne: three years, we've been looking for her. At least we can knock her off our list, now. Just a shame the disc got full before the end. Would have been handy for a time-of-death if we'd been able to see when she stopped showering.'

'Yeah,' he says. 'Sorry about that. You must be way pissed off.'

'Oh, look. She would have been a good witness. Well, of course, we don't know if she would have or not, really. She might have played dumb if we *had* got to her. But she's not our only lead. Tony Stott's a player. He'll bring himself down eventually, with or without Lisa Dunne.'

'Hope so,' he says.

'Bet the rest of them are pissed off there's no one left to sue, though,' she says, moving the subject backwards. 'That would be a nice little nest egg, the compensation for that sort of thing. Might've got our Cheryl a studio flat, when she grows up.'

'More like enough crack to kill herself, I should think. Better off without it, I'd say. These people. Not everybody can be trusted to make the right choices. And don't we just know it.'

'Don't we just. So what's going to happen to her, then?'

'Back to Liverpool,' he says. 'Armed guard of social workers and back into care until they can turf her out again.'

'Another one for us to be processing in three years' time, then,' she says. 'Pity she's so thick. She could be nice-looking if her jaw wasn't always dangling.'

'Yeah. Sad, though. Crappy parents, hopeless kids, and all the rest of us having to pick up the pieces.'

'You know what, Chris?' she says. 'If I cried about all of them I'd have no tears left for myself. In the end, there's just some pro-portion of the population that's hopeless and always will be. And that's why we're there. Keep the rest of them safe.'

They reach her car and she bips it open with her remote. Pops the boot and puts her case files in it.

'Well,' he says.

She opens the car door and turns to smile at him. 'Well. Thanks for this, Chris. We appreciate all the help you've given us.'

He gathers his courage and throws it to the wind. 'I don't suppose,' he says, 'you fancy popping out for a quick one, do you? I could do with a wind-down.'

DI Cheyne looks uncertain for a moment, then smiles. 'Not tonight,' she says. 'Sorry. Busy.'

'Oh.' He's crestfallen.

'Another time, though?'

Her cheers up again. 'Oh, okay, sure. I'll give you a bell, then, shall I?'

Her smile gets wider. 'Sure,' she tells him. 'That would be great. Not for the next couple of weeks, though. My caseload's a nightmare.'

'Don't I just know *that* feeling. Okay, couple of weeks it is.'

'Brilliant. I'll look forward to it,' she says, and flirts up at him through her eyelashes for such a brief moment he's only half sure she's done it.

She gets into the car and drives off, and he stands in the car park to watch her go. The black metal gates slide open, powered by an unseen hand in the control office, and she bumps her way out on to the pavement. Raises a hand in farewell, and he raises one back. He walks back into the station, feeling happy about his day's work. That's something to look forward to, he thinks, in a couple of weeks.

DI Cheyne turns left into the one-way street and drives up three blocks to the main road before she pulls in to a meter space and gets out her phone. Sighs, and dials, waits three rings before it answers.

'It's me,' she says. 'Yep. It's her. No doubt about it. Kid confirmed it. Thick as butter, but she recognised the photo, after about ten minutes of drooling. And there's absolutely no doubt that those were her fingers they found in the freezer compartment. They're definitely hers. And there was a watch. Gold watch, in among the trophies. Engraved from her mother to her. I mean, I suppose there *could* be other Janines and Lisas, but it doesn't seem likely, does it? Plus, there's hours of video of her in the shower, from the Landlord's little sideline.'

She listens for a moment, and smiles.

'Yes,' she says. 'Yes. I think you can stand them down. Lisa Dunne's gone and got herself slotted and we never had to do a thing. Looks like you're in the clear, Tony. At least for now.'

He says something at the other end of the line and she laughs. 'Sure,' she says. 'I'll drop in on Saturday. Just make sure the Cristal's on ice for when I get there.'

Postscript

The youth worker likes everyone to call him Steve, but behind his back the kids all call him Wicked, because that's his favourite word. She sees him Monday and Friday lunchtimes, which is good because it means that no one asks where she's going when she leaves school to do it. She's got into the habit of dawdling on her way back, dropping in to Poundland and Primani, or just having a couple of ciggies by one of the duck ponds in Sefton Park, and she's found that the words 'youth worker' seem to be enough to stop anyone asking questions as long as she doesn't actually skip the whole afternoon. The school has classified her Special anyway, and in her case 'Special' seems to mean 'not much point bothering as we all know where she's going to end up', so a bit of dawdling is neither here nor there.

He's bent over a piece of paper when she comes in, looks up and says, 'Cheryl. Wicked. I won't be a moment, take a seat,' the way he always does, and goes back to ticking boxes, the way he always does.

Cher plonks herself on the padded bench against the far wall of the office and starts picking at a patch of seat foam exposed over the years by her waiting peers. She's been picking at it for two months and has managed to make a hole that's almost six inches wide as she's waited for Wicked. The office is small – more of a cubicle than an office, really, its temporary walling covered in posters of smiling teenagers and exhortations not to catch chlamydia – and cluttered with piles of paper and box files. She kicks her duffel bag into the space beneath the bench and crosses her legs in front of it.

'And ... there! Sorted. Wicked,' says Steve, and sweeps his clipboard up from his desk. Comes over and perches on the other end of the bench, one foot on the floor and the other tucked beneath his knee. Props an elbow on the back of the bench, rests his temple on his knuckles, and gives her his understanding smile. Steve likes to meet your eye. All the time. He's like one of those pictures that follow you round the room. It's disturbing, really, though he probably thinks it makes him look like he's *down wiv da kidz*.

'So how's it going, Cheryl?' he asks.

'Okay,' says Cher, and plucks at the foam.

'Wicked,' he says. 'Minted.'

She carries on staring down at her plucking hand, because she's afraid she'll laugh. He ticks something off on a box. His eyes stray down to her moving hand, but he refrains from reproving her. Everyone, she's noticed, refrains from reproving her, these days. The last person to tell her off was Vesta, and she misses it. She's had enough of boys who've not been told off enough, for a start. 'And school? How are you settling in? Made any friends? Got any *homies*?'

'Homies?' She shoots him her fierce glare. Don't Homie me, white bhoy. You're thirty-six and you've got a degree in sociology.

You'll be asking me if I dig my crib, next. Who d'you think you are? Quentin Tarantino?

She shrugs. 'It's okay,' she says again, though school is basically a mix of the ones who avoid her because she's the runaway from the Murder House and the ones who think that such an exotic history lends her promise. Either way, she's not interested. She was past hanging with a bunch of fifteen-year-olds by the time she was twelve.

'Sweet,' he says. 'And your teachers?'

'They're trying to teach me to read better.'

'Awesome!' He ticks another tick.

'Not really. I'm not learning. It makes my head hurt.'

'Oh.' The tick is crossed off. He puts the clipboard on his lap and leans forward sincerely. 'It takes time, Cheryl. It doesn't happen overnight. Just keep trying and you'll get there in the end. And it's really worth it. If nothing else, it's good to have a goal, isn't it? You don't want to spend your life with nothing to aim for, do you, hmm?'

She shrugs again. 'Whatever.'

'Have you thought about what you might like to do when you leave?'

'Not really. It's not like there's any jobs around here, is it?'

'Oh, now,' he says. 'Never say die.'

This time, she looks up and meets his eye. 'I saw a man die three months ago, Steve. You know what he looked like as he slid down that roof? Surprised. That's what. Just surprised, all the way down to the edge. I guess *he* never said die, either. But he did, didn't he?'

A little spot of colour appears in his cheek. Nothing to tick off on your form there, she thinks. Go on. Say 'sweet' to that one.

'Er,' he says. Then: 'There's still counselling, if you want it, Cheryl. The offer's still open.'

'No, you're all right,' says Cher. 'I had counselling before.'

He ticks another box, this one to the right hand side of the form. Whatever he was looking for, she's failed. Oh, well, she thinks. Whatever. It'll just go in a drawer anyway.

'And the home? How's that? How are you doing?'

'Wicked,' she says, to encourage him.

He looks pleased. 'Cool!'

'I've got a new room-mate,' she says. 'Sylvia. She's nearly sixteen. She's really fat.'

He's so sunk into his slang that he automatically puts a ph on the front of the word and beams. 'Great!' he says.

'Yeah,' she tells him, 'she's a *playah*.'

Plays One Direction on her iPod, plays Angry Birds every chance she gets. While eating Mars Bars and crisps sent in by her fat brother, and staring at Cher with red-rimmed eyes when she tries to start a chat. Sylvia wants to be a hairdresser, or a manicurist. Personally, Cher thinks there might be too much standing up involved in hairdressing, and some of those cubicles are mighty small.

The pen moves back to the left-hand side of the page and he does another tick. 'Wicked,' he says. Checks his watch. Her allotted five minutes is up. 'Sweet. Great, well. Good to see you. Monday as usual, then?'

'Oh, yes,' says Cher.

'Maybe,' he says, adding it as though it were an afterthought, 'you and Sylvia might like to come to the Youth Centre one night? Down on Chester Street? I'm down there quite a lot, cause I sort of co-run it, so there'd be a friendly face, if you were worried.'

Like a hole in the head, thinks Cher. 'What goes on there?' she asks.

'Oh, it's cool,' he says. 'Lots of young people. There's a pool table and table tennis. And just, you know, places to sit and chillax. Be with your people. Come tonight. It's open from seven on a Friday, and there are *tunes*.'

'I think it's too late to get permission for tonight,' she says, and gives him her innocent eyes. 'I need my care worker's permission to be out after seven. And then they're – you know. Cause I ran away before, they're ...'

Steve looks sympathetic and tips his head to one side. 'I know, Cheryl. Would you like me to give him a call? I'm sure I could work out a way to keep them happy, if you'd like.'

Cher beams at him. 'Would you? Oh, *would* you? That would be *wicked*! That would be *super*cool!'

He looks pleased. The first piece of enthusiasm she's ever shown him, and it works. Three ticks go down the side of his form and he returns her smile with triumph. It was the chillax, he's thinking. I got her with the chillax.

'Well, *great*!' he says. 'I'll do that, then!'

'Sweet,' she says, and pulls her bag out from beneath the bench. Her school bag, issued along with her uniform and a selection of modest nightwear when she arrived back in Liverpool and was placed. She's not put a lot in it. Didn't want to raise suspicions. 'See ya Monday! Have a good weekend!'

He looks surprised. She sees him register pleasure at the thought that he might have had a breakthrough, and feels a tiny twinge of guilt. Tiny. 'Thanks, Cheryl,' he says. 'You too.'

She slopes down the stairs with her bag over her shoulder and turns left as she leaves the office block, shrugging up her collar against the cold. It's half a mile to school, and the bell won't go for another forty minutes – stacks of time. There's a nasty estuary drizzle in the air, but the Friday lunchtime street is full of people. Less than a month until Christmas, and holiday panic is already beginning to fill the air. Office workers push their way, harassed, into Boots in search of perfume and bubble bath and hair straighteners. Five men in hi-viz jackets stand outside the Bricklayer's Arms, with pints and fags clutched in hands that are still swathed in work gloves against the weather. She sees four girls from her year turn, giggling, through the door of Top Shop – the snotty girls, all shiny hair and little heart-shaped studs in their ears, the ones who literally back off when they see her coming, as though her past might be catching. There's a school disco at the end of the week. Cher's never been to one of those. Doubts she ever will, now.

She walks on towards the school, passes the steamed-up windows of McDonald's and sees some more of her peers stuffing down Big Macs and milkshakes, two of the boys throwing handfuls of fries at each other, lining themselves up to be thrown out. After so long away, the voices she hears around her are alien to her ears. Suddenly she knows how she, herself, must have sounded to the people in the south: all Dees for Tees and Ees that sound like the speaker has smelled a bad smell. She hadn't even noticed that she'd lost the Mersey 'gh' till Craig Caffey, a boy who looks a bit like he's been extruded from a putty machine, turned round and called her Poshgirl just before he tried to pin her against a wall and stick his tongue in her mouth.

I don't fit in here any more, she thinks. I'm not a perky Scouser. I've lost the we-suffer-but-we-laugh-through-the-tears thing and I don't know if I'll ever get it back. Do I fit in anywhere, though? I'm not a Londoner. Not really. I thought I would be, but I don't suppose I'll ever go back there, now. But here? There's nothing that keeps me here apart from the fact that the council wants me back. And even they don't really want me; they've just got to take me, and resent me, and eventually turn me into a statistic. But everyone who ever loved me here is dead, or in prison, and apart from my Nanna the love thing was never exactly obvious.

It's only one o'clock, but night is already drawing in. The day never really got light at all through the misty rain, and what brightness there was has long since given up trying to penetrate the clouds. A long, northern winter: salt wind off the Mersey, institutional Christmas dinner and a single present picked out by someone who's been paid to choose it. Coca-Cola and the sound of Sylvia crying for New Year, then the long grey wait till the end of the school year and sixteen-ness finally sets her free. I can't stay here. There's no point; it's just more loss of time and the long, long slide to nothing.

Cher reaches the turn that leads to school, and stands looking up the road towards it. I could go back, she thinks. At least it's warm inside the Special Needs block, and they mostly just let you sleep on Friday afternoon. I could go back there and suck it up.

She dips her head and walks past the turning. Walks on into the darkening streets. As she walks, she strips off her stripy tie and hangs it, damp and droopy, from the spike of a railing as she passes it; stops for a moment by the greengrocer's and digs in her bag for her denim jacket. Strips off her school blazer and pulls the jacket on in its stead, then drops the blazer in the clothes collection bin outside Age UK. She leans against the blank window of the bookie's to kick off her black school trainers and replace them with a pair of red patent wedges. Uses the window of Burton as a mirror to paint her lips dark red. Feels in the bag once again and finds her raspberry felt cloche, with the mauve rose over her temple, and pulls it over her hair. It was far too big when her nanna gave it to her that last birthday, but she's kept it with her ever since, and now it fits just right. By the time she turns the corner once again, Cheryl is gone for good.

She steps up her pace. Just a few hundred yards to the station, now. They won't be looking, she thinks. You don't have to worry. It's ages until the bell. But still she looks over her shoulder, fearful that a teacher will be out prowling for stragglers, that Wicked Steve will have taken it into his head to escort her back to the gates. The road is empty. Here, away from the shopping crowds, she might as well be in the country, for all the company she's got.

The lights of the station loom up ahead. Drab little suburban station, nothing but a waste bin and a timetable and an empty grey platform. She climbs up on to the footbridge and looks down on the tracks. Oh, well, she thinks, easy come, easy go, and walks on down to the southbound platform.

A gate on the platform leads out to the car park. Cher passes through it and stands on the pavement, looks left and right. Over by the exit, an old transit van, white paint, rust on the bumpers, turns on its headlights. She tosses her head and walks towards it. As she nears, the door on the side slides open and shows a dark, box-filled interior. She doesn't hesitate. Doesn't think. Just reaches the van and climbs inside.

Vesta slams the doors and clambers into the front seat. 'We thought you were never coming,' she says.

'I know,' says Cher. 'Fucking social workers. Talk, talk, talk.'

'Language, Cher,' says Vesta, and Cher feels a big smile spread across her face.

'Hiya,' she says.

'Hi,' says Collette, and puts the engine into gear.

'How's your hand?' asks Cher.

'Bloody horrible,' says Collette, 'and I'll never play the piano again. How's your collarbone?'

'Bit less broken,' says Cher. 'Thanks for asking.'

'Great,' says Collette, and starts to reverse. 'Sit down, there's a good girl. Don't want you killing yourself before we even get there.'

'Where are we going, again?' asks Cher.

'Ilfracombe,' says Vesta. 'You'll love it.'

'If you say so,' she says, contentedly. 'Sounds like crap to me.'

She settles down on one of Vesta's sofa cushions, next to the sports bag Collette's been carrying with her for three long years, and allows herself a sigh of contentment.

'By the way,' says Vesta. 'Your cat's in that crate. Bloody nightmare, he is.'

The Wicked Girls
Edgar Award Winner

On a fateful summer morning in 1986, two eleven-year-old girls meet for the first time. By the end of the day, they will both be charged with murder. Twenty-five years later, journalist Kirsty Lindsay is reporting on a series of sickening attacks on young female tourists when her investigation leads her to interview carnival cleaner Amber Gordon. For Kirsty and Amber, it's the first time they've seen each other since that dark day so many years ago.

Gripping and fast-paced, with an ending that will stay with you long after you've read it, *The Wicked Girls* asks the question: How well can you know anyone?

ISBN 78-0-14-312386-6

"...e suspense keeps the pages flying, but what sets this one apart ...the palpable sense of onrushing doom." —Stephen King, "...he Best Books I Read This Year," Entertainment Weekly

**PENGUIN
BOOKS**